I0549576

Published by Regina Bumbrey | www.authorrbumbrey.com

ISBN-13: 978-0-6927-1247-4

Front and Back Cover Design | Honor -N-Respect

Editor | Keira J. Northington | It's The Write Stuff

Interior Design | Strawberry Publications, LLC | www.StrawberryPublications.com

For information regarding special discounts for bulk purchases, please contact Regina Bumbrey at www.authorrbumbrey.com

Printed in the United States of America

CHAPTER ONE

The dark street was illuminated by the strategically placed streetlights. The neighborhood of Baytree was made up of modest families. It consisted mostly of people that worked and went to school during the day, so when nighttime fell, activity outside was at a minimum. The quiet was interrupted by the screeching tires of the white BMW driven by Lanai Wilson, as she barreled into the development and came to a stop in front of Sade's townhouse. She was drunk, too drunk to be driving anywhere, especially to fight someone that she didn't know. She knew it was juvenile, but she didn't care.

Sade was the woman that had called and taunted and provoked Lanai, and Lanai never backed down from a challenge. She had fought females before and nothing made this woman any different. She reached for the door handle and shoved it open. The front door to the townhouse came open at the same time that she was climbing out the car. Lanai was about to walk up to the house, but stopped dead in her tracks when she saw a crowd of people pouring out of the house, and coming down the steps in what seemed like slow motion.

The fight that had bubbled to her surface turned to fear, but she was too scared to move. As the people came towards her, she started recognizing faces. Most of the faces looked angry and vicious, some of them with their lips curled and their teeth exposed like a pack of hungry wolves. The first face that Lanai recognized was Keisha's, a girl that she had fought a few years ago. This girl had taunted her over the phone just as Sade had. Keisha's two beefy brothers were shoulder to shoulder with her. Carmen, the woman that had introduced Lanai to cocaine, came from around one of the beefy brothers and spoke in Spanish with a smile on her face, a mirror with coke on it in her right hand, and her left hand outstretched.

Lanai recognized the face of her "friend", Tameka that she'd partied with, standing behind Keisha, along with a swarm of people that she didn't recognize, but was sure that she'd known them from that partying life. Sade stood on the step, with her daughter on her right hip, and a gun hung from her left hand. Lanai began to panic. There was no one out here that she felt that would be an ally to her, and she knew she had two options; fight or flight. She chose flight, but her legs wouldn't move. She cursed under her breath and she stood at the end of the driveway, with less than fifty feet between her and a mob of people. She looked around her in a panic, praying for something or someone. She really couldn't believe that her legs wouldn't work.

She looked back at the mob of people that continued to advance. She looked up at the step and saw that Sade had a menacing look, slowing descending the concrete steps. Lanai could physically fight anyone, but there was no way she was fighting a bullet. Besides, what kind of woman would come out of a house to shoot another woman with her baby on her hip? And where the hell did all these people come from? Lanai hadn't seen some of them in years. She could've sworn that she heard her sister, Katara, calling her name and she looked around anxiously trying to find her.

Panicked, she grabbed ahold of her right leg and tugged, trying to make her legs move. When that didn't work, she tugged at the left one. *Shit,* she thought. She felt a little relief when she saw her mom, Vi, emerge from the crowd. That little relief fleeted when she saw that Vi was holding hands with her stepbrother, RJ, and her stepsister, Maria. Her father, Ramon, was behind her mother. The four of them were laughing together, but none of them seemed to be paying Lanai any attention. Lanai's heart sank. *How could she? How could she do this to me?* Lanai was Vi's own flesh and blood and she wouldn't even look at her.

Katara's voice got louder and sterner. Lanai couldn't see Katara, but she heard her say, "Lanai, you got to let go. You can't keep doin' the same shit and expectin' a different result. That's stupid."

Lanai looked around, completely puzzled. *You gotta be kidding,* she thought. What the hell was going on? She saw Sade making her way through the crowd, and knew it was just a matter of time before she made it to her and killed her. In a flash, the faces in the crowd turned into zombies and everybody's outstretched hands were clawing at her. She wanted to scream and run, but her stupid legs wouldn't move, and she couldn't open her mouth. She was paralyzed standing up.

Makai seemed to appear out of nowhere and he didn't look like a zombie. He was tall, dark, handsome, and looked like a life raft right now. He stood directly in front of her with his hands outstretched, as if expecting her to give him her hands. Her heart swelled and tears came to her eyes. She loved this man with all of her being. She felt as though he was her heartbeat, literally, even though he was the reason for the fighting, drugs, and abuse. She still loved him as if none of it had happened. He smiled at her and her heart melted. She felt her lips begin to curl up and for just a moment, that mad pack of zombies didn't matter. She knew he would protect her; he always did.

Over Makai's shoulder, she saw Sade come through the crowd with a baby on her hip, that looked like a female version of Makai and that pain was like a kick in the chest. Lanai's left hand went to her heart as the baby smiled at her. She felt as if her heart was breaking inside her chest, and she'd die right there. The one thing she wanted was a baby and that's what Sade carried on her hip. She still held the gun, but instead of it being by her side, it was now leveled at Lanai's head.

Lanai looked back to Makai for help and she saw that he held her dead son in his outstretched hands. She looked up into Makai's accusing glare and looked back down at her dead baby in his hands.

The tears that had welled up in her eyes spilled down her cheeks, and she reached out to touch her son. Before her fingers could touch the corpse, a gunshot rang out.

CHAPTER TWO

Lanai bolted upright in the bed, sweating and panting as if she'd just run a 10k. She looked around the dark room, unsure for a moment where she was. Looking at the flower print La-Z-Boy in the corner by the window, and taking in the smallness of the room, reminded her that she was in Katara's guest room. She'd been staying there for the past six months, since Sade, Makai's baby's momma, had shot her in the chest. That one moment had changed the course of her life forever.

After realizing where she was and there were no zombies, guns, or dead babies in the room, Lanai's breathing slowly returned to normal. She could tell that her blood pressure was up, because her head thumped as if she had a 50-piece band playing in her head. Bringing her knees up to her chest under the covers, she rested her elbows on her knees and put her head in her hands, closing her eyes. Usually when she had a dream, whether it was disturbing or not, it took her a while to remember what she was dreaming about. However, the details of this dream stuck out like a bull in a china shop.

The doctor had told her that her damaged lung would repair itself for the most part, and she had to go through the process of physical therapy and recovery. Even though it had been six months and overall, she felt like she was back to her old self, there were times—especially when she had nightmares or ran—when breathing regularly was a task. She would have to focus on slowly breathing in and out, in order not to have an anxiety attack because she would hyperventilate.

From outward appearances, Lanai didn't look like she had gone through anything horrific. She was about average height for a female, with a slender, athletic build, latte-colored skin, and full lips. She used to have long, coal-black colored hair, until she got it cut short like Halle Berry. Makai used to love her long, wavy hair, and she loved it because he did. After everything that she'd been through because of him, she knew that cutting her hair would make their break-up final.

Lanai had given Makai more than ten years of her life. Her life had not been her own since getting involved with him and she had been okay with it. Nevertheless, as she grew and time passed, things seemed to spiral out of control and neither of them seemed to know how to get it back. After Sade had shot Lanai in their confrontation and Lanai made it out of surgery, Lanai made one of the hardest decisions in her life. She decided that it was time to move on from him and the chaos that being with him brought. She still loved him like the air she breathed, but she knew that it wasn't healthy, and life after recovery had to be about being healthy.

When she felt like her breathing had returned, she slowly pulled the covers off her legs and eased herself out the bed. She quietly padded to the door and peeked out to make sure she hadn't awakened anyone. When she saw that the house was quiet, she crept down the steps and went into the kitchen. Katara shared the house with her daughter's father; it was three bedrooms with a family room, living room, dining room, and kitchen. It was a nice house and since Katara was an interior decorator, it was definitely decorated beautifully. It was small, compared to the six-bedroom house that Makai had bought Lanai in Wild Quail, but Lanai definitely liked it. The house that Makai had bought felt like just rooms in a building structure; Katara's house felt like home.

Lanai got a bottle of water out the refrigerator and sat in the windowsill of the bay window. She opened her water and took a drink, looking out the window at the pool in the backyard. She was lost in her thoughts as she stared at the pool water. She thought back on all the things she'd been through from her father not really being in her life, to the babies that she'd lost, to the man that she thought was hers, and almost losing her life. She didn't understand it, but she knew it had to be a purpose for her. There was no way that she was supposed to be living after all that heart-break, if there was no purpose.

She never heard her sister come into the kitchen. Katara was about an inch or two taller than Lanai and she was a mix of black and Korean, which was apparent in her slanted eyes, cocoa-colored skin, long off-black wavy hair, and hourglass shape. Her hair was wrapped up in a scarf and she had on a pair of Larry's flannel pajama pants and the pajama top to match. Lanai had joked with her several times that it was no point in even buying the pajamas for Larry when Katara wore them all the time.

When Katara had come downstairs, she had intended to just get a bottle of water and go back to bed. She wasn't sure of what had awakened her from her sleep, but normally a cold bottle of water and a walk through the house to make sure everything and everybody was okay, normally did the trick to put her back to sleep. Seeing her sister sitting in the bay window, clearly lost in thought, caused her eyebrows to furrow. She and Lanai weren't blood sisters, but they were raised together and they were as close as any blood sisters could be. She constantly worried about Lanai and seeing her up in the middle of the night was definitely a cause for concern.

Katara eased over to the bay window and sat down near Lanai's feet. Lanai jumped a little, startled by Katara's presence, and smiled slightly. Lanai said, "Hey. I didn't know you were up."

"Didn't know you were up, either," Katara responded.

Lanai asked, "Did I wake you?"

Katara shook her head. "You okay?"

Lanai looked back out the window. "Yeah, just had a bad dream."

Katara put a comforting hand on Lanai's knee. Her voice softened, "The same dream?"

Lanai pressed her lips together and nodded. She was afraid to speak for fear that her voice would crack or she'd start crying. Part of her just wanted to get over being shot; she'd lived so she felt like she should just be over it. She struggled with nightmares of being shot; in some of her nightmares, she would be on the outside looking at her own corpse either in the morgue or on the ground. She would sometimes wake up in tears because she had nightmares about the babies that she aborted, the son that she'd had to bury, and the babies that she'd miscarried.

She was sure that other people had things way more difficult than she did, but she could not, for the life of her, figure out why she had to endure so much pain. She saw women that handled so much more than she did and didn't bat a lash. She'd folded so many times with drug abuse, drinking, and just running away from her problems. She'd spent more than ten years trying to fill a void that always seemed too big to fill. She'd wasted so much time and energy, only to still feel empty so many years later.

Katara replied, "Oh, sweetie pie. Are you okay?"

Lanai smiled. Katara was such a mom. Lanai had witnessed Katara talking to her daughter, Sariyah, countless times, and Katara's voice always changed when she spoke to her daughter, unless she was disciplining her. When Katara was comforting a loved one, the mommy in her came out. Lanai had experienced more mothering from her sister than she had from her mother in her entire life. Lately, she didn't know whether she missed the lack of a relationship from her mother or her father. Being shot and becoming clean from a life of drug abuse had a way of opening things up that she hadn't felt in a long time.

Lanai nodded her head. She said, "I told you I don't know how to make it stop."

"Did you pray," Katara asked gently.

Lanai shook her head. She knew who God was and she'd heard about the relationship that other people had with Him. Katara had been trying to convince her to go to church with her, Larry, and Sariyah. Since Lanai had admitted herself to rehab more than a year ago, Katara had decided that she needed to grow in her faith, strengthen her relationship with God, and protect her family. Katara had told Lanai that she wanted to make sure that her family stood on the strongest foundation and in her opinion, God was it, and she wanted her sister to hop on the bandwagon.

Lanai didn't have anything against God; she just had a lot going on. She felt like a walking mess a lot of the time and didn't know where to start with a relationship with God. She didn't know how to pray and she wanted to get herself together before she approached God asking for anything. She felt like she had to be ready and have her life in order. She was too ashamed to tell Katara that she didn't know how to pray. She felt like with her being 26 years old, she should know how to pray, since everybody made it seem like something so simple.

She let out a breath, pushing her thoughts and fears deep down as she always did, and looked at Katara with veiled eyes and a plastered smile. She said, "I'm good. Just needed some time to think."

To make her sister feel better about it and drive her point home, Lanai swung her legs over the edge of the windowsill and planted her feet on the floor. She said, "I'm gonna go back to bed."

Katara eyed her sister suspiciously, not believing that Lanai was all of a sudden over something so traumatizing. She reached over and pulled Lanai into an embrace. She hugged her sister tight, silently praying that she could absorb all the negativity, hurt, and pain.

Both of them stood up and Katara made her way to the refrigerator to get her bottle of water, while Lanai headed for the steps, neither of them saying another word. Lanai went up to the room she'd been sleeping in and softly closed the door behind her. She climbed back in the bed out of habit, but she knew sleep was not going to come for a long time. Unfortunately, she was wide-awake and alone with her thoughts.

She adjusted and readjusted the pillows and with her back to the door, she stared blankly at the wall as she lay down. She had no idea what she was going to do. She'd thought that making it out of surgery, rehab, and cutting all her hair off was going to be the brand new start that she needed. In her mind, that was all she needed to do to move on from a bad relationship and get her life together. However, she had not figured in the time and energy that it would take to get from one point to another. It sometimes seemed impossible.

As her thoughts ran a mile a minute in her head, she barely heard the soft knock at the door. She turned to see Katara entering the room, with something in her hand and closing the door behind her. Without turning the light on, she made her way to the bed and Lanai sat up and pulled back the comforter and sheet. Katara climbed into the bed and with the sliver of moonlight that came from the window, Lanai was able to see that Katara had a pint of ice cream and two spoons. Her brain wanted Katara to leave her alone to her misery, but her stomach and her heart were grateful that her sister didn't know how to leave well enough alone.

Katara passed Lanai one of the spoons and removed the lid, placing it upside down on the comforter that she'd pulled over her legs. She dug into the ice cream and Lanai followed suit. Lanai tasted peanuts, caramel, and vanilla ice cream. Her taste buds did a dance and her stomach grumbled in anticipation. For a little while, the two of them enjoyed the ice cream in silence.

Lanai was the first to speak. She asked, "You just couldn't let it go, could you?"

With a mouthful of ice cream, Katara answered, "Nope. You know me."

Lanai chuckled, "I sure do."

"I know you, too," Katara pointed out.

Lanai admitted, "I know."

With her spoon in hand, Lanai all of a sudden lost her appetite. She was just waiting for Katara to start in on her. She held her breath, anticipating the lecture that she knew was going to come. She knew that her sister only wanted the best for her, but she just didn't want to hear the tirade that she knew was coming.

Katara asked, "So, did the doctor say you were finished with therapy?"

Lanai nodded her head. "Yeah. Finished up last week."

With the spoon to her lips, Katara inquired, "So, what now?"

Lanai contemplated the question for a moment. She really hadn't counted on the conversation going in that direction. With a shrug of her shoulders, she answered, "Keep working, I guess. I mean, I know it's time to get my own place and things."

In the dark room, Katara turned to her sister. She asked, "You know you don't have to leave, right?"

"I know you and Larry said I'm welcome to stay as long as I want," Lanai began. "I just feel like it's time. I appreciate you guys being there for me. But the more I think about it, the more I realize that I need to do things on my own."

Lanai could feel Katara nodding her head next to her as she continued to eat the ice cream. Katara said, "I understand. I just don't want you to rush it."

"Six months is not rushing it," Lanai chuckled.

Katara pointed out, "Nobody is rushing you to leave. Nobody is telling you you're not welcome or you have a time frame."

Lanai nodded, "I know, but I'm ready. I'm ready to start doing things on my own. It's important to me."

"Then that's all it is," Katara conceded. "Have you started looking?"

Lanai shook her head, "No, but I'll start tomorrow."

"You heard from the prosecutor?"

"No," Lanai answered quietly.

"I wonder what they're doing. They know who did it."

"The person from Victim Services said someone would be in touch with me."

"How long will that take?"

"Could take like a year."

"Really? A year?"

"Uh huh."

"A year for what?" Katara asked.

Lanai said, "If she doesn't take a plea agreement, it can get drug out."

Katara huffed, "She shouldn't get that option. She didn't give you an option when she shot you."

Lanai decided not to answer. She had mixed emotions about the whole situation. Sade was the mother to Makai's daughter, who bore a striking resemblance to their dead son. Makai had been cheating on Lanai with Sade for years, while Lanai had been gone on her drinking and drugging binge. Lanai was upset when she'd first seen Sade and the baby in the mall. She didn't know anything about Sade or the baby, but the minute she laid eyes on that little girl, she knew. She'd run out of the store, throwing up on the way, and she'd lost it when she confronted Makai at his shop about it.

Lanai had spent that evening getting drunk, trying to make sense of the situation. She had to be realistic with herself. Even if Makai didn't know the extent of her actions when she was running the streets and partying, she knew what she did. She had told herself that he'd had every right to move on, because they were barely at home at the same time, let alone behaving like a couple. She honestly hadn't been as angry with him as she was hurt. After all the heartache, pain, abuse, and lost babies, the only thing that she'd wanted from him was a child. It was more than the ultimate betrayal, and she'd ended up being shot and almost died that very same night.

She thought about that night every day and replayed it in her head a million times. She asked herself repeatedly what she could've done differently. She blamed Sade for having a gun and shooting her, but she placed most of the blame on Makai and herself. Makai should've never become involved with Sade, because he knew how crazy Lanai could be. Lanai blamed herself for her getting shot because she should've listened to Katara and stayed home, instead of trying to be Billy Badass and fight everybody that blinked at her twice.

Katara sensed the change in the atmosphere and reassured her sister, "It'll work out, Nai."

Lanai nodded her head. She'd been struggling with being alone and going back to sleep before Katara had come into the room. Now that those memories had been resurfaced, she really wanted to be alone. She hated feeling exposed, even to her sister, who was her best friend, and she felt that way now.

Katara put the lid on the container and said, "Alright, momma. I'ma let you get your rest."

Lanai nodded and embraced her sister. Katara kissed Lanai's cheek, got off the bed, and quietly left the room. When Lanai had left rehab a little more than a year ago, she'd had a plan. She'd been taught how important having a plan and putting it into action was. She'd never anticipated having her life derailed after getting it back on track. She'd been under the impression that once she got out of rehab, she and Makai were going to rebuild their lives together and live happily ever after. She knew that neither of them were perfect, but together, they could've worked out anything. However, she ended up sleeping in the spare room at her sister's house, because she'd reacted to his lies that were exposed.

As she leaned back against the pillows, she made up her mind that she wasn't wasting anymore energy on the past and the what-ifs. She wasn't sure how she was going to do it, but she knew that it was time to utilize what she'd learned in rehab about taking control of the situation and coming up with a plan that would be accessible. She could waste her life on wallowing in regret, but she decided to be productive and turn her life into what she wanted it to be. She refused to be a victim of circumstances.

CHAPTER THREE

Lanai sat at her desk in the interior decorating office that she owned with Katara, twirling her pen back and forth in between her fingers. She had her notepad in front of her that she'd been writing in, as she looked at the computer screen. She'd been alternating between responding to emails from clients and looking at apartment and condo listings. She'd wanted to stay near the office so that she wouldn't be too far from work and her sister, but the pickings in the Dover area that fit her personal criteria were slim.

Lanai and Katara had offices on separate sides of the building, towards the back. They also had desks in the front where there were samples of their work, books filled with designs and ideas, and a clear view of the customers that came in. They made sure at least one of them were at one of the front desks at all times during business hours. Lanai had told Katara that she would sit out front and keep an eye on the door, while Katara went over some contracts with a customer in her back office.

Lanai heard the door open as she used her mouse to scroll down the page of listings that she was looking over. She glanced up briefly and looked back down at the screen. She said, "Hello, how are you? Please feel free to look around and I'll be with you in one moment."

"Take your time," a baritone voice responded.

Pressing control, alt, delete, and enter, Lanai locked her computer screen, pushed her chair back from her desk, and stood up. For a moment, she stopped in her tracks. The man that had entered the office was tall—really tall—brown-skinned, with a low haircut and he wore a tailored navy blue suit, with chocolate brown dress shoes. He had a goatee and thick black eyebrows, with thick, kissable lips. He looked like new money.

Lanai composed herself in the blink of an eye and strode over to him in her black, six-inch Gucci heels with the pointed toes. She extended her hand to him and his massive hand swallowed her tiny hand. She noticed that his hand was soft and warm, but the smile that started in his eyes and spread across his lips, was twice as warm and welcoming. She smiled, feeling like she could get lost in those brown eyes. She said, "Hi, my name is Lanai."

Holding on to her hand, he said, "I'm Mike. Mike Stranton."

Easing her hand out of his, for fear that hers would start sweating, she asked, "How can I help you, Mr. Stranton?"

"I was referred to your business by a friend of mine and his wife," he answered. "Trent Michaels."

Lanai smiled wider and nodded, "Yes, I know the Michaels. I worked with them on decorating their home and office."

"I know. He told me. He said you were awesome."

"I do what I can."

"I've seen your work and I saw what it looked like before," Mike revealed. "You do great work."

Lanai blushed. She loved what she did; she just didn't brag about it. It did warm her heart to know that her clients did the bragging for her. She asked, "So how can Interior Designs help you?"

"I don't want Interior Designs to help me. I want *you* to help me," he clarified.

"Well, what can *I* help you with," she answered.

Placing his hands in his pockets, he said, "I have a brand new home that I need decorated. I have no idea where to start or what to do."

Well, by looking at you, I can't tell, she mused to herself. Her brain had to remind her eyes to stay on his handsome face, and not travel down what looked like a chiseled body underneath his perfectly tailored suit. She smoothed her hands over her camel-colored, leather, calf-length pencil skirt, to get herself back into business mode and directed him over to one of the books that contained designs and samples. Her long-sleeved, off-white silk Michael Kors shirt she wore tucked into the skirt, added to the business look, but was also sexy. She wasn't trying to look sexy; she just liked what she liked.

Mike stood next to her as she opened the book and explained the pages that she flipped through. She could smell his inviting cologne, but she couldn't place the name of it. Whatever it was, it had the power to make a woman snuggle up right next to him, regardless of whether she knew him or not. It seemed like everything about this man was welcoming and had the potential to be intoxicating. She knew that combination all too well; Makai had had the same effect on her. Remembering what that combination had done to her, she mentally slapped herself, reminding herself she needed to keep her distance from men like him.

She wasn't sure exactly how tall he was, but with her having on six-inch heels, he still towered over her. He put a hand on her hand, sending what felt like an electric shock up her arm. She looked up into his handsome face and he suggested, "Why don't you just come look at the house and tell me what you think it needs?"

Lanai blinked. It took a moment to find her voice. She quickly came to her senses, and when she did, she said, "Let me go check my planner and see what date I have available."

She hesitated for a moment, then moved away, going around her desk to have a seat and cross-check her planner, with the schedule that she had on her computer. She said, "Mr. Stranton, you can have a seat."

As he made his way to the seat across the desk from her, he asked, "Please call me Mike?"

"No problem, Mike," she replied, looking for her earliest opening in her schedule. She looked up from the book and checked the computer for the matching date. When she found it, she asked, "How about next Wednesday at 4:30?"

"How about today? Right now?"

Lanai looked at him. He looked like he had money and expensive taste, and a closer look at him told her that he was used to getting what he wanted. She wasn't about to be on that long list of people that did whatever he wanted whenever he said. She never wanted to insult a customer, but she'd be damned if she'd let him come in and run her.

She answered, "The earliest opening that I have is next Wednesday at 4:30. If that day and time doesn't work for you, then I can see when my next available date is. I don't have anything sooner."

Mike chuckled and nodded his head. He said, "I can double your fee if you come today."

"You can keep your money and go to someone else," she challenged, crossing her legs under the desk and folding her hands on her planner.

He laughed heartily, leaning back in the chair. "Nah, I want you."

Her steady gaze didn't waver, despite the flop that her stomach did when she heard him say he wanted her. She made a mental note that he was referring to business.

He chuckled again, "I guess next Wednesday it is."

Picking up her pen, she scribbled down his name in the time slot, and as she wrote, she said, "I need the address of where you want designed."

He answered, "118 Glenda Way."

"Zip code?"

"01."

"Here in Dover," she asked, not hiding the surprise in her tone. She knew the Dover area and she knew that there were only certain areas where people with money lived. She'd never designed for an address of someone wealthy in the 19901 zip code.

He slowly nodded his head.

After writing down the entire address, she put down her pen and looked up at him. She smiled, extending her hand, "I look forward to working with you next Wednesday at 4:30."

He accepted her outstretched hand as they rose and he shook it. "Can't wait."

Lanai rounded her desk to walk him to the door. She said, "Now if there is something that you want in the way of designs or patterns that you come across or envision in the meantime, please don't hesitate to give me a call."

She gave him a card that she'd retrieved from the holder on her desk after she'd made it around to his side. He looked over the card then looked at her. "Can I just call you, anyway?"

"No," she answered without hesitation as she escorted him to the door. "I don't mix business with personal."

Once they reached the door, she extended her hand again. He accepted and she said, "It was great meeting you."

"Likewise," he returned, allowing his strong fingers to linger on her slim wrist.

She felt electricity shoot up her arm again from his touch and she pulled her hand away. He smiled a knowing smile, realizing the effect that he had on her. She was a hundred percent sure that he had the same type of effect on every woman he came in contact with. She plastered a fake smile on her face and pushed open the door. As he left, she could hear him chuckling to himself. She stepped back and allowed the office door to close, watching him go to his car, parked at the curb. It was a very nice car. She shook her head; working for that man was going to be a problem.

CHAPTER FOUR

"**M**s. Wilson, glad you could make it," Mike said, standing up from leaning on his car.

Lanai grabbed her briefcase and purse and rushed out of her 2013 white BMW with cream and woodgrain interior. She pushed the door closed as she strutted towards Mike in the horseshoe-shaped driveway. She smiled and apologized, "I'm so sorry I'm late. My GPS had different ideas about where I should go."

He accepted her extended hand and apology. He said, "It's fine. This is a fairly new development."

The development that his new home was in was called Wolf Creek and it was located off South State Street. Lanai was surprised to see how close in proximity this development was to everything in Dover. It was right behind the Wolf Creek business park. The outside was breathtaking with redbrick and tan vinyl siding. It looked like it sat on at least an acre of land, that by the way was in desperate need of attention from a landscaper. The stone steps and white columns that led up to the double cherry wood doors were beautiful.

Mike offered, "Well, let's go see the inside."

Lanai nodded and followed his lead. She unconsciously watched his body move as he led the way to the front door. He walked with confidence, but he wasn't stiff. His shoulders were broad and she could see his muscular back through this black silk button up. He didn't have the shirt tucked in and he had on black dress slacks, but she could see that he had a nice butt. It wasn't big and it wasn't flat; it was perfect.

She shook her head at her thoughts and moved slightly to the left of him. She knew it had been a long time—seven months to be exact—since she'd had sex, but she had to compose herself. No matter how sexy or inviting this man was, she had to keep things strictly professional. She couldn't afford to lose sight of her goal and get caught up in another man. The last thing she wanted to do was lose herself in someone else again.

After they climbed the steps, she waited to his left, while he used his key to unlock the door. She also noticed to the right of the front door what looked like glass French doors. He pushed it open and stepped to the side, allowing her to enter before him. She stepped into the open, spacious foyer and immediately noticed the chandelier that hung from the ceiling. From where she stood, she could see a room to the left, a spacious open room to the right, and a room with wonderful lighting from the windows.

Lanai ventured further into the house and went to the right, through the open space, which would probably be the dining room. She slowly walked through the room and took note of the fact that there were two other entry-ways, one leading to the room with the windows, and the other leading into the kitchen. As she neared the kitchen, she was surprised by a little area tucked away with a sink, marble counters, and wood cabinets. Two of the cabinets had glass doors, to display their future contents.

Instead of going into the kitchen, she went left and across the little hallway into the room with the windows and the lights built into the ceiling, pleasantly surprised her. She noticed the columns that separated the room with the carpeted floor from the glossed hardwood of the hallway. She walked through the doorway that led into the kitchen. It was marvelous with its marble countertops, cherry wood cabinetry, and even the refrigerator door was made out of wood. There was a stainless steel range top and two oven units built into the wall. There was a built-in china closet, with a marble counter attached to it. Lanai absolutely loved the windows in the area off the kitchen with the columns. There was also a fireplace with a mantle to the right.

She left that space, went upstairs, and entered what she assumed to be the master suite, with its plush carpet, columns, and fireplace. There were ceiling to floor windows and a TV mounted on the wall. *Come to think of it,* she thought, *there are TV's mounted in just about every room.* She absolutely loved the raised ceilings and French doors that led outside to a redbrick area. This house was just beautiful.

Lanai's mouth dropped open when she entered the master bath. In the home that Makai had bought for her, she'd had her own vanity area, complete with the mirror and sitting area. However, this bathroom was like none she'd ever seen. She gasped, taking in the protective glass door that extended from the top to the bottom and was framed by white wood. There were sinks on either side of the doorway, with each having three mirrors and cherry wood cabinetry.

The tile floor was handsome and added a hotel feel to the room; a chandelier hung in the middle of the ceiling. The shower stall had a double glass door, with a marble seat and tile walls and floor. The marble-encased garden tub next to it had a nice sized window, with two marble steps that led up to it and a column on each side of the steps. She thought that the toilet being in a stall with a door that closed was necessary and unique. The walk-in closet with all the shelves and spaces made her head spin with all the possibilities. This room had a mounted TV as well, which made Lanai roll her eyes.

"It is not that serious," she mumbled.

As she advanced towards the doorway, she made a mental note that every doorway within the house was curved, and not the traditional square-shaped at the top. She left the kitchen area and walked towards the steps, observing that there was a nice little office with windows to see out onto the street. The beautiful cherry wood and iron staircase had a staircase that led to the upstairs, and a staircase that led to the basement. There was a window in each staircase's landing, allowing natural light in.

The steps were made of the same hardwood as the floors of the first floor. The first space she entered had a desk, cabinetry, and hooks. She understood what the hooks would be used for when she advanced further to see the washer and dryer. *Awww, that's cute,* she thought. *They added a mini laundromat.* She walked through the four bedrooms and the three bathrooms on the top floor, making note of the beautiful carpentry used to construct this house. She knew Mike had paid $100,000 easily, if not close to it.

She went down to the basement, admiring again the beauty of the combination of wood and iron in the staircase. She was not surprised to see a pool table, bar setup, and a projector screen, with six plush leather movie theater chairs. The carpeting in the basement was the same plush carpeting as in the bedrooms. She shook her head, going back upstairs to head towards the three-car garage.

Captivated by the house's beauty, she'd almost forgotten that Mike was following behind her quietly from room to room.

Her six-inch red and black Jimmy Choo's click-clacked across the cement of the three-car garage. She could hear Mike's shoes on the cement behind her. Slowly making a circle, taking in the emptiness of the garage, she faced him and asked, "Did you want to do something with this space other than park your cars here?"

He shook his head no. "I have enough space in the house."

Lanai nodded her head. "Yes, five bedrooms and six baths would definitely be enough. How many square feet?"

"Six thousand four hundred and fifty-four square feet."

Lanai whistled and nodded, "Impressive."

Folding his hands in front of him, he asked, "Any ideas?"

"Lots," she answered immediately. "Do you have a direction you want to go in?"

He shrugged. "Whatever you want to do."

"Do you have a figure in mind for the budget?"

He shook his head again.

She warned, "Not giving me a budget and no direction can be dangerous."

He smirked, "How so?"

"I have expensive taste," she warned.

He motioned towards her shoes, "I can tell. Jimmy Choo is definitely high fashion, unless they're knock offs."

Lanai made a face and put a hand on her hip. "There's nothing fake or knock off about me, what I wear, or what I represent."

He nodded, saying, "Well, you do what you want. Send me the bill."

Hearing those words made her moist between her legs. She had to concentrate hard not to show her arousal. She had a fetish for shopping and any opportunity to spend money—especially someone else's—was a major turn on. She readjusted herself, switching her briefcase from one hand to another, while he dug into his pants pocket. He produced a key and handed it over to her.

He told her, "You can come and go as you need to."

She nodded, keeping her lips and legs together, and tucked the key into the back pocket of her briefcase. They stood there in the silence of the garage, among the concrete, wiring, and metal. After a few moments, she cleared her throat. "Well, I'll get started immediately and keep you updated."

He nodded and before the awkward silence could return, she moved around him and headed back into the house. She was more in a hurry to put space between them, than she was about starting to decorate. She noticed that when he looked at her, his eyes liked to linger a little longer than they should. She knew that he was attracted to her, and she thought he was attractive. If she allowed it, she knew that it could be something between them. By the looks of it, he was financially comfortable, he knew how to dress, and he appeared to be successful in his career.

The physical part of her was aching to give in to him. It had been a long time since she'd been in the company of a man. However, the hurt that she felt from her failed, ten-year relationship kept her from entertaining any thoughts of being near another man in the personal capacity. She wanted to live her life the safest way possible, which meant that she needed to stay away from men and they needed to stay away from her. She needed to remember to live by the guidelines she'd been given while she was in rehab. She had to take things one day at a time, she had to let go of what she could not control, and she had to make the necessary changes in her life that she could.

A thought hit her as her heels click-clacked on the tile of the kitchen floor. Besides him looking at her, Mike had never said anything to indicate that he had any interest in her, other than wanting her to decorate his house. She realized that she could be jumping the gun with assuming that he wanted her, and imagined sexual tension between that she needed to avoid. Reflecting for a moment with a hand on the marble breakfast bar, she smiled a little as she thought about it all being in her head, and she was just horny.

Shaking her head and laughing at herself aloud, she told herself, "I need to get a grip."

Lanai waited for Mike to come back into the house from the garage and leave before she took another walk through the house by herself. She worked better when she could feel the house, which meant that she needed to spend alone time in every room, to decide what she wanted to do with it. She walked slowly through every room with her notepad and pen that she took on every visit. Since her time in rehab, working at the business she shared with her sister meant more to her every day.

She loved being able to take a bare house or business, and turn it into a work of art that the owner would be proud to show off. It was a form of therapy for her, an escape from her not-so-happy reality. She hated that she needed to escape, but it was all she could do to keep from going crazy. She'd decided not to see a therapist or counselor to work through the horrific experience that she'd been through. Interior Design was her only option, other than talking Katara's head off. She was beginning to feel like she'd worn her welcome out in many ways with her sister, despite Katara constantly telling her that it wasn't a problem.

As Lanai got to work making phone calls to begin the project, she made her mind up that she wasn't going to continue to use Katara as a crutch. She knew that being dependent upon any person or anything would be detrimental to her recovery, and the last thing she wanted was to be back in that dependent state. She was going to get on her feet and stay there. Finding a mate wasn't a priority;

neither was having sex. *After all, that was the reason for vibrators, right?*

CHAPTER FIVE

"**M**akai, I need to talk to you," Sade's voice demanded through the phone.

With his cell phone wedged between his shoulder and left ear, he counted the money from the day's close of business. He said, "So talk."

She said, "Not over the phone. I need to talk to you in person. How about I come by the house after you leave the shop?"

"How about no," he retorted. Since Lanai hadn't been home, no other female except his daughter, Makayla, and the maid had stepped foot in his house.

"What do you mean," Sade whined. "I need to talk to you."

"About what," he asked, not hiding that his patience was running thin.

"About our daughter."

"What about her?"

"Why can't I talk to you in person?"

"Look, Sade, I don't have time for the back and forth. Either you tell me what you wanna talk about now or we don't talk," he said, fully prepared to hang up the phone.

He heard her huffing on the other end. She answered, "I need more time with the baby."

Makai had been allowing Sade the opportunity to see their child for about an hour at the home daycare that Makayla went to. He was completely aware that part of Sade's conditions of being released from jail on bail was that she didn't go near any children. This included her own child, whom she'd endangered when she'd shot Lanai more than six months ago. He knew when he'd agreed to let Sade go to the daycare that she'd want to push the envelope. He didn't blame her, although, because she was Makayla's mom.

He offered, "I can talk to Ms. Hazel about you staying later or coming earlier."

She paused for a moment, and then asked, "Why can't I pick her up from daycare earlier and you get her from me? Or instead of paying a daycare provider, she could just be with me until you get done working."

"Did you forget you're not supposed to be around any kids at all," he inquired.

"She's my daughter," she replied, her voice going up an octave.

"I let you go see her every day," he reminded her. "I'm risking her by letting you see her."

Makai could imagine the offended look on her face when she said, "What do you mean? I would *never* do anything to hurt my baby."

He knew he could tell her that she had indeed done something to hurt Makayla, when she'd shot Lanai while Makayla was upstairs. That bad decision had taken her away from Makayla for almost six months, until Sade's family was able to bail her out, after three bail reduction hearings when the judge lowered it. He had never wanted to keep Sade away from the baby, but when it came down to potentially losing his daughter and giving in to Sade, the choice was obvious. Sade was grown; she'd get over it.

He clarified, "I'm talking about legally risking her. I could lose my daughter by letting you see her."

"Makai, who would find out," she asked incredulously.

He'd lived a good portion of his life doing illegal and immoral things, so he definitely knew how to hide things. Nevertheless, when it came to his daughter, he didn't want to do anything that could take her away from him. When Lanai had made the decision to go to Sade's house and Sade had shot her, Sade had been taken to jail. Makai wasn't going to allow the Division of Family Service to take their daughter, so he stepped in kept her with him from that point on.

Being a single parent had never crossed his mind. When he'd thought of being a parent, he'd always envisioned Lanai being a stay-at-home mom and he the breadwinner. His choice to cheat on Lanai with Sade and having child conceived out of that relationship seemed to kill the possibility that there would be any children with Lanai. He hid his pain every day, but the pain of Lanai not being a part of his life was very real. It felt as if a big, cold steel butcher knife was embedded into his heart. The only time he got a little relief was when he was busy working and taking care of his daughter.

From the moment that he'd left Kent General Hospital after Lanai had come out of surgery, he'd made up in his mind that he was going to win her back; he always did. She would be mad for a while, but she'd always come around. It had never taken six months to win her over before, and he was beginning to get agitated. His calls to her sister's house went unanswered, the gifts and flowers he sent were returned, and he no longer had a way to get to her. He used to communicate with his best friend, Larry, Katara's boyfriend. Makai no longer felt comfortable going through Larry, especially since he could hear it in Larry's voice that he was between a rock and a hard place.

Makai didn't blame him; he knew the importance of a happy home and there was no way Larry would continue to go against Katara. Makai knew that Katara didn't want him and Lanai together. He fought the urge every day to go down the block and talk to Lanai. He wanted to know why she was ignoring him; he'd apologized a thousand times. He'd even gotten to the point of walking around the corner to the front of his barbershop, on the corner of Loockerman Street and Queen Street, to go down and talk to her. He'd stopped in his tracks halfway there when he'd saw Katara and Lanai entering their business together.

He could tell whom Lanai was from a thousand miles away with his eyes closed, but his jaw had dropped when he saw her. She'd been dressed in designer clothes and shoes as usual. He could see from the distance that she'd maintained the couple extra pounds she'd gained in her hips, thighs, and butt after rehab. She'd filled out the black pencil skirt and peach-colored, button-up blouse perfectly. He'd imagined the light makeup that she'd probably had on, because he couldn't see her face. The thing that had his mind blown was the fact that her long, beautiful silky black hair was gone. She'd had a close, tapered cut.

Sitting at his desk in the second-floor office of his barbershop, and remembering seeing her that day, he imagined what her perfume might've smelled like. He could never remember what the name of her perfume was, but he'd never forgotten what it smelled like. She'd always smelled like warm vanilla and cocoa butter, and her skin was always so soft. Remembering how soft and warm her body was, he didn't even realize that he'd gotten hard. He missed that woman like he'd never missed anyone in his entire life.

Thinking of her made him want to go down the block, and make her talk to him. She had a power that no other woman had over him. Her ignoring him made it almost impossible to focus on anything throughout the day except her. The one thing that seemed to keep his head above water was that he had to provide a stable life for his daughter. He knew that if it had not been for having to go on with life for Makayla's sake, he'd probably be a funky mess in a dark and empty house.

Hearing his name called repeatedly brought him out of his daydream. He'd forgotten that he'd been on the phone with Sade. He blinked a few times and asked, "What?"

"Who would find out?"

"I'm not doing that," he answered flatly. "She's fine where she is, and you can take the arrangement like it is, or leave it. That's up to you."

Sade whined, "She's gonna forget who I am."

"No, she won't."

"That's not something that you have to worry about. She sees you all the time," she pointed out.

"If the roles were reversed, you'd do the same," he countered. "You probably wouldn't even let me see her."

"Yes, I would. I would never keep you away from her."

"You can't," he retorted with a confident chuckle.

"You know what I mean. I'm in a horrible position. A baby needs her mother."

He said, "She has her mother. As soon as this situation is resolved, we can figure out a different arrangement for you to spend more time with her."

Sade was quiet for a few moments, then she breathed heavily into the receiver. She relented, "Okay. I'll stick to it for now. But as soon as this is over, I need my baby back home with me."

"I don't know about that," he said. "But you definitely can see her more often."

"I'm her mother, Makai," Sade insisted.

Makai retorted, "I know who you are. I'm her father. I have legal custody."

She screeched, "Really?! You're gonna throw that in my face?!"

Patience running thin, he said, "Look, I'm not doing this with you. I gotta go."

"Makai, wait," she pleaded.

He ended the call before he could hear her say anything else and placed the cell phone onto the desk. He finished counting the money brought up to him from the clothing store that he owned, which was next door to the barbershop. It was the beginning of the month, so the barbers had given him their chair rent. He was also counting his profits from the heads he'd been cutting all day. When he was finished counting and recording, he placed all the money in a blue bank bag, zipped and locked it. He placed the bag inside his laptop bag, with the laptop that he never used. He only had the laptop and bag to disguise the bank bag. He never let anyone openly see him moving money.

When he stood, his semi-hard manhood reminded him that it had been a long time since he'd had sex, and the thoughts of Lanai only made it worse. He had to physically readjust himself so that he could walk and not draw attention. He stood at six foot four, with a muscular build, beard and mustache that he tapered himself, a low haircut, thick eyebrows, dark brown eyes, and thick lips. He knew he had a lot to offer any woman financially, sexually, and from any other aspect. However, truth be told, he didn't want to offer anything to anyone except Lanai. Sometimes he felt physically sick from her absence.

Pushing thoughts of Lanai to the back of his mind, Makai snatched up the laptop bag and keys, heading for the door. He turned off the lights as he made his way through the barbershop to lock up. He was usually the last one to leave and he was grateful to Ms. Hazel for keeping Makayla, sometimes until10:00 pm. She always took such good care of his princess and he knew that he wouldn't be able to get that type of quality care for his daughter too many places. He showed his appreciation to Ms. Hazel financially, taking care of anything she needed, in addition to paying her twice as much as she charged weekly. When she needed something fixed or something for her daycare kids, Makai handled it. She was almost like the mother he never had.

Makai locked the back door that led to the second floor of the barbershop, checked the back door of the lower floor to make sure it was locked; he walked around to check the barbershop's front door and the clothing store. Everything was locked up tight and the lights were off, just like he liked it. He was about to cross the street to his black Cadillac Escalade, with the Presidential tint and all black butter-soft leather interior, and then remembered that he needed to pick up the Jamaican food that he'd ordered from the restaurant down the street before Sade had called.

He made his way to the restaurant, paid for his food, and then went back outside to wait at the curb for the cars on Loockerman Street to pass, so that he could cross. As he waited, his eyes wandered to Interior Design. He saw that there was one light on and as he crossed the street, it was turned off. As he got to the other side of the street, the same side that Interior Design was on, he saw the door open and Lanai stepped out with an armful of stuff. She was occupied with trying to balance her purse, briefcase, and file folders while locking the door.

His palms began to sweat as he stood on the sidewalk, frozen, looking at her. He'd involuntarily imagined running into her thousands of times, but in his mind, things had never gone past running into her. He felt like a school-aged boy, staring at his crush with sweaty hands, dry mouth, and a million thoughts in his head. For a moment, he forgot that he was a thirty-year-old man that was doing better financially than anybody he'd ever met. He had to remind himself of who he was and to get it together.

Seeing that she was having a hard time with the door, he closed the distance between them. He switched hands with his laptop bag and took the files out of her hand without a word. She looked up and jumped back, alarmed. Her hazel eyes had grown to almost the size of a silver dollar and she clutched her briefcase and purse to her, leaving her keys in the door. He saw the recognition slowly register in her beautiful eyes and face. He stood only inches from her and inhaled her warm vanilla and cocoa butter scent, a scent that almost made his eyes close as if he had been feigning to smell that fragrance.

He saw a smile begin to tug at the corner of her pretty mouth, before the darkening of her eyes stopped it. He knew everything that he'd done to her over the years came flooding back to her, because of the guarded look that she gave him. His heart sank. He'd been hoping that she'd put it aside and give him one more chance, like she'd done so many times before. All he wanted was one more opportunity to make things right. She quickly finished turning the key to lock the door and snatched her files from his hand, stepping around him. She walked away from him with a purpose, leaving him looking and feeling stupid.

Recovering quickly, he turned around and caught up to her. He called, "Lanai."

She stuffed the files into her briefcase, increasing her pace to almost running. He'd always been amazed at the way she could move in her six-inch heels; she made it look easy. She fumbled with her keys, and with his free hand, he touched her left elbow. Without breaking her stride or pace, she angrily snatched away from him. She made it to the driver's side of a white BMW, and attempted to open the door after hitting the button on the keypad. He was right behind her and as she tried to open the door, he pushed it closed.

To the back of her head, he pleaded, "Nai, can you just give me five minutes? Please? I'm sorry."

Her body was tense and he could see her anger had her breathing heavily. With her back to him, she said, "Let me get in my car."

"I will," he promised. "Just give me five minutes."

"Thirty seconds," she spat.

"Four minutes," he bargained.

"A minute and a half."

"Three and a half minutes."

"Two minutes."

"Three."

"Get back or I hit the panic button on my keypad," she threatened.

"Okay, two minutes," he said.

With a stern voice, she said, "Back up."

"Turn around and I'll back up."

"Back up and I'll turn around," she countered.

Trusting that she was still a woman of her word, he took a step back. She hesitated for a moment, then slowly turned around, leaning against her car. She folded her arms against her chest, her eyes still guarded. He looked her over and thought, *Damn, she's sexy.* Her beauty seemed to stand out more with her short haircut, and with anger and attitude oozing from her. He never knew why her anger turned him on. The mint green satin blouse that she wore, with her black slacks and leather heels made her look like a business model. Involuntarily, his eyes lingered for a few moments on the way her shirt cascaded over her breasts and dipped into her flat stomach.

"A minute and a half," Lanai replied impatiently.

He snapped out of his reverie and said, "I just wanted to tell you I'm sorry."

She said, dryly, "You said that already."

The coldness in her eyes and tone was different and hard for him to adjust to. In the past, he'd always seen at least a glimpse of warmth and he would work that to his advantage. The coldness was like a brick wall that he didn't know how to maneuver around. He wasn't surprised, however, that she was going to make things hard for him. It was in his nature to rise to a challenge, and there was no challenge better than Lanai.

"Why won't you return my phone calls?"

"What phone calls," she asked, seemingly uninterested.

"I call your sister's house all the time. If anybody answers, they say you're not there," he revealed.

She seemed to brush it off as if it weren't important. "I don't know anything about any phone calls."

He tried a different angle. "Why'd you send back the gifts and flowers? They were for you to keep."

A look of confusion covered her face, causing her brows to furrow. "What gifts? What flowers? You never sent me anything."

"I did," he answered quietly. "I've been sending you something to your sister's house and here at the office, at least once a week for the last six months."

She was quiet for a second and a look passed over her face. Before he could figure out what she was thinking, the guarded look returned and she raised her chin in defiance. She said, "It doesn't matter. I didn't get anything."

"I sent it," he said, almost above a whisper.

She stared in his eyes momentarily, and in a low voice, she said, "Makai, I can't be bought."

He nodded. "I know. I'm not tryna buy you. Just wanna say I'm sorry."

He saw that her body relaxed a little and she revealed, "Then just say it. Gifts don't mean anything anymore. Actions mean more."

He thought he saw a glimpse of an opportunity to gain some leverage getting back into her life. He took a step closer and touched her elbow, "I've been trying to tell you for six months."

She visibly tensed when he touched her and she moved away. She said, "We have nothing to talk about."

She made a move to try to open her door again. He stopped her, asking, "What do you mean we have nothing to talk about? I love you."

With pain etched all over her pretty face, she said just above a whisper, "You loving me left me childless, strung out, hopeless, and almost dead."

Makai was at a loss for words. Everything that she'd said was true. All he could do was stand there with nothing to say. Over the years, he'd used every trick that he knew to keep her where he had her and it had worked. He'd become accustomed to and dependent upon her forgiveness that never seemed to end. He didn't know what to do with things as they were, which was unlike him, because he was always in control.

After a few minutes of silence, Lanai said, "I have to go."

He didn't stop her from getting into her car, starting its engine, and driving away, leaving him standing in the parking lot next to where she'd been parked, looking stupid.

CHAPTER SIX

Lanai absentmindedly used her right thumb to push the ring on her ring-finger around in a circle over and over, as she drove to her sister's house in Camden, DE. It was only about a ten to fifteen-minute trip, but tonight it seemed to be the longest ten to fifteen minutes of her life. She knew she only worked down the street from Makai and there was always the possibility to bump into him. However, she hadn't been prepared to actually run into him and have a conversation with him. She also hadn't been prepared for the emotions that flooded her afterwards.

He'd scared the life out of her when he appeared out of nowhere and tried to help make it easier for her to lock the door. Throughout their tumultuous relationship, he'd always been there to do gentleman-like things, such as opening doors, pulling out chairs, and carrying things for her. Things had gotten to a point where she'd forgotten that she could do things for herself, so him trying to help her wasn't a surprise.

Initially, she'd thought that she was about to be attacked. When she'd looked up into his handsome face, she'd been relieved for a second. That was, until the memories came flooding back. It seemed as though the last ten years of her life had flashed before her in a matter of seconds, and reminded her of why she shouldn't be happy to see him. With him standing that close to her, as he had been, she smelled his familiar Cool Water cologne. He'd been wearing that fragrance from the time that she'd met him. She remembered times when she'd bought him different colognes to get him to try something else and he never would.

The way he looked at her, reminded her of what being with him felt like. She remembered what it felt like to have his soft, strong hands and soft lips on her flesh. She was also reminded of the end result of being with him. Her empty arms and womb were constant reminders of what being with him brought. Her near-death experience and having to learn how to use her lungs all over again were ever-present reminders.

Something that Makai had said was nagging at her. He'd said that his calls went unanswered and the gifts were returned. She'd never asked Katara or Larry if anyone had called their house for her, because if there was someone calling for her, they would call her cell or business phone at the office. She posed the possibility to herself that he could be lying and just trying to rope her back in. However, she knew him and she knew that while he'd lied about a lot, he didn't lie about calling and sending gifts. He was serious about his effort to get her attention.

Lanai turned into Katara and Larry's development and parked along the curb in front of their house. She knew Katara was the one that had intercepted the calls and sent back the gifts. She couldn't be mad at her sister for trying to protect her; she understood completely. She knew that Katara only wanted the best for her, and keeping her away from Makai was Katara's idea of protecting Lanai. While Lanai felt like she didn't need protecting, it was in Katara's nature to protect Lanai. Lanai had grown to appreciate Katara's protectiveness, especially in her times of weakness.

Lanai turned the engine off, gathered her things, got out, and headed to the door, locking the doors with the keypad on the way. She searched for her door key on the way to the door, unlocking it and entering the house. She could hear Katara and Larry playing with Sariyah as she locked the door. Instead of going into the kitchen where they were, Lanai headed for the steps.

As if she could smell her sister, Katara called, "Nai, is that you?"

Lanai stopped on the steps, "Yeah."

"You want some dinner?"

"No. I'm going up to do some work," Lanai said, as she resumed her climb the steps to her room.

Lanai entered her room, kicking her shoes off immediately and pushing them up against the wall with her bare feet. She put her briefcase and purse down on the bed, as there was a tapping at the door. Knowing who it was, Lanai called, "Come in."

Katara entered the room and eased the door closed, asking, "Are you okay? Did something happen?"

"I'm fine," Lanai answered. She opened her briefcase and took out the files that she'd brought home from the office. She'd planned to get some work done, especially now that she needed to occupy her brain to keep it off Makai. She could feel Katara looking at her. She looked up at her and assured her, "Tara, I'm fine."

Katara narrowed her eyes and accused, "No, you're not. What's wrong? What happened?"

"Nothing," Lanai insisted, sitting on the bed with her favorite pen that she'd fished out of her purse.

Katara sat on the bed and positioned herself in front of her sister. She said, "I know you. Something happened. You saw somebody or something."

Lanai knew that her sister was unrelenting, and she was not going to back down until she got the information she was after. Lanai blew hot air and gave in, "Alright. I did run into somebody."

"Who?"

Lanai paused for a moment; mentally bracing herself for the reaction she knew was to come. She said, "Makai."

She allowed the one word to soak in. Katara's mouth went from a smile anticipating good news to a hard line. The light in her eyes disappeared as if someone had flipped a switch. She asked, "Where'd you see him?"

"He saw me struggling and helped to keep me from dropping everything."

Attitude and disgust were etched all over Katara's face. She batted her eyes repeatedly, "I don't understand. Why would he be at *our* office? He works up the block."

Katara sounded like Lanai was cheating on her or something. Lanai answered, "I don't know why he would be on our end of the block."

Katara waved a hand dismissively. She asked, "So what did he want?"

"He wanted to talk," Lanai answered quietly.

"Talk about what," Katara spat.

"He wanted to say he was sorry."

"Sorry," she screeched. "Sorry?! What the fuck is saying sorry going to do?! Does sorry take away the experiences that you've been through because of him?! Does sorry change the fact that you almost *died*?! The fuck outta here with this 'sorry' shit!"

"Tara—"

"No, don't 'Tara' me," Katara interrupted. "This nigga says sorry and you just fall for it every time. Sorry ain't good enough."

Lanai took a deep breath. When Katara got going, it was hard to get a word in. Lanai took advantage of the brief silence. "I'm not falling for anything. You asked me who I saw; I told you."

Katara nodded, "Yeah, that's normally how it starts."

"Nothing is starting," Lanai chuckled. "I gave him a minute and a half to say what he had to say. I'm not falling for anything. There's nothing to fall for. I'm done."

Katara let her sister's words soak in. The look on her face said that she was weighing in her mind whether or not what she was hearing was true. Again, she nodded her head. "Okay. Just don't say I didn't tell you so when he comes snooping around, trying to break you down."

"Have you been shot before," Lanai asked incredulously.

"No," Katara answered cautiously.

"Well, hush," Lanai replied jokingly. "I have it under control."

Katara nodded her head and put her hands up in a gesture to surrender. Lanai laughed and she remembered something that Makai had said to her. She said, "Speaking of trying to break me down, he said that he sent a bunch of flowers and gifts and they were all sent back. I never saw anything."

Katara admitted, "I sent it all back. I intercepted the calls, too. I threatened Larry's life and told him that if he delivered any messages from him, he was cut off."

Lanai burst into laughter. She was not surprised at all. She knew that if given the opportunity, Katara would shut Makai and his efforts down quicker than he could get the thought formed in his head. She asked, "Did you have to threaten to cut him off, though?"

Katara looked at Lanai with her lips turned up and her hand on her hip, as if she was crazy for even asking the question. She replied, "You need to know it. I ain't playing with him."

Lanai shook her head. She said, "Well, I'm about to get to work on these patterns."

"Now, who I *thought* you were gonna say you ran into was Mr. Mike," Katara revealed, with a sneaky smile on her face.

"Why'd you think that?"

"Because he's been trying to find every and any reason to run into you."

Lanai blushed. "No, he hasn't. He knows that it's only business between us."

"So, what does sending flowers have to do with business?"

"He just wanted to say thank you."

"Well, if he wanted to say thank you," Katara countered, "he coulda just said thank you. He likes you and you know it. You like him, too."

Thinking about it for a second, Lanai admitted, "He is kinda cute."

"Uh huh..."

"And he can dress, too."

"Looks like he got money."

Lanai looked up from the swatches of fabric and tile samples in front of her. In almost a whisper, she leaned forward and said, "He's an investment banker."

Katara leaned forward, her face almost touching Lanai's. She whispered, "He does have money."

Lanai nodded and giggled.

Katara asked, "How many kids does he have?"

Lanai sat back and shuffled around some papers. She said, "I don't know. I didn't ask."

"Why not," Katara demanded.

"Because it's just business," Lanai reminded her.

"Just business, my ass," Katara huffed. "You better give it to that man. He looks like he'll make some pretty babies, too."

The mention of babies would always hit like a gut punch for Lanai. She knew that every time had not been her fault, but she did play a role in the babies that she'd been pregnant with not making it. The last baby's movements before she aborted the pregnancy still haunted her the nightmares of her getting shot. Babies were nowhere on her agenda or in her plans. She needed to stay focused on work and that was it.

As she looked through tiles and swatches of fabric at the same time, Lanai re-stated, "It's just business."

Katara noticed the change in the atmosphere and quietly reassured her, "You'll have babies one day. It just wasn't meant to happen at that time with that person."

Not wanting to go back down memory lane, Lanai said, "I don't wanna talk about it. I just wanna get this stuff done."

Katara decided to leave well enough alone and said, "Okay, well, I'll leave you to it. I'm gonna go make sure Larry didn't let Sariyah tear the kitchen apart."

Lanai nodded, never looking up from what she was working on. As Katara got off the bed and walked towards the door, Lanai remembered the news that she'd had for her sister. She said, "Oh, Tara. I almost forgot. I'm going to be late to the office tomorrow. I have to go sign the papers for the apartment."

Katara stopped at the door with her hand on the knob. Her eyes looked sad as she asked, "So you're gonna go ahead and go through with it?"

Lanai answered, "Yes. I told you I need my own place. I appreciate you guys, but it's time. I'll only be about twenty minutes away."

Katara nodded. "I understand. Do what you need to do."

She left the room and left Lanai to her work, to keep from thinking about things that she couldn't fix.

CHAPTER SEVEN

"**T**hank you again, Lanai," Mike smiled.

"You don't have to keep thanking me," Lanai said, writing something in her notebook.

"Yes, I do. My home is lovely, thanks to you," he replied, standing across the desk from her.

"I did what you paid me to do."

"You outdid yourself."

Lanai laid her pen down inside her notebook and looked up at him. She asked, "What do you want from me? I did what you asked me. I did what you paid me for. My job is done."

With his hands crossed in front of him, he said, "I want you to let me take you to dinner."

"My job is done," she repeated.

He moved around the side of the desk and took her hand into his. His big warm hands covered her tiny hand. She looked up into his warm brown eyes and he asked quietly, "Can I please take you out to dinner?"

Her brain told her to say no, because she'd been through so much and had been hurt so many times. However, her heart wanted the reminder of what spending time with a man felt like. Her heart screamed yes. She whispered, "Just dinner."

He smiled. "That's all I need."

He continued to hold her right hand in his left and covered it with his right. After a few moments, it began to feel awkward, so Lanai eased her hand out of his. She liked him and she found him attractive, but there was something underlying that she couldn't put her finger on. She kept telling herself that her past hurt was the reason for her being cynical, but her gut was whispering something to her that she couldn't detect just yet.

Mike said, "I got something for you."

With her attention on the notebook that she'd been writing in, she said, "I keep telling you that you don't have to buy me stuff. I do my job without incentives."

He walked toward the door, saying, "I'll be right back."

He was gone for a few moments and returned with a box wrapped in wrapping paper and a bow on it. He eased it onto her desk and stood back, waiting for her to open it. She looked from the present to him. He encouraged, "Go ahead and open it."

"Mike—" she began.

He interrupted, "Look, I know I don't have to. I want to. Open it, please."

She let out a breath. The gifts, cards, flowers, and visits were a bit much. She wanted to remind him as she always did their relationship was professional only. The professionally wrapped box, was wrapped in beautiful, soft paper. She ran her manicured fingers over the wrapping; everything about this man screamed money, even down to the damn wrapping paper. With her curiosity piqued, she slipped her fingers under the red ribbon that created the bow, slid it over the corner of the box, and unwrapped the ribbon from around the box.

She turned the box over and slid her finger under where the paper was taped, loosening the tape from the length of the box. She carefully removed the paper from the box and laid the box on her desk. The black lid and gold embossed letters let her know it was something from Gucci. She *loved* Gucci, almost as much as she loved Tiffany & Co. She didn't realize that she was smiling at the name on the box as she lifted the lid. Inside was a briefcase, made from the softest brown leather she'd ever felt. It had a single handle, double gussets, push-lock closure, and it was larger than the briefcase she carried every day.

She eased the briefcase out of the tissue paper it was wrapped in and ran her fingers over it. Gucci leather was straight from Italy and every time she touched Gucci leather, she felt like she had a slice of heaven in her hands. She carefully unclasped it and opened it to look inside. It had an interior zip pocket, two interior penholders, and a card case for her business cards. The interior also had the infamous Gucci label on the interior fabric. The briefcase was breathtaking.

She felt the inside of the case. She knew this thing was close to $2,000; it brought her back to reality when she realized how much it cost. She didn't feel comfortable accepting flowers, cards, and small gifts from him. She absolutely could not accept a $2,000 briefcase from him. She closed it and carefully laid it back down in the box. She said, "I can't accept this."

"Why not?" He inquired. "Is it the wrong color?"

She shook her head. "It's too much. I can't accept it."

He sat down in the chair across from her and took her hands into his over the box. "You deserve it. Please accept this gift. I ordered it just for you."

His eyes could convince anybody of anything, and when he added those big soft hands, it was almost impossible to say no. She tried to resist, saying, "But it's expensive."

"I can afford it," he said, rubbing her knuckles with his thumbs. He added, "It has your initials on the back. You have to accept it. They won't take it back."

He released her hands so that she could look, and there her initials were, embroidered into the back of the briefcase. The beautiful stitching looking like it belonged there, with the thread perfectly matching the case. She ran her fingers along the stitching, thinking aloud, "This is hand-stitched."

He nodded. "Special order for a special lady."

She smiled. She'd been bought gifts, more gifts than she could ever count. Makai had bought her things to apologize for the million times that he'd messed up. However, she'd never had a gift that was personalized with her initials on it. She said, "Thank you."

With his deep baritone, he said, "My pleasure. Now, can I take you to dinner?"

"Now?" she asked, completely unprepared. "I have so much work to do. I have a few new accounts that need my attention."

"And all of it can wait until tomorrow," he said, standing and coming around to her side of the desk again.

He took her hands and pulled her out of the chair. She protested, "Wait, I can't leave. My desk is a mess."

She tried to pull her hands out of his and move back to the desk. He pulled her to him, causing her to look up at him. He said, "Learn to let go."

She blinked; surprised that he had a little aggression in him. It was appealing, almost as appealing as the scent of his cologne that wafted up her nostrils and danced around in her brain. Her palms began to sweat and she couldn't think of a thing to say. She was sure he knew that he had an intoxicating type of effect on her. It was so hard to keep her guard up when he was so close.

She heard someone clear their throat and she took a step back. She smoothed her cream-colored, wide-legged dress slacks and composed herself. She heard Katara say, "Nai, I'll see you in the morning."

Lanai cleared her throat. "You leaving?"

"No, you are. You're going to dinner," Katara answered. "I'll clean your desk off and close up."

Lanai leaned to the right, looking around Mike and shooting her sister a look of death. Katara knew Lanai hated to leave her desk a mess and she hated it even more when people touched her stuff. Katara stretched her eyes and twisted her lips. The two exchanged looks that allowed them to have a conversation without a word. Katara ended the exchange with a roll of her eyes, and a flick of her hair over her shoulder. With finality, she said, "I'll see you tomorrow."

Defeated, Lanai sighed. She squared her shoulders and retrieved her turquoise Michael Kors bag from her desk drawer, along with her keys from the top of her desk. Following Mike's lead out the door, she shot her sister another dirty look and Katara crossed her eyes and stuck out her tongue. Lanai giggled as she made her way out the building. She knew that Katara meant well and just wanted to see her happy. Lanai figured that going out with Mike couldn't be that bad; he seemed like a nice enough man and he was definitely attractive. She figured that it wouldn't be too bad if she only spent time with him. Hanging out with him didn't mean that they had to be in a relationship. She had to remind herself that even though Mike and Makai shared similarities, that didn't make them the same.

As she made her way to her car, she mentally reminded herself that things would only go as far as she wanted them to go. She reminded herself that the only thing she needed to concentrate on was getting her life back on track and have fun. It was lonely being single, but the single life was even worse at times, since she'd gotten her own apartment. She'd moved out of Katara's house a few weeks ago, and she felt better about having her own place. However, she missed hearing the constant sounds of a busy house. In her apartment, it was just her, her extensive wardrobe and shoes, and her music.

Mike followed her to the car and they stopped at the driver's side door. He said, "You know you can ride with me."

"Yeah, but I'd feel better driving myself," she responded.

"Why do you have to be so hard?"

"I'm not being hard. I just feel more comfortable in my own car."

Mike chuckled and ran a hand over his face. Lanai's stance and facial expression let him know that she was not budging. She was not opposed to trying new things and beginning to let her guard down, but she was not going to be forced into doing it any faster than she was comfortable with. She remembered when she'd moved at the pace that others wanted her to go in the past; part of the reason why she'd spiraled out of control and ended up in rehab. She was taking her sobriety serious.

He said, "Fine. It's going to be a bit of a drive, though. I wanted to take you to the DC area."

"That's a bit far for dinner," she noted.

"But it's a really nice area and there are more options," he pointed out.

She nodded, hitting the button on her keypad to unlock her door. She said, "Okay. Lead the way."

He held his hand on the door like a gentleman and waited while she slid into her seat. He closed her door as she put her bags on the passenger seat and started the engine. She waited patiently as he made his way across the parking lot, and got into his own car. She put her car in gear and followed his lead out of the parking lot. As she followed his car navigating through the streets, she thought about the last time that she remembered being in Washington, DC. She'd been partying with a bunch of people that she barely knew, drunk and high beyond belief. She remembered that she'd also been pregnant with a baby that wouldn't stop growing, despite the toxic amount of drugs and alcohol she kept filling herself with. Every time she thought of the last pregnancy, she'd get a pang in the pit of her stomach. She still had nightmares about the abortion that she'd gone all the way to New York to get, because she'd had no clue whom the father was.

Remembering the shame she'd felt, caused her palms to sweat and her stomach to turn. Suddenly, she didn't feel like eating anymore. All she wanted to do was go back to the office to immerse herself in work, in order to direct her attention elsewhere, so she wouldn't have to think about it. Shopping and work had been her ways to escape the thoughts and memories that haunted her. With her left hand on the steering wheel, she dug around inside her purse, feeling for her cell phone. Her fingers closed around the device and she removed it from the bag, preparing to call Mike and cancel. She felt like she really needed to redirect her energy. Going to dinner in a town where she'd done so much wrong was definitely not the way to do it, either.

Before she could divide her attention between the road and dialing Mike's number, her cell phone began vibrating in her hand. Katara's face and phone number popped up on the screen. Lanai had always felt like her sister had a sixth sense when it came to her. As she slid the green icon to answer, she almost knew what Katara was going to say.

"Hello?"

"Hey, mama," Katara sang into the phone.

"Hey."

"You better not be headed back to the office."

Lanai laughed. Katara was always in her head. "Why'd you say that?"

"Because I know you. You get to thinking too much and then you wanna back out. You better go have fun."

"I was thinking about all the work that I have to do, the clients I have to prepare for, and a couple clients that I have to finish up," Lanai lied.

Katara retorted, "Yeah, right."

"I do have a lot of work to do."

"And it can all wait. You need to get out. Honey, your past is your past; leave it there. You have a man that is interested in getting to know you, he wants to spoil you, and you're pushing him away," Katara pointed out. "Enjoy being treated the right way for once."

"Buying me things is not treating me the right way."

"And I'm not saying it is," Katara rebutted. "What I *am* saying is you never know until you give it a try. I hate that you are always alone."

"I'm not alone. I have you and my love bug."

"Girl, you need a man. Every woman needs a man."

"I need to get my work done."

Katara tried a different tactic. "Well, how about this? You're not welcome back here until tomorrow, and only if you go on this date with him. If you don't go on the date, and I will find out, I'm gonna have a locksmith change the locks, not give you a key, and you'll never get in this building again."

"Ugh," Lanai responded. "Do you have to be so dramatic?"

Both women laughed and Katara said in a lower tone, "You need this. Go enjoy yourself. I love you."

Knowing that there was no more argument to have, Lanai answered, "I love you, too. See you later."

Lanai ended the call and placed her phone in the cup holder. Whenever she talked to her sister, she always felt better. She would go along with going out to dinner in DC and be a little more open and receptive. She would try to let her guard down and stop letting her past control her. She was a new woman now and she needed to behave as such.

CHAPTER EIGHT

It had been months since Lanai and Mike's first date, but that date had not been their last. As the time passed, spending time with him became even easier. She actually looked forward to it. He would take her on dates out of town more than in town, but they would go to the movies, dinner, dancing, museums, and aquariums. She'd even met up with him to spend time with him when he'd gone out of town for business a couple times. She was definitely beginning to learn to trust again, and he was helping her with that.

She looked forward to his sweet emails, phone calls, and text messages that she got on a daily basis, throughout the day. She looked forward to the cards, candy, flowers, and balloons just because. They spent so much time together and she felt so comfortable with him that she didn't even mind that he'd been to her apartment, but she'd never been to his house. She really didn't mind, because she felt more comfortable in her own place anyway.

They'd never done more than kiss, which sometimes made it harder for her to maintain her composure. However, she'd been thinking about it, and she felt like she was ready to change that. She'd written off the nagging feeling in her gut, as just her unwillingness to trust. She'd given herself multiple pep talks and she felt like she might be ready for a weekend getaway with Mike to take things to the next level. She knew she wouldn't be able to get anywhere being scared all the time, so she was ready to step out on that limb.

Lanai sat at her desk, scrolling down the screen with the mouse and looking over the packages that the hotel in Atlantic City had to offer. She'd been so involved in her search that she hadn't noticed the tall, thin, light-skinned woman that came through the door, with a full-length dark brown mink coat on. It was autumn and there were certain days that the weather was a little nippy, but it was definitely not cold enough outside for a full-length mink coat in Dover, DE.

Katara was helping a client pick out some tiles from one of the sample boards in the showroom, so it was Lanai's responsibility to handle whoever came in. Lanai pushed her chair back from her desk and got up, smiling. She advanced towards the woman with her hand outstretched and said, "Hello, and welcome to Interior Designs. My name is Lanai. How can I help you?"

The woman briefly shook Lanai's outstretched hand. Lanai noticed that the woman's cold hand matched the cold look in her blue eyes. By the woman's light complexion and blue eyes, she could pass for being Caucasian. The texture of her light brown hair, which was swept on top of her head in a mass of curls, was an indication to Lanai that either she was mixed with something, or she was a very light-skinned black person. Her cheekbones were high and her nose was narrow. She looked like an uptight librarian that liked to flaunt the fact that she had a lot of money.

The woman's thin lips were in a hard line. She cleared her throat to speak. "I'm looking for the woman who is cheating with my husband."

Lanai's mouth dropped open. Take aback, she stammered, "Uh, um, I'm sorry?"

Squaring her shoulders and lifting her nose in the air, the woman repeated herself a little louder, "I'm looking for the woman that is cheating with my husband."

Lanai looked over at Katara, who was now looking at the woman in the mink coat. Katara shrugged her shoulders to indicate she didn't know the woman and Lanai directed her attention back to the woman. "Ma'am, I'm not sure you're in the right place. My sister and I own this business and just she and I work here."

"Then one of you is cheating with my husband," the woman replied arrogantly.

Trying to keep from causing a dramatic scene, or running Katara's customer away, Lanai offered, "Ma'am, would you like to have a seat?"

Without a word, the woman went to the seat at Lanai's desk and sat down as if she had a board inserted in her coat. She sat on the edge of the seat as if she was prepared to take flight at any moment, and it seemed as if her nose had inched further in the air. Lanai returned to her seat across the desk from her. Lanai sat on the edge of her seat because she wanted to know who this woman was, and why she'd stumbled into their business with this nonsense.

Lanai scooted her chair in, as if it would help her to listen better, and crossed her hands on top of her desk calendar. She asked, "Ma'am, what's your name?"

"My name is Cecilia Stranton and I am looking for a woman with the initials L.W.," Cecilia revealed.

Maybe this is a coincidence. This has got to be a coincidence, Lanai thought. She wanted to say something, but she couldn't get a coherent thought to form in her head. Things were not making any sense to her. She'd never heard that last name before meeting Mike. When she'd began spending more time with him, she asked and he'd looked her in the face and said that he was not married and had no kids. She had no reason not to believe him.

Cecilia went on to explain, "My husband, Mike, is an investment banker and we have four children together; two boys and two girls. I tracked the expensive gifts, constant flowers, and other things from a credit card receipt I found. Everything was coming here. The engraving bills specify the initials L.W., as well as the floral shop cards, which always have those initials too."

Lanai's head began to spin. She squinted her eyes and waved her right hand in the air in an attempt to communicate the question that her lips formed, but never left her lips. Her right hand went to her chin, which she rested it on. Her brows furrowed and she asked, "Huh?"

"Are you L.W.?"

She nodded confused confirmation, and said, "But he told me he wasn't married and didn't have any kids. I asked."

Cecilia calmly fished around in her purse that she'd had resting on her right forearm the entire time. As she felt around in her purse, she asked, "Did it ever occur to you that something wasn't right when he never took you to his home?"

Lanai's hand dropped and she involuntarily shrugged. "I didn't think anything of it."

"Most women don't," Cecilia retorted, pulling out what she'd been looking for. "You women generally see what you want to see."

You women? Lanai's head snapped back as if someone had thrown water in her face. Her eyes narrowed and she was about to tell this stiff bag of bones about herself, until Cecilia slid a picture across the desk to her. Lanai slowly picked up the picture and six smiling faces stared back at her. Those kids were his all right. It looked like other than their complexion, Cecilia had little to nothing to do with their conception. Mike's genes were strong; each of his children looked like a replica of him. They were a beautiful family, even with Cecilia smiling like she was truly happy. The boys took their broad shoulders and strong forehead after their father, with the girls having a softer version of their father's features.

"Are they quadruplets?" Lanai asked, looking up from the picture in her hand.

Cecilia shook her head. "The boys are twins and the girls are twins."

Looking at the picture again, Lanai couldn't fathom why Mike would deny such a lovely family. All the children looked to be in their teens. *Why would he lie to me,* she asked herself internally. She mentally slapped herself. Why wouldn't he lie to her? Realistically, there was no way he'd come out and say he was married with four children. Lanai's blood began to boil. She'd begun to let her guard down, just to get betrayed again.

She handed the picture back to Cecilia and as she tucked it away, Cecilia explained, "I know his job takes him away and he's a good provider. But I can always tell when his roving eye is at work. He follows the same stupid pattern all the time."

"So why do you stay with him?" Lanai heard herself ask, before she could press her lips together as she'd intended.

"My children and I are well taken care of, we want for nothing, and after all these years, I see him as an investment. The man that you women see is what I created," Cecilia answered smugly. "I cultivated him and molded him into what he is today. I'll be damned if a newcomer is going to come in and take away, what I've worked more than half my life to create."

"Okay, listen," Lanai began, not hiding her irritation. "This *you women* mess is bothering me. If I had known he was married, I would've never spent time with him or gone anywhere with him. I actually kept my distance from him for a long time. I'm not a homewrecker, so please get that out of your head. I knew nothing about him being married with children. Period."

"So what did you think he was when he never stayed the night, other than being out of town, if he took you with him?" Cecilia shot back.

"I have gone out of town with him, but I have my own money and I got my own hotel room," Lanai clarified. "Let's be clear, I don't need a man for anything. Also, I've never had sex with your husband."

Cecilia chuckled, "You'd be the first."

Pushing back a little from her desk because she was growing more irritated with this woman, Lanai said, "Look, I understand you're upset. But you have no right to take it out on me. Take it out on your husband, who is the one obligated to you, not me. I don't owe you anything."

"Did he tell you he's HIV positive?"

Lanai's eyes widened and she sat up straight in her chair, looking like she'd just seen a rat run across the desk. She croaked, "He's *what*?"

"HIV positive," Cecilia repeated with an even tone and straight face.

"He looks healthy," Lanai whispered, more to herself than anyone else.

"Are you sure you didn't sleep with him?"

"I'm positive. I wasn't ready to take that step."

"Thank God," Cecilia retorted. "He gave it to me twenty years ago. I thank God that my children were all born without it."

Lanai's eyes roamed over the face across the desk from her and it made more sense. *She was so skinny because she was dying. This raggedy nigga,* she thought. It was bad enough that he'd lied about having a family, but to add insult to injury, this clown had the audacity to have a deadly disease and not tell her about it. She was ready to go to his office and confront him.

She said, "I'm so sorry to hear that. You don't have to worry about me ever saying another word to him."

Seemingly satisfied, Cecilia rose from the chair and quietly made her way to the door. She left without another word. Lanai furiously gathered her purse and keys without saying another word also. She had lied to Cecilia. She had one more thing to say to that low-down, dirty, son-of-a-bitch, and she was going to do it in person. She stormed out the door and headed to her car. Hitting the button on the keypad, she climbed into the car and threw her bag on the passenger seat, started the engine, and was about to speed out of the parking lot, until she remembered that she'd forgotten her briefcase that Mike had brought her. She shoved the door open and stormed back into the office, flinging the front door open and going to her desk with a purpose.

She snatched the expensive bag out of her desk's bottom drawer, practically ripped the flap off the bag, and dumped the contents onto the desk. She heard Katara say, "Now, Nai, calm down. I know you're upset..."

Spinning on her heels and storming toward the door again, she murmured, "You have no idea."

She made her way to her car again and it never registered in her mind that she'd left the engine running. She climbed in, slammed the door, and sped out of the parking lot. Breaking every traffic law except running red lights, she focused intently on going to her apartment to gather every little thing that he'd bought her. She vaguely heard her phone buzzing in her purse, but she ignored it. The otherwise ten-minute drive to her apartment took about five minutes. She barely put her car in park after she screeched into the parking space. She angrily shoved the car door open and snatched her keys out of the ignition, this time remembering to turn it off.

She climbed the steps of her apartment building as quickly as her four-inch, pointed-toe Gucci heels would allow. She'd rented a two-bedroom apartment on the second floor from the Greens at Cedar Chase. She paid $950 a month in rent, but she felt it was reasonable with the amount of space she had, the amenities, and the fact that she didn't need a roommate or a kid to get a two-bedroom. Using her key, she let herself into the apartment and began snatching things up, from the living room all the way back to the master bedroom that Mike either bought or reminded her of Mike.

She made a pile of stuffed animals, shoes, clothes, jewelry, cards, belts, and other things in the living room floor. With a recent dozen of roses in her hand, she remembered that he'd bought a Versace travel bag for her. She went into the spare bedroom and pulled open the closet door, looking around for the signature Versace design. She located it on the floor, snatched it up, and tossed it on the bed. It was a decent-sized bag; everything would probably fit in it. She opened the bag and threw the roses in it. With the bag still open, she carried it into the living room, throwing the bag on the floor next to the pile that she'd created.

She stuffed everything in the bag, grabbed her keys, and headed back down to her car. After tossing the bag in the trunk, she climbed in and backed out, heading for Mike's office in downtown Dover. It took her minutes to get there, weaving in and out of traffic like a mad woman. She retrieved the bag from the trunk when she got in the parking lot and strutted to the door with a purpose. Once inside, the receptionist smiled and greeted her, asking how she could help her.

Lanai plastered a fake smile on her pretty face and asked, "Mike Stranton, please?"

"Yes, ma'am," the receptionist answered, picking up her phone and ringing Mike's office. She told him that a young lady was in the lobby for him and hung up. She gestured down the hall and said, "You can go down to his office."

Lanai had been hoping that he'd come out so that she could embarrass him, the same way she'd been embarrassed in her place of business because of his lies. She declined, "No, you can have him come out. I don't have much time."

The young lady behind the desk nodded, picked up the phone, and relayed the message. Within moments, Mike came down the hall and into the lobby. When he saw Lanai, a smile spread across his lips. The fake smile that she'd plastered on her face stayed in place as he advanced towards her.

Before he could get within arm's length, she said, "Hey, your wife, Cecilia, came by my office today. She took the liberty of showing me a lovely family photo, which you denied having, and made me aware of you giving her HIV twenty years ago."

Mike's eyes grew huge and his jaw dropped. It took him a second to recover and when he did, he turned to the receptionist, who was looking at them in awe, and ordered, "Call security!"

He turned back to Lanai and said, "I don't know what you're talking about. I don't have HIV."

As she spoke, she'd closed the space between them. She asked, "Oh, no?"

With her right hand, she pushed gave his forehead a hard shove, sending his head back, and then slapped him hard across the face. The slap was so hard that it seemed to quiet any movement in the office. He stared at her in disbelief, and within moments, that disbelief turned into anger. His brown eyes were smoldering and he looked like he wanted to hit her back. She stood her ground, hand on her hip with her facial expression begging him to try it.

He bit his lip and bellowed, "Renee, call security! You better get your crazy ass outta here. Now!"

"Crazy," she screamed. "I'll show you crazy!"

She balled up her fists and began swinging. He was a little more prepared, barely sidestepping the blows and managing to grab her wrists. She managed to pull her left hand loose, punched him in the left side of the face, and screamed, "Get the fuck off me, you AIDS-infested bitch!"

He grabbed ahold of her free hand before she could knock him in the head again and tightened his grip. She writhed against him, trying to get free. She was kicking and screaming obscenities as he stepped around the travel bag and moved her towards the door. She kicked him hard in the shin, causing him to let her go immediately. Security rushed into the lobby from another part of the building and a big, burly, baldheaded black man, scooped her up off the floor as she socked Mike in the face again. The security guard led her out the door, kicking and screaming.

She screamed, "You worthless, lying, dying, dirty-dick son-of-a-bitch! You tried to kill me! I hope you die slow, you motherfucker! I'm gonna fuck you up! You wait!"

The guard put her down once they were in the parking lot and said, "Ma'am, you gotta calm down. They already called the cops."

"I don't give a fuck!" she yelled. "It's against the law to have a life-threatening disease, pursue someone, and not tell them you have it. That bastard has HIV and would've given it to me if I slept with him."

Standing between her and the building, the guard said, "But he didn't. You didn't sleep with him, right?" When Lanai nodded, he continued, "Then get in your car and leave. Don't make things worse."

"That crazy ass girl cut me!" Mike yelled, coming out the building with the travel bag and the shorter security guard.

Hearing that, Lanai frantically began checking herself for any signs of blood. She didn't see any, but she made a mental note to scrub thoroughly when she got the chance. She tried to move around the security guard in front of her, but he was quick on his feet. He blocked her from advancing toward Mike. She said, "Nigga, I'll show you crazy!"

"You already did that," Mike retorted.

He took the bag and tossed it across the small parking lot towards her. He said, "Bitch, take your shit and get off of my property."

Lanai's head snapped back and cocked to the side. She echoed, "Bitch?"

With blood trickling from under his left eye, he spat, "Bitch!"

"Oh, yeah?" she asked. She moved to the right and the big guard moved too, as she expected. She quickly went left, leaving him scrambling. She had on four-inch heels, but for her, that was like having on flats. She scooped the bag up off the ground and hurled it at Mike's head. He and the other security guard ducked, and the bag that was aimed at his head slammed into the glass door, causing it to shatter. When she threw the bag, she'd begun to advance towards him again. She wanted to kill him and she probably would've done her best to achieve it, if the big guy hadn't grabbed her again.

He scooped her up off the ground again and spun her around towards the street. She screamed, "Put me down!"

He placed her on the ground, but kept his grip on her. She demanded, "Let me go!"

He said, "I can't do that. You just damaged property. I'm supposed to put you in handcuffs."

"Let me go!" she repeated.

Mike yelled, "I'm gonna kick your ass! You broke my fucking door!"

"Bitch, come do it!" Lanai taunted over her shoulder.

The shorter guard placed himself between Mike and the other guard holding Lanai. He had his hands on Mike's chest, trying to encourage him to calm down and relax. The people that were coming and going in the surrounding businesses had stopped to observe the spectacle. Two Dover police cars pulled into the parking lot and both officers were out of their cars before they could come to a complete stop. The white officer with red hair went to Mike and the short security guard, telling him to relax. The black officer went over to Lanai and the big security guard.

Mike hollered, "This lunatic came ranting and raving into my office, causing a scene, and she threw that bag and broke the door! The bitch is crazy! I want her off my property!"

"Call me another bitch!" she screamed, trying to wriggle out of the big guard's grip.

The black officer extended his hand. He advised her, "Ma'am, if you don't calm down, I'm going to put you in handcuffs and put you in the back of the car. Calm down and tell me what happened."

"He's a lying, cheating, AIDS-infested coward bastard!" she spat.

The officer asked, "Did you break the glass?"

"Yes, I did," she admitted. "I was aiming for his head."

"Well, you know I can arrest you for assault and destruction of property," the officer informed her.

She looked the officer in the eye and challenged, "Then you need to arrest him for reckless endangerment and attempted murder for trying to unknowingly spread HIV!"

The officer said, "Listen, I don't want to have a conversation with you being restrained by this security guard. I'm going to give him permission to let him go, but the minute that you so much as *twitch*, I'm going to put you down and put cuffs on you. Are you calm enough to have a conversation unrestrained?"

Lanai huffed. "Yes."

The officer gave the guard a look and he released her, but only backed up a step, prepared to restrain her again. She was little, but she was definitely a problem. She stood between the officer and the guard with her arms crossed under her breasts, tapping her foot impatiently. The officer pulled out his small spiral notepad and a pen. He asked, "What's your name?"

"Lanai Wilson."

"Spell that."

"L-a-n-a-i Wilson, like the football."

The officer nodded. "Date of birth?"

"December 6, 1989."

"Address and phone number."

Lanai rolled her eyes and blew hot air. She rattled off her information. The officer looked up from the notepad, "Lady, don't give me grief. I'm here to help."

"Help who?" Lanai asked, rolling her neck with attitude and putting her hand on her hip.

"Just answer the officer's questions," the big guard admonished. "Lose the attitude. If he wanted to arrest you, you'd be in cuffs by now."

Lanai rolled her eyes again and returned her arms to being crossed beneath her breasts. Nobody was going to tell her how she needed to act, no matter who they were. The officer asked her to explain her version of what happened. With attitude and contempt pouring from her, she rattled off what happened. She made sure to tell the officer how it started with his wife coming into her office, and telling her about the important information Mike excluded.

When she was finished, the officer asked, "Did you sleep with him?"

"No, but I could've," she answered.

The officer and the guard exchanged a look and the officer looked at her, "But you didn't. Be grateful you didn't."

The white officer came over to join them and said, "Mr. Stranton said he won't press charges on you, if you leave and never come back."

"Oh, he don't have to worry about that!" she replied incredulously. "I'll *never* come anywhere *near* him and his AIDS-infested ass!"

"Okay, ma'am," the white officer said, "he said that he doesn't have AIDS or HIV and legally, you can't spread that rumor unless you have medical proof."

"His wife told me he gave it to her," she shot back.

"Did she show you medical proof?" the white officer asked, looking like he was taking the situation personal.

Lanai looked at him as if he had sprouted a second head. "She's his wife. She doesn't need medical proof."

The black officer asked, "She found out you were seeing her husband, right?"

Lanai nodded. "But I didn't know he was married."

The black officer waved his hands and shook his head, as if to erase what she'd said. "Doesn't matter. She found out you were seeing her husband. She could've made it up to scare you away from him."

Lanai pondered on what he'd said for a moment, looking at the ground. It was possible. She looked back up at the officer, a confused look causing her brows to furrow. She asked, "Why would she lie about that? She looked sick, though."

"And she may have," the officer said. "Point is, though, she didn't show you proof. She could've said what she needed to say to make sure you stayed away from her husband. She could be telling the truth; none of us know. What we do know is unless you have medical documentation, you can't go around saying that in public places."

"If you are caught on this property for any reason again, you will be arrested for trespassing. Ma'am, you have to leave the premises. Now," the white officer insisted.

"Gladly!" she retorted. She felt around in the pocket of her slacks for her keys. She looked down on the ground around her feet and patted her pockets to be sure she wasn't losing her mind. She couldn't remember if she'd taken her keys out of the ignition when she'd gotten there. She made a move to go towards her car and when she did, both officers and the security guard moved with her. She stopped and looked at each of them. "Do I need an escort?"

All three replied in unison, "Yes."

She rolled her eyes, and went to her car with the black officer on her right, the security guard on her left, and the white officer behind her. The security guard asked, "Are you a stunt woman?"

She scrunched her face up at the weird question and said, "No. Why?"

"Because you are *killing it* in those heels," he replied. "I've never seen anyone move that quick in high heels before."

"Quick on my feet," she smiled.

She opened her car door, which was an indication that her keys were probably in there, and leaned in to find them dangling from the ignition. She climbed into the driver's seat and the white officer reminded her, "Stay away from this office, ma'am."

"Oh, don't worry. I will," she assured him, closing the door and starting the engine. She carefully backed out, careful not to hit anyone and resisting the urge to hit Mike, and then headed in the direction of her office, a few blocks away.

She never thought for a second that Cecilia would lie about having a deadly disease, but the truth of the matter was, some women were so desperate to keep what they thought was theirs that they would stoop to any level. Waiting on the red light, she sadly shook her head. She couldn't believe that things had played out the way that they did. When the light turned green, she drove though it and turned left into the parking lot outside of her office.

She got out, making sure to take her keys with her, and headed into the office. Katara was sitting at the desk writing something in her agenda book as Lanai headed for the bathroom. Once inside, Lanai immediately began scrubbing at her hands and fingers after pushing the button on the dispenser multiple times. She wanted to make sure that she scrubbed off any of Mike's blood, if it had gotten on her. She wished that she could scrub away the memory of every meeting him.

She stood over the sink with the hot water running, furiously scrubbing from her fingers all the way up to her elbows. Every few seconds, she would add more soap and scrubbed hard. She looked up at her reflection as she scrubbed. She recognized the fear in her eyes that she'd had when she'd gone to rehab and had to endure an HIV test. She'd been so afraid of the results, not because of the test, but because of the lifestyle that she'd lived. In the back of her mind, she knew that she deserved to have it, with all the unprotected sex she'd had with strangers.

"What happened?" Katara questioned, standing in the doorway of the bathroom.

Her question had broken into Lanai's thoughts and bought her back to reality. Lanai looked back down at the suds that covered her hands, arms, and filled the sink. She continued to scrub without saying a word. She had no idea where to start. Her adrenaline level was almost back to normal, and it was beginning to register in her mind what her actions could've gotten her.

"Did you kill somebody?" Katara breathed, coming into the bathroom.

Lanai laughed, "No, Tara. I didn't kill anybody."

Katara returned, "Well, why are you in here scrubbing like you're tryna get rid of evidence, or you're about to go into surgery?"

"Mike said I cut him, so I wanted to make sure I don't have any of his blood on me," explained Lanai.

"What did you do to him?"

"I molly-whopped his ass," Lanai replied, scrubbing her hands.

Katara laughed. "Are you serious?"

Lanai shot her a look, confirming that she was very serious. Katara laughed and said, "Nai, you can stop scrubbing. Whatever was on there is off now, along with the top layer of your skin."

Lanai chuckled and went about the process of rinsing off the arms, hands, and the sink. It took a while to get all the bubbles to go away, but when she did, she saw that she had scrubbed her hands and arms raw. She noticed that her knuckles were sore from making contact with his face. She still couldn't believe that she'd socked him in the face. Katara stood there, waiting patiently for Lanai to spill the beans about what happened with Mike.

Lanai went about the task of telling her sister every detail of what happened. When she was finished, Katara breathed, "Wow...your temper still has not changed."

Lanai chuckled again. "I guess you're right."

"No, I mean, you are angry...like really angry. You're lucky they didn't arrest your ass," Katara said.

"Wouldn't you be angry if you were dating someone with HIV?"

"Yes, yes I would," Katara answered quickly. "I understand *why*; I was just making an observation. So you've gotten banned, huh?"

Lanai shrugged. "I really don't care. I don't intend to go back to his office or anywhere near him. He's lucky that guard had a hold on me, though, 'cause I was gonna go tear some skin off that face."

"Then you really woulda been scrubbing," Katara laughed.

Lanai thought for a second and the thought of his blood being on her made her cringe. "Oh yeah, you're right. Not doing that."

They laughed together briefly. Katara's expression turned serious. She asked, "Are you okay, though?"

Lanai nodded. "I'm good."

"No," Katara pressed, putting her hand on Lanai's arm, forcing her to make eye contact. "I mean are you really okay?"

Looking her sister in the eye, she insisted, "I'm fine. I didn't expect this and I was mad that he'd lied so much, but at the end of the day, I knew something wasn't right with him. Shoulda followed my gut."

"This doesn't mean that you go into hiding," Katara reminded her on the way out of the bathroom. "Every man is not a lying cheater."

Lanai grunted. She found that hard to believe. She sat down at her desk and said, "Listen, I don't have the energy to deal with a man right now. I have other stuff to focus on."

Katara looked like she had so much more to say, but she decided to leave the situation alone. She'd allow her sister time to heal and move on. She returned to her desk, saying a silent prayer that Lanai didn't give up on finding love.

CHAPTER NINE

Makai sat in his clothing store's office, in the executive, black leather chair behind his desk, with his head back and eyes closed. He didn't need anything to confirm that he was in charge, but he always felt like a boss every time he sat in one of his office chairs, with the head of a gorgeous young lady in his lap. He couldn't remember the name of the most recent one, but she was sucking on his manhood as if her life depended on it. He felt like he was on cloud nine.

He gripped a fistful of her hair and felt the tracks glued into her scalp. *Shit, that shit almost ruined the mood,* he thought, resting his hand on the back of her head. She sped up the pace, performing her award-winning oral sex, taking him to his peak faster than he expected. It happened so fast that he couldn't even react or let her know it was happening. He ejaculated in her mouth and she kept going until he was completely drained. With his head back and mouth wide open, he left his hand on the back of her head. He wasn't holding her in place, but his brain needed a minute to function and direct his body parts to move.

She simultaneously removed his hand from her head by his wrist, and his penis from her mouth with a loud slurping sound. She stood up and went to the bathroom, wetting some paper towels in warm water. She returned to wipe him off gently, and then turned to go back in the bathroom, taking her purse with her to tend to her makeup.

The blood had finally returned to Makai's brain, allowing him to blink a few times. He readjusted his clothes, tucking himself inside his boxers and watched her from the chair. She had a wonderful body with a flat stomach, perky C-cup breasts, firm butt, and toned legs. Her face was pretty; she had full lips, brown eyes, cute nose, and her face had a youthful roundness to it. He hated that she had weave in her head; he hated the feel of it. He was a natural hair kind of man. It really didn't matter to him what she did with her hair, because she was nothing to him. She'd come and relieved him all times of the day several times and he was certain she'd told him her name, but he couldn't remember it to save his life.

He couldn't figure out what she got from it, because they'd never had intercourse, he didn't take her out, and they didn't talk outside of her periodic visits. He didn't give her any money, either. The day that he'd met her had been in his store a few months before and they'd exchanged glances and smiles. They'd made small talk and when he'd gone into the back office, she'd followed him grinning. He didn't say anything when she'd closed the door and locked it. He didn't fight her when she'd dropped to her knees, after pulling his button loose and zipper down.

That was something else that didn't matter to him, because he had no further interest in her. She dropped her lipstick and compact back into her purse, zipped it up, and turned off the light as she came out of the bathroom. She slid her purse strap on her right shoulder, smiled and winked at him, and quietly left the office. He continued to sit at the desk in silence. He absently swiveled slightly in the chair, with his chin resting on his thumb and forefinger on his cheek. He sat deep in thought, contemplating the current state of his life.

His daughter Makayla brought a different kind of light and joy to his life. He imagined that his life as a single parent would be harder without Ms. Hazel in it, but it was difficult enough to have a toddler to do everything for on his own. He was running four businesses in two different towns and still tried to juggle maintaining business contacts. His activities had been dramatically limited, due to having Makayla full time. His social life was nonexistent and he barely was able to mingle with his business contacts after hours as he used to. He had to take her with him to Wilmington on a weekly basis, sometimes a couple times a week to make sure that things were running smoothly.

His best friend and business partner, Larry, was normally in Wilmington at their barbershop and clothing store, but Makai always wanted to make sure everything added up. He hated surprises and definitely didn't want an IRS kind of surprise. His personal life suffered because of having a child, as well. He took being a parent seriously. He didn't want just anybody around her or at the house. He wanted to make sure that whoever was around his daughter would be stable and permanent people in her life.

The thought of Lanai ran through his mind, causing his heart to feel a twinge and his stomach to drop. Her absence was hurting him to the core. He hated it. Why wouldn't she just give him another chance? He had promised that he wouldn't hurt her again, and he really did mean it. He wanted to give her the world. He wanted to make her happy for the rest of her life and she just wouldn't let him. He hated the feeling that her absence gave him, because he couldn't control it. All he wanted to do was love her and she wouldn't even let him talk to her for more than a few minutes.

Angry at the fact that he was even thinking about such nonsense, he slammed his fist on the desk and yelled, "Fuck! I hate this fucking girl!"

He spent more time and money sending more flowers and more thoughtful gifts, just for them to be returned. If he thought that it wouldn't hurt Lanai, he would pay somebody to get rid of Katara. He knew she was the reason behind the gifts and flowers being sent back and not being able to win her back. He needed Lanai in his life. Why was it so hard for her to get that? The thought of her not wanting to talk to him, listen to him, or see him brought tears to his eyes. His heart literally ached for this woman. He never loved or wanted anyone like her; no one else had been important to him other than Makayla.

Not one for being emotional, he shoved the chair back and stood up from the desk, snatching up his keys. He needed to do something more constructive with his time and energy than sit around and think about a bitch that didn't care anything about him. Pushing his emotions way down, he left the office and closed the door behind him. He needed to go to the store and get some things for Makayla. He figured he'd better make good use of his time since he'd had his last customer of the day reschedule. He'd done all the paperwork he was going to do for the day, so sitting around was pointless. He didn't want to waste his energy on something he couldn't change.

He nodded his head at the manager of his store and she asked, "Leaving for the day?"

"Yeah, daddy duties," he called over his shoulder as he opened the door.

He pushed the door closed and started towards his truck, but was stopped in his tracks. It was the middle of fall, although it wasn't too cool outside. He spotted Lanai coming out of her office with her briefcase and purse in a skirt, sweater, and heels. Every time he saw her, time seemed to slow down and everything around him moved in slow motion. He imagined her scent and feeling how soft her skin was. He literally had to fight the urge to not cross the street and make her talk to him. He just wanted to take her home and keep her there forever.

"Man, fuck this shit," he grumbled to himself.

He pretended as if he hadn't seen her and proceeded to his truck, climbing in, and speeding off. He needed to hurry up and get this grocery mess out of the way, go get his daughter, and hit his basement gym while Makayla played. He was beginning to be angry all the time over nothing. Drinking didn't make things better, but he damn sure tried after he would put Makayla to bed. Smoking weed in his basement when she was asleep was a pointless exercise, because he couldn't get high enough. Oral sex was only a momentary distraction; shit, everything for him was a momentary distraction.

As he whipped his SUV into a parking space, he came concluded that it was time to move on. It was time to stop trying to get Lanai to give in and focus his energy on a woman that wanted his attention. There were plenty of them. He'd never had an issue with getting the attention of women. He was a good-looking businessman, and a good father to his daughter. He knew he was the cream of the crop, especially in a small town like Dover. He would just have to find a babysitter, get out, and go meet people.

He walked into Food Lion, which was a few minutes west of Loockerman Street. He scooped up a basket and headed to the baby food aisle. He tossed some things into the basket, looking for Makayla's favorite snacks and foods. He didn't even notice the woman that was eyeing him from the other end of the aisle. She came closer to him with her cart, trying to be noticed by him. When she got close enough for him to hear, she asked, "Picking up some things for a friend?"

Makai barely looked up from what he was doing and absently said, "Uh, no. Shopping for my daughter."

"Aww," she commented. "That's sweet. I know your wife absolutely loves having a dutiful husband."

He read the label on something called Apple Puffs and chuckled, "Nah, I'm not married."

"Well, then that makes you a good boyfriend," she said, clearly flirting with him.

He put the container in the basket and looked the woman over. She was brown-skinned with beautiful, flawless skin, perfect makeup and eyebrows, slim frame, and long black hair. He couldn't tell if it was a weave or not. The stylists were getting so good with putting weaves in that it looked like natural hair. Her eyes were a grayish color, which was a contrast to her milk chocolate skin and made her look more intriguing. She wore a gray pantsuit that complimented her eyes and seemed to fit her in the right places. Her hands were small, with polished medium-length nails. He didn't see a ring on her left ring finger.

He smiled slightly. "No, I'm not in a relationship. I'm a full-time single father."

One of her petite hands went to her slightly exposed cleavage and she batted her long lashes. "Oh my, that's so rare."

His eyes roamed over her again, taking in more of her features a little slower than the first time. She was shamelessly flirting with him and he found it appealing. He was visibly amused. Holding the basket in his left hand, he folded his arms across his massive chest and waited while he watched her eyes slowly travel the length of his six foot four frame. He almost laughed aloud when her eyes lingered in his crotch area a little longer than anywhere else. Almost every woman that he'd come across had done that.

He heard her make a satisfied grunt under her breath. He unfolded his arms and extended his hand. He said, "Makai."

"Lynette," she answered, placing her hand inside his.

He noticed that her hand was cold, but that was probably because the temperature was beginning to drop, the closer it got to winter. He said, "Nice to meet you."

"Pleasure's all mine," she smiled. The look in her eyes told him that she meant her comment in the most explicit way that he could imagine.

He ended their handshake and returned his arms to their folded position across his chest. He asked, "So, who are you shopping for?"

"Myself," she answered. When there was silence, she added, "Yeah, no kids, no husband, just me."

"Why's it just you? You're a beautiful woman."

"Looks don't guarantee anything."

He nodded, "True. So are you single?"

She nodded in agreement. "Are you?"

"I am," he answered.

"You're a good looking man," she pointed out.

"Well, like you said, looks don't guarantee anything."

"But I find it hard to believe that you're single. I know you have women falling at your feet."

"The same could be said about you."

"Touché."

After a few moments of silence, Lynette said, "Listen, I'm a forward kinda girl. I really don't do small talk and pussy footing. I like what I see. I'd like to get to know you."

Makai blinked. He'd anticipated her leaving it to him to say that. He answered, "Okay."

She reached in her purse and pulled out her cell phone. "What's your number?"

He chuckled and rattled it off to her. He liked the feeling of being pursued. All he had to do was stand there, and be his handsome self. He felt his phone vibrate in his pocket and she announced, "I just texted you my number. Save it."

He promised, "I will."

"We should get together for lunch or dinner some time. If you can find a babysitter," she added.

He smiled. "I'm sure I can work something out."

"Great," she said with an award-winning smile. "I look forward to it."

With that, she pushed her cart past him, her heels clicking on the tile with a purpose. She put a little extra switch in her walk, because she was certain he would be looking. He did notice that she had a nice butt. He laughed to himself at her directness and proceeded to get what he needed for Makayla and some things for himself. He mused to himself that Lanai could take a chance and miss out on him if she wanted. He knew that he was a good catch.

CHAPTER TEN

"**M**ake sure you text me when you get home," Lanai called after Katara walked out the door. They alternated between opening and closing the office, but Lanai ended up closing up more often than Katara. She would always volunteer to do it, unless she had pressing business with a client or a meeting with a client ran over.

"I will. Get home safe," Katara called back.

With it being wintertime, it got dark outside around about 5:00 pm. Their office was located on Loockerman Street, but New Street, the street that crossed Loockerman, was not a good street to be on at night. She wasn't too concerned about the people that were on New Street, because she figured that if she didn't bother anyone, they wouldn't bother her. She and Katara had talked about closing earlier during the winter months, but there was nothing waiting for Lanai at home but furniture, so she didn't mind staying until their regular time of 7:00 pm.

She'd been working on scheduling clients and fitting in a conference that she wanted to attend, into her agenda book and calendars on her desk and computer. She had been receiving requests from people all over the country to decorate their houses or businesses, thanks to either her work, her sister's work, or their work combined. She felt there was always room to learn to improve her craft, so anytime there was a seminar or conference that she could attend; she would make it an extra effort to juggle her schedule.

She loved her career and meeting the new people, but she felt that her life was lacking. It had been months since she'd barely escaped being arrested after acting a pure fool at Mike's office. She'd taken on more work to keep her mind occupied. The harder she worked and the longer hours that she kept, the more tired she was when it was time for her to go to sleep. That meant less time for nightmares and dwelling on what her life didn't have. Regardless of the amount of work that she burdened herself with, she still felt like she had a gaping hole inside of her.

When she noticed that her brain was going in the direction she didn't want it to go, she decided that it was time to wrap up what she was doing and finish it at home. Maybe at home she could Google a class or research picking up a hobby. She clearly had too much time on her hands. She made a point to gather her things, put on her wool pea coat and scarf, and separated her keys to find the key for the office door.

After turning off all the lights and making sure the back door and windows were locked, she exited the building, not paying much attention to anything past the door. She locked the office up and tugged at the door; just to be sure it was securely locked, and then turned to walk to her car. Someone stumbled past her, bumping into her slightly, and she jumped and screamed. The man hunched over, grunted something, and continued to stagger down the sidewalk.

Lanai put a hand to her chest, trying to settle her breathing and heartbeat. She said to herself, "I gotta get my ass home."

As she neared her car, she felt like someone was following her in the dimly lit parking lot. Her heart was still beating fast and seemed to increase in its pace. Her hands began to sweat and she clutched the handle of her briefcase in her right hand. She had the keypad prepared in her left hand, pushing the button to open her doors with her thumb. She always parked her car as close to the building entrance in the parking lot as she could get. It was probably a thirty-second walk, but it seemed like it was taking an hour to make it to her driver's side door.

She had almost made it around the front of the car, before she felt a cold, strong hand, grip the back of her neck and slam her on the hood of her car. She involuntarily screamed as her hands slapped the hood of the car hard. She'd forgotten to put her gloves on before she'd come out, so the cold hood and the impact of being slammed, caused her hands to sting. She felt a face next to her ear and heard him breathing heavily. His breath smelled like hot garbage and it burned her ear as he whispered, "Scream again and I'll fucking kill you."

Lanai's eyes darted back and forth, and all she could see was the gravel of the parking lot and tires. He held her in place on the hood of her car, pressing harder against her neck, pushing her further into the hood. Barely above a panicked whisper, she asked, "What do you want?"

"I want you," he answered.

She shuddered. Her mind raced with possible options. Loockerman Street was almost a ghost town in the winter months after dark, so there was probably not going to be a passerby that could help her. He'd already said that if she screamed again he would kill her. His breath was beating him to it. She tried to turn her head in the opposite direction to keep from inhaling that putrid smell. He made his grip on her neck tighter.

His voice sounded excited when he asked, "Oh, you wanna fight?"

With his free hand, he began feeling for the bottom of her coat. Feeling his cold, hard hand roaming over her body, she tried to buck against him. All she managed to do was kick her legs apart, allowing him to be able to put one of his legs between hers, and get him more excited. He encouraged, "Go ahead and fight. I like when you fight."

He dug the elbow of the hand that was gripping her neck into her back, causing her to yelp in pain. She begged, "Please, don't! If you want money, I'll give you money! Just please don't hurt me!"

She felt him find the waistband of her gray wool slacks and he tugged at them. When they didn't move, he reached around and snatched the button loose. She tried her hardest to fight him and began crying. She managed to get her arms to go back and tried to grab at him, but the way he had her pinned, kept her from being able to grab him or push herself up. She pleaded, "No, please don't hurt me! Please let me go!"

She heard his zipper opening and began sobbing. He was going to rape her right there on the hood of her car, outside her business, on a street where businesses where still operating and there was not one soul to help her. She tried to push against him, screaming, "Help! Somebody help me!"

His fingers dug into the flesh of her neck, but she didn't care. She hadn't heard or felt a weapon, so she was going to take her chances, calling his bluff on his promise to kill her to keep him from raping her. She felt him pulling at her slacks and she felt the material begin to give way. She tried to hold on to her ripping pants with her fingertips. She silently prayed, asking God to stop this man and then she continued to scream.

"Stop fucking screaming!" he ordered, spitting on her ear.

She thought that she might throw up. She screamed, "Oh, God! Somebody help me!"

She heard someone yell, "Hey, yo!"

There were fast footsteps on the gravel and within a few moments, the weight that had been holding Lanai down suddenly released. She heard something hit the ground. Feeling that weight removed, she wasted no time scrambling away from the spot where she'd been pinned down. She tripped over her own feet, trying to get to the driver's side door, a nervous mess with her hands shaking and tears everywhere. She struggled to get the door open and when she finally did, she climbed in, almost closing the door on her own foot. She slapped the automatic lock button and tried to start the engine.

Panicking, she frantically looked around for her keys. Then she remembered that she'd dropped them with her purse and briefcase on the ground in front of the car. Getting back out of the car was not an option. She felt terrified, like a trapped animal. She saw movement in front of the car and for a second, it looked like he was coming for her again. She leaned over and snatched open the glove compartment. She had no idea what she was going to find, but she needed something.

She sat up and took another scared peek. She realized that he wasn't coming towards her. He was getting the shit kicked out of him. The movement that she'd seen had been him trying to shield himself from the punches and kicks that he was receiving. She watched as this other man worked him over. There was something familiar about the guy delivering the beating. She leaned closer to the steering wheel and squinted through her tears. *Dammit, it's Makai*! It looked he was trying to make the guy a permanent part of the ground, with the way that he was kicking and stomping him.

She was relieved to know that someone had come to her rescue, and it was someone that she knew. She whispered a thank you to God for sending him, even though Makai had never crossed her mind. Makai didn't stop kicking until the man stopped moving. He was breathing heavily, fuming. He gave the guy what looked like one last kick to the head and cursed at his motionless body. As one final gesture, he spat on the motionless man and stepped over him.

Lanai watched in stunned amazement. She'd never seen that type of anger come from him in the eleven years that she'd known him. She stared at the motionless body of the man that had begun to assault her, wondering if he was dead. The banging on the driver's window made her jump almost into the passenger seat and scream. She looked up to see Makai, motioning for her to roll down the window. She stared at him, petrified, unable to comprehend what he was trying to say.

He said loudly, "Roll down the window!"

Looking in his eyes and watching his movements with his hands, her brain finally caught up and she slapped the button for automatic unlock for the doors. He pulled the door open and crouched down. His eyes searched her face and body.

He asked, "Are you okay?"

She heard him speaking and saw his lips moving, but her brain really couldn't make out what he was saying to her. She stared at him as if she were an invalid. He cupped her face in his hands, causing her to jump again. He whispered, "Relax, babe. I'm here."

Feeling his warm hands on her face, hearing his reassuring tone, and looking into his eyes caused a fresh flood of tears. She grabbed his wrists and began crying hysterically. He pulled her to him and let her cry on his shoulder, wrapping his arms around her. She clung to him, crying uncontrollably. He rubbed her back soothingly, patiently waiting for her to let it out. After a few minutes of her heaving and crying loudly, he took her by the shoulders and eased her back.

He said, "Lanai, calm down. It's over."

Looking down, she sobbed and heaved, sounding like she was about to have an asthma attack. He touched her face again, trying to wipe away the never-ending tears. He continued to encourage her to calm down and stop crying. It was a slow process, but she eventually calmed down to the point where he could talk to her.

He asked, "What happened?"

"He came up behind me and tr-tried...t-to...he tried...t-to...rape...me," she stammered.

"Where's your sister?"

"Home," she sobbed.

"Why are you here by yourself at night?" he questioned.

"I always close by myself."

Using the pads of his thumbs, he wiped more tears. "That's not safe."

She looked up into his eyes and whispered, "Did you kill him?"

With a shrug, he replied, "I should've."

She looked over the steering wheel at her motionless attacker. She was terrified that he might get up and have some sort of weapon that could hurt both her and Makai. She didn't realize that she was shaking until Makai asked, "You want my coat?"

She glanced down at his coat and her own. She said, "No, I'm fine."

"C'mon. I'm gonna take you home," he said, removing his hands from her face and taking her hands into his. Before she could protest, he gently pulled her from the car. He moved her between himself and the wall in a protective gesture as he closed her door. He asked, "Where are your keys?"

Still shaken, she pointed to the front of her car. Holding her hand, he led the way and she held onto his strong arm, with both of hers like a little child. They moved to the front of the car. The closer she got to the body on the ground, the more terrified she became. She held her breath and her eyes were as big silver dollars. She was quickly shuffling her feet along the gravel of the parking lot, trying to be careful about moving too close to the motionless attacker and quickly moving away from him. She was so scared, she felt like she was going to pee on herself.

Keeping an eye on the motionless body, Makai bent down with his free hand and picked up her keys, purse, and briefcase. He stepped over the man and Lanai had just about bunny-hopped over him. Makai moved her away from the car towards the road, pushing the button to arm the locks and alarm. As they got to the curb, Makai had slid his arm out of her grasp and around her shoulders. He navigated them across the street to his truck, but Lanai kept looking over their shoulders to see if the man had gotten up.

Makai ushered her into the truck, putting her bags on the floor in front of her and placing her keys in her lap. He went around the front of the truck, checking for traffic before he climbed in. As he pulled away from the curb, he asked, "Where am I going?"

"Uh..." Lanai tried to remember which direction she lived in, blinking a few times. She said, "Turn right. I live in the Greens at Cedar Chase. Behind the old Walmart."

He nodded and drove in the direction of the highway, turning right at the intersection of Division and Queen Streets. Lanai had wrapped her arms around herself and stared out the window. She couldn't believe that she'd been on the verge of being raped. She was still shaking from the experience. Makai noticed out of the corner of his eye and reached over, turning on the heat. The last time he'd seen her shake like that was when they'd been on their way to drop her off at rehab. He hoped that wasn't the reason now.

There was a constant buzzing coming from the floor. He said, "Your phone's ringing."

It took a moment for it to register in her brain what he was saying. When it did, she began to look around for her purse. She bent down and rummaged around in her purse until she found her phone. She unlocked the screen to see that she had ten missed text messages, multiple emails, waiting voicemails, and five missed calls. She went into her call log and saw that all the missed calls were from Katara. She knew that if she didn't call her back immediately, she'd probably call in the SWAT team.

She pressed the screen, calling Katara's phone. It seemed like there was only a half of a ring before there was a break in the line.

"What the hell are you doing that you can't answer your phone," Katara screeched. "Do you know how worried I was?"

"I was almost raped," Lanai answered flatly.

"You were *what*?" Katara's voice seemed to go up three octaves. "Where are you? What happened? Who was it? Did you call the cops? Where is the son of a bitch? Why didn't you call me? Damnit, Nai, why didn't you answer the phone?"

As Katara rattled off her questions, Lanai had moved the phone away from her ear. When Katara had taken a break, Lanai returned the phone to her ear and answered softly, "I called you as soon as I could."

Katara was quiet for a moment, but Lanai knew that the wheels in her mind were turning. Katara asked, "Are you okay? Where are you?"

"I'm on my way home," Lanai answered, ignoring the first question.

"I'm on my way," Katara announced.

Without another word and no energy to argue with her, Lanai pushed the red button at the bottom of the screen to end the call. She knew that Katara would cut the fifteen-minute drive at least by half. She slid the phone into her coat pocket and rested her head against the leather headrest. She hardly listened as Makai talked on his phone, telling somebody that he was going to be late, but he was still coming. She wrapped her arms around herself again, trying to regain some sense of security.

When he reached her development, she directed him to her building and he jumped out, almost before putting the truck in park and turning off the engine. He walked around to her side, opening the door. He grabbed her things and slowly helped her down. He guided her towards the door and asked, "You got your keys?"

She nodded, allowing him to guide her up the steps with his arm around her. When they got to the door, she unlocked it and pushed it open. He reached inside and felt along the wall for the light switch. He didn't allow her to go inside, until he was able to flip on the switch and peered inside. After he was satisfied with the safety of the entryway, he guided her inside and closed the door behind them. He let her walk to the couch on her own. He immediately went to check the sliding glass door that led to the balcony to make sure that it was locked.

He placed her bags on the couch next to her and took it upon himself to go through her apartment, without her permission, to make sure no one else was there. She curled up on the couch, with her feet tucked underneath her, still in her coat and heels, and wrapped her arms around her stomach. He came back into the living room and asked, "You wanna go in your room or stay out here?"

When she didn't respond, he went over to the couch and moved her belongings over, sitting next to her feet. He unfolded her legs, stretching them across his lap. Taking her by her elbows, he pulled her to him, taking her into his arms and holding her. She didn't even realize that she was crying again. They sat there silently with him holding her and her staring blankly at the arm of the couch across from her. He was well aware that whenever something traumatic happened to her, she'd shut down. There was no forcing her to open up before she was ready; he'd just have to wait it out.

Lanai was numb. Her mind kept replaying what happened in her mind. She was trying to figure out what she could've done differently before leaving the office. She tried to think of different ways that she could've fought him off. In her mind, there had to have been something she did wrong or could've done differently. Her brain was going a hundred miles per minute, but couldn't focus on one single thought for longer than a moment. She wanted to be able to just disappear. She let him hold her while she silently cried on his chest.

She didn't hear the front door open or close, but she did feel her sister touch her face gently. With her other hand, Katara gently rubbed Lanai's back and spoke encouraging words softly in her ear.

Lanai had no idea of how to process what she was feeling or going through. She wanted to scream, but she couldn't. She wanted to curl back up into a ball and die. So many bad things had happened to her over the years, when all she'd tried to do was be a good girl and life right. She just wanted to quit, because quitting was easier than living and she was tired of trying.

CHAPTER ELEVEN

"**T**hank you, Makai," Katara whispered, standing outside Lanai's bedroom door with her hand on the handle of the partially opened door.

Makai dismissed it. "No need to thank me. I'm not gonna let nobody hurt her."

"I just wanted to say thank you," Katara insisted. "Only God knows what would've happened if you hadn't been there."

"He would've raped her," he answered bluntly. When the tension grew thicker in the air, he said, "Listen, I gotta go get my daughter. My number hasn't changed. Tell her to call me if she needs me. I'm coming back to check on her tomorrow."

With that, he left Katara standing in the hallway and left the apartment, locking the bottom lock behind himself. As he drove to his daughter's daycare, he called and gave Ms. Hazel another update on where he was. He informed her that he would be there in about ten minutes and Ms. Hazel promised to have Makayla ready. He dropped the phone in his lap and turned the volume on his radio up. He needed something as a distraction to keep the sights and thoughts of earlier out of his mind. He wasn't sure if he'd killed that guy or not, but the mere thought of it had him ready to go back to see if he was dead. If he wasn't, Makai was prepared to finish the job. He didn't want to relive those homicidal thoughts, because he had a daughter to think about. Her mother was in enough trouble for the both of them.

Makai's mind went back to how detached and upset Lanai was. He hated to see her like that. He'd been the cause of it so many times and it ate away at him, but he wasn't going to tolerate anybody else hurting her. He felt helpless when she was hurt in any kind of way and he hated the helpless feeling. He didn't know what to do with it. He knew what to do with anger, but not to have control of the situation was foreign to him. The only person in the world that left him with the feeling of him not having control was Lanai.

His phone vibrated in his lap, snapping him out of his thoughts. He glanced down from the road to see Lynette's picture and phone number across the screen. He'd been dating her for a few months after meeting her in the Food Lion. She was cool, but she seemed to be lacking something. She was high maintenance, which he didn't care about, and she made her own money. She seemed educated and well-rounded. He liked spending time with her, but there were times when his mind would drift during their conversations. She chatted nonstop sometimes, which would work his nerves. The more he got to know her, the more he found himself looking for excuses to stay busy and stay away from her.

He suppressed a groan and answered, "Hello?"

"Hey, honey," she chirped into the phone. "I'm on my way over. Do I need to pick up anything?"

He rolled his eyes. "Look, tonight's not a good night."

"But you promised," she whined. He could tell by the sound of her voice that she was pouting. He hated when she pouted, because he felt a grown woman shouldn't be pouting.

"I know, but something came up," he said.

"What is it? Is everything okay?"

"Yeah, just had a family emergency."

"Oh, my goodness. Can I do anything to help?"

He said, "No. I got it under control. I'm just not in the mood for company right now. I gotta get the baby and put her to bed and everything. I just wanna get her settled and go to bed."

"I can come help with that," she pressed. "You know, I still haven't met her yet. Every time I come over, she's sleeping. It's almost as if you synchronize my visits to her bedtime."

It was funny, because that was exactly what he did. He would never allow Lynette to come over while Makayla was awake. If, for whatever reason, Makayla decided she wanted to be a butthole and not to go bed when she was supposed to, Makai would call or text Lynette and cancel. He would ask her to come on a different day. He avoided her comment and said, "Listen, I gotta go. I'll hit you tomorrow."

She was saying something as he hit the end button and tossed the phone into the passenger seat. He knew this nonsense with Lynette wasn't going to last much longer. He didn't like to be annoyed and she was annoying as hell. She was nothing like Lanai. The thought of Lanai caused him to blow hot air and run his free hand over his face.

"This fucking girl," he grumbled, wishing that he could keep Lanai out of his thoughts.

He pulled up to the curb in front of Ms. Hazel's home daycare. When she opened the door, he could see that she had on her housecoat, rollers in her hair, and slippers on her feet. He hated when he had to come after she had gotten ready for bed. She told him all the time that she didn't mind and he could take as long as he wanted, but he still tried his best to get there at a decent hour. Ms. Hazel had an alert and energetic Makayla on her hip all bundled up.

Makai opened the storm door and Makayla practically jumped into his arms, "Da-da!"

He kissed her cheek. "Hey, Princess." He kissed Ms. Hazel's cheek and said, "I'm sorry it took so long."

"Baby, I told you, you're fine," Ms. Hazel answered. She squeezed Makayla's cheek and added, "I love my Tinker."

"Yeah, but you need to be in the bed by a certain time," he argued, picking up the diaper bag by the door.

She pointed out, "I told you she was fine here. I could've kept her overnight. You wanted to come."

He nodded, "Because she's my responsibility."

"Speaking of responsibility," Ms. Hazel began, looking into her glasses that were always at the end of her nose. She only looked through her glasses when she wanted to chastise someone or make an important point. Makai waited and respectfully gave her his undivided attention. She continued, "You know I don't mind her mother coming to spend time with her. I think it's a good thing. But I will not have her bringing company that I don't know with her."

"What company?" he asked, with a confused look. His blood began to boil again.

"Some man. Today was the second time she brought him here," Ms. Hazel revealed. "I wasn't sure if you knew him or not, but I don't like the vibe I get from him, or the way he talks to her."

"Talks to who? My daughter?"

"Now, baby, you know I'm not having nobody come in here talking crazy to my Tinker. I'd take my cast iron frying pan and knock that nigga out," Ms. Hazel replied.

Makai could picture her swinging her heavy fry pan at somebody and at any other time, it would've been a comical thought. At that moment, he wasn't in the smiling mood.

Ms. Hazel continued, "No, baby. He talks to her mother in a nasty tone. I don't like it around any of my babies here. Now, I mentioned it to her the first time she brought him. I told her I didn't want him in here, and then she brings him back. If she thinks she's gonna disrespect my house, she's got another thing coming."

Stopping her before she could upset herself, Makai assured her, "I'll take care of it. Tonight."

Ms. Hazel nodded her head, looking like she wanted to say more, but she left it to him. She knew that Makai was a man of his word.

He said, "If she comes back, call me. I'll come handle it. Now, you get inside. It's cold out here and you'll catch a cold."

"Alright, baby," Ms. Hazel said, backing away from the storm door to close the front door. "I'll see you tomorrow. Y'all get home safe."

Makai waited until she closed the door and he heard it lock, before he closed the storm door and made his way to the truck. He put his daughter in her car seat and fastened her in. Before she could act a fool, he whipped out her sippy cup from the outside pocket of the diaper bag and gave it to her. She happily kicked her feet and drank from the cup as he closed the door.

Once he was in the driver's seat and began to pull away from the curb, he picked up his phone from the other seat and called Sade's phone. It rang about seven times before there was a break in the line. He heard sniffling on the other line before she asked, "Hello?"

He barked, "Who the fuck did you bring around my daughter?"

"What," she asked, sounding confused.

"Who the fuck did you bring around my daughter," he repeated.

"When? What are you talking about?"

"I'm talkin' about that disrespectful nigga that you brought to my daughter's daycare. Don't play dumb with me!" he warned.

"Marcus is not disrespectful," she replied, sniffling again.

He heard a male yell something in the background. He said, "Don't bring that nigga back around my daughter again."

Her response to the man in the background was muffled. Then she said to Makai, "I'm her mother. She needs to get used to her stepfather."

He took the phone away from his ear and stared at it as if it was a foreign object, then put it back to his ear and said, "Fuck what you talkin' about? That nigga ain't *nothin'* to my daughter! And as a matter of fact, you pullin' that dumb shit got you banned, too!"

"Banned? What do you mean banned?"

"I mean you can't go to daycare and see her no more," he clarified. "You wanna do dumb shit, you can't see her."

"Makai, I'm her mother! I have the right to see my child!" she screamed.

"When did you get married?" he asked, switching gears.

"Huh?"

"Huh, hell. When did you get married?"

"Uh, well...we haven't *officially* gotten married *yet*. But we will," she added.

"So, if you're not married, how is he Makayla's stepfather?"

Sade stammered and stuttered, "Well...uh...um...h-he...w-we...he asked me. And...and...we...and we're gonna get married. Soon."

"Uh huh," Makai replied suspiciously. "Like I said, you can't go to daycare. If you do, she's gonna call me. You don't want her to call me."

Sade's voice dropped almost to a whisper. She pleaded, "Kai, please don't do this to me. I need to see my daughter."

"I didn't do this. You did."

"Makai, please."

"I'm done with it. Answer's no. You can thank yourself."

There was more muffled talk, and then he heard Sade say, "I'm trying. Just hold on a minute."

The man in the background yelled, "Who the fuck you tellin' to hold on a minute? Who the fuck you talkin' to?"

It sounded like the man might've hit Sade and her scream confirmed it. She pleaded, "Marcus, baby, please! I'm trying! No! You said you wouldn't hit me again!"

Makai blew a breath of hot air. He asked into the air, "What the fuck is this? Captain Save-A-Hoe night?"

He turned his truck in the direction of Sade's house, which was in the opposite direction of his own. From where he was on the highway, it took him about five minutes to get to her house. He ended the call and threw the phone in the passenger seat. He pulled into the driveway of her townhouse in the BayTree development off White Oak Road. He left the engine running because it was cold outside, and he wasn't taking his daughter inside with the madness that he'd heard. He looked back to tell her he'd be right back and she was sleeping soundly.

He got out, retrieving one of his spare sets of keys from the console and locking the doors as he walked up the driveway to the steps. The last time he'd been here, Lanai had been shot, and he'd picked her bloody body up off the ground, and drove her to the hospital. Once at the top of the stairs, he pounded on the door. He heard yelling and screaming, so he pounded harder.

Through the door, he heard a man yell, "Who the fuck is it?"

"Nigga, open the fucking door!" he ordered.

The door swung open and a dark-skinned, burly looking man stood there with no shirt on. The scowl on his face made him look darker than he was. The look on his face and his size was enough to scare most people. Makai wasn't most people, though. He knew with somebody that big, he had to surprise him. He did just that, swinging his right fist with all his might and landing it against the left side of Marcus's face. Marcus stumbled back into the house. Makai took advantage of his opportunity and went into the house, using his Timberland boot to kick Marcus, which sent him crashing to the ground.

Makai had expected him to get up and fight him, but Marcus cowered on the floor, just as Makai imagined Sade had been when Marcus had been beating on her. Marcus lay on the hardwood floor, bleeding in the fetal position, with his arms shielding his face. Makai couldn't even swing anymore. It was one thing to beat the man that had attempted to rape Lanai unconscious. However, looking at this huge man on the floor like a little baby was pathetic. He didn't feel like it was even worth a fight.

Makai stepped back and growled, "Keep your fuckin' hands to yourself and stay the fuck away from my daughter!"

He saw Sade curled up on the couch, with blood running from her lip and nose. Her hair was all over her head and her shirt was ripped. She had old and new bruises on her face and neck. She didn't have any pants on and her eyes were huge. Makai looked a little closer at her as she began trying hard to focus her darting eyes. He looked at the coffee table littered with beer cans, liquor bottles, bags of weed, a jar with embalming fluid-dipped blunts in it, and a white, powdery substance all over the table and floor. She was obviously high.

He looked at her again, shaking his head. He pitied her, too. *What was it with these weak ass women*? They couldn't handle life so they turned to drugs, men that abused them, and ran from their kids like his mother had when he was little. He was disgusted. He said sternly, "Stay the fuck away from my daughter until you get yourself together! And I mean that!"

He turned and left the house, closing the door on what he thought was a strong woman. He descended the steps and hit the button to unlock the doors. When he got in, he looked back at his sleeping daughter. She looked more like him, but he could see her mother in her, too. He reached back and gently rubbed her face. He'd make sure she didn't end up like the tragedy her mother had become.

CHAPTER TWELVE

"**H**ey," Lanai greeted Makai as he walked into her apartment.

He carried a large bouquet of pink and white roses, along with a bag in his hand. He handed her the roses and kissed her cheek. "Hey. How you feeling?"

"Good," she answered, inhaling the sweet scent of the roses. She set about finding a vase to put them in with water. It had been a couple months since she'd been attacked, and Makai had been coming by every day without fail. He'd started bringing her roses every day in the beginning, until she told him to stop. She'd told him that all the flowers were annoying and he was overdoing it. He'd scaled back to bringing them once a week, but instead of a dozen, he'd bring her two. She didn't realize that she'd grown accustomed to his visits and their time together, until she inhaled the scent from the roses a second time, as she carried the vase outside on the balcony.

She was looking into the bouquet, but her mind was a million miles away. She absently ran her finger around the inside of one of the roses, remembering what falling into a routine with him did to her. She couldn't let that happen to her again. She had grown so much and come so far, that going back would be the equivalent to committing suicide. Her heart felt differently, though. Life without

Makai had been just existing, not living. Even with all the stress, drama, and lies, her heart felt as though it came alive and felt complete when he was a part of her life. She was so conflicted.

"You hungry?" Makai called from the kitchen, taking food out of the bag that he'd carried in.

Lanai snapped out of her daze and answered, "Yeah. What'd you bring?"

She came back into the apartment, closing the screen door behind her. It was the beginning of spring and flowers and trees were blooming, birds were all over the place chirping, and the weather was warmer than it had been in a while. She welcomed any opportunity to have her sliding glass door and windows opened.

"Stopped by the Olive Garden and got you a Tour of Italy," he said, folding up the bag.

She looked over the food and asked, "And what'd you get you?"

"Fish."

"Hmm." She tore off a piece of his fish. She remarked, "This is good."

He laughed, "You know you the only person in the world that can eat off my food, right?"

She smiled and climbed on the stool next to him in the kitchen. She replied, "I must be special."

He dug into his food as if he hadn't eaten all day. With a mouthful of food, he answered, "You are."

With her fork, she pushed her food around. She looked at him and asked, "Why do you do that?"

He looked up at her with a packed mouth and innocent eyes. "What?"

She laughed. "That. You eat like somebody's gonna take your food."

He shrugged his shoulder and continued to attack his food. When he noticed that she wasn't eating, he washed down the food he had in his mouth with a big gulp of iced tea and asked, "Why you not eating? I thought you were hungry."

"I am," she said, continuing to push the food around with her fork.

He dropped his fork on the plate and put his glass down next to his plate. Taking a napkin, he wiped his mouth and asked, "What's the matter?"

"Nothing," she lied, not looking at him.

"C'mon, man," he said. "What's the problem? What's on your mind?"

She placed her fork on her plate and looked up at him. "What are we doing?"

He looked down at their food and back at her. "Eating lunch."

"No, really. What are we doing?"

It took a moment for it to register in his brain that she wasn't talking about the food. He let out a defeated breath. He looked like he really wasn't in the mood to have this conversation. She needed to have it, though. She didn't want it to turn into an argument, but she definitely needed to have the conversation with him. He said, "Lanai, not this again. I thought we were in a good place."

"We are," she assured. "I just don't know what we are. What is this?"

"This is us."

"Which is what?"

"What do you want it to be?"

"Don't answer my question with a question."

"Are you really gonna do this?" he asked.

Crossing her arms, she said, "You can go."

"You're really gonna do this," he replied, more to himself than to her. She waited for his answer. He breathed heavily. "I asked what you want it to be, because I'm ready to give you what you want. Whatever it is you want."

"And what do I want?" she probed.

He cut her a look, letting her know that she was treading on thin ice. He asked, "What do you want?"

"I want to know what we're doing. What is this? You coming by here every day, bringing me flowers once a week, bringing and sending me gifts. What is this? Are you trying to date me?"

"Yes," he answered.

"So, that's the only reason you've been coming around?"

"No."

Lanai looked at him expectantly, rolling her hand in a gesture for him to continue.

He rolled his eyes and blew an exasperated breath. "Look, you know I don't like doing this shit. You know why I'm here. You know why I've been coming. Cut me some slack."

"No," she answered bluntly. "You talk now or we don't talk at all."

He said, "I've been coming to make sure you're okay. I like spending time with you, and I want it to lead to us working things out. I want to be with you, but that's your call."

She thought for a moment on his answer, looking carefully into his eyes. She felt that he was being genuine, but she wanted to continue to push the envelope. She asked, "So, I'm just supposed to forgive and forget?"

"No," he said. "You're supposed to eat your lunch before it gets cold. Have you been out of this apartment yet?"

She knew he was an expert at dodging uncomfortable conversation. She would let him slide for the moment, but as far as she was concerned, they were going to stay in the same place until he decided to either walk away for good or follow through. Though she didn't trust him, she still loved him and was in love with him. Her heart and head were in two different places.

She picked up her fork and began to eat her food. She answered, "Nope."

Following her lead, Makai resumed eating. He pointed out, "You know you can't live the rest of your life in this apartment."

She eyed the lasagna on her fork before putting it in her mouth. She said, "I know."

"Are you going back to work?"

She nodded.

He asked, "You got an attitude now?"

She shook her head. She replied, "I work from home. I don't need to go in the office."

"You don't need to see your clients?"

"Katara is handling the face-to-face. I'm doing all the research, calling, emailing, and paperwork," she explained, taking a drink of tea.

She felt him looking at her as she ate. He asked, "So you givin' up?"

She shook her head. "I'm working."

"You're hiding," he rebutted.

She shrugged her shoulder. "Call it what you want."

She heard his fork hit the plate. He asked, "Yo, what is goin' on with you? You ain't scared of nothin'. All of a sudden this nigga almost raping you, got you too scared to come out the house?"

She chose not to respond to his callous question. She didn't need anybody's approval or permission to live her life as she wanted to. When she was ready to leave the apartment, she would. He didn't experience what she had, so he couldn't judge her. She thought to herself that she didn't need him to keep coming around, no matter how much she looked forward to it. She unconsciously shifted her body away from him.

His voice softened, "All I'm saying to you is you're a fighter. Don't let one situation keep you from living your life."

She nodded her head, eating in silence.

"Yo, you stubborn as shit." She laughed and he continued, "You are, and you know it. Spoiled ass."

She looked at him and saw something in his eyes. She looked back down at her plate. She knew that he loved her and could see it in his eyes. She was afraid of seeing it though, because of the dark places the obsession with that same look she saw in his eyes had led her.

He asked, "Are you worried about running into him again?"

"I didn't *run* into him," she clarified.

"Are you worried about that situation happening again?"

She sighed, "Yup."

"I'm right down the street," he reminded her.

"That didn't stop him before," she said softly.

He assured her, "I'm not gonna let anything happen to you. I'll take you to work and pick you up. Your sister will be there with you. You gotta get outta this apartment, though."

She thought about what he said to her. In her mind, it wasn't feasible for him to take on more responsibility for her than he was. He was already taking time out of his day and losing money, and she didn't want to inconvenience him further. She knew that she couldn't live life depending on someone else to protect her. She thought about Katara's suggestion for her to finally go see a counselor. She'd thought about it a few times, but always decided against it, because it made her feel weak. She realized that it might not be a bad idea to talk to someone, outside of Makai and Katara, and begin the healing process. The last thing she wanted to do was to begin to use anyone or anything like a crutch again. She also realized how selfish it was of her to continue to consume so much of Katara and Makai's time.

She decided, "I'm gonna make an appointment to see someone."

Looking up from his food to her and then back to the food, he asked before putting a forkful of food in his mouth, "See who?"

"A counselor or therapist."

He chewed thoughtfully then shrugged his shoulders. "Whatever you wanna do."

They continued their meal with light conversation, laughing, and joking. He cleaned up the kitchen as she went to the couch and checked her laptop to see if she had any instant messages or emails waiting for her. She hated to admit it to herself that she liked the little routine that they'd fallen into. As she typed away, answering the message that she'd missed, Makai came into the living room. He came over to her and leaned down, kissing the top of her forehead, and said, "Babe, I gotta go. Got business to deal with."

She nodded and without looking up, she said, "Thanks for lunch."

On his way out the door, he called, "I'll see you tomorrow night. I'm locking the bottom lock."

His usual time to come by was in the middle of the day; he rarely came at night unless she was extremely scared. She preferred him to come in the daytime, because it made things easier. They both had work to deal with, and he always would have to leave because he had business and a child to tend to. Lanai stopped typing in mid-sentence at the thought of his daughter. She'd seen the little girl once and she'd been a beautiful little girl. She had huge cheeks, jet-black curly hair, a cute little nose, and big bright brown eyes. She was about a shade lighter than Makai was, and she looked like the female version of Makai Jr., their dead son, which bothered Lanai.

She didn't have anything against the little girl; she was only a baby. The negative feelings that she harbored about the baby had been towards Makai and Sade, more towards Makai. He knew having a baby was all that she'd wanted and that was the ultimate betrayal. She hadn't thought of that betrayal since he'd saved her a few months ago. Since they'd been spending time together, she hadn't thought of much else than the time they spent. However, remembering that he had a daughter made her feel uneasy.

They never talked about his daughter and he never brought her with him, but Lanai knew that he took good care of her. Makai took good care of everyone that he loved. Lanai thought about it for a moment. She wasn't sure if the baby was with Makai or her mother, so she thought that it might be easier for him to move the way he wanted to, because he didn't have the full-time responsibility of a child all the time. Either way, there was never a mention of the baby, the arrangements concerning the baby, or how his life has changed since the baby's birth. Lanai was somewhat relieved that he didn't mention her or bring her around. She wasn't sure if she was ready to handle that can of worms.

She pushed thoughts of the baby, her mother, and Makai to the back of her mind. She decided that dwelling on a situation that she couldn't control was not how she wanted to use her energy. She switched gears and began researching names of reputable therapists in the area. She refused to let anything keep her cornered or afraid, even if it was something that haunted her nightmares and daydreams.

CHAPTER THIRTEEN

Makai kissed his sleeping daughter's head, and laid her in the toddler bed in her room at Ms. Hazel's house. Makayla's room had originally been one of the spare rooms. After arguing with Ms. Hazel about not wanting to leave her overnight, Makai lost the fight. Ms. Hazel had put her foot down and told him that when he had late nights or something to do at night, he was not taking Makayla out of the house. She had given him a curfew of 8:00 pm, and had explained to him that it was an appropriate bedtime for a toddler.

He'd tried to fight her on it, but realistically, the only times that he wasn't there by 8:00 pm to pick Makayla up, were the few times that he'd gone over Lanai's house in the evening. It wasn't that often that Makayla stayed the night, but she loved it either way because Ms. Hazel spoiled her rotten. When she did stay the night, if he wasn't able to get there before she went to sleep, he would stop by and hold her for a little while as she slept, before he went home alone. Otherwise, he'd put her to sleep and then leave her with Ms. Hazel, who had told him repeatedly that he could always stay the night if he wanted to. He had told her that he would rather be in his own bed. He left his daughter there because he trusted her and sometimes he did need that little break.

As he covered Makayla up with the Dora the Explorer blanket that she loved so much, he turned out the overhead light, leaving on the little Dora lamp on the dresser. He quietly left the room, leaving the door slightly ajar. He was leaving her tonight, because he was going to watch a movie with Lanai. She had begun going to see her therapist several times a week, and ventured out to the office a day or two out of the week. She was making small steps to resume her life as normal, and he'd made it a point to be there with her every step of the way.

He knew that subconsciously, he was trying to make up for all the times that he'd messed up, as well as for the times that she'd needed him and he hadn't been there. He was working hard to make sure she saw that he was serious and wanted to make amends. As he came down the steps, he went into the kitchen where Ms. Hazel was making her tea for the night. He kissed her cheek and said, "She's sleeping. I'm gone."

"Alright, baby. You have fun," she answered.

"What makes you think I'm gonna have fun?" he asked, amused.

"Your cologne is fresh," Ms. Hazel pointed out. "Usually I gotta threaten you to get you outta here when she stays. Tonight, you're flyin' through here like you on skates. Whoever this young lady is, she makes you happy."

He chuckled. "Goodnight, Ms. Hazel. Come lock the door behind me."

As he left the house without acknowledging what she'd said to him, his phone buzzed in his pocket. He pulled it out and checked the screen. When he saw Lynette's face and number had popped up, he pushed the button on the right side of the phone to lock the screen again and returned the phone to his pocket. He had been dodging her calls, and rushing her visits to the store or barbershop whenever she would show up. He knew that the best thing for him to do was to be honest with her, and tell her that he didn't want a relationship with her. He just couldn't bring himself to do it yet, because he wasn't sure exactly where things stood with Lanai.

He strode towards his truck at the curb, taking his keys out of his left pocket. He noticed movement from a car parked behind his truck. He squinted his eyes to better see whom it was moving in the darkness as he slowed down his pace. He wasn't afraid, but he wasn't stupid, either. It took a few moments for the figure to emerge. When it did, he saw that it was Lynette in sweats and sneakers. She glared at him and with an accusatory tone, she asked, "So you're just gonna keep ignoring my calls?"

He looked her over carefully, taking in her demeanor. Her breathing was hard, nostrils flared, and her eyes looked a little wild. He asked, "How did you know I was here?"

"You look nice," she replied in a sarcastic tone, looking him up and down. "And where's the baby? You come here to pick her up and come out of there with no baby?"

He put his hands up, "Whoa, hold up. Why are you here? Are you following me?"

"I'm *here* because *you* have been avoiding my calls, instead of being a man and answering," she retorted, her tone and eyes shooting darts at him.

"Yo, don't ever come to my daughter's daycare again!" he warned.

He attempted to move around her, not wanting to continue the conversation, but she moved into his path to keep him from walking past her. He looked at her confused and annoyed. He asked, "What's your problem?"

"Where are you going?" she demanded.

"Minding my business."

With her hands on her hips, she repeated, "Where are you going?"

He chuckled a little to keep from snapping, because he could feel his temper rising. He tried a different approach. "Really, Lynette? What's the problem? Are you this mad because I didn't answer the phone? I told you I'm busy. You know that I'm busy."

Gesturing towards the steps behind him, she pointed out, "You just ignored my call coming out of the daycare. How busy are you really?"

"I'm on my way to see a family member that hasn't been feeling well lately," he lied. "I didn't answer, because I'm running late after putting Makayla to sleep. Ms. Hazel keeps her after a certain time."

"You never told me that," she replied, her expression softening. "You know I wouldn't mind helping you out. I love little Makayla."

He nodded his head, noting the sudden change in her demeanor. "I know. But I'm not fighting Ms. Hazel. She said she's keeping the baby after a certain time. She's good, I just wanna make sure that I see her, before she goes to sleep or at least kiss her goodnight."

She touched his arm. "You know you can rely on me. Just trust me. I would never do anything to hurt her. I'm here if you need me."

He nodded. He would never take her up on it, but he knew that if he needed her, she would fall all over herself to get done whatever he asked. He'd noticed a while ago that she was clingy, and that was something he couldn't stand in a woman. Every day that he spent with Lanai made him dislike Lynette more. He didn't want to string her along, but he really wasn't interested in having anything between them. Seeing the love in her eyes kept him from telling her how he really felt, because he really didn't want to hurt her. He'd always been a sucker for a fragile woman.

Taking advantage of the change in the atmosphere, he said, "Listen, I gotta get going."

With eyes filled with concern, she asked, "Do you want me to come with you? I can take some of the burden off you."

Where is your hobby? he asked himself, beginning to feel annoyed again. He shook his head no. "I'll call you. Probably tomorrow."

She allowed him to pass and he made a beeline for his truck. She called after him, "I'll text you later to check on you."

He threw his hand up to acknowledge that he'd heard her and got into the truck. His phone began vibrating in his pocket again as he pulled away from the curb. He checked his right side view mirror to see if Lynette was calling him again. He saw her making her way to her car, but she didn't have her phone up to her face. Steering with his left hand, he dug inside his pocket with his right, and pulled the phone out to see Lanai's name and number on the lit up screen. He silently said a thank you to the sky. Her timing couldn't have been more perfect. She'd refused to let him take a picture of her and he had none of her in his new phone. He'd decided that if she didn't let him take a picture soon, he'd sneak and take one.

He slid the green icon to answer the call. "Hey."

"Hey," she answered, sounding like she was smiling. He loved when she smiled. It did something to his insides.

"I'm on my way."

"You ate already?"

"Yeah, I had a burger and fries from Simaron's," he replied, navigating the streets of Dover near the Air Force Base, to get to the highway. "You hungry?"

"No," she said. "Just wanted to know if I needed to pull something out. I didn't wanna wait too late."

He looked at the time on his radio. It was about 9:30 pm. He said, "Well, it's kinda late to be cookin' anyway, right?"

She retorted jokingly, "Well, next time, I won't think about whether you've eaten or not."

"Yeah right."

"So when should I pop the popcorn?" she inquired.

"In about ten minutes. I want my popcorn hot."

"What are we watching?"

"I dunno. You pick."

"You are the worst."

"And it better not be no chick flick, either," he warned.

She reminded him, "You told me to pick."

"C'mon, man. Don't be pickin' no bullshit."

"You'll see when you get here," she replied, her tone teasing.

"A'ight. I'll be there in like ten minutes."

"Okay."

They ended the call and he dropped his phone into the cup holder. He had to admit to himself that he'd been waiting for, and wanting this interaction and opportunity for a long time. He felt like he was getting back to being complete again. He had messed up a lot and he knew he had a lot of work to do. However, all he'd wanted was the opportunity to prove to her that he was serious, which was what she was giving him.

He made it to her apartment in ten minutes flat and almost forgot his phone in the cup holder as he got out. He grabbed it and closed the door, arming the alarm. The only reason he even took it with him was on the off chance that Ms. Hazel called because of something wrong with herself or Makayla. He always kept his phone on and nearby. Business was important, but nothing was more important than the ladies in his life.

He made his way up the walkway towards the steps, thinking of how important Lanai and Makayla were to him. He never thought that he'd have a baby with anyone other than Lanai. However, since her birth, he couldn't imagine his life without Makayla, regardless of who her mother was. He hadn't been pressed to introduce any woman to his daughter; he'd actually avoided it. Lynette had gotten the chance to meet and be around her, but he really didn't consider to her to be anything more than just a friend.

It bothered him to think about how he was going to introduce Lanai to Makayla. He knew that Lanai was uneasy about Makayla being another woman's child. It made the situation worse that Makayla's mother had been the one that had shot Lanai and almost killed her. He figured meeting his daughter officially would be hard to accept, considering the fact that her own baby didn't make it; he knew she lived with that every day. Realistically though, it was inevitable that they would meet. He wasn't going to hide his daughter and he wasn't going to stop seeing Lanai. In his mind, Lanai was going to have to get over some things, adjust, and accept some shit.

He knocked on the door and within a few moments, the door came open and he saw her walking away, leaving it open for him to enter. He watched her disappear around the corner into the living room or kitchen as he closed and locked the door. He came around the corner, watching as she did something on her phone, and pressed buttons on the microwave. She had on a pair of sweat pants that hugged every curve and a white T-shirt that barely came to the top of the sweats. When she reached up to push buttons on the microwave, the small of her back was exposed.

Goddamn it, he thought, remembering how soft that skin was. She was sexy before, but it was something about her short haircut that made her sexier. She was the epitome of feminine and ladylike to him. Sometimes he found himself holding his breath when she came near him, and he would find reasons to be near her to breathe in her scent, which hadn't changed in all the years he'd known her. Standing just outside the kitchen area, he fought the urge to go over to her and stand behind her, just to feel her body heat. Sometimes he wondered if he was obsessed.

"You're right to the second with that ten minutes," she observed.

The sound of her voice brought Makai out of the trance that her butt had him in. He continued to look, though. He replied, "You know I'm always on time. You're the one with the late problem."

"For good reason," she replied, typing away on her phone.

His eyes traveled slowly up her back to the top of her head, then back down. The chef's island was preventing him from seeing anything lower than her backside, but it really didn't matter, because that was all he really wanted to see. He said, "Hmmm."

She turned around and leaned against the counter. She looked up and smiled. She asked, "What does 'hmmm' mean?"

Allowing his eyes to rove slowly over her body and up to her face, he stared a little longer at her luscious lips. Finally, he shrugged. "Nothing."

While he'd allowed his eyes to take a tour of her, she continued to type away on her phone. Without looking up, she asked, "What's the matter? You're not very talkative tonight."

"Who you talking to?" he asked, slightly changing the subject.

She looked up at him and gave him an incredulous look. "You," she laughed.

He smiled slightly. He really did love it when she smiled. It caused a light to twinkle in her eyes, which was something he'd thought at some point that he'd never see again. He said, "I'm talkin' about on the phone. Who are you talking to?"

"Oh," she said, scrolling and typing. "Katara. We're comparing schedules and she's telling me about my niece and Larry. She's got something to do in the afternoon and needs me to cover for her with this new client."

The microwave beeped three times, signaling that the popcorn was done. She turned around, took the hot bag out with two fingers, using the other three to close the door. She sat her phone on the counter to pull apart the bag and empty the popcorn into the waiting bowl. She tossed the empty bag into the trash, resumed what she was doing on her phone, picked up the bowl and headed for the living room.

As she was about to pass by him, he slyly took the phone out of her hand. She stopped in her tracks with her mouth open. She asked, "Really?"

He didn't even attempt to look at the phone. He pushed the button on the right side of the phone to lock the screen and put the phone in his pocket. He walked towards the couch, saying, "No business tonight. Your rules, not mine."

Following him in disbelief, she said, "I know what I said. But I at least need to finish the email to the supplier."

He sat down on the couch and draped his arm over the back of it. "It can wait. Sit down."

She stood for a moment, looking perplexed, like she couldn't function without her phone. She'd told him the night before that she wanted to watch movies with him, and she didn't want any interruptions. He was only giving her what she asked for. Looking at her standing there between the coffee table and the couch, he had to fight the urge to slap her behind. *It's just sittin' there,* he thought, leaning his head to get a better look.

Lanai turned to face him fully, narrowing her eyes. She asked, "What are you looking at?"

Trying to think of something quick, his eyes darted around the room. His eyes landed on the remote on the coffee table. He said, "I was looking for the remote."

"Uh huh," she said, regarding him closely.

He laughed as she sat down and simultaneously slid the remote off the table. He asked, "Why you lookin' like that?"

She hugged the bowl of popcorn with her leg crossed. She over-chewed the popcorn that she'd put in her mouth and looked at him out of the corner of her eye. She rolled her eyes. "You ain't slick."

With mock innocence, he asked, "What? I ain't do nothin'."

"Uh huh," she repeated, handing him the remote.

He took the remote and hit the power button. The wall-mounted TV across the room powered on and he asked, "What are we watching?"

She shrugged her shoulders, putting more popcorn in her mouth. She said, "You pick."

Pushing the guide button, he said, "I told your ass to pick. You just don't listen." She giggled, eating away at the popcorn. He asked, "Damn, are you gonna save me some? You were supposed to have a movie picked out and ready to go so I could enjoy hot popcorn."

She laughed. "Oh, shut up. The popcorn is still hot."

"You over there hoarding it," he joked, reaching for the bowl.

She gave him the bowl and he sat it in his lap as he continued to scroll for something to watch. He finally settled on an old movie called *Tombstone,* showing on one of the movie channels. He dropped the remote in the small space between them and began munching on the popcorn. He was glad that the movie was just coming on. It was rare that he got to watch TV with his life being so hectic and when he did, movies like *Tombstone* was exactly what he liked to watch.

She asked, "Are we really watching this?"

He nodded, shoving popcorn in his mouth. He asked, "Why not?"

"Why do you always talk with a mouthful of food?" she asked, staring at him in disbelief.

He shrugged his shoulder, packing his mouth again.

"You eat like a savage," she replied.

"Get me something to drink," he ordered around a mouthful of popcorn.

With perfectly arched eyebrows raised, she asked, "Who are you talking to?"

"You," he answered, looking at the TV.

After staring at him for a few moments, she got up and went to the kitchen. She returned with a bottle of water that she opened after she sat back in her seat. She removed the lid and took a sip. He asked, "Where's mine?"

She looked at him over the bottle with an amused look on her face, as she deliberately took another drink of water. She returned the lid to the bottle and tightened it. He could tell she was being a smart ass to show him that she didn't have to do anything that she didn't want to. Without any warning, he snatched the bottle from her hand and took the lid off. She tried to take it back, but he used his left arm to keep her at bay, while he drank almost the whole bottle's contents in one gulp. He burped loudly, then handed her the almost empty bottle.

She smacked his arm. "Really, Makai? You drank all my water."

"Stop bein' a smart ass," he replied. "I asked you to get *me* something to drink. You come back with one bottle."

"Your legs ain't broke," she pouted, sitting back on the couch with her arms crossed.

He saw that she'd shoved her bottom lip out for emphasis. To further agitate her, he flicked her lip with his pointer finger.

She laughed. "Stop."

He smiled, "You stop. Watch this movie."

"I don't wanna see this."

"Have you ever seen it?"

"No."

"Then watch it," he said. "It's a good movie."

CHAPTER FOURTEEN

Four hours and two movies later, Makai and Lanai were stretched out on the couch. They'd started out sitting next to each other. Makai had been right about the movie being good; she definitely didn't expect it to be. She'd almost regretted letting him pick the movie, but after it was over, she'd tucked her feet underneath her and had curled up next to him. He'd taken off his wheat-colored Timberland boots and his button-up Polo shirt, and had draped his arm over her. He'd placed the popcorn bowl on the table and had slid deeper into the couch.

By the time the second movie that had come on the same channel was almost over, he'd reached over and pulled the throw blanket that she kept on the couch and covered them with it. She hadn't needed a blanket, because the heat that exuded from his body was like a furnace. The combination of his body heat and the throw blanket had her drifting off to sleep. She felt him tapping her arm.

On the brink of sleep, she asked, "Hmm?"

"Stretch out," he said softly.

She did as he said without hesitation, uncurling her body and stretching out her legs, and laying her head in his lap. She readjusted the blanket and moved a little to get more comfortable. She was ready to give in to the sleep that was calling her name. She felt him moving beneath her. Initially, she pretended as if it didn't bother her because she wanted to go to sleep. However, when he kept moving, trying to get more comfortable, she sat up on the couch, annoyed.

She scowled at him, waiting for him to get himself together. He moved around in his seat, still looking uncomfortable. Impatiently, she asked, "Can you come on?"

"What?"

"Get comfortable. You're messing with my sleep," she explained.

"This couch ain't the most comfortable," he pointed out.

She sucked her teeth and with the blanket wrapped around her shoulders, she stood up. She snapped, "Lay down." He hesitated for a moment and she stretched her eyes and ordered, "Lay down."

He followed her orders and laid down on the couch, trying to adjust his jeans and T-shirt and get into a more comfortable position. She sucked her teeth again and lay down in front of him on the couch, spreading the blanket over the two of them. She made his bicep into a pillow and squirmed until she was comfortable. She felt his hand on her hip.

He said, "Stop moving."

Ready to drift off to sleep, she noticed how warm it was where his hand had been. She resisted the urge to push her butt into his stomach, certain her movement was bothering him for a reason other than annoyance. She felt enveloped in the scent of his cologne. *God, he smells good,* she thought. She decided that going to sleep would be the best bet, because she was not going to give much thought to his scent, or how good he looked, or even how good lying next to him felt. She knew that if she did, she'd never go to sleep.

She closed her eyes tight and laid there pretending to be asleep, until she really did drift off to the steady rise and fall of his breathing. As sleep tugged at her once again, she noticed that their breathing had fallen in line with one another. She remembered that he snored, so while he wasn't far from sleep, she knew that he wasn't there because he wasn't snoring. The last thought she remembered having was that he still had her cell phone in his pocket and she hadn't sent the email to one of the suppliers.

Lanai was awakened by something rubbing on her shin. For a moment, she had forgotten that she'd been lying on the couch with Makai. She was ready to jump up off the couch, until she realized that the rubbing was Makai's foot rubbing on her shin. She'd forgotten that that was what he did to help him to go to sleep. The rubbing was persistent; it was sporadic, which meant that he was close to being asleep. She could it blame it on it being late at night or sleepiness, but she really just wanted to mess with him.

Pretending to try to get comfortable, she wiggled and squirmed, moving her butt up against his stomach. His hand went back to her hip, but instead of steadying her, his hand slid around to her flat stomach and rested there. She took her soft, pedicured foot and slid it up and down his lower leg under his pant leg. She felt him move around behind her, trying to get comfortable. She wiggled against his stomach and heard him murmur something. He moved his head, and opened and closed the hand of the arm that she laid her head on.

He unconsciously rubbed her belly, causing an electrical sensation in the pit of her stomach. She thought for a moment that messing with him probably wouldn't be a good idea, because he was the only man that had the ability to make her body come alive. It had been so long since she'd had sex, she was thinking it was a bad idea to play with fire. She wasn't sure she'd be able to keep from giving in to him. There were times when she'd catch him looking at her and she thought her panties might melt off her.

She decided to lay still and leave him alone, but it was too late. She felt his lips on the space behind her left ear, which sent a shock directly between her legs. He was still on the brink of sleep. She could feel his labored breathing on her neck and ear, and it was sending chills down the left side of her body. She knew she had to do something to stop what was happening, because she knew it was quickly going to get heated. Her nipples already felt like they were trying to come out of her bra. She wondered if he was dreaming of another woman.

That thought caused her to flip over onto her back. She was ready to kick him until he woke up, and then kick him out of her apartment. His hand slid over her stomach, causing a ripple effect inside her stomach and her back to arch. She hated how her body responded to him, regardless of the amount of time since their last encounter. If there was any truth to the statement that someone could own another person's body, she knew it had to be true with him, because he definitely owned her body. When her brain wanted to do one thing, her body would always betray her when it came to him.

With his warm lips on her forehead, Makai asked, "What's wrong?"

Involuntarily, her eyes fluttered shut. His hand had gone from rubbing across her stomach to sliding down her right thigh. She whispered, "Nothing."

He pulled her body to his by gripping her thigh and put his hand on the small of her back underneath her T-shirt. He asked, "Why ain't you sleep?"

"Uh..." she tried to think of something to say, but nothing came to mind. It was hard to think with his fingertips gently sliding across her skin. His touch caused her back to arch again, which pushed her breasts against his chest and caused her to slightly moan.

He lightly kissed her temple. "You can't sleep?"

Her breathing quickened. "Uh-uh," she breathed against his face.

She'd been trying to keep her hands to herself, but with his face in such close proximity to her own, she couldn't resist touching his face. He always kept his beard and mustache so well groomed. Hell, he always kept his whole body well groomed. She'd been fighting the urge to touch his face for months. She loved the feel of his facial hair under her fingertips. She slid her thumb from the side of his mustache, along his beard. It was almost as if her hands had a mind of their own. Her right hand had wiggled itself free and found its way to the other side of his face.

He kissed her right jawbone and his left hand slowly crept up her back. The fingers of his left hand rested underneath the clasp of her bra and she felt his right hand on the small of her back. Her right thumb slid across his thick bottom lip, causing her to bite her own bottom lip. Memories of how it felt to kiss his lips came flooding back to her. She put her head back, trying to get ahold of herself. She felt his manhood growing stiff against her leg. Remembering how he'd felt inside of her, caused the moistness between her legs to turn into what she was sure would be a puddle.

She felt his lips on her neck where her pulse had tripled in speed. Her right leg had involuntarily crept up his leg. His left hand left her back to go to her right leg, caressing her butt on the way. He gently kissed where her pulse was, making a moan escape her lips and her head to come down quickly, and her shoulder to go up to protect that spot. Her hands had found their way to his ears, then his head. It was almost as if they couldn't get enough of caressing his face and head.

Good sense was trying to peek through the lust overtaking her. She really wanted to give in to the physical, but in the back of her mind, she remembered what giving in to that lust had gotten her. She really did want different results, which meant that she had to do something different. Giving in to the man that had caused her so much pain and grief would be stupid, according to what she knew Katara would think and say. She had to get control of herself and the situation.

As if he could sense she was about to pull back, he kissed her. The first kiss was light, almost hesitant. He kissed her again, the second time lightly nibbling on her bottom lip. Her breath caught in her throat, unsure of how to respond to that other than to return the kiss. When he kissed her lips again, she couldn't help but to kiss him back, their tongues remembering the familiar dance and falling in rhythm with one another. Completely caught up in his intoxicating kiss, she moved on top of him. He moved so that he was flat on his back and she was straddling him, still locked in their passionate kiss.

His lips left hers to make a trail down her face, then down her neck. She felt his hands on her butt, then up her back under her shirt. She pressed her eyes closed and reveled in the feeling of his lips and hands on her body. Her brain told her she needed to put a stop to what was going on, while her body told her brain to shut up, because it was much needed. As usual, he'd unclasped her bra with almost no effort. *He is too damn good at this*, she thought.

She had her palms flat on his chest, and in an effort to stop him; she patted on his chest. She hoped that would let him know that she wanted to stop what they were doing. His hand came around her back and cupped her breast. His thumb sliding over her nipple, caused her to shiver and say, "Oh."

She knew that if he got her shirt off, there was absolutely no turning back for her. She had to get it together. With her hands flat on his chest, she pushed back against him, trying to sit up. Trying to keep her close to him, he used his hand on the small of her back to hold her in place. He never took his hand off her breast and his lips were doing a number on her neck and collarbone.

Finally finding her voice, she whispered, "Makai."

Nibbling on her earlobe, he asked, "Hmmm?"

"St-stop," she stuttered.

With his breath tickling her ear, he asked, "Why? I know you want it."

"I do," she breathed.

Caressing her with his hands and tongue, he asked, "So why you want me to stop?"

Her eyes rolled back in her head. "God," she whispered. She said to him, "I need you to stop."

"Tell me why," he demanded in a low voice, massaging her hips.

She groaned. He was not going to make things any easier. "This is wrong. Baby, I need you to stop. I'm not...uh...oh, Makai. I'm not ready."

He chuckled, "You ready. I know you ready."

She shook her head no. "I'm not."

He stopped momentarily and she sat up straight on top of him. His hands were still on her hips and she could feel beneath her that he was ready. His dark eyes were darker as he looked at her, confused and frustrated. She dropped her eyes down to his T-shirt. She didn't want him to see that the same desire in his eyes was also in hers. She wanted to do what was right and this didn't feel right. She had too many unanswered questions and she still didn't trust him. For all she knew, he was still screwing broads in the office of his store.

She bit her lip and looked up at him. She whispered, "I'm sorry."

With genuine concern in his eyes, he asked, "What's wrong?"

"I'm just not ready," she replied.

His eyes went to her breasts, which told a different story. He looked up at her again and said, "You seem ready to me."

"My body is ready," she explained. "I'm just not ready. Not yet."

He questioned, "So what's it gonna take for you to be ready?"

She shrugged.

It looked like it was hard for him to ask, "Is there someone else?"

She shook her head no.

"That situation a few months ago?"

She knew he was referring to the almost-rape. She answered, "That's part of it."

"What's the rest of it? The bigger part of it?"

"Us."

"What do you mean?"

"It's hard. I don't trust you."

He nodded his head, but kept quiet. The look on his face told her that he already knew it before she said it.

She continued to explain, "Too much has happened. I spent a long time overlooking and ignoring."

"But that's the past," he said.

"The past that kept repeating itself," she reminded him.

"Am I ever gonna live it down?" he asked, looking like he genuinely wanted the answer. "Are you ever gonna let me live it down? Can I get a fresh start?"

"There are a lot of unanswered questions...a lot of unresolved issues," she said, trying to dodge his questions.

She made a move to get off him, but he held her in place. He said, "Uh-uh. Answer my questions. You corner me with your questions and when I don't answer, you put up a stone wall. I wanna know if I'm tryin' in vain. 'Cause I am tryin'. You know the old me wouldn't have cared."

Lanai nodded. "I see effort, but Makai, I saw effort before. I almost died. You had a baby with somebody else. I don't know if I can get over that."

"Nobody's askin' you to get over it," he said. "I'm askin' you to give me a real chance. I changed everything for you."

"I didn't ask you to," she pointed out, getting offended.

"And you didn't have to. I wanted to," he pointed out. "I wanted to show you that I'm capable of changin' for real; no bullshit." He let his words soak in for a minute, and then continued, "I'm not livin' without you. So you tell me what it is I need to do and I'ma do it."

"It's not that simple—" she began.

He cut her off, "What you mean? It is that simple. Somethin' wrong, you tell me, I fix it. Period. Somethin' you don't like, you tell me, I change it. Done."

"What about your daughter?" she asked quietly.

"What about her," he shrugged. "She ain't goin' nowhere." When he saw that his response had caused her to shut down, his voice softened. He said, "Listen, I never wanted a child with anybody but you. I fucked up and I'm sorry. But I love my daughter and she's my responsibility."

"How would you feel if I had a baby with someone else?" she asked, remembering the last abortion that she'd had and the fact that it hadn't been his baby.

"I'd kill that nigga," he answered bluntly. "But I'd have to deal with it. You're always gonna be in my life. I told you...you're my wife and I meant that. I would have to accept that child." After a moment, he added, "But don't go gettin' no ideas. Don't be the reason a nigga don't make it home."

She wanted to believe that what he was telling her was the truth, but he'd lied to her so many times over the years, that her brain just wasn't believing it. Her heart wanted to believe that he was going to do right and she should give him another chance. He touched her face, sliding the pad of his thumb across her cheek. Her eyes closed and she sighed. It was more than just her body responding to him; it was her soul.

She heard him say, "Lanai, I love you."

She felt the tears form behind her closed eyes. Her heart had been waiting to hear him say those words. She kept her eyes closed, hoping that the tears would go away. One tear, however, betrayed her and slipped from under her right eyelid. He immediately wiped her tear and pulled her down to him, kissing her cheek and forehead.

She laid her head on his chest and listened to his heartbeat. Tears quietly slid out of her eyes and onto his shirt. He wrapped his strong arms around her after pulling the blanket up to her shoulders. She didn't realize that while she stared blankly at a spot on the couch until she went to sleep, Makai had stared at the ceiling for the rest of the night. He held her like a baby and never went to sleep until the sun came up.

CHAPTER FIFTEEN

Makai felt like he'd just closed his eyes when the vibration in his pocket woke him up. Lanai was still sleeping peacefully as he patted his pockets, feeling for the cause of the disturbance before it disturbed Lanai. He pulled the phone from his pocket and looked at it. He definitely didn't have a phone with a pink case and he'd forgotten that he'd taken Lanai's phone the previous night. He looked to see why it was vibrating. He saw that it was her alarm. He silenced it and gently tossed it onto the coffee table. He'd let her sleep a little while longer.

He craned his neck so that he could see her face. He knew that before she'd gone to sleep, she'd left a puddle of tears on his shirt. There was nothing that he could do except hold her. He'd stayed awake the majority of the night, thinking about everything that had happened in the past and the state of their relationship. He'd never wanted to be a better man for anybody, until he'd felt what it was like to lose Lanai, and when he became a father. He wanted to be the kind of man that his daughter would marry. He wanted to be the kind of man that Lanai would marry.

A part of him kept telling him that he was too young to think about marriage; he still had living to do. His ego told him that there were still a million women out there that he had the potential to have sex with. He'd been a player for so long, that was all he knew.

He didn't know what it was like to grow up with a mother, or in a household with two parents. His mother, Mya, had left his brother, his dad, and him when he was about two years old. She'd decided that she wanted to be free and Makai's dad, Roger, had let her be free.

Roger had done a great job raising both boys, stressing to both of them the importance of education and following their dreams. Makai hadn't been proud of how he'd begun his businesses with drug money, but he'd needed quick money. No banks were willing to loan to a young black man fresh out of college, and he wasn't waiting for anybody's handouts. His dad had shown him how to "get it from the muscle". Makai knew that Roger had women that he dealt with, but he had kept those women away from the house and his sons. Makai could sometimes see the pain in his dad's eyes from missing Mya.

He'd never understood that pain until Lanai had told him in the hospital that it was over. Over the time that'd passed since then, his pride had been worn down, his resistance was nonexistent, and he was ready to give in to whatever she wanted. He'd laughed at guys that said that mess in his barbershop or his store. Deep down, now he understood where they were coming from and why. No amount of money or new pussy that could take the place that the woman sleeping on his chest held. If he had to wait forever, and he prayed that he didn't, he would.

His phone began buzzing in his pocket and he retrieved it. Lanai began to stir on his chest as he looked at the screen. He had five unread text messages. He knew they were from Lynette, because Ms. Hazel didn't text. She barely knew how to work a cell phone. He also noticed that the time on his phone read 7:47 am. He pushed the text message icon and went into the thread attached to Lynette's phone number.

The first text read: "*Hey, baby. Just wanted to check on you. Call me when you get this.*"

The second message read: "*Hey. Not sure if you are able to call or not, but at least send me a text letting me know you're okay.*"

Messages three through five read: *"Look, Makai. This is just fucking ridiculous. If you're really with a sick family member, why can't you answer a text message? Any time that you're with me, that damn phone is virtually GLUED to your hand or your head. Now you're too good to answer me? I don't know what's going on with you or this supposed sick relative, but the least you could do is answer the text or call me like I ask. YOU OWE ME AT LEAST THAT MUCH! If you don't respond or call me, I WILL FIND YOU!"*

He pushed the back button and returned to the home screen, making a mental note to cut her off completely. There was no other way around it. He knew that if he didn't, he'd end up in jail. Lanai's phone began buzzing on the coffee table. He picked it up to see that it was a phone call. He kissed her forehead and said, "Nai, wake up."

She barely moved, until he kissed her forehead two more times. She moved around on top of him, causing a part of him to begin to awaken that he wanted to stay asleep, at least until he got the chance to get in the shower. He said, "Nai, get up. Your phone is ringing."

She stirred in her sleep, looking up at him, confused. He repeated, "Your phone is ringing."

Her face registered what he was saying to her and she asked, "Where is it?"

He took it off the coffee table and gave it to her. She caught the call just before it went to voicemail. Lying back on his chest, she cleared her throat and asked, "Hello?"

He could hear a male's voice through the receiver and after a few minutes of listening, she sat up on Makai, listening. She asked, "Is the Attorney's General's Office even open this time of morning?"

Her brows were furrowed together and she wedged the phone between her ear and shoulder, trying to get her hands behind her back to re-fasten her bra. He moved her hands away and had it fastened, almost as fast as he'd unfastened it the previous night. She swung her leg over and climbed off him and the couch. She paced as she listened, adding an occasional, "Uh huh," here and there. He got up from the couch and readjusted his jeans, trying to think of something to take his mind off Lanai. He folded the blanket and draped it on the arm of the couch where he'd found it last night.

"Okay, thank you. I'll be in there shortly," she replied, ending the phone call. She immediately went to texting.

Makai asked, "What's wrong?"

She looked up from her phone, "The ADA wants to meet with me about the upcoming trial."

He nodded his head. He asked, "You need me to go with you?"

She shook her head. "I can handle it."

"You sure? You look upset."

"I'm fine," she returned, not sounding too convincing.

He decided to leave well enough alone. He said, "If you need me, let me know. Text me or call me when you get there."

"I gotta go get dressed," she announced to the room, but it was directed at herself. She put her phone on the coffee table and headed for her room.

Makai went to the kitchen and set about making breakfast. If she wasn't going to let him physically be there, the least he could do was make her breakfast. He felt his phone buzz in his pocket, letting him know someone was calling. He pulled it out far enough to see who was calling. When he saw that it was Lynette, he dropped the phone back in his pocket and ignored it. When the phone stopped buzzing, there was a double buzz, letting him know he had a text message. He was certain it was more "hate mail". He made a mental note to deal with it later.

As he scrambled eggs and flipped the bacon, he took his phone out to call Ms. Hazel. He was sure Makayla was awake. After the normal seven rings, Ms. Hazel picked up the phone. She sounded like she'd been up for hours. She asked, "Hello?"

"Good morning, Ms. Hazel," he called into the phone.

"Oh, hey baby," she cooed. "You calling to check on the baby?"

"Callin' to check on both of you," he corrected.

He heard movement in the background as she moved around. She said, "Oh, baby, Ms. Hazel is just fine. Spent some time with my Lord and Savior this morning. Perfect way to start off my day. You know my dumpling likes listening to me read the Word and praying.

She prays with me every morning that she's here. You know, you two are still welcome to come to church with me."

The tone she'd used let him know that she was expecting him to attend church with her sometime soon. "Yes, ma'am. I know," he said.

"So when you coming?" she asked.

"Soon, Ms. Hazel. Soon," he promised, with no definite answer in mind.

She said, "Well, I'll give the phone to my dumpling."

His heart fluttered when he heard Makayla's baby talk through the phone. This little girl had him wrapped around her little finger. He smiled, "Good morning, princess."

He couldn't make out everything she was saying, but she was excited about it, whatever it was. He listened for a moment, taking the toast out of the toaster and smearing butter and jelly on it. He could listen to her little voice all day. He said, "I love you, baby. I'll see you in a little bit."

Ms. Hazel took the phone back and he promised her that he would be over there in a little while to feed Makayla breakfast. He appreciated her help and he appreciated it even more that Ms. Hazel allowed him to have certain things, like coming over and feeding her breakfast and putting her to sleep when she stayed the night.

He ended the call and placed the phone on the counter, putting the food on two plates. He turned around to place the plates on the chef's island as Lanai came from the back of the apartment. She had on a pair of wide-legged gray slacks and a scoop neck white shirt that fit her like a glove. The shirt could've been a bodysuit, for all he knew. As she approached the chef's island, she dropped her black, red bottom heels next to the stool. She tied the strings at the waist of her pants into a bow, commenting, "Are you on the breakfast express?"

He knew she was referring to the tail end of his conversation. He hadn't been trying to hide his conversation. He wasn't stupid. He wasn't going to call another female or answer another woman's call, anywhere near where he thought Lanai might be. He said, "I gotta go cook my baby girl breakfast. Gotta feed my ladies."

Adjusting her watch on her wrist, she asked, "Oh, yeah? And how many ladies are you feeding?"

He'd retrieved the orange juice from the refrigerator and poured a glass for each of them. He answered, "Just you and my daughter."

She took a piece of toast off the plate, took a bite, and put it back on the plate. He sat on the stool and started eating, watching her put her jewelry on. She looked in the small mirror on the kitchen wall and finger-combed her hair. He watched her go back and forth, gathering what she needed for the day. She plopped her over-sized, black Michael Kors bag on the chef's island and looked through it. She went to another purse and took out a wallet and a pouch-looking thing. She dropped the wallet into the bag on the island and opened the pouch-looking thing, which he saw held makeup. He didn't like her wearing makeup; she was beautiful without it.

She quickly applied a little here and little there, scrolling through and checking her phone in between pencils and pads she used on her face. He took his time eating his breakfast, which was probably the first time in a long time. She glanced over at him quickly, then back to the mirror. Sliding the black pencil back and forth under her eye a couple times, she asked, "What's wrong?"

"Why do you wear that shit?" he asked.

"I like it," she laughed, putting the clear lid back on the pencil.

"You don't need it," he said, not hiding his disgust.

"You never complained before," she pointed out.

"Didn't notice before," he quietly answered, still watching her.

She said, "The things you will see when you pay attention." She raised an eyebrow at him, checking to see if he caught her drift. She zipped her makeup container and dropped it into her bag on the island. She reached down and positioned her shoes to step into them. Her shoes gave her about five inches of height. He knew when she put her shoes on, that meant she was about to leave out the door. He said, "I cooked you breakfast."

She smiled, "I know. Thank you. I gotta go, though."

He frowned. In a low tone, he ordered, "Sit down. Eat."

She looked at him carefully, and then looked at the food. He didn't want to tell her what to do, but he wasn't going to let her be inconsiderate and walk out the door, without trying to at least to do more than nibble on the toast. His gaze was unwavering, and she finally gave in and took a seat on the stool across from him. He bit off almost half of the piece of toast. They ate in silence for a few moments.

She finally said, "This is good. Thank you."

He didn't respond, but continued to eat his food in silence.

She asked, "What's wrong? I thought you were in a good mood. You had to be to cook breakfast."

He looked up at her and said, "I'm fine. Just didn't want you leavin' without eatin'. It's not good to start your day without a good breakfast."

She shook her head, taking a drink of juice. In between bites of food, she accused, "Something is wrong with you. I can feel it."

"Oh, you can," he asked with a raised brow.

"You know I can. What's wrong?"

"Nothin'."

"Okay," she began, "so are we gonna dance around the problem, or are we gonna confront it and get it out in the open?"

"There's no problem."

"So we're lying to each other?"

"No lies."

"So what's with the change in your demeanor? When you were talking about feeding your ladies, you were happy. I go to walk out the door without eating and it's World War III," she observed.

He shrugged. "It's inconsiderate to walk away from a breakfast somebody cooked for you."

She tried apologizing, "I'm sorry."

Again, he shrugged. "No big deal."

"You're gonna let this ruin your day? I'm eating, aren't I?"

He nodded and asked, "Can we talk about something else? This is workin' on my nerves."

She raised her hands in mock surrender. "So, what are your plans today?"

"Work, go get my daughter, tie up some loose ends," he answered vaguely. "What're your plans?"

"After meeting with the ADA about this nonsense, I'm going to work, dealing with clients, suppliers, and stuff. Then I gotta go meet with Katara's client up in Wilmington for her," she chatted. He pretended to listen to what she said as he watched her lips move. *Damn, she has some sexy lips.* His mind went back to what was about to happen the night before. She was lucky that he respected her, but if she were anybody else, he would've used his power of persuasion to change her mind.

"Hello," he heard her call. He blinked and focused on her whole face to see her waving her hands at him. She gave him a confused look and asked, "Where is your head? Do you need a hug or something?"

"Why you ask?" he asked, going back to eating his food.

"It's like your brain is somewhere else."

He shook his head no. "My brain is here."

"And what's with the short answers?" she asked. "Like all up until last night we were having conversations. Now you're being short with me. Are you mad?"

"No, Lanai, I'm not mad," he assured her.

Throwing her hands up, she replied, "And now you're using my first name. You only use my first name when you're mad."

He laughed and sat back on his stool. "I'm not mad. I promise you. You wanna wait, so we'll wait. No rush."

She looked at him for a moment, checking to see if he was telling the truth. "Are you really able to wait? Is that what you wanna do?"

He folded his arms across his chest. "I'm good. It ain't like I've never had it before. I am only human, though."

"Awww," she gushed. She climbed off her stool with her arms outstretched and her lip poked out. She came over to him and wrapped her arms around his neck, pressing her body against his and rubbing the back of his head. "Poor baby. Is it gonna be too hard?"

With his arms around her waist, he said, "I'll show you hard."

They both laughed and she leaned back to look into his face, with her hands interlocked behind his head. Her face was serious when she said, "I want you to know that I notice your efforts. I'm scared, that's all. I really do appreciate your patience."

She leaned her forehead against his and he moved his mouth up to kiss her on the forehead. In the past, kissing a woman on the forehead had always been a tactic to get what he wanted. Lately when he kissed her forehead, it was an indication to her that he respected and wanted to protect her. He wanted her physically, but he knew that if things continued to be on her terms, it would make things easier between them. He hugged her tight and felt her relax in his arms. He knew that it would take time to rebuild the trust fully, but he also knew that she trusted him more than she wanted to admit.

They slowly released each other from their embrace and she eased back to where her plate was. She went about the task of clearing off their dishes and scraping things into the trash. While she moved around the kitchen, he debated about whether or not he should tell her what was on his mind or not. He said aloud to himself, "What the hell."

She asked, "Huh?"

"I want you to meet Makayla," he blurted.

She was at the sink, putting the dishes in for her to wash later. He heard her movement stop when he'd said that. Tension filled the air and he waited while her brain processed his words. When it seemed like it had been an eternity, he pointed out, "Y'all are gonna meet, anyway. I'd rather it be sooner than later."

She moved around him and went into the living room to get her briefcase. She returned to the kitchen to get her purse off the island. He called, "Yo!"

Her head snapped up and she looked at him.

He asked, "What the fuck?"

She gave him a questioning look. "What?"

"Yo, don't play dumb with me. I said I want you to meet my daughter."

"I heard you."

"So respond to it. This shit is corny. She can't help who her parents are."

"I know she can't," she answered softly.

"So stop actin' like an asshole!" he yelled. "Every time I say something about her or barely mention her, you got a problem! She's a fuckin' baby!"

She warned, "Stop yelling at me!"

He stood up from the stool and said, "I don't get it. I fucked up. I've been apologizing from the gate for it, but I can't take it back. Stop holding this shit over my head. My daughter is always gonna be my daughter and I'm not choosing."

Crossing her arms under her breasts, she reminded him, "I never asked you to."

"Your fucked up attitude towards a situation that we can't change, is askin' me to!" he yelled.

"Makai, stop yelling at me," she repeated, sounding like she was nearing her own breaking point.

"No, fuck that! I'll yell all I wanna yell! I'll be humble about a lotta shit, but I'm not gonna be humble about you actin' like you too good to meet my fuckin' daughter!"

"I never said I was too good!" she yelled back. "I need time to think about it! Too much shit has happened! There's no point in me meeting her if you and I aren't gonna work!"

He lowered his voice, "We're gonna work."

"Oh, really?" she asked in a taunting voice. "Like we worked over the last ten years? Like all the lies, games, and bullshit worked?"

"You lied, too," he reminded her. "You played games, too. You ain't a hundred percent innocent."

Putting her hands on her hips, she craned her neck to emphasis her point, "I never said I didn't. Stop putting fucking words in my mouth. I know I contributed to how things played out. I'm not just afraid of you hurting me, I'm afraid of hurting you or your innocent daughter. But you don't see that. You don't care about that. All you know is what you want and how you feel."

He was quiet as the weight of her words settled on the room. Her eyes were shooting darts at him. Still seething, she snatched her purse off the island and spun around on her heels, saying, "Fuck this shit."

Not wanting her to leave the apartment angry, or for them to part ways angry, he started after her and caught up to her at the door, pushing it shut and blocking her between him and the door. She demanded, "Move so I can go."

"I'm not letting you leave like this," he replied.

"You can't stop me."

"I'm stopping you," he said, choking back the laugh that almost escaped.

She turned around to face him and looked up at him. She asked, "What do you want from me?"

"I want you to let go," he answered.

"Every time I let go—"

"Goddamnit, Lanai," he interrupted her. "Stop with this 'every time' shit. That was the past. We can't live there. I was wrong, you were wrong, but we need to move forward. I fucked up more times than I can count, but I'm promising you that I won't hurt you anymore. *Give me a chance.*"

She blew an exasperated breath and stress lined her forehead. She rolled her eyes up to look at him, "It takes time."

"Time, not roadblocks," he reminded her. "You keep puttin' up roadblocks."

"I know," she whispered.

"Then stop doin' it," he whispered back.

She promised, "I'll try."

He kissed her forehead. "It's not that hard."

He pulled her to him by her waist and enveloped her in his arms. She hugged him back and rested her head on his chest. She asked, "So when do you want this meeting to happen?"

He kissed the top of her head, "Whenever you're ready. Just wanted you to understand how important it is to me. I feel like I'm torn between my two favorite people."

She leaned back and peeked up at him through her lashes. "Am I one of your favorite people?"

Kissing her nose, he said, "Absolutely. You're my favorite sexy woman."

She smiled up at him with her arms wrapped around his waist. She asked, "You think I'm sexy?"

"Is water wet?" he asked.

"It sure is."

Nuzzling her neck and causing her to giggle, he said, "I know somethin' that gets wetter."

He kissed her neck, then her earlobe. When he kissed her lips, she kissed him back and their lips lingered on one another for a moment. He kissed her again, deepening the kiss and pushing her up against the door. Their breathing had quickened and he felt her grip a fistful of his T-shirt. He wanted to resist being near her and touching her, but he couldn't. There was this irresistible, undeniable pull of attraction. He felt the need to be inside her as much as he needed to breathe. He couldn't hide his excitement; his hard-on pressed against her. He'd beg if he had to, and he didn't beg anybody for anything.

Her hands found their way to his chest and she pushed at him. He groaned in his throat. With his lips against hers, he asked, "How long you gonna make me wait?"

"You know I have a full day," she said, her lips brushing against his as she spoke.

He outlined her bottom lip with his tongue, causing her to moan softly and her back to arch. The sound of her moaning was what he looked forward to. He wondered how fast he could get her out of her clothes. He brushed his lips across hers. He promised, "It won't take long."

"Yes, it will."

"I promise it won't," he countered.

Her voice turning sexy, she said, "I don't want it if it won't take long."

"Well, shit. We can take as long as you want," he offered.

With her thumb caressing his beard, she said, "I want you to wait."

"Why," he said, clearly frustrated. "It's not like we don't know each other."

"Please?" she begged, barely above a whisper.

Her begging was having the opposite effect on him. He imagined her saying please to something else.

She reminded him, "You have a breakfast date with your daughter."

He groaned, "You ain't playin' fair. Don't mention the kid at a time like this."

She smiled against his mouth. "I promise. I'll let you know when it's time."

He blew hot air and hit the door over her head, causing her to jump. He backed away from her and headed to the living room, adjusting himself in his pants for the second time that morning. Trying to hide the fact that he wanted to act like a little kid, and throw a temper tantrum because he couldn't have his way, he put on his boots and shirt. He searched around for his keys, which he found on the end table next to where he'd been sitting the previous night. He wasn't sure how they got there, but it really didn't matter. He looked up to see Lanai looking at him with a concerned expression.

His demeanor softened. He asked, "You ready to go too?"

She nodded, clutching her purse in front of her.

He noticed that her phone was on the chef's island and grabbed it on his way past. He took her briefcase off her shoulder and handed her the phone. He said, "Let's go."

Turning off the lights, he led the way out of the apartment and waited while she locked the top and bottom locks. He led the way down the steps and walked her to her car, waited for her to unlock the doors and opened the driver's door for her. She slid into the driver's seat and he handed her the briefcase. He dropped down on his haunches, so that he was almost eye level with her. He leaned in and kissed her. He asked, "I'll see you later?"

She smiled. "I hope so."

"You wanna do dinner?"

"I wanna go out to dinner."

"It's gonna have to be an early dinner, 'cause I can't keep leaving Makayla with Ms. Hazel. She says it's no problem, but she's old and I don't wanna put too much on her," he explained, trying to hide the stress that the juggling caused.

She had a thoughtful expression for a moment, and then suggested, "Well, how about you bring her with you? I don't know what time I'll be done in Wilmington, but we can meet up there. They have better food up there."

"Look," he began, not hiding his exasperation, "I don't want you to think you gotta rush yourself to do what you're not ready to do. We just argued about it and I damn sure ain't tryna have an argument later. I don't want a stressful situation around her."

Looking him in the eye, she promised, "It won't be. I realize how hard it is for you and I see how hard you work. I wanna work with you."

He looked at her for a moment, trying to read if she was actually ready or if she was just trying to please him. He finally said, "Okay. If you ready..."

"I'm ready," she said with finality.

"Alright. So where you wanna meet?"

"Arner's in New Castle?"

He nodded. "What time?"

"Don't know. The appointment in Wilmington with the client is at five, I believe. These appointments normally take anywhere from a half hour to an hour, typically," she explained. "Depends on how much they want or how much they know."

"You're sexy when you talk business," he replied.

She laughed. "We're not starting that mess again. I'll call you when I get to the client. I'll make sure it doesn't take more than an hour."

He nodded. She leaned towards him and he met her halfway, kissing her puckered lips. He stood up and said, "Watch out." After closing her door, he added, "Drive safe."

She mouthed, "You, too."

He stepped back onto the curb behind him and stood there, waiting for her to back out of the space and drive off. She smiled and waved at him as she pulled away. He smiled in return and held up his hand as he made his way to his truck, pulling out his phone. He made a call to his favorite florist and ordered a single pink rose, wrapped in pink paper, to be delivered to Lanai's office at noon. He figured her meeting with the ADA shouldn't keep her too long. He didn't want a card sent, because he didn't want to give her hating ass sister a chance to send it back.

CHAPTER SIXTEEN

"**H**ow'd it go?" Katara called from her seat behind her lobby desk.

"It went okay," Lanai replied, making her way around her desk.

Katara looked up, expecting more information. She asked, "What happened?"

"I had to go over the details of what happened and he explained the process of trial and everything," Lanai answered.

Concerned etched all over her face, Katara asked, "Are you okay?"

Lanai nodded. "I'm fine. I've had to go through this a couple different times."

"You know if you needed me, I would've gone with you," Katara reminded her.

Lanai looked at her sister. She said, "I know. But you know you don't have to hold my hand through everything, right?"

Katara reiterated, "I'm here if you need me."

"I know," Lanai smiled.

She set about going through messages that Katara had written down for her. A few moments later, a delivery person walked in with a single pink rose wrapped in pink paper. He asked, "Lanai Wilson?"

Katara pointed at Lanai's desk at the same time that Lanai raised her hand. The man handed Lanai the rose, smiled, and told her to have a good day. As she accepted the rose, she noticed the logo on his shirt was the florist that Makai used. She inhaled the scent of the rose and smiled. The single rose meant more than eight dozens of roses at one time.

Suspicious, Katara asked, "And who sending you a single rose?"

"Noneya," Lanai retorted.

"It better not be that raggedy ass, Makai," Katara warned. "I know he used that situation as a way to weasel back in, didn't he?"

Lanai tried to ignore her sister. She knew her silence was telling, but she didn't want to argue, either.

Katara looked at her sister incredulously. She accused, "It *is* from him."

Lanai asked, "So what if it is?"

"He's a raggedy piece of shit!" Katara yelled. "Why would you want to accept a rose from *him*?"

"It's just a rose," Lanai said.

"Did you sleep with him?" Katara demanded.

"We *slept* together," Lanai admitted. Katara groaned and flopped around in her seat and on her desk. Lanai said, "We didn't have sex. We just slept. We fell asleep watching a movie."

Katara warned, "And that's how the bullshit starts. Why are you settling for less? You're a beautiful, intelligent, vibrant woman. You can have any man you want."

Lanai finally admitted aloud, "I want that man."

In disbelief, she asked, "Even after all that he's done to you?"

Lanai tried to get her sister to understand. She said, "Tara, I love him. I'm in love with him."

"Sometimes love ain't enough, sweetie," Katara answered. She had a look of pity on her face.

"This time it is," Lanai returned, not backing down. She really wanted her sister's understanding and her blessing, but she was not changing her mind because Katara hadn't forgiven Makai. That was something they'd have to hash out between them.

Katara held up her hands in surrender. She said, "Honey, this is your life. You do what you want. But when he breaks your heart again, don't say I didn't tell you so."

Changing the subject, Lanai said, "So you never told me who this 5 o'clock client is."

"Jamal."

"Jamal who?" Lanai questioned, looking up from rearranging her desk.

"The bartender."

Lanai thought for a moment and then remembered her friend Jamal from years ago that Makai had forced her to stop seeing. They'd only been friends, but Makai had felt threatened because of all the dirt he'd done. She remembered that he had been a student at Temple University, also. She asked, "And why can't you make it to the meeting?"

"Gotta take Riyah to the doctor and Larry is taking us to dinner," Katara said. As if she could sense Lanai wanting to back out, she reminded her, "You already said you would do it."

"What makes you think I don't have plans?"

"Well, if you did, you wouldn't have agreed to cover for me," she began. "And anyway, if you have plans, they ain't with nobody but that raggedy ass Makai, and I'd be happy to ruin them." The smug, fake smile let Lanai know just how sorry Katara was not.

Lanai laughed and shook her head. She hadn't been prepared for the client being Jamal, but it didn't matter. She'd be going in a business capacity. Her gut instinct told her that Katara had purposely worked her way out of being able to make it, just because of who he was. She was always so pressed to set Lanai up with someone, anyone. Lanai understood that it was from a genuine place, which was why she had put up with it for as long as she did.

The next few hours flew by with all the phone calls that Lanai had to make and return. She multi-tasked, researching things that clients had specifically asked for, and answering and sending emails. She and Makai were texting each other all day, which kept a smile on her face. She would occasionally look up and catch Katara looking at her and shaking her head in pity. Lanai had begun laughing at her, causing Katara to laugh, too. Katara had never been able to stay angry with Lanai for long.

Katara left the office around 3:30 pm and Lanai was busy moving around the office when 4 o'clock came. She was in the supply closet in the back of the building when she heard the bell to let her know that someone had come in the front door. Grabbing the box of tile and other samples that she needed, she called out, "I'll be right there."

"Babe, it's me," Makai called back.

She released a breath she didn't know she was holding and closed the locked door. She made her way to the front of the office with the box in tow. Makai stood in the showroom, looking around as he did every time he waited for her to finish and lock up. He saw her carrying the box and immediately relieved her of it, asking, "Where's this going?"

"In my car," she answered. "I'm taking it to the meeting."

"You ready to go?" he asked.

She went around the showroom, turning off lights, and shut her computer down. As she packed up her things, she asked, "Do you schedule your clients to coincide with my schedule?"

He nodded his head.

She smiled, "That's so sweet."

"I told you I'll be here for you."

"Thank you for my rose," she said, picking it up off the desk, along with her keys and purse.

He took her briefcase and waited for her to lead the way out. He said, "No need to thank me. I'm glad you like it."

"I love it," she clarified. She locked the door behind them and pressed the button on her keypad to open the trunk.

He dropped the box inside the trunk and she deposited her purse in the passenger seat. He put the briefcase on the passenger seat and closed the door, as he grabbed her elbow and pulled her to him, before she could walk away. With her back to him, she covered his hands on her stomach with her own. He leaned down and kissed her neck, then kissed her temple. Still holding her, he leaned against the car. She leaned her head back against his shoulder. She felt so safe in his strong arms.

He asked, "Why don't you reschedule your meeting? I can cook dinner or we can leave together from here to go up to Arner's."

She said, "You know I can't do that. My business reputation is important."

"More important than spending time with me?" he inquired. He sounded like he was pouting.

She reassured him, "No. But just like you have to handle business, I do, too. I told you it won't last any longer than an hour."

He sighed and finally gave in. "Okay," he said, in a defeated, tired tone.

He released his hold on her and she took a couple steps and turned to him. She looked over his handsome face. She told him, "You look tired."

"I am," he admitted, standing up from the car.

"We can reschedule," she offered.

He shook his head no. "If you're not gonna reschedule business, we're not rescheduling dinner."

She touched his face and pouted, "Poor baby. You should get a quick nap."

Looking at her with dark lustful eyes, he bit his bottom lip and said, "I wanna get a quick something else."

She playfully pushed his face. She asked, "Do you ever think of anything else?"

He laughed when she'd pushed his face. He said, "Money."

"That's it for you, huh? Sex and money."

"That's 'bout the size of it," he joked.

She shook her head. She said, "Well, I gotta go. I'll see you in a couple hours."

He walked her around to the driver's side. She had to admit that she loved him treating her like a lady; he didn't even have to think about it. He held the top of the driver's side door and waited while she got in to close it. He waited for her to put the window down as she started the engine. He bent down and leaned into the car, kissing her. He said, "Drive safe."

She nodded and he stood there and watched as she pulled away, waving. He always stood and watched her until she was out of sight. She wasn't sure if he knew it or not, but she would watch him in her mirror until he was out of sight. She loved how he protected her. It seemed as though he was a little more appreciative of her, which was all she'd wanted.

She drove the fifty minutes to the address that Katara had given her to meet Jamal and she arrived right on time. She got out and collected her belongings, making her way to the door. She balanced everything in her arms as she pulled the handle with her fingers, and pushed the door open with her foot. She made it inside without dropping anything, and it took a second for her eyes to adjust to the inside lighting of the bare bar, because she'd forgotten her sunglasses in another purse.

She put everything down on the first open table and went back to the door to push the lock button on the keypad. She heard a male's voice ask, "How can I help you?"

She turned around and walked over to him with purpose, and an outstretched hand. She shook his hand, saying, "I'm Lanai with Interior Design. My sister couldn't make it today."

Jamal shook her hand, smiling. He said, "I know who you are. I talked to your sister already. She told me. I know it's been a while; you may not remember me."

Her smile widened, "I remember you, Jamal. How've you been?"

"Good," he answered, nodding his head with a smile. His smile was still nice, his teeth were straight and white and his lips were still full as she remembered them. His dreadlocks had grown; they were now shoulder-length. He was light-skinned with gray eyes, and he still had an athletic build. With her five-inch heels on, she was slightly taller than he was, but he was still handsome.

He pointed at a chair at the table where she'd deposited her things. He offered, "Have a seat?"

She followed his lead to the table and they sat down. He said, "So tell me. How've you been?"

"I asked you first," she reminded him.

"Yes, you did," he laughed. "Not much has changed with me, except I got tired of working for someone else, and decided to go into business for myself. Uh, I'm divorced with two kids, college graduate, and multiple-business owner. Not much else to tell. What are you up to?"

"My sister and I own a business together," she began, stating the obvious. "No kids, no college education, just work, work, work."

"I see you cut off all that pretty hair," he said.

She self-consciously rubbed the back of her neck, smiling sheepishly. She said, "Yeah, it was time for a change."

"Are you married?"

She shook her head no. There were a few moments of awkward silence, but then she reached for her briefcase, taking out her notebook and pen. She asked, "So I take it this is the business you want decorated?"

"What was your first clue?" he joked.

They got down to business rather quickly, Lanai not allowing much room for anything else. They walked around the bar, Jamal expressing his vision to her. She made notes as he talked and showed her around. At the end of the appointment time, she said, "Well, let me track down what you specifically want, get everything together, and then I'll give you a call."

She gathered her things as she spoke. He said, "It was nice seeing you."

She smiled, "Yes, it was. Nice to see you're doing your thing."

Once she had everything together, he asked, "Do you have plans later?"

She replied, "I actually do. I'm headed to dinner straight from here."

He made a face and nodded his head. He said, "I should've known the answer to that."

She said, "We'll be in touch. We're doing business together, remember?"

He nodded his head and held the door as she maneuvered her way out to her car. She dropped the box into the backseat, purse and briefcase on the passenger seat, and made a beeline for the driver's seat. She waved to Jamal, who stood in the doorway waving. She pressed a few buttons to call Makai as she put her seat belt on and backed out of the parking space.

He answered, "Hello?"

"What's your location?"

"About ten minutes away."

"Me, too," she said, navigating through the beginning of rush hour traffic. She figured that if she drove like a bat out of hell, she'd probably get there almost the same time that he did. Newark, which was where the restaurant was, was about fifteen minutes from where she was in Wilmington, and that was with light traffic. She knew she'd have to drive like Danica Patrick.

"How was the meeting?" he asked.

"Good. He's waiting for me to get back to him," she answered. She was debating on telling him who the meeting was with, but she figured that it would definitely put a damper on their night, and she wanted to put forth an actual effort to make the night run as smoothly as possible.

"What are you decorating?"

"A business. He just bought a bar that he wants to be upscale."

"Uh-huh."

"Well, I just wanted to check and see how close you were," she said. "I'll see you there."

"Okay," he responded and the call ended.

After driving as if her life depended on it for twenty minutes, she finally pulled into the parking lot at Arner's Restaurant. She saw that Makai's truck was parked and she craned her neck to see if he was still inside. She parked and got out, grabbing her purse, looked inside and saw that no one was in the truck. The parking lot was full, so she was certain that it was going to be a busy night. She hoped that the line wasn't long.

She opened the door to the restaurant and the lobby area had people waiting to be seated. She saw Makai standing against the wall, pretending to be eating his daughter's fingers, while she giggled and smacked his nose with her other hand. She couldn't help but smile at what she saw. He looked natural playing with a baby.

The overwhelmed hostess asked, "Ma'am, do you have reservations?"

Lanai smiled and pointed at Makai. Makai looked up and saw her coming. He moved the baby to the right side, bouncing her. He whispered something to her and she giggled and squealed, clapping her little hands. Lanai went over to him, embracing his left side. He bent down and kissed her cheek. He stood up straight and said, "This is Makayla. Kay, say hi."

Makayla blew spit bubbles and smashed them with her hand against her mouth. Makai frowned. "Don't do that. Nasty."

He fished a cloth out of his pocket and wiped her hand and mouth. Again, he told her, "Say hi, princess."

Instead of saying hi, Makayla leaned forward and almost leaped out of Makai's arms, trying to get to Lanai's necklace. Her little hands reached out for Lanai and Lanai couldn't resist cautiously taking the baby from her father. She gingerly bounced Makayla, just as she'd done Sariyah when she'd been that small. Makayla touched the necklace, and then touched Lanai's face. She tried to put her fingers in Lanai's mouth, but Makai moved her fingers away. He said, "Stop that."

Makayla pulled her hand away from him, with her little face frowned up, and attempted to offer her fingers to Lanai again. Lanai was a little uncomfortable with allowing the toddler to put her fingers in her mouth. Makai moved her hand again and she started fussing, stretching her little body out. Lanai put her free hand behind Makayla's head to keep her from falling out of her arms.

In a stern voice, Makai said, "Hey. Cut it out."

Almost as quick as her tantrum started, it ended. At the sound of his voice, Makayla straightened up. She reached for him and when he took her back, she patted his face with her chubby hands. She leaned down and kissed him, then clapped her hands, squealing. Lanai said, "Looks like somebody is spoiled."

"Rotten," he added, trying to talk around Makayla's fingers in his mouth.

Lanai asked, "How long have you been waiting?"

Around the fingers in his mouth, he said, "Like ten minutes."

"Jackson, party of three," the hostess announced.

"C'mon," Makai said, allowing Lanai to go ahead of him to follow the hostess to their table. The restaurant was buzzing with conversation, busy staff, and the after-work crowd. People seemed to be thoroughly enjoying themselves. They were seated at a booth that seemed a little exclusive, in an area of the restaurant that was quieter and a little bit away from everyone else. As she sat down, Lanai was sure that he'd had extra pull somewhere to make that happen.

He tipped the hostess before she could walk away, after she'd given him a booster seat for the baby. Lanai picked up her menu and began looking it over, feeling a little uncomfortable. Makayla began to fuss again, trying to get out of the seat. She squirmed and reached for Lanai, whining and whimpering. Her big brown eyes pleaded with Lanai to save her from that seat.

"Awww," Lanai said. "Come here, sweetie."

She leaned over and picked Makayla up. Makayla stood in Lanai's lap and then positioned herself to sit down between Lanai's lap and the table. She tried to move the menu around on the table, swinging her hands. Lanai laughed as the baby played with the menu that she couldn't get off the table. Lanai leaned over to the left to get a better glimpse of what Makayla was doing, and Makayla leaned her head back against Lanai's chest. She touched Lanai's lips and nose, slightly squeezing her nose. Lanai giggled and Makayla laughed with her.

Makayla turned her attention to her father, who was watching. She said, "Da-da."

"What?" he asked, smiling at her.

She smacked the table and screamed, "Da-da! Da-da!"

"What, girl?" he asked.

She talked in her toddler language, with the only thing understandable being Da-da. Lanai laughed hard at the rambling and the swinging of her hands. She was an animated little girl. Makayla clapped her hands, slammed her head against Lanai's chest to look up at her, and clapped her hands again. Lanai figured, *what the hell? Might as well entertain her*. She clapped her hands, too, following the baby's rhythm, causing more pleased squeals. The sound of her delighted squeals and laughter made Lanai laugh, too.

She looked up at Makai and saw that he was watching them with a slight smile on his lips. She said, "She is too cute."

"She is," he agreed.

They had somehow managed to order dinner and drinks over Makayla's gibberish, which got louder when the waiter came over and asked for their orders. When dinner came, Lanai had to get creative to keep Makayla from digging her fingers in the mashed potatoes. Makai offered, "You can give her to me so you can eat."

Lanai shook her head no. "She's fine. We'll eat together, right, munchkin?"

Makayla smacked her lips together, tasting the potatoes that Lanai had given her and looking for more. Lanai managed to eat and feed Makayla fast enough so that that there wasn't a mess or a tantrum. She also noticed that Makai ate in peace and he wasn't rushing, which was rare. Her heart went out to him. He was always somewhere, doing something, and he went especially hard for the people he loved. It felt good to know she was one of those people, and he'd gone so far out on a limb to be there for her lately.

He caught her looking at him and asked, "What?"

Feeding Makayla some vegetables, she said, "Nothing. Just noticing how you seem to be enjoying your meal."

Breaking apart his roll, he reminded her, "I told you I would take her. I'm used to eatin' and havin' to fend her off."

She shook her head, carefully wiping Makayla's mouth as she chewed. She said, "I got it. You look like you don't get much of a break."

He chuckled, "I don't."

She admitted, "I thought this would be hard."

"What? Eating with a kid in your lap?"

"Meeting her."

He shook his head. "She's a lovable kid. It's hard to not like her."

"She's such a cutie," she said, hugging Makayla. "She looks just like you. I mean, she looks like you had her."

Putting a forkful of food in his mouth, he replied, "Strong genes."

For the rest of their meal, they talked, and when Makayla thought it was a good idea to try to turn the gravy on the plate into finger paint, Lanai pushed the plate away and cleaned her up. Makai gave her the sippy cup that he'd had in his back pocket earlier. As she drank, she laid her head on Lanai's chest and watched her daddy.

"She's going to sleep," Makai said quietly.

"Should I move her?" Lanai asked, ready to turn her around.

He shook his head. "You move her and she won't go to sleep. She's fine."

Within minutes, Makayla's head slid to the side and Lanai carefully slid the cup out of her sleeping hands. The waiter came and began clearing the table. He asked, "Can I interest you guys in dessert?"

She looked at Makai and he winked at her. She smiled and mouthed, "Nasty."

He raised his eyebrow and asked in a suggestive tone, "You want some dessert?"

Mocking him, she asked, "Do you want some dessert?"

"I sure do," he answered without hesitation.

She laughed and shook her head. "You're funny."

The waiter left with the dirty dishes and returned with his pen and pad ready. Lanai asked, "Do you really want dessert?"

"I said I do," Makai said.

"*Dessert*, Makai," she said.

He leaned forward in his seat and stretched his eyes, "I said yes, *Lanai*."

"Well, what do you want?" she challenged, sliding Makayla into a cradling position.

He mouthed, "You." He looked up at the waiter, "Chocolate ice cream, please."

Lanai laughed and shook her head. She asked, "Can I have the apple pie à la mode, please?"

Scribbling down their orders, he said, "It'll be out shortly."

When the waiter was gone, Lanai gave Makai a look. She asked, "Is that all you think about?"

Taking a drink of his water, he said, "I answered this question already today."

She laughed and looked down at Makayla's sleeping face. Looking at her reminded Lanai of when she'd held Makai Jr. in the hospital, and how much the two of them actually looked alike. She used her forefinger to trace Makayla's thick eyebrow. She had held in the hurt of the loss of her son, and the babies that followed. For so long, she felt that having a baby would fix her. She was thankful for the growth that she'd experienced because without it, she wouldn't have been able to be mature enough to hold the baby of the woman that shot her.

"Beautiful, ain't she?" he asked, breaking into her thoughts.

Lanai hadn't noticed that her eyes had filled with tears. She blinked a few times and looked up him with a smile. She admitted, "She's gorgeous. She looks like our son did."

"Yeah," he said quietly, watching her with concern. They'd never really talked about Makai Jr. She wasn't sure how he'd dealt with it, because they never talked about it.

She assured him, "I'm fine. I used to think about him and be sad, but I don't anymore. I still miss him, but I'm good. I'm glad to see she looks so much like him. Maybe that's what makes tonight easier, too."

Makai was quiet for a while. Their desserts were brought to the table and he finally said, "Lay her down on the seat. Enjoy your food."

Lanai made a face. She asked, "You know how many butts have sat on this seat? That's nasty."

Makai laughed. "Lay her on her back. Her face doesn't have to touch the seat."

She thought about it for a minute, and then decided laying her on her back probably wouldn't be too bad. She carefully positioned and repositioned Makayla, until she was able to move her to the seat on her back. She kept her close to her, putting her little feet in her lap. She said, "You need to bring a diaper bag. If you had a bag, you could have a blanket in there to lay her on."

"I'm not doing that," he replied quickly.

"You're too masculine for a baby bag?" she teased.

"Too much work," he said. "I can just put her cup and diaper in my pocket."

"What if she throws up?" she challenged.

"I'm not doing it," he said, with finality. He ordered, "Eat."

She asked, "Why you always tryna feed me? You want me fat or something?"

Tasting his ice cream, he said, "Nope. You gotta eat to survive. Plus, you phat where you need to be."

With her spoonful of vanilla ice cream and hot apple pie in mid-air, she stopped and tilted her head. She asked, "Are you calling me fat?"

"P.H.A.T.," he said, giving his full attention to his ice cream.

She tasted her dessert, and when she looked up her eyes went to his lips. He was sexy, but his lips took that sexiness to another level. She loved his lips and the way they felt on hers. She watched as he ate the ice cream off the spoon, as if she was in a trance. She wanted to see if the chocolate ice cream would taste different on his lips.

He caught her staring again and she couldn't do anything, but be caught. She looked up at him, not realizing that she'd been staring with slightly parted lips. He read the expression in her eyes and grinned, his confident, sexy grin. He put ice cream on the spoon and offered it to her, "Want some?"

His tone indicated that he was talking about more than just the ice cream on the spoon. She barely shook her head no. She really felt that she was stuck in a trance. She wanted him so bad that her stomach hurt. She knew that it would be good, too.

He asked, "Sure?"

Again, she barely shook her head no. She'd forgotten about her dessert and the ice cream was melting at a faster pace because it was on top of hot apple pie, which was growing cold. He shrugged and ate the ice cream. She needed to get some fresh air and get herself together. She'd been fine with spending time with him and taking things slow, but the burning desire that she felt in the pit of her stomach, had just hit her like a ton of bricks. The feeling made it difficult to breathe.

She hated that he could read it in her eyes. She wanted to keep it to herself. When she was home alone or at work, she could find something to busy herself until the sensation passed. She'd be asleep and wake up distorted and disheveled, because she'd dreamt of what his lips would do to her body, but she was the only one in her bed. She'd been tempted so many times to call him when she woke up feeling that way. However, she reminded herself that she needed to be consistent, and continue to take things slow, just in case he was full of shit.

She forced herself to stop looking at him, and looked down at the melted mess in the bowl in front of her, using the spoon to push the pie and ice cream around in the bowl. She really wanted to run out of the restaurant, but she knew she couldn't do that. Running away from him wouldn't solve anything, anyway. She was going to need to confront her feelings at all times; something she'd learned from rehab and counseling. She wasn't confronting her feelings at that particular moment, but she did make the decision not to run.

"Why you doin' this to yourself?" he asked, sounding amused.

Looking up, but not looking at him, she asked, "What do you mean?"

"You know what I mean."

"No, I don't."

"Stop playin' dumb."

"I don't know what you mean."

"I mean, I can see you want me, but you keep playin' this game."

Lanai felt her face growing hot, her skin flushed. She looked up at him, trying to convince him that she was more in control than she actually was. She said, "It's not a game. I told you I wanna take things slow."

"We go any slower and we'll be standing still," he retorted, pushing his bowl away. He pointed out, "You're torturing yourself." When she didn't respond, because she didn't know what to say, he continued, "But if you wanna play this game, I'm with it. You'll give in eventually."

She dropped her spoon and looked up at him. She asked, "Why do you keep saying I'm playing a game? This is serious to me."

"Clearly," he said dryly.

"You are not funny."

"Not tryna be. Ain't we grown?" he asked.

"Yeah."

"So why you wanna pussyfoot around?"

"Did you have to use that word?"

"I like that word."

"You would," she replied, making a face.

He said, "Answer the question."

"I don't wanna pussyfoot around. I wanna make sure it's right; the timing, everything. I told you, I don't wanna be hurt," she explained.

"That's a bunch of bullshit," he countered. "You ain't that scared of being hurt. You scared you gonna be stalkin' me."

His comment caused her head to snap back. She asked incredulously, "What?"

"You heard me."

Recognizing reverse psychology, she said, "You're not tricking me into that. You and I both know I never stalked you."

He laughed, "Never say never."

"You're foolish."

"And you're playin' yourself."

"How?"

"Why not give in to what you know you want?" he asked.

"Because it's not good to always get what you want."

"I ain't never had a problem with it," he replied.

She laughed, "I bet you haven't."

"Like I told you," he said. "I'm waitin' on you. Whenever you ready for me to scratch that itch, you need to know I'ma scratch the shit outta that motherfucker. Patience is key."

She pushed the bowl away from her and announced, "I'm ready to go."

With a surprised, hopeful expression, he asked, "You ready for me to scratch that itch?"

"No," she said, leaning over and picking the sleeping baby up. "I'm ready to go home."

"Aww shit," he said, sounding disappointed and going into his pocket to pull out the money for the bill and the tip. He taunted, "Can't handle talking about it, either?"

Lanai had gotten up and balanced a sleeping Makayla in her arms. Sounding annoyed, she said, "Just come on."

He slid the money in the black wallet for the bill and dropped the tip on the table. He got up and they walked to the front of the restaurant, where he gave the wallet to the hostess. He held the door for Lanai to carry the baby outside. Lanai noticed that the late spring air was somewhat chilly and Makayla didn't have a jacket on. They walked together to his truck and he opened the back door. Lanai carefully deposited the sleeping child into her seat and waited off to the side while he strapped her in. She wrapped her arms around her body and waited patiently to say goodnight.

Makai opened the passenger door, leaned in and started the engine. He suggested, "Leave your car and I'll drive you home."

Lanai's eyebrows furrowed. "Absolutely not. I'll be fine."

He leaned against the side of his truck and asked, "So now we're back to you being distant? I offended you with the conversation?"

She made a face, as if to dismiss the idea, and shook her head no. "I didn't realize I was being distant."

"You are. You way over there," he joked.

She laughed. "I forgot you like me all up on you."

He reached out and grabbed her arm, pulling her to him. He admitted, "I really do. I like how your body feels."

She fell into him and looked up at him. He wrapped his arms around her waist and she asked, "You are going to make this as difficult as possible, ain't you?"

He nodded. "That's my job."

She smiled and shook her head no. "That's not your job. Your job is to be understanding and patient."

His hands slowly rubbed up and down her back. He said, "This is the only way I know how to be understanding and patient."

They stared into each other's eyes and she knew she was going to lose the battle. Breathing in his cologne and looking into his dark eyes was a horrible combination for standing her ground. His body heat was always so warm and inviting. He lowered his head and she tilted her face upward, anticipating the kiss that she knew was coming. His lips were a breath away from hers, but he didn't let his lips touch hers. Their warm breath mixed and she could smell the chocolate ice cream. His face hovered over hers and she found herself holding her breath, waiting for his lips to make contact.

He lightly brushed his lips across her cheek and his nose brushed against her forehead. His fingers had begun to massage her back and the combination of the feeling that his teasing and fingers caused made her lean into him. She inched her face closer to his, wanting to kiss him. He slightly pulled back, purposely playing with her. Her hands were trapped between their upper bodies and when she tried to move them, he held her in place. She knew he was going to make things harder for her, since he'd seen it in her eyes that she wanted him. He was going to turn into a game.

She whispered, "Now you're gonna play?"

"Why not?" he asked, allowing his lips to hover over hers again.

She bit her bottom lip as his lips grazed her eyebrow and forehead.

He asked, "You ready to go?"

She nodded. She said, "You don't play fair."

"Neither do you."

"I can't leave with you holding me," she said.

He suggested, "You should ride with me. I can bring you back to get your car tomorrow."

She shook her head no. "I'm gonna drive home. But if you didn't have to take the baby home, I would offer for you to come over."

"For a nightcap?" he asked, leaning back and looking at her.

Still biting her lip, she nodded.

"You got two rooms, right?" he asked.

She nodded her head again.

"Is it a bed in the other room?"

Again, a nod.

"A nightcap it is," he announced.

"You sure?" she asked.

"Is water wet?" he returned.

She smiled. "You gonna follow me?"

He nodded and released her. "Let me walk you to your car."

He took her hand in his and walked her to her car. She pulled her keys out of her pocket and unlocked the doors. He held the door for her while she got in, leaned into the car and kissed her, then closed the door. She could taste the chocolate ice cream on his lips.

The drive back to Dover seemed to take half the time that it took to get to Wilmington. As she neared her apartment, a sign for the last liquor store before she got home caught her eye. She quickly turned her signal light on and jumped over onto the shoulder of the road, turning into the small shopping mall. She pulled into the parking space in front of one of the doors. Makai pulled up next to her and she put down her passenger window. He gave her a questioning look.

She said, "You said a nightcap. A nightcap is a drink, right?"

"It can be," he said, a little confused.

She said, "I'll be right back. I'm gonna leave the car running."

She put her window up, snatched her wallet out of her purse, and made a mad dash for the store. The last liquor she remembered him drinking was Hennessy, which they kept behind the counter. She grabbed a cold bottle of Moscato with the green label and went to the counter. After asking for the pint of Hennessy and presenting her ID, she paid for her purchases and darted out the door, almost before the clerk could completely bag up the bottles. She slipped into the car and headed back onto the highway.

Her brain wasn't too sure of what her body was doing. She was still afraid, but she was tired of hiding behind that fear. She felt that if she was serious about wanting to make things work with him, then it wouldn't kill her to let go and trust him. On the drive down, she had mused to herself that she was going to give it to him, anyway, so she might as well just do it. The waiting was more torture for her than it was for him.

She turned into her development and parked in front of her building. As she got out and gathered her things, Makai was taking Makayla, her sippy cup, and some diapers out of the truck. She led the way up the stairs and balanced her bags as she unlocked the door.

Makai said, "If you wasn't movin' all fast, I could've helped you with the bags."

Pushing the door open and flipping on the light, she said, "I'm fine. You got enough to handle with Sleeping Beauty."

After he was inside the apartment, she closed and locked the door. She said, "The blankets and sheets on the bed in the guest room are brand new. Is she going to be okay in the bed by herself?"

He nodded and made his way to the guest bedroom and Lanai headed for her room, taking her heels off on the way. She tossed the shoes near her closet, and began unbuttoning her blouse. She went into the bathroom and turned the water on; making sure it was as hot as she could stand it. She tugged the ends of the shirt out from the waistband of her A-line, black, knee-length skirt and finished undoing the buttons. Lanai went back into her room, pulling the blouse off and tossing it into the hamper that she kept outside the bathroom door.

She went over to her dresser and pulled out underclothes and pajamas, making her way back to the bathroom. She was so used to being by herself that she never closed any of the doors in her apartment, except the front and sliding glass doors. After placing her clothes on the counter, she reached behind her to unzip her skirt and jumped at the feel of hands already back there. She was so caught up in her routine that she'd almost forgotten that Makai was in the apartment. With one of his hands, his pushed her hands away and slowly unzipped her skirt.

Lanai's heartbeat sped up as the steam from the shower poured out from behind the shower curtain. She felt his warm fingertips on her skin as he pushed the skirt and it fell into a puddle at her feet. She felt the heat from his body even though he was fully clothed as he closed the space between them. Her eyes fluttered shut when she felt his warm lips on the back of her neck. His fingertips whispered across her flesh, making their way up to the clasp of her teal lace bra. She felt her bra come loose and he slid the straps off her shoulders, kissing her left shoulder. The fluttering in the pit of her stomach turned into what felt like tidal waves.

She let the bra fall to the floor and turned to face him. He cupped her face with his hands and kissed her deeply, pulling her to him. Their tongues locked in an intimate dance. She stood on her tiptoes and held onto his forearms. The spark that he'd started turned into a flame that seemed to consume both of them. Her hands went to the hem of his shirt, pushing it up. He took the hint, breaking the kiss momentarily to pull both his shirt and his T-shirt underneath over his head at the same time. As he was taking off his shirts, she began unbuckling his belt and jeans.

She could see the print of his erection through his jeans. She could never get over how well-endowed he was, even after over ten years; she didn't realize that she was biting her lip as she pushed his jeans to the floor. He stepped out of his jeans and boxers. A gasp escaped her when she saw how ready he was. It had been a long time since she'd had sex, and she was thinking that it probably would've been a good idea to get the dildo that Katara had told her would help her in rough times. At least if she had, she wouldn't have been standing in her steam-filled bathroom, gawking at Makai's penis like a virgin.

He took her hand and pulled her to him, his hard on poking her in the stomach. Tilting her face up to kiss her lips, he caressed her face with his thumb; he knew that his touching and kissing her would distract her. The feel of his soft, warm lips against hers made her mind swirl as she felt him slip her teal-colored lace panties off. She wrapped her hands around his neck and interlaced her fingers behind his head. Putting his hands on her hips, he lifted her off the floor and her legs wrapped themselves around his waist, as their tongues did the familiar dance. His lips abandoned her mouth to leave a trail of kisses from her chin to her nipples. His left hand held her where she was, while his right hand cupped her left breast. His mouth and tongue on her breast was sending shock waves through her, causing her to arch her back and moan into the top of his head.

She wanted him inside her so bad that she could feel her vagina throbbing. She kissed the side of his face and lightly bit on his earlobe. The teasing that he was doing to her was about to drive her crazy. She felt him walking, and then felt the cold wall against her bare back. She felt him move and within a moment, she felt him begin to enter her. She was wet enough to probably fill the tub, but her tightness made it a little bit of struggle for him. She bit down on her lip, trying not to tense up or scream. She wanted it bad, but if the pain was going to outweigh the pleasure, she'd just have to keep waiting. She dug her nails into the flesh of his neck, mouth wide open and unable to make a sound.

The girth of him filled her up and she was sure that he was touching her cervix. She leaned her head against the wall, trying to get her bearings. She felt him move slow and steady inside her and he kept that pace, until the movement of her hips matched his. His face hovered over hers, their lips a breath apart, as he made love to her against the wall of her bathroom. He was so gentle and she could feel the love in his touch; it seemed like he couldn't stop touching her face. They looked into each other's eyes and Lanai fell in love all over again, seeing the depth of his love for her in his eyes. She hated looking into his eyes, for fear of what she would see, as well as a fear of being let down yet again.

She couldn't look away from him or blink if she wanted to. She'd been afraid to look into his eyes for a long time, because of all the things that she'd done in the past. However, she was no longer scared to bare her soul to him, because she felt as though she could see his. She'd waited over ten years to be able to see what she'd felt for the entire time and it was worth it. With him moving in and out of her, and her movements matching his, she felt whole again. Her moans went from barely above a whisper to almost screams, as he delved deeper into her. She had no place to run and certainly not hide, because he had her pinned against the wall.

She could barely hear his moans and murmuring, or him cursing under his breath. With his lips against hers, he whispered, "Shhhhh."

She panted, "I can't."

"You have to," he whispered.

It felt like he was trying literally to become one with her. She shook her head from side to side frantically. She felt her climax coming, with her legs beginning to shake. She tried to keep the climax at bay. Even though he was hung like a horse, after the initial shock of him getting inside, she loved the feeling of him being inside her. She wanted to cherish that feeling forever. He was bringing out feelings that she'd forgotten she'd had. His pace increased, which was an indication that he was close to his peak, too. Unable to hold it any longer, she bit down on his lip, which was against her mouth.

"Ahh, shit," he grumbled.

She screamed against his mouth and dug her nails deeper into his flesh. She could feel him explode inside of her, causing his body to shake. After his release, he rested his forehead against hers, gently sliding his lip from between her teeth.

He said, "Dammit. You bit the shit outta me."

She smiled sheepishly, "I'm sorry." He began to ease out of her and she squeezed her muscles around him and tightened her legs around his waist. She whined, "No. I wanna stay like this."

He laughed. "We can't stay like this."

Reluctantly, she allowed him to slide out. She knew that they both needed to clean up. If she didn't quickly get into the shower, what was left of the hot water would be gone and she would be a sticky mess. She definitely couldn't go to sleep like that. She unwrapped her legs, prepared to get down, but he carried her to the shower. He pulled back the curtain and stepped into the tub with her in his arms.

He let her down and asked, "Where's the soap?"

She pointed behind him and snatched down the washcloth from the shower curtain rod that she'd hung there earlier that morning. She held out her hand for the soap, but instead of him giving it to her, he took the washcloth. He reached around her and lathered up the washcloth with the soap and water, taking it upon himself to wash her.

She tried to take the washcloth, saying, "I can wash myself."

He pushed away her hand. "Shut up."

For once, she did as she was told. It felt a little weird, getting bathed like a baby, but it also made her feel special. She felt herself getting aroused again as he washed her most sensitive spots. She giggled and tried to snatch back her feet as he bent down and gently scrubbed each one. He turned her around, washing her back and butt. The water rinsed away the soap on the front of her, and he reached around her to rinse the soap from the cloth. He repeated the process a few times, using the cloth to rinse off the back of her.

While she let the water, which had begun to cool off, run on her skin a little longer, she closed her eyes and enjoyed the feel of the water pulsating on her skin. She sensed him moving behind her, but she stayed under the showerhead with her hands on either side of her neck. She felt a light smack on her butt. With her eyes still closed, she asked, "Hmm?"

"You wanna move so I can rinse off?"

She opened her eyes and attempted to move, but there was nowhere to go. She asked, "Where am I gonna go? The shower ain't but so big and you're blocking the way out."

He reached up and angled the showerhead higher so that he could rinse off, getting her hair wet in the process. She was about to get upset, wiping the water from her face with her hand, but then she remembered that she didn't have long, difficult hair anymore. It would take no time for her hair to dry. He finished rinsing within a few minutes and then he told her to turn off the water.

He pulled back the shower curtain and asked, "Where the towels?"

She climbed out, pulling out one of the fluffy, oversized white towels and wrapping it around her body, then handing him the other one. She unwrapped herself from the towel, slowly drying herself. She debated in her mind whether her nightly routine was worth going through, with her energy level being on zero. Every night, she made sure to moisturize. She looked at the container of body butter that she normally used, thought about how she'd have to apply it to her whole body, and decided against it. She reasoned with herself that it wouldn't kill her to skip one night as she slipped into her underclothes and pajamas.

While she'd been debating with herself, Makai had taken his clothes and left the bathroom. She went into the bedroom to find him underneath the covers, looking like he was almost asleep. She followed his lead, dropping the clothes that she'd picked up off the bathroom floor into the hamper. As she slid underneath the covers next to him, she felt him reach out for her and she gladly slid over next to him. She fell asleep almost immediately, wrapped in his arms, her breathing matching his, and feeling as if she was on cloud nine.

CHAPTER SEVENTEEN

"**T**hank you, Ms. Wilson, for coming today," ADA Justin Montclair said, rounding the table where he sat in the courtroom.

Lanai nodded her head, trying to remain as calm as possible. She was nervous as hell, as if it was she on trial for her life. She could feel the twelve pairs of eyes from the jury box staring at her, along with everyone else in the courtroom. She wanted the day to be over already. She'd been called to testify in Sade's trial, who'd pled not guilty, due to self-defense. Lanai caught a glimpse of Sade sitting at the defense table with her public defender.

Sade was chewing on her bottom lip, looking like she barely could keep it together. She looked nervous and fidgety, with dark circles under her red eyes. Her clothes were loose fitting and hair was pulled back into a non-fashioned messy bun. The poor girl looked a hot mess. Her eyes kept darting around the room. If Lanai didn't know any better, she could've sworn that Sade was on something. The woman Lanai remembered seeing in the mall and at the door a little more than a year ago was beautiful. The woman that sat at the defense table was a shell of the woman she remembered.

"Ms. Wilson, will you please tell the court what happened on the night in question," ADA Montclair asked, approaching the witness stand.

"Well," Lanai began, "I received an antagonizing phone call from the defendant at my residence at the time. I was shot after I arrived."

"How did you know where she lived?" he questioned. "Had you ever been there?"

She shook her head. "She told me over the phone where she lived."

"And why did she do that?"

"She was angry that her daughter's father is still in love with me."

"So she almost killed you over a man?"

Lanai nodded her head. "Yes."

"She's a fucking liar!" Sade exploded, standing up from the table.

The judge banged his gavel, yelling for order. The public defender stood and grabbed Sade's arm, forcing her back into her seat, and whispering something in her ear. The two of them looked as though they were having a heated conversation. The judge warned, "Counselor, instruct your client to respect this courtroom, or I will hold her in contempt and have her removed."

Lanai could hear the public defender and Sade loudly whispering. When the judge banged his gavel one more time, and gave the public defender a warning look, both Sade and the public defender straightened up. Sade shot Lanai an evil look, but Lanai wasn't fazed at all. She didn't care where they were. If Sade wanted to try her, Lanai was going to give her exactly what she was after. The dumb bitch couldn't even fight, which was how Lanai ended up shot.

"No further questions, Your Honor," ADA Montclair said to the judge. As he walked back to his seat, he said to the public defender, "Your witness."

The public defender got up out of his seat, looking as if he'd slept in his suit. He had more of a bald head than he had hair, but the little bit of hair that he had was holding on around the sides and back for dear life. He wore brown, wire-framed glasses. His shoes looked cheap and the button holding his suit jacket closed was screaming for release. He approached the witness stand, asking, "What was it that brought you to my client's house?"

"She gave me her address," Lanai repeated.

"But why did she give you her address?"

"Ask her."

"Ms. Wilson, I'm asking you. Please answer the question."

"I did," she retorted.

"Your Honor, can you please instruct Ms. Wilson to answer the question that was asked?" the public defender asked, looking over the top of his frames at the judge.

The judge looked at Lanai and said, "Ms. Wilson, please answer the question."

Looking directly in the public defender's eyes, she retorted, "Because she called my house antagonizing me, and I asked her for her address, so that we could handle the situation face-to-face."

"So you were threatening my client and she was in fear for her life?" the Public Defender asked, trying to trap her into saying that Sade had just cause to shoot her.

Lanai replied, "No, I did *not* threaten your client."

"Isn't it true that you went to my client's house and punched her in the face on her doorstep?"

"Yes, I did."

"So isn't it an accurate statement to say that my client feared for her life, and the life of her daughter?"

"No, it's not accurate."

"What would you call it, then?"

"I would call it trying to kill me, and endangering the life of her own child," Lanai stated matter-of-factly. "As a public defender, you should know that there is no self-defense or stand your ground laws in Delaware. The closest thing to self-defense in the state of Delaware is if the person with a gun or weapon, attempts to flee from the situation, then they use deadly force. Your *client* answered the door with a gun in her hand, with the intention of shooting me."

"Objection, Your Honor!" the public defender called out.

Lanai continued, "Your *client* was completely aware of the risks of brandishing and using the deadly weapon that she chose to come to the door with. She chose to put her child, herself, and me in danger, just to prove a point, which I have yet to figure out what that point was."

The public defender yelled, "Your Honor, objection. I object!"

The judge repeatedly banged his gavel, which Lanai had initially ignored. She was determined to get her point across and let the truth be heard. The judge called, "Order! Order!"

When Lanai finally sat quietly, the judge told her, "Ms. Wilson, you and no one else will treat my courtroom like a circus. You answer the questions that you are asked and nothing more. Do you understand me?"

Lanai defiantly but barely nodded her head. She didn't know whom he was talking to, but judge or no judge, he was going to get his life together, talking to her as if she was a child. The judge turned his attention to the public defender. He asked, "Are you done with this witness?"

The public defender, in a defeated tone, said, "I am, Your Honor."

The judge turned to Lanai, "Ms. Wilson, you may step down."

She gladly got up and left the witness stand, making a beeline for the doors that led outside the courtroom. She went straight for the bathroom, and when she got inside, she yelled, "Uggghh!"

Who the hell did these people think they were? That public defender had a lot of nerve, trying to make it seem like his retarded client had every right to shoot me! Scared or not, when Sade answered the door, she should've just taken her beating like a woman, or she should've kept her big mouth shut. Shooting Lanai was a weak, stupid move and in Lanai's mind, Sade needed to pay for it. Lanai knew that if the situation were reversed, the judge would be ready to throw the book at her, no questions asked.

She paced back and forth, balling and un-balling her fists and fuming. She was trying to suppress the urge to punch the wall or the mirror. She wished that Sade were in the bathroom with her, so that she could punch her in the face; that was what she really wanted to do. As she paced, she noticed that it wasn't helping with her anxiety, but she did get a metallic taste in her mouth. Whenever she was upset and couldn't calm down, her body would crave cocaine, which was where the metallic taste would come from. There were times when she would go for months without even thinking about the drug. However, there were also times that she would crave it, just as someone would crave a cigarette.

Needing to shake the feeling and get her mind on something else, Lanai stormed out the bathroom, making a beeline for the exit. Instead of waiting for the elevator to come to the second floor as a few other people were, she headed for the large marble steps. She moved so quickly down the steps that everything around her was a blur. She had to get out of that building and get some fresh air. She barely made out that the security guard at the entrance and exit doors was asking if she was okay. She nodded her head, but didn't slow down her pace.

She felt her hands sweating, as she tried to be patient with the detector that allowed people to exit the courthouse. She walked through the detector and almost ran out the doors to the right. She ran down the marble stairs that led to the courthouse doors and almost sprinted to her car. She had to force herself to stop on the sidewalk where she was, take in the sights and sounds of traffic and people moving around her, and acknowledge that she was outside in an open space. She wiped her sweaty palms on her black dress slacks. She counted in her head, her lips moving simultaneously to keep her distracted. She hadn't even noticed that her breathing had become erratic. She looked around the busy street that Superior Court was on, not focusing on anything in particular, but just looking at different things.

She forced her mind to focus on a squirrel that was scrambling to get where it was going. She watched as it moved quickly and tried to go unseen. Sometimes she could sympathize with that creature. There were times when she wished she could go unseen or unnoticed. There were also times that she wished she could go back in time and redo her past. She stood on the sidewalk, wishing that she could go back to the night that she'd fallen and hit her stomach, causing her son's premature birth and subsequent death.

She felt that if she could go back to that night and just stay home, she would've never gone to the barbershop and saw what she'd seen. She felt that if her son hadn't died, her life wouldn't have spiraled out of control the way that it did. She wouldn't have had so much hurt and regret to live with, if she'd never lost her son. The empty feeling that she used to have, driving her to get high to escape, crept into her body like the spirit of the Grim Reaper.

It was rather warm outside, but she started to feel chilly, which was the feeling that the emptiness gave her. She had to do something; she felt would soon consume her again. The emptiness always pushed her to do things that would have her hating herself, which would start that vicious cycle that she'd fought so hard to end. She knew exactly where the road would lead her if she allowed that feeling to take over.

Determined not to keep letting that feeling take over, Lanai mentally shook herself and physically straightened her shoulders. She had so much going for herself and she couldn't sink to the old person that she used to be. She had to keep in the forefront of her brain that regardless of where she was, or what pressure she was under, she was a survivor. She was not a victim of her circumstances. She was determined to not live in the "what-ifs" and the "shoulda, coulda, woulda's". What was in the past had to stay in the past and she had to move forward.

After giving herself a mental pep talk and assuring herself that she would be okay, she made her way to her car. She still had the metallic taste in her mouth, but maybe checking her messages would further distract her. Taking her keys from her pants pocket, she unlocked her doors and climbed into the driver's seat. She retrieved her cell phone from the center console and proceeded to see whose phone calls and text messages she'd missed.

She had text messages from both Katara and her mom, asking her to call them immediately. There were voicemails from the two of them. Lanai knew something was seriously wrong, because Katara didn't leave voicemails unless it was business related. Holding her breath, Lanai pushed the button to play the voicemail from Katara. She carefully put the phone to her ear and listened cautiously.

Katara said, "Nai, I need you to call me back ASAP. Dad is in the hospital in Arizona. He had a heart attack and stroke. He's in a coma and Mommy is upset. Call both of us. I love you. Bye."

Lanai's mind tried to make sense of the message. She'd heard the words, but she didn't understand. Every time she'd seen her father, he'd always looked healthy. Neither of her parents had told her that he'd had any health issues. She pushed the back button to exit out of her voicemails without listening to her mom's, and dialed Katara's number.

After half of a ring, Katara answered, "What the hell took you so long? You love scaring the shit outta me, don't you?"

"I was in court," Lanai explained. "I can't take my phone in there."

"Well, call Mommy on three-way," Katara ordered.

Lanai pushed the button to add a call and dialed her mom's number. She couldn't merge the calls until Vi picked up, which took about five rings for her to do. In a weak sounding voice, Vi asked, "Hello?"

Lanai pushed the "Merge Calls" button, bringing Katara on the line. Lanai asked, "Mommy, what's wrong?"

"It's your dad," Vi answered. "He's in the hospital. He slipped into a coma the other day. The doctors aren't expecting him to make it."

"Where are you?" Lanai questioned.

"At the hospital," Vi answered incredulously, as if her daughter should've known the answer to that question before asking it.

"So, why am I just finding out about this now?" Lanai inquired, sounding irritated.

"Nai, we can talk about that later," Katara said, trying to diffuse the situation that she knew was about to get out of hand. She knew Vi didn't know about Lanai's feelings towards them, for not being the parents that she felt they should've been for her.

Vi asked, "Who's that?"

"Katara," Lanai answered absently.

"Hey, baby," Vi said.

"Hey, Mom. I just wanted Nai to call you, so you could hear her voice and not worry," Katara explained. "I have all the information and we'll take the first flight out."

Lanai was about to ask Katara exactly who was flying out, because it wasn't going to be her. She had a life in Delaware, a business to run, and neither of her parents had cared enough to inform her from the beginning. She had no interest in going to sit by the bed of a man that barely was in her life, even if he was her father.

Vi spoke before Lanai could, saying, "You girls call me when you get to the airport. Be safe."

Lanai opened her mouth to oppose, wanting to let her know that she wouldn't be coming to Arizona. Katara must've felt it, because she jumped in, "Okay, Mom. Love you. Talk to you later."

Vi ended the call, but Katara and Lanai were still connected. Lanai asked, "Just what the hell did you just volunteer me for?"

"We're going out there," Katara replied.

"*You* can go out there," Lanai clarified. "I'm not going anywhere."

Katara breathed into the phone. "Lanai, don't do this. He's your father. He could be dying."

"So what?" Lanai asked defiantly. "Where was he when I needed him?"

Katara asked softly, "Nai, honey? Please don't do this. Not now. I know you're upset and you have every right to be, but I need you to do this for Mommy. She needs us."

"She's with the person that matters the most," Lanai spat, tears filling her eyes. "He's always mattered the most."

Katara's voice softened even more. She said, "I know. Please go out there with me. I need you to do this for me. I can't go by myself."

Katara had never asked Lanai for anything. Lanai had never heard in her sister's voice what she heard over the phone. Katara had never needed anyone and had been the rock for everyone else. However, Lanai heard in her sister's voice that she really did need her to be there for her. She sounded as if she was beginning to get weary. There was nothing in the world that Katara could ask Lanai for that she wouldn't get.

Pulling herself together, Lanai took a deep breath and wiped at her eyes with the back of her forefingers. She relented, "Okay. I'll do it for you."

It sounded like Katara was smiling. She said, "Thank you. I'm gonna text you the flight information. It leaves in four hours. We have two hours to get to Philly."

"Really," Lanai groaned. "Okay. I'll meet you there. I love you."

"Love you, too," Katara responded, ending the call.

Before Lanai could gather her thoughts, her phone vibrated in her hand. Makai's picture and number popped up on her screen. She answered right away, "Hello?"

"Hey, babe," he answered.

"Hey."

"What's wrong?" he asked, concerned.

She hesitated for a moment, and then explained, "My dad is in the hospital. I gotta fly out to Arizona."

"What time does the flight leave?"

"I'm waiting for Katara to send me the flight information. She said I have two hours to get to Philly."

"I'll meet you at your house in forty-five minutes," he said.

She was trying to come up with an argument, but truth be told, she really did want him to at least be there to see her off. She needed to draw some strength from somewhere. She never had to be the strong one and when her source of strength—Katara—sounding as though she was getting weak, Lanai felt like she owed it to her to be strong. She answered quietly, "Okay."

He ended the call and Lanai sat in her car in complete silence for a moment, mulling over in her mind the conversation she'd just had. She didn't know what it was like to grow up with a father. All her father had done was take care of her financially and fly out to Delaware twice a year. The little bit of time that he spent in Delaware was spent with Vi, as if she and Katara didn't exist. The older the girls got, the more frequently Vi would take trips to be wherever Ramon was. His trips to Delaware had dropped off completely after they'd grown up.

She had mixed emotions about the whole situation. She was angry with both her parents for caring more about each other, than they did her and Katara. She wondered where his two kids in Arizona were, and why she and Katara needed to go all the way out there. She didn't feel her responsibility was to take away from her life, just to be there for a man that didn't care. He never took away from his life for her, not even when his grandson died. She told herself for years that it didn't matter that he wasn't there for her and tried to convince herself that it was something that she'd gotten used to.

A part of her longed for the relationship that she'd missed with her father. She knew that her sister in Arizona had gotten plenty of time with him and he'd been to plenty of, if not all of, her school functions and other events. Deep down, she wished that she were able to have regular conversations with her dad, or form the father-daughter bond that every daughter deserved. She'd found out when she had been in rehab that part of the reason she'd turned to drugs and dealt with the way Makai had treated her, was because of the lack of relationship that she'd had with Ramon.

She wanted to know what it felt like to be her daddy's little girl. She thought that she'd confronted and dealt with those feelings and issues a long time ago. The tears that slid down her face let her know that she hadn't. She had asked herself for years why she wasn't good enough for him to want to be a part of her life. What she'd done that was so wrong. She had wondered if she wasn't beautiful enough or smart enough. She'd even asked herself why the relationship with her mother was more important to her father than establishing one with her. She didn't want to admit it, but her heart hurt. It really did hurt that she had never been special or important enough for him to be there.

After a few minutes of allowing the tears to stream down her face and come together under her chin, she decided that enough was enough. She angrily wiped away her tears, pissed off at herself for allowing that man to get to her in any form. What was in the past was done; she couldn't change it. She wasn't going to allow it to ruin her present or her future, either. She'd go to Arizona as a favor to her sister, but the tears that she'd just dried were the last that she would shed.

CHAPTER EIGHTEEN

The plane to Glendale, AZ landed at Glendale Municipal Airport at the same time that the sun was setting. Lanai looked out the window where she sat, thinking about how beautiful the skyline was. She wished that she were able to get away and see the sun set for a better reason than the one that she was there for. The plane came to a stop and the flight attendants were making the announcement, instructing passengers about how to exit the plane.

She looked over at a sleeping Makayla on Makai's chest, admiring how beautiful and peaceful she looked. Makai had surprised her by coming along. He'd met her at her house with a bag and Makayla in tow. When she'd asked what he doing, he told her that he was going to be there for her, no matter what. He'd also joked that he could use the trip as a reason to get out of Delaware. She didn't argue any further, because she really wanted him there with her. She appreciated not having to go through the experience by herself.

Larry, Katara, and Sariyah sat across the aisle from them. Lanai had called and told Katara that Makai was going with them. Lanai could hear the begrudging tone, but Katara promised to get another ticket for him. They all rode up to the airport in Philadelphia in Makai's truck and Lanai was halfway expecting Katara to say or do something ignorant. Surprisingly, she didn't. She had just stared out the window at the passing scenery. When they'd boarded the plane to leave Philadelphia and almost the entire plane ride, Katara had been quiet. As they prepared to get off the plane, Lanai made a mental note to pull her sister to the side and talk to her to find out what was bugging her.

Once inside the airport terminal, Lanai observed that it was a nice building, with floor to ceiling glass, nice carpet, and nice, comfortable-looking chairs. It was somewhat quiet for it to be an airplane terminal. Lanai took in the beauty inside the building, forgetting that she had to get her bag. She had taken her briefcase, which contained her laptop on the plane with her as her carry-on bag. When she realized that she needed to go get her bag, she looked over to see Makai with his bag on his shoulder and her bag in his free hand.

She smiled. "Can I help?"

He shook his head. "You can get the door."

Larry followed behind him with his family's luggage and Katara carried a sleeping Sariyah. Lanai led the way out of the terminal where a van was waiting. Lanai asked Katara, "Did you organize this, too?"

Katara nodded her head, looking tired. Lanai went over to her and took the sleeping toddler. She wanted to help out as much as possible. She said, "Get in the car. They'll manage the bags and stuff."

Once all the bags were in the trunk, Larry and Makai got into the van. The driver asked if everyone was good. When everyone confirmed and Katara gave him the name of the hotel, he took them in that direction. When they reached the hotel, Katara said to Larry, "You guys can go up with the kids, and Lanai and I will go on to the hospital. Mom has been waiting for us to get here for a while."

Larry kissed her and followed her directions after she kissed her sleeping child. As he took the luggage out of the trunk, Makai kissed Lanai, saying, "I'll see you when you get back. Call me if you need me."

She said, "I will. I love you."

"I love you, too." He closed the door and the driver took Katara and Lanai to Banner Thunderbird Medical Center.

They were quiet on the way there, with Lanai holding Katara's hand. Lanai rubbed Katara's knuckles with her thumb soothingly. Neither of them knew what to expect, but they were both sure that it wouldn't be anything they couldn't handle together. Being the support that Katara needed was more important to Lanai, than her personal feelings about the situation. The van came to a stop in the horseshoe at the entrance of the emergency room. Katara and Lanai looked at one another, and Katara smiled a reassuring smile, which made Lanai smile and they got out. Vi had texted Katara the room number, so by reading the signs posted on the wall, they were able to locate the third-floor room Ramon was in..

As they approached, they saw a small -ramed, short woman, with a younger female and a male standing on either side of her in the hallway. The three of them were standing across from where Vi stood, just outside Ramon's room. Lanai felt uneasy about the interaction that they were approaching, and she increased her pace to keep up with Katara, who was by Vi's side in the blink of an eye.

Katara asked, "What's the problem?"

The younger female asked, "Who are you?"

"Her daughter," Katara returned, gesturing towards Vi. Vi's brow was furrowed and she looked upset.

Lanai stood on the other side of her mother. She noticed that the guy that was standing there looked exactly like her father, just younger. He had the jet-black hair and Cuban features. He and the younger female had the same light complexion that Lanai had. The younger female looked exactly like Lanai, but with the long hair that Lanai had cut off. It was an eerie feeling, as if she was looking in a mirror. Ramon's genes were definitely strong. Looking at the wife standing between her kids, Lanai could tell they barely had any of her physical features.

"Who are you?" Katara asked.

"*I'm his daughter,*" the younger female spat. "What are *you* people doing here?"

"You people?" Katara and Lanai echoed simultaneously, both of their heads snapping back.

"Yeah, *you people*," she repeated, her tone challenging. "It's bad enough that his mistress is here and then his bastard children come, too?"

"Look, girl," Lanai began, taking a step forward. "I don't know who you think you're talking to, but I'll slap the taste outta your mouth."

The young man stepped in between his sister and Lanai and said, "Listen; there's no need to get upset. Everybody just calm down."

"No, they need to leave!" the girl yelled.

Her mother began talking in Spanish, and Vi and Katara were trying to calm Lanai down, telling her to just back off. Lanai said to the girl, "I'm not going anywhere. I'm just as much his child as you are. You *make* me leave."

Lanai was just waiting for her to blink too many times and she was going to knock her into the wall behind her. This girl didn't even know it, but she was going to catch a beat down for everything and anyone that had ever upset Lanai. Lanai was going to unleash all the anger that she'd held in, on this girl. The young man stood between them, but Lanai watched the girl intently, as a panther would its prey before pouncing.

Vi said, "Lanai, stop it. This is not the time or the place."

Katara had her hand on Lanai's arm. She said, "Nai, relax. Don't upset Mommy."

"This bitch is not gonna stand here and talk to people like she has any more entitlement than anybody else, and she's not gonna disrespect my mom," Lanai retorted.

"Your mom was my dad's *whore*! You're the bastard child that none of his family knows about!" the girl snapped, as she antagonized Lanai from behind her brother.

Lanai was much quicker than she looked, and in the blink of an eye, Lanai had reached around the young man and grabbed a fistful of hair, snatching her from behind him. With the fistful of hair, Lanai put her free hand around the girl's neck and slammed her into the wall behind them, causing a loud thud. There was screaming and yelling, Vi screaming at Lanai to stop, and the wife screaming and crying in Spanish. The young man attempted to grab Lanai, but

Katara was quicker than he was, jumping in between them and shoving him back.

In a threatening tone, she said, "Don't put your fucking hands on my sister!"

"She's choking my sister!" he tried to reason. "She can kill her!"

"I'll get her," Katara said, eyeing him suspiciously.

Lanai had a death grip on the girl's neck and still had a fistful of hair. Through clenched teeth, she dared her, "Say something else! Call my mom another whore! I dare you!"

The girl struggled to get her breath, clawing at Lanai's wrist with wide, scared eyes. Seeing how angry Lanai was seemed to scare the girl even more. All the noise and commotion caused security to be called and two security guards came running down the corridor. Katara was in Lanai's ear, trying to calmly talk her into letting the girl go.

Katara said, "Nai, security is coming. Let her go. Please let her go."

"Fuck that!" Lanai spat. "This bitch wanna talk shit! Talk shit now!" With the adrenaline thumping through her veins, she squeezed the girl's neck tighter, taunting through clenched teeth, "Talk shit now. Call my mother another whore."

Katara grabbed Lanai's arms and tugged at her, saying, "Lanai, let her go. Now!"

Katara tugged at Lanai, but she wouldn't release her hold on the girl's hair and neck. When Katara tugged Lanai, it caused the girl to be jerked off the wall and slung around like a rag doll. Security was yelling at her to let go and it was just chaotic in the hallway. More security guards came running down the hall, trying to assist in bringing order to the otherwise quiet hospital. Katara grabbed ahold of Lanai's hands and tried to pry her hands off the girl. A security guard grabbed Lanai by the waist and tugged at her, yanking the girl with him. He yelled, "Let her go!"

Katara worked at removing Lanai's hands until she succeeded. Lanai pushed at the security guard's arms that were wrapped tightly around her small waist. He walked down the hallway with a kicking and struggling Lanai, and Katara following behind him. She heard the wife yelling at Vi to leave, and telling security that she wanted Vi to leave. Lanai yelled, "Fuck you, bitch! My mom don't need to be here!"

Katara chastised, "Lanai, shut up! It's bad enough that you're getting carried outta here!"

Lanai saw security escorting her mom in the direction that she was being carried in. Once the elevator came open, the guard carried her inside and wouldn't put her down until Katara, Vi, and a couple other security guards boarded the elevator and the doors closed. When the elevator began to move, the guard put her down. She snatched away from him unnecessarily, mumbling obscenities under her breath. The elevator reached the first floor and the doors came open. The guard that had carried her took hold of Lanai's elbow, escorting her off the elevator.

There was a Glendale police car outside the doors and Lanai's stomach dropped, knowing how things were going to go. The three ladies were escorted to security's office. The officer ordered, "Sit!"

Lanai looked up at him defiantly and rolled her eyes.

He repeated, with his voice more forceful, "Sit!"

She defiantly crossed her arms across her chest.

He warned, "You don't sit and I'ma make you sit, then I'm gonna cuff you to the chair."

"My God, Lanai! Sit down," Vi screamed. She was visibly shaking, her eyes bloodshot red and bottom lip quivering.

Katara touched Vi's arm and whispered to her, "Mom, calm down. You're shaking."

"I'm sick of this fucking girl!" Vi yelled, her eyes shooting daggers at her daughter.

Lanai's head jerked back in disbelief. She asked, "You're sick of me? That girl disrespected you! I defended you, and you're sick of me?"

"You don't know how to act," Vi accused, her voice going up another octave. "Every time I turn around, it's something with you. Your father is in a *coma*, Lanai. For once, pretend that I raised you better."

Lanai thought about it for a second. She wanted to go off on Vi when she said she didn't know how to act, but she thought better of it. When she told Lanai to pretend she was raised better, something in her snapped. Lanai asked, "Oh, so you *raised* me now? Last time I recall, you spent all your time with that clown in the coma."

"Don't you disrespect your father," Vi admonished.

"He's not my father," Lanai countered. "He's my sperm donor. A father spends time with his children, regardless of the circumstances that they were conceived under. A father makes an effort. I bet you he was there for his daughter upstairs. And you were so busy following behind him that you didn't teach me anything."

Vi replied, "I taught you better than the way you're behaving. I taught you manners and respect. Why do you have to be so damn ignorant everywhere you go? Why do you always have to fight? Why the hell are you so angry?"

"You!" Lanai screamed at her mother incredulously. "You're the reason I'm so angry, you and that nigga upstairs! It was so important for y'all to be together that you didn't give a damn about me. You spent almost thirty years chasing behind a man that is married to someone else. You're stupid!"

Vi chuckled cynically, "No, stupid is getting hooked on drugs after causing the death of your baby, and allowing your life to spiral out of control."

Katara gasped, "Ma!"

Lanai retorted, "No, stupid is chasing behind a man that's married to someone else for almost three decades, leaving your child to be raised by herself and her sister, and being escorted out of the hospital because the *wife* said so. You dedicated your whole life to this man, just to end up with nothing. You don't have a leg to stand on. When he dies, unless he specified in his will otherwise, you get nothing, dummy!"

Vi's breathing became ragged, her chest rising and falling rapidly. If looks could kill, Lanai would be dead. Katara hollered, "Both of you, stop it!"

Vi asked, "So what do you call the ten plus years that you were in a relationship with Makai and all the hell he put you through? All the hell you put yourself through? How smart are you?"

"Look at my example," Lanai returned, gesturing at her mother. The angrier Vi got, the calmer Lanai was. Lanai continued, "You can *never* say anything to me about how I lived or continue to live my life. *You are someone's mistress.* Not the wife; the mistress. You get no benefits. All you get is the money he spent on you and the trips he took you on. Regardless of what you think of Makai, at least he wants to marry me. Why did you settle for the life of a mistress? What do you get out of it?"

"Just because your father was married to that woman, that doesn't mean that he didn't love me," Vi argued. "I never wanted to be tied down to a man. My needs were met and that was what was important to me."

"Clearly," Lanai retorted dryly, "more important than being a parent, too."

"I was a parent to you."

"You were there more than him physically, but you weren't there emotionally," Lanai explained.

"I was there," Vi insisted.

"Who told me what to do about my period? Who was there when I started my period? Who told me about boys? Who came to my school functions? Who was there for me when my son died?" Lanai screamed, leaning forward with tears in her eyes. She continued to fire off her questions, "Who loved me enough to walk me through my addiction? Who has been there every single step of the way, and ain't but a few months younger than me?"

Vi stood there quietly and Katara rubbed Lanai's back soothingly. Lanai cried, "I *needed* you to be a mother to me. All you ever cared about was being there for *him*. He was all that ever mattered!"

Katara pulled Lanai to her and hugged her. She said, "Shhhh, momma. Don't cry. It's okay."

With her head on her sister's shoulder, Lanai sobbed, "It's not okay, Tara. I'm a broken woman because of them."

None of them paid attention to the fact that the security guards that had come in with them were openly watching and listening to their display. Vi blinked a few times and finally looked around at the people looking at her. She took a step back, visibly distancing herself from her child that needed her. She left Katara to clean up the mess, yet again. She went over to one of the security guards and had a brief conversation with him, while Lanai cried on Katara's shoulder. One of the other guards took some tissue to Katara. She mouthed a thank you and gently pushed it into Lanai's hand.

Lanai clutched the tissues and cried like a baby. She cried for the years lost that she'd wished that she could get back. She cried for all the times that she'd needed her parents, and they had been too wrapped up in what they wanted to put her needs first. She wanted to be over those feelings so bad. She wanted to be able to get over it and move forward with her life in a positive direction. The emptiness that never really left her began to feel as if it was consuming her. It always got worse when she was sad or upset. She needed to do something to get ahold of that feeling.

Lanai finally pulled herself together, taking the tissue and wiping her eyes and nose. With her hands on Lanai's arms, Katara asked, "Are you okay, honey?"

"Yeah," Lanai answered, barely above a whisper. She didn't sound convincing, but they both knew that pushing the issue wouldn't help.

Everyone looked at the door at the sound of someone coming into the room. Lanai noticed that her mom had left the room. Two male police officers came into the room and walked over to Lanai. The taller officer asked, "Are you Lanai Wilson?"

Lanai nodded, knowing what was going to happen. The officer informed her, "Ma'am, you're under arrest for assault. Turn around and put your hands behind your back."

"Wait, what?" Katara screeched. "What do you mean she's being arrested for assault?"

Turning around as she was told, Lanai looked Katara in the eye and calmly said, "Tara, calm down."

Hearing the handcuffs being fastened around her wrists, Lanai swallowed hard. She'd never been arrested, but hearing and seeing what was going on in the news lately with the police brutality had her extremely calm and cooperative. She didn't want to do anything that would set them off or make them feel like she was a threat.

"Where are you taking her?" Katara asked, sounding weak and small.

"Glendale Police Station," the officer guiding Lanai by the crook of her arm answered.

CHAPTER NINETEEN

"**S**ay what?" Makai looked up from the basketball game that he had been watching with Larry. Both Makayla and Sariyah were asleep on one of the queen-sized beds in Larry and Katara's room.

Annoyed, Katara repeated, "Lanai got arrested and she's at Glendale Police Station."

Makai instantly reached over and pulled his boots on his feet, standing up. He asked, "Do you know where it is?"

"The driver does," she answered, looking and sounding nervous and worried.

"Let's go!" he ordered, going to the door.

"What do you mean 'let's go'? I don't know what their requirements are to bail people out here," she argued. "I gotta call somebody. I gotta find a lawyer, call a bail bondsman, and find out how much it's gonna cost to get her out."

"You gotta come on!" he replied. "I have a lawyer and I got money. Let's go!"

Katara looked at him as if she'd forgotten whom she was talking to. She looked at Larry. He said, "Go get your sister."

Makai was already out the door and halfway down the hall by the time Katara decided to follow him. He knew Makayla would be okay with Larry if she woke up. As they got into the van, he asked, "What happened?"

"She snapped," was Katara's reply.

"Snapped how?" he demanded. When she didn't respond, he said, "Listen, I know you don't like me. You have every reason not to. I hurt your sister and I left you to clean up the mess, but staying mad at me won't fix anything. She and I are working on it and I'm gonna do right by her. You might not believe me and I don't blame you. But you're making things harder on her, because she feels like she's caught in the middle."

Katara rolled her eyes and looked out the window at the passing scenery, with her arms crossed over her chest. Makai always knew that she was a hard ass. He wasn't surprised that she wasn't going to talk to him, but he didn't care. His concern was to get Lanai. He could find out from her what happened when they released her. He was just as stubborn as Katara was. He attempted to have a conversation with her and bury the hatchet for Lanai's sake and sanity. He wasn't going to beg her, though. That was the first and would be the last time he'd try to make amends with her.

Makai pulled out his phone, scrolled through his contacts, and pushed the name of his lawyer. He had his lawyer's personal cell phone number, making it possible to get in touch with him anytime. He waited while it rang, and then there was a break in the line. "Hello?"

"Hey, Marty," Makai asked.

"Makai," Marty replied, sounding like he was smiling through the phone. "How are you?"

"Good," Makai answered. "What about you?"

"Can't complain. I'm working, as usual. What's up? What can I do for you?" Marty asked.

Makai answered, "I got a situation in Glendale, Arizona. My girl got arrested for whatever reason and they took her to Glendale Police Station. I'm headed over there now."

"Gotcha," Marty replied, sounding like he was moving around in the background. "Do you know what happened? What's her name?"

"Lanai Wilson. I don't know what happened, but I'll find out when they let me bail her out," Makai said.

"I know a judge in Glendale," Marty offered absently, talking more to himself, than he was Makai. "Hold on a second."

It sounded like Marty had moved the phone away from his mouth to place a call on his office phone. It was a little muffled, but Makai could hear him talking to someone else on the other phone. He was making small talk for a while, but then he got to the point. He asked about the situation with Lanai's arrest and asked what her bail was. He told the other person that he would be representing her, and he wanted her release fast-tracked. He thanked the other person that he was talking to and came back to the phone with Makai.

Marty said, "They'll be releasing her on R.O.R. within twenty minutes."

"Thanks, Marty," Makai smiled.

"When are you going to be back in town?" questioned Marty.

"Not sure. Why?"

"I need to put you on the schedule for lunch. We have some business to discuss," Marty reminded Makai.

At that moment, Makai couldn't recall exactly what he was talking about, but he agreed, "Okay. I'll hit you when I get back in town and we can set that up."

"Good. I'll do everything I need to do on my end here, and when I find out the court date, I'll notify both of you. She's not a flight risk, is she?" Marty inquired, sounding a little worried.

"Nah," Makai assured him. "You ain't gotta worry about that."

"Great," Marty replied. "Make sure you let me know when you get back to town."

"I definitely will," Makai promised, ending the call.

He checked his missed calls and text messages as they pulled up to the Glendale Police Station. He saw that he had some threatening messages from an unknown number, which he was sure was Lynette. He'd changed his number three times and the last time paid for it to be unlisted, so it was beyond him how she continued to get his number. He'd told her face-to-face, over the phone, and through text message, that he wanted nothing to do with her. She insisted on harassing him, which caused him to ignore her. He made a mental note to call the general manager, Asia, after they got everything situated with Lanai.

When the van came to a stop, Makai and Katara climbed out. He headed for the door, as she told the driver to wait for them while they were inside. He waited and held the door for her as she approached. They went to the front desk together and she gave the officer behind the bulletproof glass Lanai's name, and said they were there to bail her out. The officer looked up Lanai's name and said, "She's in front of the judge now. Just have a seat over there."

Reluctantly, Katara dragged herself to the chair to the right with Makai behind her, leaving a seat in between them. They prepared to sit and wait forever, despite the fact that Marty had said twenty minutes. Makai recognized that they were in a completely different state across the country. Marty was good, but Makai wasn't sure if he was *that* good. Pulling out his phone again, Makai decided to go online and check ESPN updates.

His phone buzzed in his hand with an unknown number. He didn't answer unknown numbers, so he slid the red dot to ignore the call. Two seconds later, Unknown Number popped up again on his screen. Again, he ignored it. After two more seconds, Unknown Number came up again. Aggravated, he answered, "Hello?"

"Oh my God, Makai! I have been calling and texting," Lynette whined into the phone. "I thought that maybe something had happened to you, or worse, the baby! How is my baby? It's been so long since I've seen her! My God, I miss her! And I miss you, too! Baby, I need to see you!"

As she rambled, Makai pitifully shook his head. His gut told him that he should have kept ignoring the phone, because he had a feeling that it was her. He said, "First, of all, my daughter is *not* your baby. Second, I've been avoiding you, because I don't wanna talk to you. I told you that a few times. When are you gonna get it through your head that I want you to leave me alone?"

"You don't mean that," she said.

"I mean that. Stop calling me, yo."

"But, baby, I love you," she whined. "And I know you love me, too. We...we just hit a rough patch, that's all. I'm only a few minutes away. I'll be at the house in no time. We need to talk face-to-face."

"I'm outta town," he answered dryly.

"Oh," she answered barely above a whisper, sounding disappointed.

Taking advantage of the pause in the conversation, Makai said, "Listen, don't call my phone anymore. Stay away from my daughter's daycare, my businesses, my house, and me. I don't love you; I never did. I never told you I did. I—"

"You don't have to say it," she interrupted. "I know you do. I can't stay away from you. I won't live without you."

He rolled his eyes. "I'm in a relationship and you need to respect that. Stop calling and texting me. Period."

He could hear her protesting as he took the phone away from his ear and ended the call. He put the phone back in his pocket, all of a sudden uninterested in what was on ESPN online. He thought that he'd been clear with Lynette from the beginning, about what he wanted and didn't want. It was annoying to him that she saw what she wanted to see. He'd ignored and avoided her for months and she still didn't get it. He knew he was a beast sexually, but she wasn't dickmatized. The bitch was crazy. No matter how annoyed or irritated he became, he made his mind up that he wasn't going to answer any more unknown calls or numbers. He knew that changing his number would be pointless, because he was sure she'd find that out, too. Frankly, he was tired of changing his number. Eventually, he figured she'd get the point.

He looked across the small waiting area at the vending machine, as his stomach simultaneously growled, and stood, walking over to get a snack. He'd wanted to wait until Lanai had come back to the room before he'd gotten anything to eat, because he wanted to eat with her. As he put a dollar in the machine, he wondered what she'd done to get arrested. He was certain it was something to do with her temper. She was a hotheaded firecracker, and he had to admit that he liked that about her. Over the years, it had begun to get on his nerves, but he thought that she was even sexier when she was angry. He also liked knowing that she could handle herself in any situation. He just wasn't sure how much her being able to "handle herself" was going to cost him in bail money.

He bent down to get his bag of Doritos and started back to his seat, when the door that led to the back opened. He looked up to see Lanai walk through, escorted by an officer that stopped at the door. Katara had looked up when she heard the door open, and when it registered to her that it was her sister, she jumped out of the chair as if someone had set it on fire. She grabbed Lanai and squeezed her as if she hadn't seen her in a hundred years. Katara pushed Lanai out to arm's length, carefully looking over her sister's face.

Katara asked, "Are you okay?"

Lanai nodded with a weak smile. Katara yanked Lanai back into a tight embrace, mumbling her thank you's to God. Lanai patted Katara's back, trying to assure her that she was okay. When Katara finally let her go, Lanai met Makai half way and allowed him to envelop her in his embrace. He kissed the top of her head, asking, "You good?"

She nodded. "They let me go on R.O.R., but I gotta come back for court in a month and a half." She stepped away from him and went to the window, asking, "Is there anything else I need to do or sign?" When the desk sergeant shook his head no, she turned to Katara and Makai and said, "Let's go."

The three of them walked outside to the waiting van and Makai waited while the two ladies got in. Once he was inside and closed the door, the driver pulled off. Lanai spoke up, "Can you go back to the hospital? I need to check on my mom."

Makai opened his bag of chips and began eating, offering her one. She shook her head no and he shrugged his shoulders, putting the whole Dorito in his mouth. Around a mouthful of Doritos, he asked, "What happened?"

"I got arrested," she answered, stating the obvious.

"No shit," he quipped. "How?"

"That bitch wanted to talk shit and call my mom out of her name," Lanai replied, her anger from the situation returning. "I bet she won't talk shit again!"

"Look, now," Katara warned. "You can't go up here wanting to fight. They may not even let you in there. You just got carried out."

Lifting her chin in defiance, Lanai said, "I'm just gonna check on Mommy. I don't have anything to say to anybody else."

"Make sure you keep it like that," Katara mumbled, crossing her legs in the seat behind Lanai and Makai.

It didn't take long to get to the hospital and when they pulled up in front, security was standing outside with a distraught Vi. She had tears streaming down her face and also wringing her hands. She looked as if she was trying to plead her case with the guard, who looked as though he was trying hard not to pick her up and escort her off the grounds. Lanai was unlocking the door and trying to pull it open, before the driver could come to a complete stop. Katara squeezed past Makai and was on Lanai's heels as she jumped out the van. Both of them rushed to Vi's side.

The other security guard that was standing there straightened his shoulders, and his face showed that he remembered Lanai from earlier. Makai climbed out the van to make sure that things didn't go south again. He heard Vi pleading with the guard to let her go back in.

The guard said, his tone pleading with her to understand, "Ma'am, we've gone over this over and over. My hands are tied."

"What is the problem?" Katara asked.

"Who are you?" the guard asked.

"Her daughter," Katara answered, gesturing towards Vi.

"Well, I've been trying to explain to your mother that I can't allow her back upstairs," he explained. "I understand that your dad is sick and everything, but she can't be in there. Her presence is upsetting his family up there, as well as the staff and other patients and their families. I don't want to call the police, but she has to go."

"Ma, let's go," Lanai said, attempting to guide her to the waiting van.

Vi angrily snatched her elbow away and yelled, "Don't touch me! If it weren't for you and your foolishness, I could've convinced his wife and daughter to let me stay!"

Lanai gave her an incredulous look. "Are you serious?"

Vi turned her attention to the security guard, pleading, "Please, let me go up and talk to his wife privately. I don't want to cause them any added grief, but I *need* to be up there. He needs me up there."

"What is your relationship to him?" the other guard asked.

"Mistress," Lanai answered dryly.

Both guards looked shocked. The first guard shook his head. "I can't do that. You gotta go."

He took her elbow and guided Vi towards the van. She pushed against him, trying to stop him from moving her. She protested, "Please, you don't understand. I have to be by his side. Please let me go up there. Please! I need to at least say goodbye to him!"

The guard ignored her pleas and guided her to the open sliding door of the van. Lanai and Katara shook their heads in pity at the spectacle that Vi was making of herself. Makai stood back and watched in amazement. He'd never seen anyone's mistress pleading to make nice with the wife, so that she could be by the dying husband's side. The guard used two hands to practically stuff Vi into the van. She tried to get back out, trying to make him understand how important seeing Ramon was to her.

Katara tried reasoning with her, begging her to just get in the van and stop making things harder. Fed up, Lanai moved around Katara and pushed past the guard, placing herself between her mother and the guard. In a threatening tone, Lanai said, "Get your ass in that van now, before I *make* you get in there! Stop acting like a goddamn three-year-old having a temper tantrum!"

For a second, Vi looked like she wanted to try Lanai, but the even more threatening look in Lanai's eyes, made her second-guess her decision to try and get all the way out. She ducked her head into the van and quietly went to the back. Katara hopped in and got in the back row with Vi, with Lanai and Makai following them. Makai pulled the sliding door shut and the driver took that as his cue to leave. There was complete silence in the van on the way back to the hotel, except for Vi's quiet sobs.

CHAPTER TWENTY

Lanai's head spun and her palms were slick with sweat. She was pacing back and forth, biting her lip and trying hard not to sucker punch her mom in the face. Listening to her mom's never-ending stupidity was making Lanai wish that she could get high. *A couple lines would definitely block her out,* she thought. She had gotten the metallic taste, the cocaine craving, when the police had locked the cell. Witnessing the spectacle that she called her mother, only made her want the drug more. She was craving cocaine so bad that her tongue felt thick and heavy, and her vision was beginning to blur.

Vi was screaming about how much of a disappointment Lanai was, and the only good thing that had come out of her birth, was the relationship that Vi was able to forge with Ramon. Lanai understood that her mom was upset and that she loved Ramon, but she was about two seconds from knocking the snot out of her, mother or not. There was only so much a human could take and Vi was pushing the limit. Lanai was so angry that she snarled, "I wish you would shut the fuck up!"

Vi stood there, wide-eyed, staring at her child. Her eyes seemed to take in Lanai's wild, bloodshot eyes, erratic breathing, and pacing for the first time since they'd gotten to the hotel. Vi had been so hell-bent on taking out her anger on her daughter that she never looked at her. Lanai didn't know for certain how disheveled she looked, but she felt crazy on the inside, so she could only imagine. Makai, Larry, Katara, Sariyah, and Makayla had gone downstairs to the restaurant to get something to eat. When a craving for cocaine hit Lanai hard, she would have no appetite. She'd told Katara and Makai that she would just wait upstairs until they came back. She had no idea her pain-in-the-ass mother would stay behind to drive her up the wall.

Unable to stop herself, Lanai screamed at Vi, "Just shut up! Shut up, shut up, shut up! I don't care about how much you love that worthless son of a bitch! Just shut up before I choke the shit outta you!"

"Who do you think you're talking to?" Vi asked, narrowing her eyes.

Lanai would normally respect her mom, regardless of what she felt or thought. But it seemed like seeing her mom reduce herself to such a pathetic low just to be at Ramon's side made her loose the respect that she'd had for her mother. Lanai had always thought of her mom as being a strong woman when she was growing up. However, wisdom, age, and maturity over the years on Lanai's behalf, had exposed Vi for the weak woman that she was. Vi's life revolved around Ramon and making sure that he was always a part of her life, regardless of the fact that he was married with children elsewhere. It didn't seem to concern her that her daughter needed her more than Ramon did.

Feeling like a lioness about to pounce on her prey, Lanai eyed her mom carefully. She had been continuously reminding herself that she couldn't choke her mom, but it reason seemed to slip away from her as every second passed. Initially, she'd been pacing from one end of the room to the other. She didn't even realize that her pacing had turned into deliberate, calculated steps, making a half circle in front of Vi. A small voice inside her that told her she needed to get fresh air to clear her head. The bigger part of her was consumed with her craving and the predator in her. The bigger part of her strategically placed her between Vi and the door that led into the hallway.

There was an adjoining door between the couples' rooms, that Vi could probably make it to; but Lanai was pretty sure that she would be able to smash Vi's face against the second door before she could get it opened. Her sweaty fingers itched as her eyes went to Vi's neck. She wanted to watch the life drain out of Vi as she applied pressure. She inched closer, her eyes on Vi's neck. Lanai never heard the door open when Makai entered the room.

Makai had been carrying Makayla in one arm and takeout in the other. Lanai was almost close enough to wrap her fingers around her mom's neck, when Makai called her name. The fog that her craving and her mom's nagging had caused was thick in her head. He was calling her name, but it only sounded like more noise that her brain couldn't make sense of. Vi stood there, looking at Lanai as if she were crazy. Vi's eyes widened, her brain registering what was about to happen. Fear paralyzed her and she was frozen in the spot she was in.

Lanai's hands slowly inched up, positioning themselves to be around Vi's slender neck. Lanai guessed that it would take about three and a half minutes for Vi to be unconscious, but she knew that if Vi put up a fight, it could take longer. The key was to choke her until she passed out, but not to kill her. Lanai knew she'd have to apply enough pressure to cut off the oxygen supply to her brain. She just wanted to send Vi a message to think before she talked, because Vi really didn't know what awaited her. Lanai was aware that sending that kind of message could go left rather quickly and Vi could end up dead. The adrenaline that pumped through Lanai's veins made her want to try it, just to see what would happen.

"Lanai!" Makai yelled, snatching her backwards.

She snapped out of her trance, looking up into his face. She blinked several times, trying to remember when or how he'd gotten into the room.

With his thick brows furrowed, he asked, "What is wrong with you?"

Absently, Lanai shook her head. She whispered, "Nothing."

Makai looked at Vi and advised, "You should go next door."

He held onto her arm until Vi had slipped though the adjoining door and closed it. He slowly released her arm. He repeated, "What is wrong with you?"

She shook her head and looked away. She was ashamed of what he would see in her eyes. She knew that even though he probably hadn't seen a fiend in a long time, he hadn't forgotten the look in their eyes. She was afraid that he'd see that look in her eyes. Whenever the cravings had hit her in the past, she'd been able to hide it and suppress it. However, it seemed that her addiction had grown from being a monkey to an oversized gorilla and it was weighing her down. She wasn't sure if hiding and suppressing it was a good idea; she just didn't know what else to do.

"You was about to fuck her up," he quietly observed.

Lanai moved away from him and said barely above a whisper, "She doesn't know when to quit."

"Something else is wrong," he observed.

She had moved over to the window that looked out over the busy street below, looking out at nothing in particular. A part of her was itching to be a part of the constant movement of the nightlife again. It was about five o'clock and she knew that the clubs in the area were preparing to open, if not already open for early dinner. She wasn't interested in getting something to eat; she wanted to feed the craving that she never seemed to outrun.

She let the curtain fall back in place and went to the closet where her clothes were. She pulled out her suitcase and tossed it on the bed, unzipped it and began rummaging through for something to wear, without acknowledging his statement. She could feel him looking at her, but she refused to look up. She'd tried her hardest to separate herself from her addiction and live a clean life. It was just too hard and her parents only made the situation worse. She needed to escape her reality and lose her mind, if only for moment.

Without saying another word, Makai went over to her and put his hands over hers, stopping her from searching through the clothes. She still refused to look up, but he quietly pleaded with her, "Baby, talk to me. Please."

Her heart dropped. She felt like she was torn in half. The whole time that she'd been lost in the world of partying and addiction, all she'd wanted was for him to care enough to stop her. She'd felt that if he cared enough to stop her one time, then she would be strong enough to stop and clean her life up. That time never came; she learned that she had to want to stop on her own. Now that he was standing in front of her, begging her to let him in, she wasn't sure that would be enough. The pull of the addiction was strong and it was calling her. She wasn't sure that she could continue to resist.

Tears had formed in her eyes and even though he couldn't see them, he pulled her to him and wrapped his arms around her. She rested her head against his chest and wrapped her arms around his waist. The only place in the world that she'd ever felt safe was in his arms. The first tear escaped her eye and slid down her nose. Just when she felt like she was getting her life together, it seemed like it was falling apart. She just wanted to get a handle on things and keep everything consistent. She hadn't been to see her therapist in about a month and a half; it was probably time to schedule an appointment.

He kissed the top of her head and said softly, "Tell me what's wrong."

"Everything is just so hard," she sobbed. "I coulda stayed in Delaware for all this."

He rubbed her back soothingly. He asked, "What is so hard?"

"My mom, my dad's family, shit, even my dad," she confessed. "I don't wanna be here. I came to help Tara, but I caught a charge, embarrassed her, and made things worse. I just wanna go home."

"We will," he promised. After a few minutes of silence, he asked, "Why were you going through your clothes? Were you tryna leave now?"

Wiping her face with her left hand, she said, "I was gonna go out."

"Go out where? You don't know anything about this place," he replied.

She shrugged. "I was gonna go just anywhere to escape this mess."

He put his hands on her shoulders and moved her back arm's length. When she wouldn't look at him, he lifted her chin with his hand, forcing her to look at him. His eyes searched hers. She saw recognition in his eyes, letting her know that he'd seen what she didn't want him to see. His thumb slid across her cheek. He said, "I'm not losing you again. If you need to talk, we can talk. You need to let some shit off your chest; we can do that, too. What you won't do is go off somewhere and I lose you."

Her eyes filled with tears again. She was at a loss for words, because that was exactly what her addiction had her about to do. She would give anything to feel normal again and not have to fight the demon of addiction. With his thumb, he wiped away the tear that had escaped. He pulled her to him again and hugged her. She could feel his heartbeat against the side of her face, a beat that almost matched hers identically. She didn't want to feel as if she needed saving, but it felt good to know that he would be the one to save her.

He told her, "Babe, I know you struggle with staying clean. I don't know the struggle personally, but I know you're trying. Don't shut me out. I ain't going nowhere and shutting me out only causes more problems for us. I wanna help you. Let me help you."

As he talked, she cried harder. He tightened his arms around her and her silent cries turned into loud sobs that shook her body. She thought that when she'd taken the step to go to rehab and survived it, things would be easier. Even though she could feel Makai's love for her, she still felt that she was missing something. She felt there was a gaping hole in her that no child, man, material things, or drugs could fill. She appreciated his love and support, but she had to fill the hole with something, before it consumed and killed her.

Her cries were so loud that Katara burst into the room. She gave Makai an accusing glare, and tried to pull Lanai away from him to find out what he'd done to her. Lanai had a grip on his shirt and she wouldn't let it go. Her sobs shook her body so hard that her knees buckled. Larry was standing in the doorway of the adjoining rooms. Makai motioned with his head for Larry to take Makayla, who was sitting on the bed, with her fingers in her mouth and eyes wide. She looked confused and on the verge of tears herself.

As Larry took the baby into the other room and closed the door, Makai sat Lanai down on the end of the bed and sat next to her with his arm around her shoulders. Katara bent down in front of Lanai and held her hands. She asked, "What's wrong?"

Lanai tried to talk, but her crying was uncontrollable. She opened her mouth and the only thing that came out was loud sobs. Her body shook violently and Katara got down on her knees in front of Lanai, holding and rocking her as if she was a baby, whispering soothingly to her and rubbing the back of her head. Makai and Katara let Lanai cry until there was nothing left. Neither of them moved; both of them allowing her time to let out what was bothering her.

Lanai stared at a spot on the wall for a long time. The tears that had gone down her face, in her right ear, all over Katara, and on the floor had dried. She knew she was loved and physically wasn't alone, but inside, she felt alone and empty. She'd thought for a long time that if she and Makai had either gotten it together or left one another alone, that would fix the lonely feeling. Nothing seemed to fix that problem. No amount of shopping, keeping busy, or getting attention from people seemed to fill the void. Counseling helped her to get things out, but it seemed like the more she got things out, the emptier she felt. The emptiness was what she'd been running from.

She allowed Katara to sit her up finally, and she looked into the most caring eyes she'd ever seen. Katara had been everything that Lanai had ever needed: a parent, sister, and friend. As looked into Katara's sympathetic, worried eyes, Lanai's heart felt heavier. She'd caused her sister so much stress and grief that it made her feel guilty. Lanai never could understand how Katara could care for and raise her, and Lanai was the oldest by a few months.

Katara asked, "What's wrong?"

Barely above a whisper, Lanai said, "I feel so empty." Her lips felt swollen, just like her eyes.

Katara answered, "Because you are."

Lanai's eyes filled with tears again. She admitted, "I don't wanna feel empty anymore. I feel so alone."

"Baby, you are not alone," Katara replied, rubbing her thumbs over Lanai's knuckles. "As long as I'm alive, you'll never be alone. But do you know why you feel that way?"

Lanai shook her head from side to side.

Katara continued, "You used to try to fill that void with Makai, a baby, material things, drugs, and partying. The only thing that can fill that void within you is God. You feel like that emptiness is eating you alive, don't you?"

Lanai nodded her head and Katara nodded, completely understanding how she felt. Lanai had no idea how much Katara could actually relate to that feeling. Katara said, "You gotta fill it with God."

Lanai had never felt like she was ready to go to God. She'd always felt that she needed to fix what was wrong before she went to God; she couldn't take an unorganized mess to God. Lanai didn't even know which church to go to. She also wasn't ready for the judgment of the congregation at whatever church she decided to go to; she definitely wasn't ready for that. She had enough to deal with; dealing with other people's issues with her past was far from her idea of how to spend her time.

Katara continued to speak. "You gotta know that the only way that God will fix it is if you go to Him. I can pray for you all day, but you gotta submit yourself to Him and pray for yourself. *You* gotta give it to Him. He's so much more capable of fixing our messes. You don't have to be perfect. As a matter of fact, no one is perfect. Waiting to go to God with it will only make your suffering worse. You're torturing yourself. You have the answer to your problems. Just take that step out on faith and trust God to do what He promised."

Unbelieving, Lanai asked, "What did He promise? Pain? Misery?"

Katara smiled. "Pain and misery are guaranteed in this life. Building a close relationship with God ensures that we can bear it. God makes everything endurable. The only way to God is through our Lord and Savior Jesus Christ. If you believe that Jesus died for our sins and that He is the Way and the Light, you will be saved from your sins. Dedicate your life to God, so that he can turn your mess into a message, baby. You can be an inspiration to someone. Your story can touch lives and even change them. Without God, nothing will work. Everything you try to establish will fail without Him in it."

Lanai looked away. She felt that if she just tried harder to stay clean, and ignore the empty feeling, she'd be okay. Going to God with her issues sounded simple enough, but she felt she was fine, she needed to just stop being so soft and emotional. She knew that she needed to pull herself up by the bootstraps and get her life together. She'd done it before and she knew that she could do it again.

She looked at Katara and gave her a half smile. "Thanks for always trying to fix everything. I'm okay."

Katara laughed. "Honey, I ain't fixing nothing. God is trying to get through to you. When He wants you to listen, you will," she replied, with complete confidence.

Lanai nodded to appease Katara, not really believing what she was hearing. She felt that if God really was trying to get to her, He would've never allowed her to go down such a dark path. If God really wanted her attention, He would allow for everything to go smooth in her life. She really had no idea what awaited her.

CHAPTER TWENTY-ONE

"**N**o, absolutely not!" Katara yelled into the phone. Lanai had to move the phone away from her ear to keep her eardrum from being damaged. "You're going! I'm on my way there right now and if I have to, I'll dress you. You're going."

Lanai had tried backing out of going to church with Katara and her family for the third time since they'd been back in Delaware. She just wasn't ready. She didn't feel that church was going to help her. Church, in her opinion, was just a bunch of people that came together on Sundays to pretend and talk about people. She'd rather just lie in the bed with Makai and Makayla all day.

Lanai sighed. "I don't feel like it. I don't feel good."

"I don't care," Katara retorted. "I'll be there in ten minutes."

Katara hung up on her and Lanai tossed the phone on the bed next to her. She didn't care if Katara came or not. She wasn't going and that was final. No one could make her do something she didn't want to. Makayla crawled from the middle of the king-sized bed to the top and picked up Lanai's phone. She pretended to be dialing a number and put the phone to her hear, saying, "Hello? Hello?"

Lanai smiled at her. She hadn't expected to fall in love with the little girl, but she was so in love. She anticipated seeing her every day. She and Makai spent practically every day with Lanai, and Lanai loved it. She felt she had something good to look forward to and worked hard on keeping thoughts of her parents out of her mind. When Lanai, Katara, Larry, Makai, and the kids flew back to Delaware, Vi had made the decision to stay. She'd decided to continue to grovel for the opportunity to see Ramon one more time before he died. Lanai pitied Vi and was disgusted by her behavior.

The bathroom door opened and Makai came out with a pair of cream-colored dress slacks, black belt, and a white wife-beater tucked into his pants. He asked, "Babe, can you iron my shirt while I get Kay dressed?"

"What shirt? Where you going?" she asked incredulously.

"You told your sister we were going to church," he reminded her. "I don't wanna keep hearing her mouth or her messages she sends through Larry. Get up. We already gonna be late."

"I'm not going," Lanai said. "I don't feel like it."

He gave her an exasperated look. "C'mon, man."

"What?" she asked, propping herself up on her elbow.

"I'm not gonna be caught in the middle of the mess with you and her," he said. "She already gives me her ass to kiss. Why don't you just go to get her off your back?"

"Because I don't want to," she answered. "I don't feel like going."

"Get your ass up and iron my shirt!" he ordered.

She pulled back the covers and said, "I'll iron your shirt, but I'm not going. You let me know how it goes."

She set about pulling out the ironing board and plugging up the iron, while he bathed and dressed Makayla. She ironed his shirt and when she was finished, she put it on a hanger and hung it from the side of the ironing board.

Makai asked, "Breakfast?"

"Yeah, go ahead."

"No, lazy ass," he retorted. "You go make breakfast. You ain't doing shit else."

She laughed at him and made her way to the kitchen. She didn't have a problem with cooking for the two of them. Breakfast was the most important meal of the day, and she didn't want to send the two of them off without eating. She had made up her mind, though. She still wasn't going.

She cooked sausage, eggs, grits, and toast, adding butter and jelly to the toast. As she added butter, salt, and pepper to the grits, there was a knock at the door. She was certain it was her sister. She made her way to the door, not surprised when she looked through the peephole to see Katara standing there, with Sariyah on her hip and Larry behind her. She chuckled as she opened the door and stood back while the three of them came in.

Katara gave her an accusatory stare, saying, "You think I'm playing with your ass."

"I don't," Lanai said. "I told you I don't feel like it."

Katara made her way to the guest bedroom, saying over her shoulder, "Yeah, yeah, yeah. You're going."

Lanai returned to the kitchen, laughing. She asked Larry, "Hungry?"

He shook his head. "Nah. We ate already."

Lanai called out to her sister, "You know you're petty. You wouldn't even let me kiss my niece."

She fixed a small plate for Makayla and fixed Makai's plate. Makai came out the room, carrying Makayla in a diaper and onesie. After giving his friend dap and saying good morning, he put his daughter in her highchair, and Lanai gave her the plate and a toddler spoon. Makayla dropped the spoon and dug her fingers in the grits, smiling at the texture of the food in between her fingers. She took a fistful of grits and put her hand in her mouth. She always seemed to have so much fun with her food.

Makai sat down to eat, telling Lanai, "You better go get dressed."

Taking a piece of his sausage and biting it, she said, "I'm going back to bed."

She headed for her bedroom, just as Katara was coming out of the guest bedroom with a pair of tan Ann Taylor Kate straight leg pants, white silk blouse, and matching tan Ann Taylor two-button jacket. Lanai took Sariyah from Katara and kissed her cheeks on her way into her room. She flopped down on the bed with Sariyah in her lap. Katara laid the clothes on the bed and put her hands on her hips, standing in front of Lanai.

She said, "You got two options. You can get dressed, or I'ma get you dressed."

Lanai laughed. "I'm not going."

Katara had a straight face. "I'm really not playing with you. You're going. You have two seconds to decide."

Katara impatiently tapped her foot, waiting for her sister to decide. Lanai laughed again, looking down at Sariyah.

"Always think somebody playing with you," Katara mumbled. She yelled, "Larry!"

"Yeah?" he called back.

"Come get your daughter!" she yelled.

Within a few moments, Larry appeared in the doorway. He came into the room and took Sariyah back into the living room with him. Katara asked, "Did you take a shower?"

Lanai nodded her head. "Took one this morning."

"Okay," Katara said, in a warning tone.

Lanai sucked her teeth and sighed. "You're petty."

"Petty is acting like my four-year-old," Katara returned. "Get dressed or I'ma do it for you."

Lanai begrudgingly snatched her clothes off the bed and stalked to the bathroom. Katara may have won the battle of going to church, but Lanai was going to make sure she didn't enjoy it. She didn't want to push her sister too far, because she wasn't that crazy, for real. She knew that Katara would dress her if she felt she had to.

Lanai took her time getting dressed, applying her makeup, and curling her hair. She took so long that Makai came bursting into the bathroom, irritated. He asked, "Can you come the hell on? Shit, I'm sick of waiting."

She tsked and shook her head, teasing her curls with her fingers and turning her head from side to side. She said, "You should really watch that mouth."

"You better come the fuck on," he warned.

Looking at her reflection one last time, she announced, "I'm ready."

She went through the apartment, turning off lights and TVs and gathering her things. Katara glared at her. "Took you long enough."

Lanai smiled slyly, "Told you I didn't wanna go."

"But you're going," Katara retorted, on her way out the door.

Lanai mused to herself that she must've taken much too long, because someone had taken pity on Makayla and put her hair in two ponytails. She figured it was probably Katara, because they actually looked decent; when Makai did it, her one or two ponytails looked messy. She locked the door behind everyone and asked, "Am I driving?"

Everyone answered in unison, "No!"

She laughed and followed Makai to his truck, continuing to take her sweet time and smiling extra wide the entire time. She loved it when she worked everyone's nerves. As she sat in the passenger seat, she kept the smug smile plastered on her face and her hands politely folded in her lap, after she'd placed her oversized Versace sunglasses on her face.

Makai was beyond irritated and she could tell by his hard jawline and silence. Her goal was to piss her sister off; he was just a casualty of war. Out the corner of her eye, she observed his rigid profile. He was pissed, but he was still sexy. His thick eyebrows were so close together that they almost looked like a unibrow. She saw the defined muscles in his right arm as he gripped the steering wheel. She had to look out the passenger window at the passing scenery to keep from biting her lip. Just the sight or smell of him turned her on, and regardless of the fight she put up about going to church, she knew that wasn't the moment to be allowing lust to take over. She needed to stay in the church mind frame.

It took about thirty minutes to get to what looked like the middle of no-damn-where. The winding road that they took led them to a little white church that was sitting on a hill with a cemetery to the right of the parking lot. The black-topped parking lot with the cute little white poles and chain-linked fence that surrounded the parking lot had a good amount of cars in it. Makai parked next to Larry's white Cadillac and everyone got out of their vehicles. Lanai took Makayla out of her car seat and Makai grabbed the Louis Vuitton diaper bag that Lanai had made him begin to carry.

Katara led the way across the parking lot and up the four steps, fussing, "I could punch you in the face for making me late, you heifer."

Larry opened the door and held it obediently, until Katara had rushed through the door. Makai took over holding the door for Lanai, who took her time getting up the steps. She noticed that there was a scripture written beautifully on the door with praying hands underneath the scripture. The entryway to the church was small, but clean and neat. She liked the red carpet that matched the seat of the pew benches in the entryway. It felt extra crowded in the entryway when Makai stepped in and they waited for the usher to open the door.

The short, brown-skinned woman in all white, with glasses and the biggest butt and breasts Lanai had ever seen on a short woman, smiled warmly as she pushed open the door and welcomed them. She hugged Katara and kissed her cheek, saying to her, "Hey, baby. It's good to see you."

She smiled and said good morning to everyone else, kissing and hugging Sariyah and commenting on how cute Makayla was. Her warm, welcoming disposition and smile was so contagious that it evoked a genuine smile out of Lanai. She followed everyone else to the third pew from the front on the left side. Lanai noticed that the majority of the congregation and choir were older black people. They were beautiful, but she'd expected to see more young people. There were a couple of kids that sat with a woman who looked like she was in her late twenties or early thirties, and a gentleman that sat in the choir box that looked to be in his thirties. There was a dark-skinned woman with dreadlocks in the choir box that also looked to be in her late thirties. But that was it as far as the younger generation, except for the people she'd come with.

When they entered, there was an older dark-skinned woman with more gray than black hair at the podium. She was reading off a list of announcements and Lanai could tell by her accent that she was from down south. She wore glasses and spoke with authority. Lanai wasn't sure what her position was in the church, but whatever it was, she took it seriously. When she finished with her announcements, she looked out into the congregation and asked with a smile, "Are there any acknowledgements of guests today?"

Her eyes seemed to go directly to Lanai. Katara had moved all the way over to the wall on the inside of the pew. She stood and said, "Good morning, church. Giving honor to God, Pastor, Co-pastor, the ministerial staff, the choir, and the congregation. I brought my sister, Lanai, her boyfriend, and his daughter with us today."

The woman behind the podium smiled and said, "Welcome. It's nice to have you here and thank you for coming. We hope you enjoy the service."

Makai and Lanai smiled in return and Lanai felt a little hot with the woman looking at her. She said a silent prayer of thanks when the woman moved on to birthdays and anniversaries. Lanai was pleasantly surprised when they moved to the Children's Expressions segment of service and the children that sat across the aisle got up and read from a children's book outlining the Bible that they passed around to each other. When they were finished, the church clapped for them and smiled their approval. They seemed to love the kids and their participation.

Sariyah squeezed past, saying, "'Cuse me, Uncle Kai. 'Cuse me, Aunt Nai."

Lanai smiled, "Of course, Love Bug. Where you going?"

Sariyah hurried to the steps and got a microphone from the lady at the podium. She stood in front of the altar facing the congregation, and after a few seconds, began singing "This Little Light of Mine". The whole church clapped and sang along with her. She was only four, but she had a stage presence and wasn't afraid to perform in front of the church. She smiled as she sang and did a couple little ad libs, causing a couple of people in the congregation to call out, "Go 'head, baby! Sing it!"

Lanai was grinning from ear to ear and clapping like it was her child. When Sariyah was done and took her bow, practically everyone in the church stood and applauded her. She smiled graciously, with her big brown eyes shining bright. She gave the microphone back, saying, "Thank you, Elder."

Elder smiled at her and said, "You are so welcome, baby. Thank you."

Sariyah ran back to her seat, being stopped by everyone on the way to get hugged and kissed. With her free arm, Lanai gave Sariyah a big hug and kissed her forehead. She said, "You did great, Love Bug! I'm so proud of you!"

"Thank you," Sariyah replied, sliding past to get a hug and kiss from Makai and Larry. When she returned to her seat next to Katara, she gave her mom a high five and Katara pulled her into a big hug, kissing her cheek. Katara was beaming brighter than the sun with her arm around her daughter. Lanai smiled at them, feeling a twinge in her belly. She was beginning to accept the fact that she was probably never going to experience that. The closest that she'd probably get to it was being an active part of Sariyah and Makayla's lives.

The offering plate went around and the usher took her place in the front of the church, instructing everyone to stand, one side at a time, to go up and place their tithes and offerings in the plates in front of the altar. Lanai felt uncomfortable not knowing the song that was sung after the offering was received. She noticed how involved Katara, Larry, and Sariyah were with singing the different songs. They looked like they actually enjoyed it and fit in. When everyone sat down, Elder stood at the podium, announced that it was time for altar call and that Co-pastor would be leading it. The co-pastor stood from his chair and stood up to the podium in the pulpit. He announced that the altar was open for anyone in need of prayer. Katara and Larry stood, with Larry picking Sariyah up, and they waited while Makai and Lanai stepped out into the aisle for them to go up to the altar.

Makai and Lanai returned to their seats. Larry put Sariyah down in front of the altar, and then he, Katara, and Sariyah all knelt down in front of the altar, a sight that touched Lanai's heart. Larry was definitely a good man. Lanai didn't have too many interactions with him outside of her sister, but she was glad that her sister had him in her life. He seemed to be an amazing support system for both her sister and her niece. Co-pastor began to pray and everyone in the church bowed their heads, except for Lanai. She was looking around at everyone, until it registered in her mind that she needed to bow her head during prayer.

She ducked her head down and closed her eyes, trying to focus on what he was saying. Her mind was going in so many different directions. She felt like she stuck out like a sore thumb, because she didn't know the processes or routines of the church. She wished that Makai and Katara had left her alone and let her stay home. She also felt like there was no reason for her to be there. She didn't know anyone and she had no idea what was going on. Her mind did grasp that the co-pastor said a prayer for everyone at the altar. He prayed specifically for the children at the altar, he said a prayer for Katara and her family, and he prayed for President Obama and the country.

When the prayer was over and everyone said, "Amen," she and Makai got up so that Katara, Larry, and Sariyah could return to their seats. The choir sang a song that Sariyah and Katara knew every word to and then the pastor stood to say a prayer. Lanai thought, *they sure do pray a lot in here.* She was beginning to feel antsy. She was ready to go and it was taking forever for the service to be over. She began to get a little hot in the collar of her shirt, adjusting her jacket unnecessarily. When the pastor finished praying, she told them which scripture she would be preaching about. Everyone searched for the place in the Bible where the scripture was, with the pastor waiting patiently to hear everyone say "Amen," to let her know that they'd found their place.

Lanai looked around Makai's arm, because he was able to find the scripture, whereas she wasn't even able to pick up the Bible. Katara had brought her own Bible and she seemed to find the scripture almost before the pastor could tell the congregation where to find it. Even though Lanai was looking around Makai's arm to see what was being read, her eyes wouldn't focus on the letters in front of her. She'd never had a problem with seeing letters before, but she couldn't make out what was in the book. She looked straight ahead, pretending to be listening to the pastor, but actually, she mentally counted down the time until it was over.

Makayla must've sensed Lanai's uneasiness, because she started to get restless. She tried to wiggle her way out of Lanai's lap, and when Lanai wouldn't let her, Makayla started to whine and stretch out. Feeling like that was her cue to leave, Lanai picked the toddler up and walked out the sanctuary. The nice usher was sitting, until she saw Lanai coming. She got up out of her seat to hold the door open for Lanai to take a fussing Makayla out into the entryway. She was thankful for any excuse to get out of there. She had no idea what the pastor was talking about; she just knew it had her restless and ready to go.

She put Makayla on her shoulder and gently bounced her, patting her back. When that didn't work, Lanai sat down in the chair, sitting Makayla in her lap. Makayla tried to slide out of Lanai's lap again. Lanai turned Makayla to face her and asked, "What is wrong, Sweet Pea?"

Makayla rubbed her eyes and whined. Lanai put Makayla back on her shoulder and said, "Awww, you're sleepy."

Makayla tried to fight again, but Lanai tightened her hold on her and patted her back a little harder, until Makayla laid her head down on Lanai's shoulder. Makayla put her fingers in her mouth and allowed Lanai to pat her back until she went to sleep. Lanai figured it had probably taken about ten or fifteen minutes to put her to sleep. The pastor was still preaching, yelling and emphasizing her point. The congregation responded with claps, yelling "Hallelujah," and "Amen," and encouraging the pastor to, "Go 'head and preach!"

After what seemed like forever, everyone stood up and sang "The Lord's Prayer". Someone was on the microphone, offering for anyone that wanted to dedicate or rededicate their life to God, to come up to the altar. No one seemed to come up to the altar and the person on the microphone again said the altar was open for anyone that needed or wanted prayer. Shortly after that, everyone was dismissed. Lanai sat in the chair, watching people hug and kiss one another. Some people chatted, while others made a beeline for the door. She wanted to be one of those people that made a beeline for the door.

Finally, Makai came through the door. He asked, "You alright?"

"I'm tired," she lied. "I'm ready to go home."

"Tired from what?" he asked, picking up a sleeping Makayla so that Lanai could stand.

She joked, "You know every time somebody opens a Bible people get sleepy."

"Your sister was looking for you," he said.

Lanai rolled her eyes. "She's gonna have to call me. I'm going home."

She made her way to the door, pushing it open and hoping that Makai had sense enough to follow her, before she acted a royal fool in that church. She'd gone against what she'd said earlier and came to the church. She refused to sit around and wait for Katara to stop running her mouth and holding her up. Katara would just have to call her and hope that Lanai answered the phone. Lanai had just about all she could take for one day.

By the time she'd gotten to the truck, Makai had unlocked the doors and opened hers for her to get in. She climbed inside and he closed the door. After strapping Makayla into her car seat, he made his way around to the driver's seat. As he started the engine, he asked, "You hungry?"

She slid on her shades and shook her head. "Just wanna go home."

"Yo, since when did you turn into a hermit," he inquired, backing out of the parking space. He carefully navigated the big SUV around the parking lot, careful not to hit any churchgoers that were slowly making their way to their cars.

"I'm not a hermit," she answered, sounding more defensive than she'd wanted to.

"All you wanna do is stay in the house," he replied, pulling out onto the road, turning left.

Changing the subject slightly, she asked, "What would you like to do? Where would you like to go?"

"To get something to eat," he answered, his tone sounding as though she wasn't paying attention to the conversation.

"Where?" she laughed.

"Anywhere but at your apartment," he retorted, navigating the curved road. "I've asked you over and over about coming to the house."

"I told you I'm not doing that," she answered stiffly, remembering all the hell that she'd endured in that house and the empty feeling of the mini-mansion.

"Why not?" he asked, not understanding. "I bought the house for you!"

"Sell it," she retorted.

She could hear the agitation in his voice when he asked, "What is your problem?"

She answered honestly, "Too many bad memories."

He was silent for a moment and she knew that he was debating whether it would be an argument worth having. He stopped at the stop sign, instead of going to the right, which was the way back to Dover. Irritated, he asked, "Where we going?"

"Let's go to Salisbury to Golden Corral," she suggested. "You know that's the closest one."

Without another word, he hit the gas to make it across the northbound side of the highway to the median where he could go south. When he saw that it was clear for him to go, he headed south. They rode for several miles without either of them saying anything, but the tension in the truck was growing thick enough to cut with a knife. Out of the corner of her eye, she saw that his body language indicated that she was on his last nerve.

She really wasn't trying to piss him off again, but she had absolutely no desire to set foot back in that house. When she'd left for the last time, she'd told herself that she'd never go back and she hadn't. Katara had gone to the house to get her belongings for her. She asked, "Makai, what do you want from me?"

"Nothing," he snapped.

"Now you have an attitude."

"No, I don't," he lied.

"You do."

"I don't."

"You do."

"Don't tell me what I have," he cautioned.

"I'm not dumb or blind. You have an attitude," she insisted.

"You're not dumb or blind, but you're a spoiled ass brat," he returned.

"How am I spoiled?" she asked in the most innocent tone she could muster.

With the hand that had been on the steering wheel outstretched, he returned, "How are you not? Don't you get *everything* your way?"

"Not all the time," she hesitantly answered in a low tone.

"When don't you?"

She thought for a few moments. She couldn't think of a time when he hadn't given her what she wanted, even without asking for it. In the past, he didn't give her attention and respect, but now he was definitely working on righting that wrong. She knew that without question he spoiled her rotten. She never wanted for anything.

He cut into her thoughts. "See? Your spoiled ass can't think of a time that you ain't get what you wanted."

She pouted. "You created this monster."

"Bullshit."

"You did!"

"You a grown woman! Act like it."

"I do act like it."

"You don't."

"I do, too."

"No, you don't. You don't get your way and you act like Makayla, throwing a fit," he said, switching lanes to maneuver around a car going too slow for him.

"And you had nothing to do with it?" she asked, accusingly.

"I know I did," he admitted. "I need your ass to compromise sometimes, though. You killing me. It's always your way or it's no way. I bend over backwards to please you."

"And I don't bend over backwards to please you?"

"In the bedroom, yeah," he quipped.

She shoved his arm. "Shut up! I'm being serious. You don't get what you need from me?"

"Not all the time, no," he answered.

Her tone unbelieving and unconvinced, she questioned, "What is it that you need from me that I don't give?"

"*Compromise,*" he said, enunciating the syllables of the word, switching lanes again.

Exasperated, she asked, "And what don't I compromise on?"

"What do you compromise on?" he returned.

She opened her mouth to answer and moved her lips, but nothing came out.

He said, "You know I'll give you the world. Just ask for it, or if I think you want the world, I'ma go get it and bring it to you. I need you to cut me some slack sometimes, though. Stop fighting me on *everything.*"

She thought for a moment on what he said. She'd been so hell-bent on making him suffer for all the wrong he'd done to her. She felt justified in making him work extra hard just to get some of her attention. She loved him and wanted to be with him, but secretly, she hadn't completely gotten over all the lies, hurt, and pain. She didn't even realize that she was putting him through test after test, making him prove himself repeatedly.

She secretly enjoyed making him jump through hoops. It was the icing on the cake to know that he would actually do it. Whenever life had her feeling bad or something was going on, she'd take it out on him and make him work harder. She never for one second thought that he'd get tired of it. In her mind, he was a human Superman; nothing bothered him. She felt that he could withstand anything, and his emotionlessness over the years had been confirmation of that for her.

Her voice softened. "I didn't know I was fighting you on everything."

"I can take it," he said. "Just compromise every once in a while."

"I can compromise," she promised. "I'm just not going back to that house."

He chuckled and momentarily dropped his head in frustration. He looked back at the road and blew a breath. He asked, "You really expect me to sell the house?"

She replied, "I don't expect you to do anything. I don't care if you sell it or not. I'm just telling you that I'm not going back in there."

Reaching his breaking point, he agreed. "Okay. I'll figure out something. I feel claustrophobic in that tiny ass apartment."

She felt like even though he accused her of not compromising, they'd reached a compromise. So what if it was on her terms? If he hadn't started with spoiling her and giving in to her all the time, then she wouldn't expect it. She didn't care what he said, he was the reason she was the way she was. If he was serious about spending the rest of his life with her, he was going to have to live with it.

CHAPTER TWENTY-TWO

Lanai bolted upright in her bed, drenched in sweat. The scream she'd let out caused Makai to reach for her. He clearly was half-asleep, pulling her to him. She pushed away from him, needing to get out of the bed. She'd had the same nightmare for the past month, unable to get much sleep.

In the dream, zombies and shadows chased her down dark streets and through alleys. Right before she woke up screaming, a zombie would touch one of her shoulders, or a shadow would almost completely cover her. She'd gotten to the point where she wouldn't sleep in the dark anymore. She and Makai had fought over the overhead light being on all night. He wouldn't back down, telling her she'd better use the lamp on the nightstand or something. She'd tried sleeping with the TV light only, but that hadn't been enough. She slept with the TV and nightstand lamp on every night to make herself feel better and it wasn't working.

She had been back to her sister's church a couple times since the first time. The more she withdrew instead of being open about the church experience, the worse her anxiety and nightmares became. She had to get a grip on things soon, because she felt like she was on the verge of a mental and emotional breakdown. Katara continued to tell her that she needed to dedicate her life to God and the nightmares would stop. Lanai continued to ignore her, but her labored breathing had her wondering if her sister was right. Whenever her breathing returned to normal and she got a moment of peace, she would push the idea to the back of her mind, and try to move forward with her life as it was.

As she made her way to the kitchen to get a bottle of water out the refrigerator, she noticed that her breathing was more shallow than it normally was, even after a nightmare. She felt lightheaded as her feet touched the tile of the kitchen floor. As she took the couple extra steps to close the distance between her and the refrigerator, she figured if she could just get the cold water into her body, she'd be fine. She reached out her hand to open the refrigerator and the room began to spin. She tried to squint to focus her vision and her hand went to the middle of her chest, where it had gotten tight. It felt like an elephant was sitting square in the middle of her chest.

With her hand on the door of the refrigerator, the room went black and she crumpled into a heap on the floor, hitting her forehead on the refrigerator that she never got the chance to open. She was enveloped in complete blackness, with no concept of time or space. There was no noise or movement. She held her breath, too terrified to blink. The last time that she'd been surrounded by such darkness, she almost died. She felt something cold slowly creep over her body, starting at her toes and inch its way up her legs. She wanted to scream, or cry, or something. Whatever it was that was beginning to cover her body was not only cold, but gave her an eerie feeling.

She wasn't sure if it was death or the devil, but whatever it was, it wasn't good. When the feeling made its way up to her stomach, she tried to fight it. She wasn't sure what was going on, but she was certain that she wasn't ready to die. It felt like old, cold, scrawny fingers making their way up to her chest. When the feeling reached her breastbone, it seemed almost to cave her chest in. The pressure she felt was the equivalent to a 400-pound man sitting on top of the elephant and bouncing up and down. As the "scrawny fingers" feeling made its way to her neck, it felt like it closed around her throat and began to squeeze.

Her labored breathing had diminished to almost nothing. She was barely able to get a half of a breath. Tears formed in her eyes and all she could think to do was call out to God in her mind quietly. She tried to focus on something to get her breath, but calling out to God in her mind, caused the "fingers around her neck" feeling to tighten. She had nothing else to cling to, nothing else to think about, except God. She could only think of the word God. Her mind couldn't form a proper prayer, no coherent thought, just repeatedly thinking God.

In her mind, she screamed, "God, help me!"

That thought seemed to make the fingers back off a little. She knew she was crying, but she couldn't feel any tears. She repeated the thought over and over and the fingers retreated further. Her lips moved and she was able to say, "God, please help me! God, I need you to help me!"

When she'd been in her addiction, she remembered calling out to God, and He'd saved her. Maybe it had been so long that she'd forgotten how powerful calling out to God actually was. Laying in the cold darkness reminded her of the cold, dark place that she'd been some years ago, and what had brought her out of it. She'd known that it hadn't been of her own accord that she'd been saved. Laying in the cold darkness, her head thumped and her chest burned, but the cold fingers fled completely.

She felt like she was sobbing, begging God to help her and save her, yet again. She heard a familiar voice calling her name, but she couldn't make it out. All she could really focus on was her lips and her mind, begging God to save her and not let her die. She felt in her heart that if she stayed with that thought, He would bring her out of the cold darkness. Whoever was calling her would have to wait. Her body shook and she screamed for God to help her and save her. She pleaded, "I'm not ready to die! Please, not yet!"

She felt a hard slap to her face and jumped back from the feeling. Her eyes were able to blink and she blinked them several times, trying to focus her eyes. Her pupils slowly focused and she was able to take in what was around her. Makai was on the kitchen floor holding her and looking at her funny. She'd never seen him look afraid before, but he looked like he'd seen the most frightening thing in his life. He yelled in her face, "Wake the hell up!"

She answered weakly, "I'm awake."

"What the fuck happened?" he asked, frantically looking over her from head to toe.

"I don't know," she answered, a little disoriented. "I—I was trying to get a bottle of water. I must've blacked out."

"Can you move?" he asked, looking to see if anything looked broken.

She attempted to push herself into a sitting position, but fell back onto his arm behind her back. He got up, pulling her up to stand. Her legs felt like wet noodles and she wasn't able to stand on her own. Noticing how weak she was, he swooped her up into his arms, carrying her back into the bedroom. He gently placed her on the bed and pulled the covers up over her.

Her mouth and throat were dry. Her throat felt like it had when the hospital had removed the ventilator, and she was able to breathe on her own. Her throat and chest were on fire. She croaked, "Water."

Makai immediately left the room and returned with a bottle of water in a matter of seconds. He cracked the seal on the bottle, held her head, and slowly gave her the water. She tried to take hold of the bottle, but her hands were too shaky. She slightly turned her head away from the bottle, letting him know she'd had enough. She still wanted more water, but the extreme coldness on her inflamed throat and chest seemed to make it worse for a moment. She knew she'd have to take sips or eat ice.

The concern that she saw in his face scared her. She wasn't sure how long she had been out or how severe the blackout had been, ut he looked terrified, which was something that he never was. He eased her head down on the pillow behind her head. He asked, "You wanna go to the hospital?"

She shook her head. In a hoarse whisper, she asked, "Call Katara?"

He took her cell phone off the nightstand and looked through the phone until he located her sister's number. He pushed the button to call and waited for the service to connect. After six rings and right before going to voicemail, there was a break in the line.

"Hello," Katara whispered, sounding asleep.

"Your sister fell and she asked me to call you," he said into the phone.

"What?" she asked, sounding like she was sitting up.

"Lanai fell trying to get some water after a nightmare," he explained. Lanai could tell by the look on his face that he was prepared for a back and forth with Katara. She knew he wasn't in the mood for it, but he was prepared.

"Oh my God," she breathed. "Is she okay? Is she at the hospital?"

He answered, "She doesn't want to go to the hospital. She wanted me to call you."

"I'm on my way," she said, just before hanging up.

He returned the cell phone back to the nightstand, asking, "What now?"

"Crushed ice," she said, trying to clear her throat.

He left the room and she could hear the icemaker on the refrigerator as he got her ice. He came back into the room and before he could try to feed her the ice, she tried to push herself up. Putting his hands under her armpits, he helped to pull her into a sitting position, propping pillows up behind her. Once she was sitting comfortably, he gave her the cup of ice from the nightstand. She slowly tried to shake ice into her mouth. He pulled the covers up to her stomach and said, "I'm gonna go check on the baby."

She nodded, chewing on the ice. After a little while, she felt like her energy level was rising and her throat and chest felt a little better. She was still scared to death over what she'd just experienced. Some people would probably say that she'd just imagined it or she was exaggerating. However, she could feel it down in her soul that she'd been seconds away from death for another time in her life. She was completely convinced that God had saved her yet again and she made up her mind that she was not going to take it for granted again. She knew what she had to do and she was going to do it as soon as she could make it back to church.

She heard an urgent knock at the door, then Makai's footsteps to open the door. Within moments, Katara came rushing into Lanai's bedroom, her tied up in a scarf with slippers and pajamas under her overcoat. She went to the side of the bed where Lanai sat, concern etched all over her pretty face. Lanai noticed a few lines around Katara's eyes that she'd never seen before and she knew it came from all the grief and worry that Lanai had caused over the years. Lanai smiled a weak smile.

Katara touched the sore spot on Lanai's forehead, asking, "What happened? Did he put his hands on you again? I'll kill that bastard."

Lanai shook her head. "I must've hit the refrigerator or the wall when I blacked out."

Katara made a face, turning her lips up. Her tone also indicated that she didn't believe her sister. She said, "Bullshit. If you blacked out, what made you black out? Where was he?"

"He was asleep," Lanai answered. "I had the same nightmare again, got up to get some water, and everything went black when I got to the refrigerator. I don't know why I blacked out, but I was lightheaded. I felt like I was dying after I blacked out."

Katara regarded her seriously for a moment, still not wanting to believe that Makai didn't hit her. She warned, "You better not be lying to me. I swear I'll fucking kill him and call the cops myself."

"Stop," Lanai pleaded weakly. "I know you don't like him; I understand. But he hasn't put his hands on me. I'm not lying to you."

Katara rolled her eyes. "Whatever."

After a few moments of silence, Lanai said, "I'm ready."

"Ready for what?" Katara asked, clueless.

"I almost died. I'm not ready to die. I'm ready," Lanai explained.

It seemed like a lightbulb went off in Katara's head. She said, "Ooohhh. Okay. That means you're going to church tomorrow?"

Lanai nodded.

Katara asked, "Are you really ready? You know that's a big step."

"I know," Lanai admitted. "But I'd rather try life with God, than to keep living without Him. I've been running and I'm exhausted. I'm out of excuses. I've tried life without Him. Now I'm ready to give it a shot with Him."

Katara nodded. She pulled out her phone and showed Lanai an app for the Holy Bible. She advised, "Start with this. Download this app and go into plans. Set up the plan to read the Bible in one year."

"Okay, I will," Lanai promised. To show her sister that she was serious, she reached over and picked up her phone off the nightstand. She went into her app store, typed in the Holy Bible, and downloaded the app. When it was finished, she showed Katara the screen, showing it was finished downloading.

Katara advised, "Nai, do this for you. Don't do it to shut me up. Don't do it just to have something to do. Do this because you really want a closer relationship with God. God is not to be played with or mocked. You gotta take this serious."

"I will," Lanai answered. "I am doing this for me. I just need your help."

Katara hugged her sister. "You know I'm always here to help. Just please take this serious."

Hugging her back, Lanai promised again, "I will. Thank you so much."

Taking off her coat and climbing over Lanai's legs, Katara got into the bed with Lanai, getting under the covers. They laughed and talked for hours, like they were teenagers again. They talked until the sun came up. Both of them yawned in unison, Katara saying, "Well, I gotta go home and get dressed. I'll see you there?"

"Yes, ma'am," Lanai said, hugging her sister goodbye.

As Katara left, Lanai took her time getting out of the bed and making her way to the bathroom. She took a shower, allowing the hot water from the showerhead to beat down on her tense shoulders and back. She felt completely drained and as she got out the shower and wrapped her body in the towel, she looked longingly at the bed. She thought to herself that it wouldn't hurt to lie back down and catch a quick nap. It would probably help her to take a nap.

She shook her head. *If I lay down, I ain't getting back up for a while. I need to stay up and that's that,* she thought to herself. After putting lotion and a bathrobe on, she went into the bathroom to apply her makeup and curl her hair, which she noticed was growing faster than it normally did. For the last couple of months, she'd toyed with the idea of letting her hair grow back. But she loved the short cut and how it made her cheekbones and eyes stand out even more. For the last month, she'd noticed the dark circles under her eyes. Her once bright gray eyes looked dull. She noticed that she'd begun to lose weight too, which wasn't a good thing. The stress of the nightmares and lack of sleep were taking a toll on her.

As she finished up her hair, she turned the curling iron and bathroom light off. She left the room and stuck her head in the guest bedroom, which had been turned into Makayla's room. Makai was stretched across the bed, snoring with his mouth wide open. Her heart went out to him because she knew that her nightmares were keeping him from getting enough sleep, too. A part of her enjoyed punishing him, but her love for him grew every day. The trust wasn't going to get back to where it was in the beginning, but he had definitely done a hell of a job earning it back.

She looked down at the rose gold Michael Kors watch on her right wrist, that he'd bought for her some years ago as an "I'm sorry" gift. She had about an hour and a half before they needed to leave for church. She decided to go into the kitchen and make breakfast. Her hands seemed to go on their own accord, cutting up peppers, onions, and potatoes. By the time she was finished, she'd ended up making omelets, fried potatoes with onions, turkey sausage, grits, and toast. Looking at the spread she'd made, she shook her head, knowing no one was going to eat all that food.

She made Makai a plate and took the food and a glass of apple juice into the room. She placed the glass and plate on the nightstand, gently shaking his shoulder. He groaned and turned to the left on his side. She shook his shoulder again and called his name. He wildly swung his right arm and grumbled. She jumped back to keep from getting hit in the face.

Irritated, she shoved his shoulder and said, "Makai, wake up!"

Angry, he asked, "What, goddamnit? I'm tryna sleep."

"I made you breakfast," she said with her hands on her hips.

He let out an angry sigh and flipped over onto his back. He glared at her. He asked, "Are you serious?"

"Do you not wanna eat?" she asked.

"Babe, I wanna sleep," he complained.

"Fine," she huffed, turning to walk away. "Let it get cold."

He grabbed her wrist and pulled her backwards. She snatched away from him, but he grabbed her wrist again, pulling her to him. Before she could pull away, he pulled her on top of him. He said, "Watch your funky ass attitude."

"Be hungry," she pouted. "I was trying to help you out."

He slipped his hand underneath the bottom of her robe, rubbing her panty line. "Help me out by taking this off."

She smiled. "No. The baby is sleeping in her crib."

"I'll be quiet," he promised, kissing under her chin.

"No," she giggled. "Get up and eat before it gets cold."

"What I wanna eat never gets cold," he replied suggestively.

She pushed against his chest until she was standing up on the side of the bed again. She said, "You are a mess."

He swung his feet over the side of the bed and smacked her on her butt. He murmured, "Don't make no sense."

She sat on the bed next to him as he picked up his plate. "You ain't cooked like this in a minute. That's what a knot on the head does to you?"

She playfully shoved him. "Shut up. I just felt like it."

He began eating, asking, "Why you got on makeup? Where you going?"

"Church."

"That's why you cooked," he said in between bites.

"Gotta feed my babies before we leave," she said, looking over the side of Makayla's crib at her sleeping.

Drinking a gulp of apple juice, he looked at her and asked, "We?"

She gave him a look that asked if he was serious. She said, "Yes, 'we'."

"I ain't going to church every Sunday," he argued. "I told you I went that first time to shut your sister up. Sunday is my day to relax."

"You can relax when we come back."

"I'm not going."

"Yes, you are."

"No, the fuck I'm not."

She whined, "You have to go."

"I ain't go the last two times," he pointed out.

"Please," she pouted.

He shook his head no. He didn't miss a beat with his food, shoveling it in his mouth, barely chewing it. He ate like he was in the military.

She straddled his lap, almost knocking his plate to the floor. She wrapped her arms around his neck. In a low voice, she begged, "Please."

"Not gon' work," he replied, trying to look around her to see his food.

She wiggled in his lap and pressed her upper body against him, nibbling on his bottom lip. She whispered, "Please?"

He looked down at her robe that had begun to come loose, which she was aware of. She wanted him to see her black lace Victoria's Secret matching bra and panty set. Sex always worked with him. She wasn't going to have sex with him, but she wanted him to think she was, so she could get her way. She heard him put his plate on the nightstand and felt his hands under her bathrobe around her waist.

She felt his fingers massage the flesh of her lower back, causing a moan to escape her lips. He had magic fingers and knew exactly how to use them. His hands slowly massaged up her back, making her feel like her plan was backfiring. Her back arched involuntarily and she felt his warm lips on her neck, where her pulse beat rapidly. He lightly bit her neck and she could feel his manhood harden beneath her. He was going to have his way; she just knew it.

"Daddy," Makayla called from the crib. "Ma."

Lanai dropped her head on Makai's shoulder. *Saved by the baby,* she thought. Pulling her robe together, she looked over her shoulder at Makayla standing in her crib and holding on to the rail. She smiled, "Good morning, Sweet Pea."

Makayla held up her arms and Lanai climbed off Makai's lap, picking the child up. Lanai asked, "You wanna eat?"

Makayla nodded her head with her fingers in her mouth.

"Little cock-blocker," Makai mumbled, picking his plate up again.

Lanai told him, "I'm gonna feed her and get her ready. I need you to hurry up so we're not late."

"I ain't going to church every single Sunday, Lanai," he warned.

On her way out the door, she said over her shoulder, "I'm not asking you to."

Breakfast and getting Makayla dressed didn't take long. Lanai managed to do Makayla's hair, get herself dressed, and iron Makai's clothes before he got out the shower. She made sure Makayla's cup was filled with juice and she had enough diapers in her bag. As Makai came out the room, she yawned.

He asked, "You sure you wanna go? You look tired."

"I always look tired," she replied.

"I can put you to sleep," he whispered, coming up behind her.

She pushed him away. "That'll have to wait until after church."

She knew he wouldn't understand the importance of her going to church, so she didn't try to explain it. She just knew that they were going, and she was going to do what she needed to do, to get her life where she needed it to be. She went through the apartment, turning off everything and followed Makai and Makayla out the door, locking it behind them.

On the way down the steps, he asked, "You driving or me?"

"You drive," she answered.

She looked around the parking lot, looking for the pair of eyes that she felt like were watching her. She'd never said anything to Makai, or even Katara, about feeling like someone was watching her, because she knew that they would say she was being paranoid. She first felt like someone was watching her, about two weeks ago. She wrote it off as a side effect of having nightmares every night of someone or something chasing her. She still couldn't shake the feeling that someone was watching her. Nothing looked out of place, though.

She put her sunglasses on, climbed in the truck, and waited for Makai to get in. He had barely gotten out of the parking lot before she drifted off to sleep. She didn't realize that she was asleep, until she bolted upright in the seat, looking around. She saw that they weren't far from Katara's church.

Makai asked, "You okay?"

Her heart pounded in her chest, feeling like it was trying to come out. She eased back against the leather of the seat. She said, "Yeah, I'm fine."

"You gotta go see somebody about those nightmares," he said. "You can't even take a nap without having a nightmare."

"I know."

They arrived at church, just as everyone else was getting there, everyone greeting everyone in the parking lot and on their way inside. Everyone gushed over how adorable Makayla was, which Makayla loved. She was always getting candy and little gifts from the people of the church. Some members even slipped her dollar bills, which went straight to her mouth, if Lanai or Makai weren't paying attention. Once inside, the usher at the door greeted them with hugs and kisses. Lanai led the way to the second pew from the front on the right. Shortly after they arrived, Katara, Larry, and Sariyah showed up and sat with them.

Church began and followed the same schedule that they followed every Sunday. The group of children read after announcements, birthdays, and anniversaries. Sariyah sang a song about God giving her two wings that Lanai was sure that Katara had taught her. Makayla clapped and squealed in Lanai's lap after Sariyah's performance. Lanai didn't realize that she'd been holding her breath and anticipating altar call, until she heard it announced. A part of her was deathly afraid, but something was pulling at her to go to the altar.

Co-pastor announced that the altar was open and Lanai absently gave Makayla to Makai, standing. She excused herself to get by. Katara stood up and stepped into the aisle. Lanai looked up when she felt Katara's hand cover hers. Katara smiled and Lanai's unsure smile met her sister's. Katara walked with her up to the altar, still holding her hand. When they got to the altar, Lanai followed Katara's lead, kneeling down and folding her hands on the altar. She didn't pay attention to Larry and Sariyah following them and kneeling on the other side of Katara.

Lanai didn't know why she was there; she just knew she had to go to the altar. Co-pastor began to pray, telling God that He knew what everyone at the altar stood in need of. He asked God to heal everyone at the altar of whatever was hurting them. Listening to him pray, Lanai felt the need to run. She was about to get up and bolt out the door, but Katara squeezed her hand tighter. Lanai could hear Katara praying to herself. She couldn't make out the words, but she knew that Katara was praying. Lanai looked around the altar, feeling out of place. She told herself that maybe it was too soon. She should just go back to her seat and wait until another time.

She heard Katara ask God to touch and bless Lanai, to heal her of her heartache. She heard Katara ask God to help Lanai to forgive herself, as Co-pastor continued to pray. Hearing Katara pray for her made Lanai try to pull her hand out of Katara's. Lanai's palms were beginning to sweat, as well as under her arms. She didn't want her sister wasting her time or prayers on her. Katara tightened her grip on Lanai's hand, telling her, "Bow your head. Let go."

She bowed her head, realizing that she was terrified to let go. She didn't know what was on the other side of letting go, and she couldn't control what she didn't know. She heard the Co-pastor move closer to her, standing over Katara, Larry, and Sariyah, praying over them. Lanai felt the cold feeling that she'd felt a few hours ago and she shook with fear. Instead of fleeing, Lanai clung to Katara's hand and pushed the negative thoughts out of her head.

She wanted to get away from the negativity that stalked her. She wanted the nightmares and paranoia to stop. She felt like she was only a breath from relapsing and she really didn't want to do that. In her mind, she said to God, *Okay, God. Fix this. Fix me.* She felt like it would be the appropriate words to say, but she really had no idea what it meant. She felt a hand on her shoulder from the other side of the altar where Co-pastor stood.

He prayed for God to unbind her spirit in the name of the Father, the Son, and the Holy Ghost. He commanded that whatever was holding her hostage to release her immediately. He encouraged her to give whatever was hurting her to God, because God is a healer. The harder he prayed, the more she squeezed Katara's hand. With her free hand, Katara rubbed Lanai's back, encouraging her to let go and let God handle it. Lanai didn't even realize that she was shaking her head from side to side. Co-pastor put a hand on each of

Lanai's shoulders, speaking with authority, over casting out anything that wasn't of God.

Lanai felt hot, but her body was shaking. She heard Co-pastor speaking in tongues, and Katara was whispering in her ear that it was okay. Tears dropped from her closed lids onto the carpet and wood of the altar. Katara whispered to her, but Lanai could no longer make out what she was saying. Lanai's lips moved, silently asking God to fix her. She asked God to forgive her for everything she'd done wrong. She apologized for being angry with God for the loss of her son, sobbing loudly and uncontrollably. She begged for God's forgiveness, because she knew she had no right to be angry with God.

She begged God to forgive her for defiling her body and her mind, trying to run away from the mess that her life was. She cried out to God for forgiveness for aborting a baby that she knew was still alive in her womb. She'd felt that baby kick and move all up until the abortion, which she knew was immoral, illegal, and not of God. She asked God to give her another chance to get things right. She repeated over and over that she was sorry, and she needed God's forgiveness. She told God that she didn't want to live in darkness anymore. She cried for every child that she'd held in her body that didn't make it from either an abortion or a miscarriage.

Co-pastor leaned over her and whispered to her, "God hears you. He told me to tell you that He forgives you. He wants you to forgive yourself."

Every confession that she'd made had been between herself and God, because she'd mouthed the words and whispered them. But getting them out at the altar and hearing from an anointed servant of God that He forgave her, let her know that it was effective. She didn't care if the congregation heard every word she'd said, but she felt like what needed to be said needed to be just between herself and God. She cried and sobbed loudly, though, wanting to let go of every bit of hurt. She felt like she was in God's presence and that He finally heard her. She felt in her spirit that He forgave her. A small voice in the back of her mind told her to leave everything at the altar.

Katara said, "Leave it at the altar. Don't take anything back with you. God won't fix it, if you continue to carry it with you."

Lanai let go of Katara's hand to wrap her arms around her sister's neck. She hugged Katara like she'd never get another opportunity to hug her again. Lanai mouthed a thank you to God for blessing her with Katara. She felt someone push tissues into her hand, which was balled into a fist on Katara's back.

Lanai said into Katara's hair, "I'm so sorry, Tara. Please forgive me for making your life harder."

"Honey, you're fine," Katara assured her. "You didn't make my life hard. You made your own life hard. Forgive yourself, though. God loves you. He forgives you."

After a few more minutes of crying and being prayed over, Lanai was able to get herself together, wiping her tear-soaked face and nose. Katara helped to wipe away her tears and helped Lanai to her feet. Katara smiled at Lanai, who was barely able to look at her. Katara hugged Lanai, then stepped back and looked at her again.

Katara asked, "You okay? Feel any better?"

Lanai nodded, wiping her nose with the wad of tissues. She said, "Thank you."

Putting her arm around Lanai's shoulders, Katara guided her back to their pew. Larry and Makai moved over to allow the sisters to sit next to one another. Katara held Lanai's hand for the remainder of the service, smiling at her encouragingly. Lanai felt like she'd left a load at the altar, making her feel a lot lighter. She actively listened to the songs the choir and congregation was singing. Her mind was open to receive the message from the sermon, which was to trust God.

At the end of service, she took another big step, and accepted Jesus Christ as her Lord and Savior, acknowledging that Jesus is the Son of God, and was born to die for the sins of the world. She left church feeling like a brand new woman, smiling a genuine smile that she hadn't smiled in a long time. She slept a peaceful sleep all the way back to Dover.

CHAPTER TWENTY-THREE

"So you'll be in Miami for the pick-up, right?" Marty asked, sitting across the table from Makai at Seacrets, in Ocean City, MD, for a business lunch to get the details of his trip to Miami.

Makai nodded, putting down his glass. He asked, "Tuesday, right?"

Marty nodded, using his spoon to help twirl the spaghetti perfectly on his fork before putting it in his mouth. A few years ago when Makai had been still moving shipments of cocaine with Carlos, he'd seen Marty at a gathering where Carlos was. He'd seen them talking and Carlos introduced a laughing Makai to Marty. Makai let Carlos know that he and Marty knew each other, because Marty was his lawyer. From that point on, Makai and Marty had a different relationship and a better understanding of each other.

Marty was a short, stocky, balding Italian that had old-world values. He was a modern-day gangster with the majority of his income being legitimate. His family had mob ties, so it seemed only natural that he would dabble in illegal activity. He knew a little bit about a lot and always seemed to have a connect somewhere. He always seemed to have someone "in his pocket". If he didn't know someone that was in a position of power, he knew someone that knew the person in a position of power, which made Makai even more connected than he already was.

Makai worked on staying away from the drug dealing, because he had much more to lose than he used to have. But every now and then, he would agree to coordinate an exchange and get a fee for it, or he would set up meetings for a fee. He hadn't been at a pick-up or drop off in a long time, but it was like riding a bike, which was something he'd never forget. He'd told both Carlos and Marty that his involvement would be minimal, because of everything he had at stake. He hadn't thought about how he would explain going to Miami to Lanai, yet. He knew that if she found out he was involved in anything to do with drugs; she would hit the roof.

She was taking the church thing serious, going to church every Sunday, with Sunday school before service, Bible study on Wednesdays, and participating in whatever the church needed her to participate in. She always did it with a smile. She was serious about faithfully reading the Bible, trying hard to complete the plan on her phone to read the entire Bible in one year. She took Makayla everywhere with her, especially to church and church activities. Sometimes she had Makai feeling like Makayla was her daughter.

He wanted to take Lanai and Makayla with him, but he knew it might be a little tricky, trying to get away long enough to handle his business. He had no idea of what he'd tell her because he was definitely going. She might not even want to go because she was so wrapped up in participating in church. She'd even started telling him that they were sinning by continuing to be together and not be married. She was beginning to get on his nerves with telling him they shouldn't be having sex unless they got married. He knew she was the one he wanted to marry; he just wasn't 100 percent sure he was ready to go that far yet.

He pulled out his vibrating phone from his front pocket and saw that Lanai was calling. He answered, "Hey, babe."

"Hey, baby," she smiled into the phone. "What do you want for dinner?"

"Don't matter," he answered, looking up at the TV that was across the room, mounted over the bar to check the score of the basketball game.

"Gimme an idea," she said.

"It doesn't matter. I don't care," he replied. "I'll eat whatever you cook."

"You always do. I need you to be decisive," she pushed.

He answered, "I am decisive. Just not about dinner. Cook whatever you want."

Blowing a defeated breath into the phone, she gave up, "Okay. Do you know what time you're gonna be home? I wanna have an idea of when to start dinner."

"Start at your normal time. I should be home by seven. I gotta go see the guy I was telling you about. You know, the guy with the car lot?" he asked.

"Yeah," she answered, sounding distracted.

"Yeah, I'ma go talk to him, see what he's talking about," he said.

"Okay...what the hell?" she asked, sounding alarmed.

"What's wrong?" he questioned.

"Oh my God," she screeched, and then it sounded like she dropped the phone.

He sat up straight in his chair and called her name through the phone. When he got no response, he yelled, "Lanai!"

His yelling caused several patrons to look at him. Marty looked up from his spaghetti dinner, which had had his full attention until Makai yelled. He heard rummaging and movement, and then she came back on the line. "Lanai, what's wrong?"

"Some sick son of a bitch sent a box with dead flowers and a burned cat in it," she shrieked.

He stood immediately. "Are you serious?"

"Yes," she answered.

"Who sent it?"

"I don't know. There's no name on it. I thought it was from you, because it came from your florist," she explained.

"The florist allowed dead flowers and a dead burned cat to be sent?" he asked incredulously.

She said, "The box has the logo on it. It was sitting in front of the door when I got home."

"It was delivered to the house!"

"Yes! Who would do something like this?"

"You ain't think it was extra heavy?"

"I did, but you always doing something extra, so..." she let her sentence trail off. "I can't believe this. Who would do some shit like this?"

Instead of him lying and saying that he didn't know, when he was completely sure who had done it, he said, "I'm on my way there."

"I'm not staying here," she replied. "You can meet me at Katara's. I'll stop by the daycare and get the baby."

He wedged the phone in between his shoulder and his ear, pulling a wad of money out of his pocket and peeling off four twenties, dropping them on the table. He mouthed to Marty that he would call him and asked into the phone, "Are you okay?"

"I will be when I get outta here," she said, sounding like she was moving quickly.

"Alright, baby. I'll meet you at your sister's and then we can go to a room or something," he promised.

"Okay. I love you," she said.

He returned her sentiment, "I love you, too."

He ended the call as he got in his truck and started his trip back to Dover. He went to his messages, scrolled through, and found the thread that he hadn't deleted yet from Lynette. He normally immediately deleted them, but he'd been so busy lately that he'd forgotten. He went into the thread and pushed the word "Call" at the top right of the screen. He waited for the network to connect the call and right after it connected, it went to voicemail. He called again, the phone ringing twice, and then going to voicemail. He knew she was sending him to voicemail, which was confirmation that she sent the box.

He knew that she was stalking him, but he just could never prove it. He'd had mysterious flat tires, scratches to the paint on his truck, and one of his back windows had been busted out. There had never been anything to involve Lanai until the dead flowers and cat. For the life of him, he couldn't understand why she would burn a cat and leave it on someone's doorstep. He didn't understand the significance of a burned, dead cat. A thought dawned on him.

Damn, I hope the poor cat was dead before she burned it, he thought. *This bitch is really crazy.*

He tried to keep as much of it from Lanai as he could, because he didn't want to involve her. He didn't want to worry her, because she had enough on her plate. He also didn't want to involve her, because he didn't want to answer the questions that would follow. He tried to keep things to himself, but Lynette was pushing him to the point of him wanting to show up at her house and knock her fucking head off. He never took pride in hitting a female, but she was a bitch that was asking for it.

His phone vibrated on his lap and Ms. Hazel's number showed up. He answered immediately, "Hello?"

"Makai, where are you?" Ms. Hazel asked, sounding stressed.

"On the road. Why? What's wrong," he asked.

"Some crazy ass girl is here banging on my storm door, screaming like a nut that she wants her daughter," Ms. Hazel said.

Makai listened a little closer and he could hear banging in the background. He was already doing 75 in a 55-mile zone. Hearing the banging, he mashed his foot down on the gas. He asked, "Is that Sade?"

"No, it ain't her crazy ass," Ms. Hazel retorted.

"It's not Lanai, is it?"

"No, I know her and she knows better. I ain't never seen this girl before. I put the kids upstairs and got my shotgun. I'll shoot her, Makai," Ms. Hazel warned.

"Ms. Hazel, I'm on my way," he promised.

"How close are you?" she asked. "I done warned her twice to get off my property. I'm about to open this door and blow her ass across the street."

"I'm a few minutes away," he lied. He didn't like lying to Ms. Hazel. He just didn't want her killing someone and going to jail behind something that involved him. He wondered where Lanai was. He knew the psycho banging on the door was Lynette and he hoped for her sake that she was gone by the time he got there.

Ms. Hazel informed him, "She sounds like she's trying to tear the storm door off the hinges. If she does, I have a right to protect my property."

He wondered if Ms. Hazel had entertained the idea of calling the police. She probably hadn't. She was a mild-mannered, lovable old woman that would turn into someone's worst nightmare if they crossed her. He heard what sounded like a shotgun pump. He called, "Ms. Hazel!"

"I'm here," she answered.

"Don't shoot nobody," he warned. "I'm coming. I'll handle it."

Getting into Greenwood, DE should've taken him more than an hour, but he was flying through the tiny town within thirty minutes flat. He knew it was supposed to take another half hour before he got to General's Greene in Dover. He glanced down at the speedometer and saw that he was going well over 100 miles an hour. He glanced around quickly, knowing that if a cop spotted him, he'd be arrested, his license would be taken, and his truck would be towed. He didn't see any police cars, but he was going so fast that everything was a blur.

He heard Ms. Hazel say, "She stopped banging. I'm gonna go see if she's still out there."

"Stay put," he ordered. "If she is, let her stay out there. I'll be there. I'll deal with it. Go upstairs with the kids and put that gun away."

She protested, "I'm not lettin' nobody come to my house actin' a fool. I ain't scared of nobody, especially not at my own house."

He blew an exhausted breath, his tone pleading with her. "Ms. Hazel, think about the kids. I know you ain't scared and you shouldn't be. But hearing a gunshot will scare the kids to death. Think about their safety. Please go upstairs and keep the kids safe."

She sounded like she wanted to argue some more as Makai flew through Felton. He knew he was treading on thin ice doing more than the speed limit through Felton, because a cop was usually sitting on the side of the highway, waiting to pull somebody over for speeding. He refused to let up off the gas, though, and just hope against hope that no cops were lying in wait to pull him over. If they tried it, they'd have to follow him to General's Greene, because he wasn't stopping.

He heard her breath into the phone. "Okay. I'm gonna go upstairs. I think I hear one of the babies fussin', anyway."

"Thank God," he breathed to himself. He said to her, "I promise I'm on my way. I'll be there in a few minutes. Call the cops if you feel like you need to."

He heard her moving in the background and assumed that meant she was going upstairs. Within a few moments, he heard little kids, which meant she was upstairs. She said, "Okay, well, I'll see you when you get here. Be care...what in the hell? I think somebody else just pulled up outside. I don't know what in the hell."

He said, "Go to an upstairs window and tell me if somebody else pulled up."

He heard more movement, and then she said, "It's Lanai. She just pulled up."

"Oh, God," he mumbled. He knew that Lanai being there, with Lynette outside acting retarded would have the same result as adding gas to a raging fire.

"This crazy bitch," Ms. Hazel screeched. "She just broke my window! Let me get my gun. I'm gonna kill this bitch."

Makai said, "Ms. Hazel, stay with the kids. Call the cops."

"To hell with that, baby. I ain't callin' no cops. She damagin' *my* property," she answered in a voice that told him she was shaking her head, and moving towards going back to wherever she'd left her shotgun.

His palms were sweating as he gripped the steering wheel. He was pushing the truck to its max as he zoomed through Camden, swerving around traffic like he was driving for NASCAR. He subconsciously prayed that no one got in his way. He didn't want to hit anybody, but he had to get there as fast as he could, before somebody ended up dead. As he neared the intersection of Route 13 and Route 10 in Camden, there was a red light with a line of cars stopped. He quickly looked over his right and when he saw no traffic on the side of the road, he quickly jumped to the shoulder of the road and sped to the turning lane.

He turned the corner so fast that he could've sworn that the truck was on two wheels. He merged onto the two-lane road after riding the shoulder for a second, and almost hitting a car that had turned from the opposite direction at the same time as him. He figured that the car had the right away, but it didn't matter. He couldn't stop. He swerved around the car and jumped into the left lane. He felt like he was racing against the clock for a third time in his life and he wasn't sure if he could get there fast enough.

CHAPTER TWENTY-FOUR

Lanai put her BMW in park at the curb in front of Ms. Hazel's home daycare. Her plan was to pick Makayla up, grab something quick for dinner, and head to Katara's house to wait for Makai. As she got out the car, she noticed a woman pacing back and forth angrily in front of Ms. Hazel's door. Lanai had no idea what could be wrong with the woman, because Ms. Hazel was one of the sweetest, funniest women Lanai had ever met.

Out of nowhere, the angry woman picked up one of the bricks circling one of her trees in Ms. Hazel's front yard, and threw it through Ms. Hazel's front window. Lanai stopped in her tracks, mouth wide open in surprise. Her hand flew to her mouth in disbelief. The woman began screaming and cursing at the apparently-locked screen door. Whoever the woman was, she was upset that Ms. Hazel wouldn't open the door and give her daughter to her.

Lanai cautiously approached the situation, not wanting to make things worse or set the woman off any further. She said a silent prayer in her head that the brick thrown through the window hadn't hit any of the children or Ms. Hazel. The woman turned around and spotted Lanai, her already narrowed eyes closing to almost slits.

The woman snarled, "*You!*"

"Me?" Lanai asked innocently.

"You homewrecking bitch," the woman screamed as she bent down to pick up another brick.

Lanai had her hands up in a gesture to surrender or cause no harm. She asked, "Do I know you?"

"I know *you*," she spat, slowly advancing toward Lanai with the brick. "You're the *bitch* that's been running around with *my man*, and he's had the nerve to have you around *my daughter*! This is *my* fucking family! You stay the fuck away!"

Without warning, she hurled the brick at Lanai's head. It was a good thing Lanai was paying attention, because she ducked in just enough time as the brick went whizzing by her head, and hitting the cement walkway behind her. She could hear the brick crumbling to pieces behind her. She knew that if that brick had hit her, it would've knocked her out cold. She stood back upright, asking, "Lady, who are you? I don't know you, your man, or your daughter."

"Oh *now* you don't know them," she asked, her tone taunting. "I see you with him all the time and now you don't know him? I *watch* both of you come and go every day and you don't know him? At least both of you have better sense than for you to have your nasty ass in my house."

Lanai thought for a second. Was this woman stalking her? Was she even stalking the right person? Or was she in love with Makai? Did Makai lie to her and play her for a fool again? Was all this a big game to him to rope her back in, and keep other women on the side? Lanai was confused. She didn't know what was going on, but she did know that there was no way a sane woman would be so mad over a situation that didn't actually exist.

Lanai said, "Hold on, I have no idea what you're talking about."

"Sure you don't," the woman said in a mocking tone.

"What's your name?" Lanai inquired.

"Lynette."

"Okay, Lynette. Who is this man you're referring to?"

"Don't play dumb," Lynette said in a threatening tone. "You know damn well who the man is that I'm referring to. I'm talking about Makai."

"And you two are in a relationship?"

"Yes. A relationship that you ruined."

"And Makayla is your daughter?"

With a straight face and raised chin, Lynette replied, "Yes."

To be sure, Lanai asked, "You're her biological mother?"

Again, with a straight face and raised chin, Lynette answered, "Yes."

"You're lying," Lanai said immediately.

Lynette's head jerked back as if she had been slapped in the face. She said, "She is my daughter."

"You may *want* her to be your daughter," Lanai accused, "but I know her biological mother. And you are not her." While Lynette struggled to find words to dig herself out of the verbal hole that she was in, Lanai continued, "I don't know what kind of game you're playing, or what you're hoping for, but coming here and disrespecting this woman's house and scaring these babies is unnecessary. If you have an issue with Makai, take it up with him."

"Because of you, he won't see me or take any of my calls," Lynette accused.

"I don't have anything to do with that," Lanai countered. "I didn't even know you existed until right now."

As Lynette opened her mouth to say something, the screen door came open and a vehicle came to a screeching stop next to Lanai's car. Lanai wanted to look and see who was in the vehicle, but her eyes were locked on a red-faced, shotgun toting, Ms. Hazel, who came busting through the screen door with the gun leveled at Lynette.

Ms. Hazel said, "You crazy bitch. You wanna break windows, do you?"

Lynette jumped back when she saw Ms. Hazel coming out the door and down the steps. Her eyes were as big as saucers and her lips moved, but nothing came out. Ms. Hazel pumped the shotgun, ready to blow Lynette clear across the street.

"Ms. Hazel, put the gun down," Makai called, running from his truck to the grass where everyone was standing. He went towards Ms. Hazel, who was shaking with anger, but she held the gun steady and had it pointed at Lynette's chest.

"You get the fuck off my property. *Right now*," Ms. Hazel warned.

Makai tried again, "Ms. Hazel, give me the gun. I'll fix your window. Just give me the gun. Think about the kids in the house."

Makai continued to talk to Ms. Hazel in a calm, even tone as he slowly advanced toward her. He slid in between the barrel of the shotgun and Lynette, forcing Ms. Hazel to look at him. He looked rather confident in his strategy. Lanai thought he'd completely lost his mind, because there was no way she was getting between anybody and a bullet. Ms. Hazel seemed to snap out of her trance and focus on the person in front of her. She allowed Makai to take the shotgun from her, but reiterated, "I want her off my property."

"I want my daughter," Lynette yelled.

With his free arm, Makai had to grab ahold of Ms. Hazel, because she had started to charge towards Lynette. Ms. Hazel said, "You're gonna leave my goddamn property. Voluntarily or involuntarily. You leave here in a body bag. That ain't the only gun I own, little girl."

Makai guided her towards the door, asking her to calm down and to check on the kids for him. He took her fussing and cussing into the house. Lynette decided to seize the opportunity and started for the steps. Lanai didn't want to get into anyone's business, but she couldn't stop herself from jumping into Lynette's path to stop her from going into the house. Lynette paused for a second, a confused look on her face momentarily. She attempted to move around Lanai, but Lanai moved with her.

Lanai said, "You're not taking Makayla."

"You can't tell me what to do with my child," Lynette replied.

"I can tell you what you're not doing with *that* child," Lanai rebutted.

Lynette attempted to push past Lanai, who shoved her back a few feet. Lanai warned, "This is your chance to leave without it being a bigger problem."

Lynette said, "I'm not leaving without Makayla."

"Oh, you are," Lanai replied, sounding like she was about to laugh, but she was dead serious. "Honey, you can leave here walking, or on a stretcher. That's up to you. But you're not getting that baby. She's not your daughter."

Lynette tried to charge past Lanai, but Lanai stopped her cold with a stiff punch to the middle of her face. Lynette's head bounced backwards and she stumbled. Lanai waited; her fighting stance ready. Lynette seemed to get her bearings and charged at Lanai again, swinging wildly and screaming. Lanai ducked and tried to dodge the hits, but Lynette managed to land one on the left side of Lanai's face. With her adrenaline pumping, Lanai barely felt the blow. She hit Lynette with another right, connecting with the left side of her face with her fist.

Lynette's nails went into Lanai's skin, clinging to her like a terrified cat, digging into her flesh. With her left hand, Lanai gripped Lynette's neck and squeezed, forcing her backwards. With her right hand, Lanai continued to punch wherever she could; trying to get Lynette's nails out of her skin. Lanai pushed Lynette backwards with her hand, squeezing Lynette's neck tighter, causing Lynette to stumble over something on the ground.

Lynette lost her balance and fell to the ground with Lanai on top of her. Lynette began slapping at and trying to punch Lanai. Lanai had an advantage with being able to sit on top of Lynette, and she used it. She released her hold on Lynette's neck, just to pummel Lynette's face, arms, and chest with her fists. Lanai's fists were coming so quick and fierce that Lynette stopped trying to fight back and tried to shield herself from the blows. She was screaming for someone to help her. Whenever someone took Lanai to a certain level, she would black out, which is exactly what happened.

Lanai continued to punch Lynette, until she was lifted into the air and up off her. She had no idea who picked her up, but she kicked and tried to fight her way down to the ground. She wanted to finish what she started and give Lynette what she'd come for. She never imagined going into protective mode over someone else's child. But when faced with the possibility that someone was going to try to take, or do something to Makayla or Makai, Lanai went into "kill mode". She wanted to teach Lynette a lesson that she wouldn't forget ever in life.

As she was being carried into the house, she figured that it was Makai that had pulled her off Lynette. He was the only one—other than security guards—that would pick her up and carry her away as if she weighed nothing. When she was put down, she was in Ms. Hazel's living room. Makai went back outside, closing the door behind him. Lanai went after him, determined to hear whatever was said and possibly to finish what she started. She wanted to know what the whole fiasco was about. The only she'd get to the bottom of the mess was to hear their heated exchange. The truth always came out when people were angry, so if he was lying, she'd find out.

She came out the door to Makai yelling at Lynette to leave.

Blood dripped from her face and her weave was a complete mess. She was crying, screaming, "I can't believe you're doing this to me, Makai! After all this time! After all that we've been through; all that we've meant to each other!"

"What the fuck are you talkin' about?" he asked, yelling. "I told your stupid ass months ago that I didn't want nothin' to do with you. I told you to stay away from my daughter and her daycare. What the fuck is wrong with you?"

"I love you, Makai," she said. "I know you love me. We can fix this."

"There's nothin' to fix," Makai replied, adamant to drive home his point. "I don't love you. I told you I don't love you."

Lanai couldn't resist the chance to ask him a question. She asked, "So were you in a relationship with her?"

Without hesitation, he looked her in the face and answered, "No. When me and you weren't together, I met her. I spent some time with her and she met Makayla. I found out that her fuckin' ass is crazy and I cut it off. She started stalkin' me and came here the night that we watched a movie the first time. I ignored her, I told her, I changed my number a thousand times, and she still won't give up. She's been fuckin' with my truck and she's the one that put the fuckin' dead cat and flowers on your doorstep."

Lanai looked at Lynette with a renewed hatred. She quietly asked, "Are you serious?"

Lynette screamed at Lanai, "He doesn't want you! He wants me! You need to go the fuck away, so we can be happy!"

"You need help," Lanai replied, shaking her head.

"Lynette, you need to leave," Makai said. "One of the neighbors called the cops and they're on their way."

"And I'll tell them I was jumped by the two of you," Lynette answered. "I'll tell them that crazy battleax tried to shoot me, too. All of you will go to jail and I'll still get Makayla."

"You touch my daughter and I'll kill you myself," Makai threatened in a low, dangerous tone.

Lanai came from around Makai and advanced towards Lynette, telling her, "You better leave willingly or I'll make sure you leave on a stretcher."

Makai grabbed Lanai by the waist and pulled her back. He said, "Babe, stop. Go in the house."

"Babe?" Lynette asked in a disbelieving tone. As if she was trying to convince herself more than anyone else; she shook her head from side to side, saying, "You don't love her. You love me. You don't want to be with her. You want to be with me."

Taking her by the wrist, Makai pulled Lanai into the house again, leaving Lynette outside. He closed and locked the door. They could hear Lynette screaming and crying through the broken window. She sounded like a little kid having a temper tantrum, because she couldn't have her way. Lanai knew that Makai couldn't handle arguing or going back and forth for too long. She thought that he would've walked away long before he did.

Ms. Hazel came into the living room with cotton balls, peroxide, and bandages, mumbling and fussing under her breath. Without Lanai's consent, Ms. Hazel began addressing the scratches that she had on her arms, chest, and neck. The screaming and crying stopped and was replaced with shattering glass. Lanai's wide eyes met Makai's eyes and both of them rushed to the door. Makai pulled open the door to see Lynette smashing his truck windows with a crowbar.

They stood on the step in shock. Lynette climbed on top of the hood of the truck and smashed out the windshield. While she was up there, with all her might, she took the crowbar and drove the pointed end down into the hood of the truck. Not that she could do much damage with her 130 pounds, but she jumped up and down on the top of the truck, trying to further damage the body. Before Makai could come off the step and react, three police cars came to a screeching stop, with the officers jumping out of their squad cars and pulling their weapons.

They were yelling at Lynette to come down slowly from the hood of the truck and to keep her hands where they could see them. She froze like a deer in headlights, slowly complying with what she was told to do. When she jumped down from the truck, she was ordered to turn around and put her hands behind her head. One of the officers put his weapon away, moving toward her and retrieving his handcuffs from his utility belt to put on her wrists. Once he had the handcuffs secured on her wrists, he moved her to the back of his squad car, helping her into the backseat by pushing her head down.

The other officers put away their weapons and approached Makai and Lanai standing on the step. One officer said, "Sir, can you step over here, please? I need to ask you some questions."

The other officer pulled out his small spiral notebook and pen, asking Lanai, "Ma'am, can you step down here, please? Thank you. Ma'am, what's your name?"

Looking over at the officer that had taken Makai off to the side and pulled out his spiral notebook, she distractedly answered, "Lanai Wilson."

"Do you live here?"

Her head snapped back around to the officer in front of her. She shook her head no, "Uh, no. I live in Cedar Chase."

"So what are you doing here, ma'am?"

The officer that had put Lynette into the back of his squad car walked past Lanai to go up the steps and knocked on the door. Lanai was distracted by watching his movements. He walked into the house without waiting for anyone to tell him to come in and called out to anyone in the house. She blinked and looked back at the officer in front of her. She answered, "I came to pick up my boyfriend's daughter. She goes to daycare here."

"Can you tell me what happened here today?"

"All I know is I pulled up to get the baby and she was—"

"She who?" the officer interrupted.

"Uh, Lynette, I think her name is," Lanai replied. "She was outside going crazy, screaming for Ms. Hazel to open the door and give her daughter to her."

"Does she have a child here?"

"No, she was talking about his daughter," she answered, pointing at Makai.

"What's his name?"

"Makai Johnson."

"And who is he to her?"

"I don't know. She says they're in a relationship and I ruined it. He says he told her he doesn't want her and they're not together," Lanai explained.

He looked up at her and asked, "And what do you say?"

"I say she's crazy," she answered quickly. "Anytime that you come to a daycare, cause a scene, endangering innocent kids and an elderly woman, something has got to be wrong with you. She told me with a straight face that his daughter is her daughter. I know who his daughter's mother is."

"So what happened after she was screaming and yelling for the daycare provider to open the door?"

"She threw a brick through the window."

"Did you see her throw this brick?"

"Yes."

"Then what happened?"

"Then she picked up a brick and threw it at me," she said.

He asked, "Is that how you got the scratches?"

"She charged at me and I defended myself," Lanai explained, waiting for the officer to say she was under arrest.

"Then she destroyed the truck?" he questioned.

She nodded her head.

He wrote scribbled some more on his notepad, then looked up at Lanai and asked, "Hold tight for me, please? I'll be back."

He walked away to the squad car where Lynette was, opened the door, and began talking to him. From where she stood, Lanai could hear Lynette go from talking loudly to screaming at the officer. She heard the officer say, "Ma'am, I need you to stop screaming at me."

"I need you to take these fucking cuffs off of me and let me out of this goddamn car," she screamed.

Without another word, he closed the door of the car and walked over to where the other officer was talking to Makai. Both officers stepped away from Makai and began having a private conversation. Makai walked over to where Lanai was standing and wrapped his arms around her. She hugged him back and he kissed the top of her head. He said into her hair, "Babe, I'm sorry."

With her face pressed up against his chest, she could hear his heartbeat. She asked, "Sorry for what?"

"Sorry you had to go through this bullshit. I swear I told that retarded girl I didn't want nothing to do with her."

She sighed. It had been a long time since she felt like she could believe what he was saying to her without questioning it. She liked the feeling of knowing that he was telling her the truth. He was really trying and she loved it. She hated that it took so long for him to get to that point, but it felt worth it. She said, "I believe you."

After squeezing her tight, he moved her back to arm's length and looked at the scratches that Lynette had left. He said, "I could fuck her up for scratching you up. It's gonna take a while for it to heal, too. You know you light as hell."

She smiled. "I'm not worried about it. It'll heal. We need to go check on Ms. Hazel and the kids."

He put his arm around her shoulder and they walked to the steps together. As they were about to go up, the officer that had been inside was coming out. They let him pass before going up the steps and into the house. As they entered the house, Lanai noticed that Ms. Hazel looked shaken. For the first time since she'd met her, Ms. Hazel looked her 82 years. Her face looked pale and Lanai could've sworn that her hair had turned grayer in a matter of minutes. Lanai walked over to her and wrapped her arms around Ms. Hazel's frail shoulders.

Lanai hugged her tight and said, "I'm so sorry you had to go through this."

"Aww, baby. You ain't go nothin' to be sorry about," Ms. Hazel said.

Lanai released her from the hug, but she took Ms. Hazel's frail, wrinkled hand in hers and held it.

Makai said, "Ms. Hazel, I'm sorry. I didn't know this dumb broad would do something like this."

With her free hand, Ms. Hazel waved off what he'd said. She said, "I want the two of you to stop apologizin'. You didn't do nothin' wrong. You can't predict what folks are gonna do. That girl is broken and there probably ain't no fixin' her, either. I'm just gonna go get me a restrainin' order, so when if she comes back, I can shoot her and it'll be legal."

Both Lanai and Makai burst into laughter. Lanai said, "Ms. Hazel, a restraining order doesn't make it legal. You have to call the police, so they can document it and arrest her."

Ms. Hazel waved her free hand again, dismissing what Lanai said. She commented, "She comes back and I'm shootin' her. Period."

Neither Lanai nor Makai thought to argue further. Ms. Hazel had her mind set on how she was going to handle the situation, and no one was going to change that. Lanai asked, "Where are the babies?"

"Upstairs," answered Ms. Hazel. "I have a little helper that comes in the afternoon to earn some extra money. She's up there with them."

"So what did the cop say?" Makai asked.

"Nothin'. He took my statement and said he'd be back," Ms. Hazel replied. "Not much he can say. She's trespassin' and destroyin' people's property. They need to take her to jail."

There was a hard knock on the glass of the screen door. The officer that had questioned Lanai came through the door and asked, "Ma'am, are you pressing charges for your damaged property?"

"Yes," Ms. Hazel answered immediately.

He looked at Lanai and asked, "Are you pressing charges for her attacking you?"

Lanai nodded her head.

He looked at Makai and said, "And I'm guessing you're gonna press charges for the damage to your truck."

Makai nodded his head in response.

The officer took everybody's personal information and told them to hold on while he put the information into his computer in his squad car. He also told them that Lynette would be taken down to Dover Police Department. She would be booked on charges of trespassing, two counts of destruction of property, five counts of endangering the welfare of a child, offensive touching, and disorderly conduct for trying to kick the window out of the squad car.

Lanai asked, "When did she try to kick the window out?"

"After you two came in. While we were talking," he answered. "She's gonna have plenty of time to cool down in that holding cell."

The officer left out to go type up the report while the other officers left. Makai pulled out his cell phone and called McKinney's Towing Company to come and tow his truck, as Lanai cleaned up the glass and brick that were on the floor under the window for Ms. Hazel.

Makai asked, "Ms. Hazel, do you have any plywood?"

"Baby, I don't know what I have in that basement," she said, lowering herself into the La-Z-Boy and lifting the footrest. "You can go ahead and look."

He headed down the steps of the basement to see what he could find to temporarily patch up the broken window. After cleaning up the mess on the floor, Lanai asked, "Ms. Hazel, you want something to eat?"

"Honey, I can't eat nothin' right now. My stomach is too upset."

"You want some tea?" Lanai offered.

"Yes, baby. Thank you. Do you need me to show you where everything is?" Ms. Hazel asked, attempting to get up.

Lanai waved her off, heading for the kitchen. She said, "No, ma'am. I need you to relax. I'll find everything just fine."

Moving around the kitchen and looking through each cabinet, Lanai found what she needed to make a cup of chamomile tea. She filled the empty blue teapot that sat on the stove with water. She straightened up the kitchen while she waited for the water to boil and when the teapot whistled, she removed it and carefully poured the hot water into one of the coffee mugs that she found. She added a   heaping teaspoon of sugar to the hot water, dipping the tea bag into the water a few times, before carrying the mug with a spoon in it to Ms. Hazel.

Ms. Hazel was asleep by the time Lanai brought the tea out. Lanai smiled at her and put the hot cup on the table, pulled the throw blanket from the back of the couch and covered Ms. Hazel with it. She headed upstairs to check on the children and to let Ms. Hazel's helper know that she needed to keep the kids upstairs, so that Ms. Hazel could sleep.

Lanai had to check every room before she found the room that the kids were in. She eased the door open and every eye was on her, because of the creaking old door. When Makayla laid eyes on Lanai, she dropped the toy that she'd been playing with and ran to her, squealing, "Ma!"

Lanai laughed as Makayla wrapped herself around Lanai's legs. Lanai bent down and picked her up, hugging Makayla back, when she wrapped her little arms around Lanai's neck and squeezed. Lanai loved the excitement that Makayla expressed every time they were apart, and Makayla would see her. Makayla made Lanai feel like a rock star, the way that she lit up, screamed, and squealed.

Lanai kissed her cheek. "Hey, my Sweet Pea, I missed you."

Makayla laid her head on Lanai's shoulder. Lanai had been worried about Makayla becoming too attached to her or vice versa. She reminded herself daily that Makayla was someone else's daughter. It no longer mattered to Lanai who Makayla's mother was, but what did matter was the fact that she wasn't Makayla's mother. She reminded herself that at any given moment, they could be separated. With every passing day of waking up to her, spending time with her, and doing things with her, it got harder and harder for Lanai's heart to accept the fact that she wouldn't be a permanent fixture in the little girl's life.

Makai had told her that they were always going to be a part of each other's lives, because he was going to marry her. Her heart wanted to believe him, but her head continued to keep things in perspective. He had yet to buy a ring and he hadn't proposed to her. Deep down, it was her dream to marry Makai and live happily ever after. But past experience and her head kept her grounded, reminding her that nothing in life was guaranteed. She'd learned over the years that she seldom got what she wanted.

Growing closer in her faith and her relationship with God, she was learning to let go of things that she couldn't control. She'd fallen apart at the altar a few times, letting go of the things that had bound her for the majority of her life. She was learning to accept what she couldn't change, and giving God control of every part of her life. When she felt like she was struggling over something, she'd pray about it and do her best to make peace with it. She'd learned through Bible study and Sunday school that if someone obsessed over something, they didn't truly trust God to work things out. She wanted her actions to show that she trusted God completely, which made life that much easier.

With Makayla on her hip, she told the young girl, Ms. Hazel's helper, "Keep all the kids up here. Ms. Hazel is sleeping."

"Ms. Hazel told me to call all their moms to come and get them," the young girl revealed.

"Okay, well, I'll go down to let them in," Lanai said.

Lanai toted Makayla down the steps just in time, as a parent was knocking on the screen door. Lanai greeted the woman in nursing scrubs, and inquired about which child she'd come to pick up. Before she sent her for the child, Lanai gave her a brief description of tonight's commotion, which had forced Ms. Hazel to need a nap, and then quietly directed her upstairs to get her child. Lanai greeted and relayed the short version of events to every parent that seemed to show up almost back-to-back, while Makai boarded up the window as quietly as possible.

Lanai went to check on Ms. Hazel after the last child was picked up and her helper went home. She was unsure whether or not Ms. Hazel was breathing, so Lanai checked her pulse on the side of her neck. It was a little faint, but it was there, although her breathing was shallow and she still looked pale. Lanai called to Makai, "Babe."

"Yeah?" he asked, driving a nail into the wood he'd found in the basement.

"Ms. Hazel doesn't look so good."

"What do you mean?"

"She's pale."

He looked in their direction and said, "She always looks like that."

"No, she doesn't," Lanai countered. "Her breathing is shallow and her pulse is light."

"Babe, speak English," he said, sounding exhausted, standing back from the window.

"She doesn't look so good," Lanai repeated.

He looked over the temporarily repaired window, absently asking, "What do you want me to do? She's breathing, right?"

Lanai answered, "Yeah, but barely. We need to call an ambulance."

"Try to wake her up," he suggested.

Lanai gently shook Ms. Hazel's shoulder and got no response. She called her name and shook her shoulder a little harder, still getting nothing. Lanai was about to panic. She said, "She's not waking up."

Makai came over to them, calling Ms. Hazel's name. He shook her shoulder roughly, calling her again. Ms. Hazel barely stirred, but she did move. Makai looked at her with a confused look on his face. He said, more to himself than to anyone else, "She never sleeps heavy. Call the ambulance."

Lanai took the phone that he had outstretched to her while he pulled the blanket off her and looked her over. As she dialed 911, she wasn't sure what he was looking for. As she told the dispatcher that they needed an ambulance at Ms. Hazel's address, Makai said to her, "Her body temperature is off, too."

Lanai relayed what he said to the dispatcher. The dispatcher asked, "What does that mean?"

Lanai looked at Makai, asking, "What does that mean?"

"Her skin is cooler than it should be."

Lanai repeated to the dispatcher what he'd said, still not completely understanding what he was saying. The dispatcher asked, "Do you mean her body temperature dropped?"

"Maybe," she answered.

"Alright, we have an ambulance on the way. It should be there shortly. Are there any health issues that she has that you are aware of?" inquired the dispatcher.

She answered, "I have no idea. Babe, does Ms. Hazel have any health issues that you know of?"

He looked up at the ceiling, trying to remember if she'd told him anything. His response was, "She's eighty-two. I'm sure she does."

"We don't know," Lanai answered into the phone.

"Okay, well, the ambulance is on the way."

"Okay. Thank you," Lanai said as she ended the call, handing the phone back to Makai.

Lanai sat on the arm of the chair next to Ms. Hazel, waiting for the ambulance for what seemed like forever. When the paramedics got there, one of them put his bag down next to the chair and checked Ms. Hazel's vitals. He said, "Her pulse is light. Does she have any issues with low blood pressure?"

Makai said, "We don't know."

The paramedic said, "We'll be right back. We're going to go get the gurney."

They left and returned with the stretcher. Both paramedics attempted to wake Ms. Hazel, with Lanai and Makai calling her name. They got nothing from her. The paramedics worked together to lift her from the chair and lay her on the bed. After strapping her to the bed and making sure the straps were secure, they rolled her out to the ambulance.

Makai followed them out and Lanai locked the door behind her. The tow truck driver pulled up as they were walking down the walkway. The paramedics loaded Ms. Hazel into the back of ambulance. Lanai put Makayla in the car seat in the back of her car, while Makai talked to the tow truck driver. Lanai stopped one of the paramedics and asked, "Which hospital are you guys taking her to?"

"Bayhealth," he said, climbing into the driver's seat.

As Makai came towards her car after signing paperwork, he had stress etched all over his face. He got in the passenger seat and Lanai asked, "We going to the hospital?"

He nodded, rubbing a hand over his face and blowing a breath. On the way to the hospital, Lanai silently prayed that whatever was wrong with Ms. Hazel was something minor. She prayed that God protected them all and would give Makai some relief from all the stress that he felt. She asked God to help her to be his strength, and be there for him and Makayla as much as she possibly could. She also asked God to be a fence around her family. She knew that they needed protection from the devil's attacks, that seemed to be extra busy.

CHAPTER TWENTY-FIVE

"**H**ey, Dad. What's up?" Makai said into the phone.

He talked to Roger on a weekly basis; however, he hadn't talked to him in a few weeks. He hadn't thought much of it with everything that had been going on. Ms. Hazel had been admitted into the hospital and was in a coma. The doctors originally couldn't find out what was wrong with her, but after they ordered tests and finally got in contact with her daughter, they learned that she had a history of low blood pressure and a heart issue. Makai and Lanai visited her as much as possible and her daughter had come to Delaware from Toledo, OH to be with her. The doctors told everyone they didn't expect Ms. Hazel to live past the end of the month. Her daughter had set about making funeral arrangements and handling things with her house and insurance.

Makai didn't want to believe that Ms. Hazel wasn't going to die soon. She was more to him than just a daycare provider. She was the grandmother and mother that he'd never had. She listened to him when he was going through the pain of Lanai not being in his life. She gave him good advice and took great care of his daughter. She had become a family member to him, Makayla, and Lanai. Lanai prayed over Ms. Hazel daily, even enlisting the prayers and presence of members of the church.

She would read bible verses to Ms. Hazel and she helped the staff at the hospital to care for her, too. Makai hadn't wanted to, but Lanai found another daycare for Makayla, telling him that it would only be temporary, until Ms. Hazel got out the hospital. His heart didn't want to believe it, but looking at her every day, seeing her not respond to anything and the machines breathing for her, he knew she wasn't going to make it. He didn't want her to suffer; he just wasn't ready to let her go yet. He wanted just a little more time with her.

He'd taken a flight down to Miami to handle the business that he'd agreed to handle with Marty. Lanai had told him she wanted to stay in Delaware to be there for Ms. Hazel, and she had kept Makayla with her. Miami was beautiful, with its gorgeous beaches and weather, the women even more beautiful, walking around with little to nothing on. But he couldn't enjoy himself, he barely registered where he was because his mind was on Ms. Hazel being in the hospital. He sat in the black Chevy Tahoe with tinted windows, waiting for the person he was supposed to meet up with, when Roger's number had popped up on his phone.

"It's not Dad," a voice said. "It's Malik. Dad's in the hospital."

"What?" Makai asked.

His brother said into the phone, "Dad is in the hospital."

"Why? What happened?"

"He was in a car accident," Malik answered.

"A car accident where? When was this? How long has he been in the hospital?" Makai fired off questions in rapid succession.

"He was here in the city. A truck driver fell asleep driving and hit him, knocking him off the road. He slammed into the guardrail on the median. The car is totaled and he's in a medically-induced coma."

Makai repeated, "When did this happen?"

"It happened at three o'clock this morning."

"Are you fucking kidding me?" Makai asked, more to himself than to his brother. "Which hospital is he at?"

"Thomas Jefferson University Hospital."

"I'll be on the first plane there," Makai promised.

Malik asked, "Plane? You're right in Delaware."

"I'm in Miami on business," Makai corrected him.

"Oh, okay. Well, let me know your flight information and I'll pick you up from the airport," Malik promised.

"Bet," Makai said, ready to hang up.

Malik said, "Kai, it's one more thing."

"What?" Makai asked, suspicious of his brother's hesitation.

"Mom is here."

Makai fell silent. He hadn't seen Mya since the day that she'd walked out on him, his brother, and his father twenty-two years before. He thought that he'd done a good job of moving on with his life without her. The majority of his friends had been raised by single mothers, but they'd had their mother's love, support, and guidance. He had never allowed himself to feel her absence in his life. Whenever he would feel like he was missing her, he would push the thought to the back of his mind and redirect his energy. When he'd crossed paths with Ms. Hazel, she seemed to fill the void that he'd forgotten was there. A void that he felt his mother should never have left.

"Kai?"

Makai replied, "Yeah, I'm here. Look, I gotta go. I'll text the flight info to your phone."

"Text it to Dad's phone," Malik told him. "My phone is broke."

"You need a couple dollars?" Makai asked.

Makai would periodically give his younger brother money, whether he asked for it or not, but there were times when Malik would ask him for money for a bill or something for one of the kids. Makai made sure that Malik stayed away from a life of drug dealing and he led a straight life. Malik had never been in trouble, got good grades in school, but decided not to go to college. He held a steady job working for one of the universities on the janitorial staff. He didn't make enough to live the way his brother did, though.

Malik sounded like he was having a hard time talking. "Nah, I'm...I'm good. I'm due...my phone is due for an upgrade soon, so I'll just...I'm gonna just wait on that."

"I'll Western Union you the money before I leave Miami," Makai retorted, ignoring what his brother had said.

Malik paused, then lowered his voice, "Kai, you don't have to keep bailing me out. I'll be alright."

"Make sure you have your wallet on you so you can have your id to pick it up," Makai continued as if Malik hadn't said anything.

"Thanks," Malik mumbled.

"Look," Makai began, "stop doing that. If I didn't have it, I wouldn't send it. You need help; you need to let me know. Don't feel bad about needing help. You're doing what most niggas would never dream of doing. You're holding your family down the right way. As your big brother, I'm supposed to be there when you need me."

"I know, Kai. I appreciate you. Let me know when you're on the way so I can be there," Malik replied.

"I will," Makai promised. "Love you, little bro."

"Love you, too," Malik returned, before they hung up.

Makai looked at the time on the radio, noticing that it was five minutes past the time the guy he was waiting for was supposed to show up. He started the engine and was about to pull off, when a pair of headlights swept over his rental truck. He didn't trust people that were late. It was one thing for a female to be late when she was getting ready for a date, but when it came to business, lateness made Makai nervous. The last thing he needed was for someone to be wearing a wire or working with the police.

The description of the guy that Marty had given him fit the guy completely. The short Hispanic jumped down from the truck he'd been driving. From where Makai sat, he could see the guy had black hair and was stocky and bow-legged. Makai turned off the engine and got out, going around to the front of the truck to meet the man. As the shorter man approached, Makai could see the scar that started at the right side of the man's forehead and went across his face, crossing his nose and ending at his left jawbone. Marty had told Makai that the scar came from a drug deal gone bad and he'd almost lost his eye.

Scarface extended his hand, "What's going on?"

Makai accepted his hand and shook it briefly. He said, "Marty sent me."

Scarface nodded his head briefly, then motioned with his hand for Makai to follow him to the back of his truck.

Makai looked around the parking lot that Marty had chosen for the meet. He'd been looking around all night, just to be sure nothing was weird or out of place. He followed Scarface to the truck, looking inside to make sure he wouldn't have to pull the gun that he carried in his waistband. He didn't see any movement or anyone in the truck. Scarface opened the back gate of the truck and there were four black duffle bags.

Scarface unzipped each bag and stood back while Makai looked into them. Each bag was filled with bricks of cocaine wrapped in shrink-wrap. Makai produced a pocketknife from his jeans pocket and cut into one of the bricks. He took a small tube from his pocket with a liquid in it, dumping the small amount of cocaine into the tube from the knife blade. He slightly shook the cocaine and liquid mixture, watching the liquid turn blue instantly. He put a plastic cork in the tube and dropped it into the duffle bag, zipping all four of them up.

He took two of the bags and Scarface took the other two, following him to the other truck. Makai pressed the button above the license plate and the back gate opened slowly. Makai put down the two bags he carried and opened one of the two bags in the back of the truck filled with money. He allowed Scarface to flip through a few of the stacks of money in each bag, then Scarface took the two bags, said goodnight, and went back to his truck. Makai closed the back gate and got into the driver's seat, continuing to look around.

Every time took part in a drug transaction, he always subconsciously held his breath, waiting for the police to jump out of nowhere and arrest him. He didn't even realize that his palms were sweating, until he gripped the steering wheel after restarting the engine. Scarface got back in his truck and threw up two fingers to Makai on his way out of the parking lot. Makai went in the opposite direction than Scarface. He had to remind himself to do the speed limit and not look nervous so that he didn't draw attention to himself. He'd been skeptical about driving around with $1.2 million in the trunk. Knowing that he had 40 kilograms of pure cocaine straight from Columbia in the trunk had his nervous-pervis.

It seemed like it took three times as long for him to get to the lawyer's office that wasn't far from the boardwalk. It was a fifteen-minute drive, but that 15 minutes felt like 45 minutes to him. He kept looking around, watching every vehicle, person walking, or anything that moved extra close. He felt like he was watching his rearview and side-view mirrors more than he was the road in front of him. When he reached the lawyer's office where he was supposed to meet Marty, he parked in the garage and turned off the engine. He waited a few minutes, watching his surroundings. He wiped his sweaty palms on the pants legs of his jeans and blew a breath. He liked to gamble, but lately he'd been asking himself if taking such a risk was worth the consequences, or even the stress.

Deciding that he couldn't sit there the entire night, he got himself together and got out. Looking around and back and forth, he made sure for the final time that nothing was out of place or different. It was a little hard for him to determine something unusual in a town that he wasn't familiar with. He hoped against hope that things went smooth, otherwise, he had no idea how he would explain to Lanai why he was in jail in Miami for moving 40 kilos of cocaine.

Taking the duffle bags two in each hand, he closed the trunk and hit the alarm from the keypad. He went to the door he'd been told to go to, trying his damnedest to remain as calm as possible. His ears were listening extra hard for any unfamiliar noises, along with the rest of his senses being heightened. When he got to the door, he rang the bell and waited for what seemed like 100 years. The door came open and Marty was on the other side of it. He smiled, holding the door for Makai to come inside.

Marty extended his hand to take two of the bags from Makai. Makai followed Marty's lead to a conference room where another short, Opie-looking, white guy in a suit waited. He looked like he did taxes for a living with his brown, plastic-rimmed glasses and two pens sticking out of his breast pocket of his suit jacket. Makai dropped the two bags on the table that he'd been carrying.

Marty followed suit and asked, "You gonna stick around?"

"Nah, I gotta take the first flight to Philly. My dad was in a bad car accident," Makai explained.

Marty offered, "You can use my jet, if you want. I just flew in."

"Flew in from where?"

"Washington State," he answered. "That's why I needed you to be here for the pickup. I wasn't sure how long it was going to take. This bitch of a soon-to-be ex-wife of mine is going to give me a stroke. Everything dealing with the divorce is in Washington State."

"What is this, ex-wife number three?" Makai asked.

"Four," Marty corrected.

"What the fuck is the point of getting married?" Makai laughed. "You keep divorcing them."

Marty shrugged. "I guess it's family tradition. Technically, the way I was raised, I shouldn't be having sex with a woman unless I'm married to her."

"When did tradition ever stop you?"

Marty admitted, "You're right. That's why all four of them divorced me. I don't care, though. I met soon-to-be ex-wife number five after court."

Makai laughed harder. "What? What kinda shit is that?"

Marty shrugged again. He said, "They want the wedding, I want the sex."

"You gotta get married to have sex?"

"No, I get what I want and I give them what they want."

"Man, that's insanity."

Again, Marty shrugged. "What're you gonna do?"

Makai replied, "I'm not gonna get in that predicament. Fuck that. I'm not getting married four and five times. If I ever get married, it'll be one damn time."

"Different strokes for different folks," Marty said, unzipping the bags. "You want me to call my pilot? My jet is always on standby."

"Nah, I'm just gonna change the date on my ticket," Makai said. "I bought a round trip ticket. I thought I was staying for a day or two. I wanted to take in some sights and do some shit."

"You can always come back," Marty pointed out.

Makai assured him, "Oh, I will. Next time, it'll be a family trip."

"Speaking of your family and trips," Marty said, wagging his finger in the air. As he unpacked the duffle bags, he continued, "That bullshit that happened in Glendale. The girl that your girlfriend almost choked to death, wanted to pursue every possible charge and add more. I talked with my judge friend and got him to lean on the prosecutor. Bottom line is she has to plead guilty to offensive touching. It's a misdemeanor and she'll have a fine to pay. I can work on helping her to get it expunged later on."

Makai nodded. "I'll call and tell her. I'm outta here. I'll talk to you later."

Marty held up his index finger, telling Makai to wait a minute. He left the room for a minute, came back with a briefcase, handing it to Makai. Makai asked, "What's this?"

"A gift to say thank you for handling this situation for me. I know how much you have at stake," Marty answered.

Makai put the briefcase on the conference table and opened it to see rows of hundred-dollar bills bundled by the paper banks used to hold stacks of money together. Makai said, "I can't take this on the plane. You know they check everything now."

"So take the jet," Marty suggested.

Makai sighed. "Call the pilot. Where am I meeting him?"

Marty said, "Give me the keys to the rental and the driver I have waiting out front will take you to the jet."

"Is there ever anything you don't have figured out?" Makai asked jokingly.

Makai and Marty shook hands while he walked Makai out to where the car and driver waited. Makai thought to himself that things were going just a little too smoothly. He was waiting for everything to fall apart, and the DEA and FBI to jump out from around every corner with guns drawn, but that never happened. The ride from the office to the airstrip where the private jet waited was smooth and quiet. There were no government officials or law enforcement waiting to stop him from getting on the jet. Before the jet took off, Makai took out his phone and made a phone call to Lanai.

It was after 11pm, but she answered on the fourth ring, sounding half-asleep. "Hello?"

"Hey, baby."

"Hey. Are you okay?"

"Yeah."

"What's wrong?" she asked, sounding like she was sitting up in the bed.

"My dad is in the hospital."

"What? What happened? Which hospital?"

"Malik told me he was in a car accident. Some truck driver fell asleep on the road and knocked him into the median," Makai explained.

"Oh, my goodness," she gasped. "Is he okay?"

He felt a lump forming in his throat and he immediately cleared it. *This is no time to be getting weak or emotional.* "He's in a coma. Marty is letting me use his jet to fly to Philly. I just wanted to let you know what's going on."

"Well, which hospital is it?"

"Uh, Thomas Jefferson University," he said. "You go ahead and go back to sleep. I know you gotta work in the morning. I just wanted to let you know and hear your voice."

"I'm getting up now. I'll meet you there," she said, ignoring his instructions to go back to sleep.

"Babe, I'm good. Just go back to sleep."

Stubbornly, she said, "That's not happening. I won't be able to sleep anyway. I'll meet you there. I'll call Katara when I think she's awake, and let her know I'll work from wherever I am."

He sighed, knowing that when her mind was made up, there was no convincing her otherwise. She was going to do what she wanted. He didn't want to admit to her that deep down; he needed her to be there. He was going to need to pull some strength from somewhere. He said, "Well, be careful. I'll let you know when and where I land."

"Alright. I love you."

"I love you, too." He pressed the end button and texted his dad's phone, letting Malik know that he was taking a private jet to Philly. Within a minute, Malik texted back, telling him to let him know when and where he landed.

He put his phone away and waited for the pilot to take off. He figured that he'd take a nap during the flight, but that didn't happen. His brain was going a mile a minute, trying to process everything that had happened in such a short time. He didn't like thinking about or dealing with emotional things. He liked to keep everything just how it was, and not deal with anything other than money. He'd gotten the most important woman to him back in his life. Makai wanted to believe that everything else was irrelevant.

He hadn't thought of his mother in a long time. All the thoughts, feelings, and questions he'd had as the eight-year-old child she abandoned, he'd put in a box in the far corners of his mind. It had been so long that he'd forgotten that they'd been there in the first place. But just like everything else in life, boxing something up didn't make it disappear. He tried to think of Lanai and Makayla the entire flight because they made him happy; he felt like he had a purpose to his life with them. He also thought of his brother and his father. His father had worked so hard all his life to make sure that Malik and Makai had everything. Makai just wanted to be half the man his dad was.

A little more than two and a half hours later, Makai was landing at Philadelphia International Airport. He texted his brother to tell him where he was, but told him he was going to either rent a car or take a cab to the hospital. He told his brother he wanted him to stay at their dad's side until he could get there. He called Lanai to see where she was and to tell her he had landed at the airport. She told him she was at the hospital, but she was on her way to the airport. He didn't attempt to argue with her about coming to the airport to pick him up. She told him that she put the information in Google Maps on her phone and expected to be there in about twenty minutes.

He figured he'd take that time to grab a cup of coffee. While he waited, he found some toys and stuffed animals to buy for Makayla, picked up a card for his dad, and bought a bouquet of flowers for Lanai. As he paid for his purchases, he remembered that he'd forgotten to send the money to Malik. He shook his head at himself, realizing that his memory was getting worse.

He walked out to the pickup and drop-off area in front of the airport. He waited for a few minutes, then saw Lanai pull up, looking around for him. She spotted him as he was walking towards the curb and she pulled up to the curb where he stopped. She popped the trunk and he dropped Makayla's gifts and the briefcase inside.

Right before he closed the trunk, he opened the briefcase, took out a bundle of hundreds, locked it back, then closed the trunk. He got into the passenger seat, giving Lanai the flowers and a kiss.

She smiled, "Thank you, baby."

"You need a truck or something. This car is small as shit," he complained, putting on his seatbelt.

She sucked her teeth. "My car is not small. You had the same car."

"I got rid of it, too," he pointed out.

"We'll talk about that later," she said. "How was Miami?"

He shrugged. "Don't know. I got the call from Malik a few hours ago. I didn't get to Miami until like seven. I didn't even check into the hotel."

Lanai shook her head from side to side in an expression of pity. "That sucks. I hear Miami is a beautiful city."

"It is beautiful," he admitted. "I just didn't get to do or see nothing."

"Well, what did you want to do or see?"

"Jet-ski, go out to eat, sightsee," he said. "Just enjoy the city."

"I bet you did wanna sightsee," she retorted.

"I wanted to sightsee, not woman-see. You're all the woman I ever wanna see."

"I didn't say anything about woman-seeing," she said, sounding like she was trying too hard to sound innocent.

"I know you. You don't have to say it for me to know what you're thinking. That ain't something you gotta worry about anymore."

She kept quiet, just nodding her head to let him know she heard what he'd said.

He asked, "Where's Makayla?"

"I got Nicky to come over and watch her," she said, pulling into the parking garage of the hospital. "I figure she's had her fill of hospitals—poor baby."

"Yeah, she's had to visit more hospitals in her little life than I have in my entire life," he mused.

When she found a parking spot, they got out the car and headed inside. He called his dad's phone and Malik answered, sounding like he was asleep, "Yo?"

"What's the room number?"

"3035."

"On my way up there."

"Bet."

Makai ended the call and he and Lanai headed to the elevator to go to his dad's room. On the elevator ride up, his stomach started flip-flopping. He knew it wasn't because of the movement of the elevator. The closer he got to being able to physically lay eyes on his dad, more afraid he became. He didn't want to admit it out loud, let alone to himself, that he was afraid of anything. He'd always felt like he had to be strong for the people he loved and if he showed fear, in his mind, he couldn't be there for them.

Getting off the elevator, he led the way to room 3035, following the signs on the walls and numbers outside the doors. As he approached room 3035, he took a deep breath and pushed himself to go inside the room. He could hear the beeping of the machines from the door. He crept around the corner, feeling like a little kid cautiously entering a room where his parent was. He saw his dad in the hospital bed with the white sheet and blanket covering him up to his chest. He was on a ventilator, with tubes and wires going in and coming out of his body. He had multiple IV's and tape to secure the wires, tubes, ventilator, and IV's.

He slowly neared the bed with Lanai at his side. The closer he got, the better he could see deep scratches and horrible bruises on Roger's face, neck, and arms. He had a nasty gash on his forehead. Tears unexpectedly sprang to his eyes as he gripped the rail of the hospital bed. He blinked a few times to chase the tears away and pressed his lips together.

He cleared his throat and called, "Dad?"

When Roger didn't respond, Makai let go of the bedrail and touched Roger's hand, which laid flat on top of the covers. In a softer voice, Makai asked, "Daddy?"

"He can't hear you," a female voice said from the doorway.

He had asked himself, when he'd allowed himself to think about it over the years, if he would remember what she looked or sounded like. Even though he wasn't looking at the door, he knew it was Mya. He instantly recognized her voice. The tears came back, but he tried his damnedest to keep them right where they were, and not let them spill over.

Mya sounded like she'd come closer to the bed when she said, "He can't feel anything, can't hear anything. The machines are living for him."

Makai stood there, stiff as a board. He wasn't sure if Lanai knew what was going on, but she moved closer to him and slipped her hand inside his, squeezing his hand reassuringly. He blinked a few more times, clearing his throat again. He was determined not to cry, especially not in front of Mya.

He asked, "Where's Malik?"

"Went downstairs to get some coffee. He's been here quite a while," she explained.

Makai touched his father's head where the gash was. He couldn't believe this was his dad—the strongest man he'd ever known and always looked up to—looking fragile and lifeless in a hospital bed. He found himself wishing Roger would wake up, if only for a second, so he could see his eyes one last time. He wanted to be able to talk to him one last time.

Not liking how his emotions had him feeling, he took his hand out of Lanai's and moved back from the bed. Under his breath, he growled, "Uggghhhh."

He looked at Lanai and said, "I'm gonna go find Malik. I'll be back."

Lanai nodded, her eyes showing concern for him.

"He'll be back," Mya said.

Makai walked towards the door as if she never said a word. He needed to get out of that room, because he didn't know how long he'd be able to hold on to his emotions. Makai didn't deal with emotions well, and he knew he could only hold them in for so long. Before he could make it to the door, Malik came walking in with two cups of coffee. Seeing his big brother, Malik immediately embraced him, coffee in hand. Makai hugged him back; feeling like someone had taken a rusted knife, stabbed him in the heart with it, and slowly and deliberately pulling it downward.

Makai stood back, asking, "You alright?"

Stress etched all over Malik's handsome brown face, a face that was almost identical to Makai's. Malik nodded. "I'm okay...considering."

Makai nodded. He asked, "Take a walk with me?"

Malik readily agreed; Makai could've asked him to take a walk off a bridge with him and he'd comply. Malik handed a cup of coffee to Mya, and walked out into the hallway with Makai. Makai reached into his pocket when he saw that no one was in the hallway, and pulled out the bundled money that he'd taken from the briefcase. Without a word, he slipped the money into Malik's jacket pocket. Malik put his left hand in his pocket and felt what his brother slipped in there.

He argued, "Kai, I can't..."

"I'm not askin' you," Makai said sternly.

"I can't take this," Malik protested.

Makai pointed out, "It's already in your pocket."

Malik was clearly uncomfortable taking any money from his brother, but this large amount of money had him ready to give it back.

Makai said, "Look, I know you, Nina, and the kids could use it. Stop being so fuckin' proud. I ain't holdin' it over your head. As far as I'm concerned, it never happened."

"You don't get it," Malik said. "I'm a man. I'm supposed to be able to provide for my family without anybody's help."

"Alright, 'Roger'," Makai joked. Whenever one of them did or said something reminiscent of what their dad would say or do, they would call each other their father's name. Makai's voice turned serious. "You do take care of your family every day without anybody's help. You know when I can, I'm gonna help you. I'm takin' no for an answer. The issue is dead."

Hearing the finality in Makai's voice, Malik decided to drop the subject. They both knew it wasn't going to be worth the argument. They walked a few feet away from the door of the room and stood up against the wall. Makai asked, "So what are the doctors saying?"

"He has internal bleeding and there's a lot of damage. They're trying to get the bleeding on the brain to stop," Malik explained. "He has damage to his spine, both his legs are broken, and several ribs are broken. They're worried about blood clots, too. They put him in a medically-induced coma to keep him from being in so much pain. If he was awake, he'd be beyond miserable."

Makai nodded, wishing there was something he could do. "So what is it that they're saying can be done?"

Malik shrugged his shoulders. "Keep him comfortable until we decide as a family to take him off."

Makai looked at him with tear-filled, hurt eyes. "They can't fix what's wrong?"

Malik's eyes filled with tears, too. He just shook his head no. When he found his voice, he said, "Certain things can't be fixed."

"Nah, man," Makai said, not wanting to accept that the last time he'd talked to his father would be the last time. "They gotta do something. There's gotta be something. Who's his doctor?"

"Patel," Malik said. "He hasn't completely given up on Dad. But they're doing everything they can. They don't have control over certain stuff, Kai."

After a few moments of standing in the hall in their own thoughts, Makai suggested, "C'mon. Let's go back in the room."

He put his arm around his little brother's shoulder and they walked back into the room. They stood on the side of the hospital bed, looking at their father's state in disbelief. The room was silent for a while, until Mya asked, "So have you guys made a decision?"

"Decision for what?" Makai asked, not looking at her.

"A decision about what you're going to do with your father's condition," she elaborated. "Whether or not you guys are going to let him suffer or not."

"What?" Makai asked, not believing his ears. "It's been barely twenty-four hours and you're ready to kill him off?"

"I'm not ready to kill him off," she countered. "I'm thinking about what he would want and not my own selfish needs. Roger wouldn't want to live like this. You know he wouldn't."

"How do you know what he would want?" Makai asked, bitterness lacing his tone. "You didn't stick around to see what *anybody* would want, like, or anything. But you know a lot about being selfish."

"Makai, I know you're angry—" she began.

"Nah, I'm not," he lied, cutting her off. "I'm pointing out the fact that since you disappeared twenty-*two* years ago, you lost the ability to vote on family situations."

"I am still your mother," she said, standing from the couch next to the bed.

"Wrong. You gave birth to me. Any animal can do that," he spat.

Mya's mouth dropped in disbelief, but she recovered. "You have every right to be upset. I know I hurt you, your brother, and your father. But think about what your father would want."

Makai finally looked at her, his eyes shooting darts of hate at her. "Why are you here? Are you the beneficiary on one of his policies or something?"

"I'm here because he would want me to be," she replied indignantly, slightly raising her chin.

"Says who?"

"Says *him*," she returned. "Your father and I have been seeing each other for the past few years. He didn't want to tell you two, because he was afraid of how you guys would feel. We were going to get remarried."

Makai let out a dry laugh that sounded more like he'd choked. "That's funny. You walk out on your kids twenty-two years ago, wait until they're grown, and then you slide back into your ex-husband's life. For what? What are you getting out of this?"

"I love your father," she said, sounded defensive.

"Bullshit," he countered. "You love you and what you can get from people."

Her face showed obvious offense at his accusations. "You *will not* talk to me that way. You *will* show me some respect."

"Look, I ain't doin' this with you," he conceded. "I give you what you deserve. My brother and I will talk about our options to do what's best for our dad. I don't care if you're here or not, just don't say anything to me. Period."

Mya came from around the end of the hospital bed. Makai looked more like Roger than he did Mya, but he'd inherited her thick eyebrows and forehead. As her forehead creased, her eyebrows came together. She was about a foot shorter than Makai was. She came within a foot of him, measuring almost a foot shorter, pointing her finger at him.

She issued him a direct warning. "I don't give a fuck what your problem is. I am the woman that carried you in my body. I brought you into this world, and nigga, I will take you out. You will show me respect or I will split your head open. Do you understand me?"

Makai didn't answer and he wasn't fazed by what she'd said, either. She was right; she'd carried him in her body and brought him into the world. But she'd also abandoned him for reasons unknown and he no longer desired to learn. She destroyed his idea of what a mother-son relationship should be like. She'd killed the part of him that she should've nurtured. Mya was the reason that he'd disrespected and discarded women the way he did, and took Lanai through everything he'd put her through.

She wasn't around to answer any questions that he had. She was nowhere to be found, when a whore he could've sworn would be his wife, broke his fifteen-year-old heart. She wasn't around when his son died or when his daughter was born. Mya had no idea she had a granddaughter, and Makayla didn't know Mya as her grandmother. He had no mother around to chastise him when he did something stupid; she was busy chasing whatever she felt like would make her happy.

"Boy, you better answer me," she said in a low, threatening tone.

Malik stepped in between them, taking her by the shoulders and guiding her back to the couch. He said, "Mom, relax. Just have a seat. You don't need to get yourself worked up and Dad doesn't need any excitement around him. Let's just focus on what's best for Dad."

Makai had a lot that he wanted to say to her, but his pride wouldn't let him. His pride kept him from asking her why she left, and to tell her how much she'd hurt him and his brother. He had no clue why his dad had begun seeing her again—if that was the truth—because what she'd done was unforgiveable. She'd gotten to live free and clear, while their dad had to sacrifice everything. Makai hated her for it. He wasn't going to show her an ounce of respect, because she didn't deserve it. *If she was on fire, I wouldn't piss on her.*

She pointed her finger at Makai and told Malik, "You better talk to your brother. You better tell him something; otherwise your dad won't be the only one in the hospital."

Makai wasn't worried about Mya doing anything to him. He turned his attention back to his father, not even acknowledging Mya anymore. It was quiet in the room for a while until someone came bursting through the door. Makai looked over to see a young girl coming over to the bed with her hand over her mouth. She looked just like a female version of himself and Malik. The right side of her hair was shaved bald and she had long wavy black and brown weave cascading down the left side. Her bracelets and necklaces clinked and clanked as she slid into the space that Makai had stepped back from.

Tears slipped down her pretty face as she mumbled, "Daddy."

"Daddy?" Makai asked, confused. He looked at Malik, who shrugged his shoulders. Malik looked just as lost as Makai did. Both of them looked at Mya, who wouldn't meet either of their stares.

The young girl laid her head on Roger's shoulder, crying softly for a few moments. With her acrylic nails, she touched his face. She lifted her head and asked, "Mommy, is he gonna be okay?"

Mya rose from the couch and went over to the bed, putting a hand on her child's head. Mya's eyes were sad and filled with tears, watching her daughter cry. She shook her head. "No, baby. He's not gonna be okay."

The young girl dropped her head back onto Roger's chest and sobbed. Makai had almost forgotten Lanai was there, until he felt her wrap her arms around his. He looked down at her and she rubbed his arm reassuringly. He looked back at Mya and the girl that was apparently his little sister. Looking at her, he would've guessed that she was a relative; their features were too similar for them not to be related. It just wasn't making sense to him how she was a teenager, she was Roger's daughter, and he knew nothing about her. Mya came around the bed and took her daughter by her shoulders, lifting her from Roger's chest and holding her in her arms. Makai wanted to trip her when she walked over.

Lanai felt his arm tense when Mya came to the side of the bed where he was standing, because she pulled his arm, pulling him back a few steps. Sick of the questions hanging in the air, Makai asked, "What the hell? What is going on?"

Mya shot him a look that he ignored. She sighed, telling him and his brother, "Boys, this is your sister, Raegan."

"Sister," Makai asked. "How old is this sister?"

She looked down and dabbed at the tears on Raegan's face, being careful not to smear her makeup. "She's sixteen."

"Okay," Makai said. "So let me get this straight. You disappear from our lives twenty-two years ago, you and Dad link up four years after that—keep it from us—and you get pregnant again? Then you all of a sudden started dealing with Dad again when? Are you pregnant now?"

Malik chastised, "Kai, stop."

"Nah, I'm not gonna stop," Makai said. "I wanna know. Shit, you should wanna know. Are you pregnant now?"

"No, I am not pregnant," she retorted, completely annoyed.

"When you think shit can't get any worse," he mumbled. "Well, we're not making any decisions about anything concerning Dad, until I talk to the doctor."

"Who died and made you boss?" Mya challenged.

"My dad made me the beneficiary of his estate, when we sat down and mapped out his will four years ago," Makai revealed. He taunted, "Or didn't he tell you that when y'all were laid up?"

He looked down at Lanai and said, "You can go back home, if you want. I'm staying until I talk to the doctor."

She said, "I'll go call Nicky. I'll tell her we should be home tomorrow some time."

When Lanai walked out of the room, Mya asked, "Who is she?"

"None of your business," Makai answered flatly.

He pushed the button on the bedrail TV remote and turned on the TV. He scanned through the channels until he found ESPN, and sat in the chair closest to the door. He looked at the time on his watch and saw that it was almost 5 am. He wanted to catch a nap before the doctor came in, but he doubted that he'd be able to do that.

Mya had taken Raegan to the couch with her and sat down. It made Makai sick to his stomach to watch Mya fussing over Raegan, who was clearly old enough to do for herself. He held no ill feelings for Raegan; as far as he was concerned, she was just a casualty of a war she had no knowledge of. Mya just seemed like she was doing too much. It was almost as if she was showing Makai and Malik that she was really a good mother. Makai would never believe that, no matter who told him.

He decided to push the questions that he had to the back of his mind, propped his head up on his fist, and watched the old basketball game that was on. His eyelids were getting heavy and he'd almost drifted off to sleep, until Lanai came back into the room with two white Styrofoam cups. She handed him one and stood quietly next to the chair that he sat in. He took her wrist, pulling her down into his lap. She rested her head against his shoulder and took out her phone, going to her Bible app.

He asked, "You ain't done reading the whole thing, yet?"

"Uh-uh," she said, bringing her legs around over his. "I read whatever the plan has for me on that day. If I need more encouragement, I'll read the devotional or I'll read *Our Daily Bread*."

He wrapped his left arm around her, put his cup on the floor, and propped his chin up on his fist. She rested her head in the crook of his arm and read while he dozed off to sleep.

CHAPTER TWENTY-SIX

"Hello," Lanai asked, answering her cell phone while she sat at her desk in the lobby of her office.

"Hi, Ms. Wilson?" a woman asked.

Lanai answered, "Yes."

"Ms. Wilson, this is Amanda from the Attorney General's office." "I was told to give you a call and let you know that the jury has a verdict."

Lanai's hands froze over the samples that she'd been going through. She said, "Okay. What now?"

"You can go to the courtroom to hear the verdict yourself, or you can wait for a call back," Amanda replied.

"I'll be right over there," Lanai said, ending the call.

Katara looked up from a file she'd been going through and asked, "What's up?"

"The jury has a verdict."

"Great. It only took them two and a half months," Katara quipped.

Lanai grabbed her purse and dropped her phone in it, taking her keys out the bag. She got up from the desk and headed for the door, saying, "I know. I'm gonna go see what it is."

"I'll come with you," Katara offered.

Lanai stopped at the door and looked at her. She said, "Okay."

Katara closed the file, grabbed her phone and purse, and followed Lanai out the door. Lanai locked up the office, then they got in her car. She drove the few minutes over to the court on Federal Street, found a parking space, and she and Katara prepared to get out and head for the court. Katara's phone went off in her purse. She said, "Hold up one second. That might be Larry." She fished the phone out of her purse and blew a breath when she saw Vi's name scroll across the screen, then answered, "Hey, Ma."

She was silent for a few minutes, then she looked up at Lanai. Lanai gave her a questioning look and Katara put her finger up to tell her to wait a minute. Katara said, "Oh, my goodness. I'm sorry... It's not that... She does... Ma, let's not do that again. You're stressed... you've gotten some horrible news, but it's no one's fault. Wow, that's crazy. It's mean, but we expected it. I know you didn't, but we did. Well, Ma, I'ma call you back. I can't take my phone in where I'm going. Okay. I love you, too."

Katara ended the call and dropped her phone back into her purse. She got out and walked with Lanai across the street towards the courthouse steps. Lanai asked, "What happened?"

"Dad's wife took him off life support. She didn't let Ma see him for the final time to say her goodbyes. The only reason Ma found out was because she went up to the hospital to see him and his room was empty," Katara explained.

Lanai looked at her with a shocked expression on her face. She asked, "Are you serious?"

Katara nodded. "As a heart attack. She won't tell Ma what the funeral arrangements are or nothing."

Lanai sadly shook her head as they climbed the steps. She said, "She shoulda known that woman was gonna do that. I don't know why she went back."

"She never left," Katara retorted, walking through the double set of automatic doors.

"What? She's been in Arizona the whole time?" Lanai exclaimed.

Katara nodded her head, waiting in line behind Lanai to go through the metal detector. "She was determined to be with him until the end. She would go every day. None of the staff told her the family was thinking about it, or that any paperwork had been signed."

"His wife got the last laugh," Lanai said, walking through the metal detector after emptying the contents of her pockets into one of the bins.

"I always knew she would," Katara said, following Lanai's lead. "That woman had put up with his infidelity for too long not to get him back in some sort of way. I'm surprised that she waited as long as she did to pull the plug."

Lanai said, "I think she loved him; that's what took her so long."

Katara made a face. "Love ain't no excuse to put up with stupidity."

Deciding not to delve further into that messy conversation, Lanai said, "Well, I pray she accepts the fact that she can't change it. I pray for her sanity."

"She said she's gonna find out where the funeral is and go," Katara revealed.

Lanai giggled and shook her head as they climbed the marble steps to the second floor. "That's your mom."

"Honey," Katara commented, shaking her head in agreement.

They arrived at the doors of the courtroom just as the ADA was going in. He smiled at Lanai and Katara, holding the door for them. "Nice to see you again, Ms. Wilson. I see you got my message."

Lanai smiled in return. "Yes, I did. Thank you for having her call me."

Lanai and Katara took a seat on one of the benches on the right side of the room, a few minutes before the court officer came in, ordering everybody to stand. Once the judge was inside and seated, everyone was instructed to have a seat. The jury filed into the room. While each jury member took their seat, Lanai tried to read their faces. Every one of them had a poker face. She looked over to the defendant's table where Sade sat. Lanai could only see the back and some of the side profile of Sade, but she didn't look any better than when Lanai had testified over two months before.

An unexpected feeling washed over Lanai. She felt sorry for Sade. She'd never imagined feeling anything other disgust or hatred. But she actually felt bad that Sade was lost in the same world that Lanai had been saved from. Lanai found herself asking God to help guide Sade through it, because she knew what it was like to be lost. Lanai had been blessed enough not to have a child be impacted negatively by her stupidity and decisions.

The judge asked, "Jury Foreman, I understand that a verdict has been reached?"

The foreman of the jury stood up and nodded, "Yes, Your Honor, we have. We the jury, on the charge of attempted murder, find the defendant guilty."

Sade gasped, as her mouth fell wide open.

The foreman continued, "On the charge of endangering the welfare of a minor child in the first degree, we the jury, find the defendant guilty."

Sade jumped up from her seat. She screamed, "I didn't endanger my daughter! I tried to *protect* her!"

The judge banged his gavel several times, yelling for order. "Counselor, get your client under control."

The public defender grabbed Sade by the wrist and snatched her down into her seat. They were arguing with each other back and forth through clenched teeth. The judge banged his gavel once more, giving Sade an evil, warning glare. Sade was quiet, but she was visibly shaking.

The judge told the court officer, "Take the defendant into custody. She will be remanded to Baylor Women's Correctional Institution until sentencing. Court is adjourned."

The court officer instructed, "All rise!"

The judge moved so fast to get out the courtroom that he was almost a blur. Lanai saw the agitated look on his face and knew that he was fed up with the disrespect shown in his courtroom. The jury was escorted out, but almost all of them were looking back over their shoulders at Sade, who was putting up a fight with the court officer attempting to put her in handcuffs. Lanai and Katara watched in amazement. Sade was yelling and screaming as the officer pinned her to the table, with her arm bent behind her back. Her face was smooshed into the wooden table.

The bailiff went over to assist with subduing Sade, after he called in a code over the walkie-talkie secured to his left shoulder. Other court officers and a state policeman came rushing into the courtroom. Sade kicked and tried to push herself up off the table. Lanai wasn't sure what she was under the influence of, but whatever it was, it was definitely making her give them a run for their money. She somehow got her arm loose and slapped one of the court officers. He jumped back, allowing her a brief second to stand up.

The state trooper took her by the wrist, slammed her down on the wooden table, and snatched her other wrist behind her back. Taking his left hand, he held her wrists in place with her hands turned upward to immobilize her arms, taking his cuffs out of the holder on his utility belt. He put the cuffs on her and had her standing upright in about 30 seconds. The court officer that she'd slapped took her by the crook of her arm and led her out of the courtroom. The other court officers and the state trooper left the courtroom as if nothing had happened, returning to their posts.

Lanai turned and looked at Katara, who had an amused look on her face. Lanai shook her head and Katara laughed. "Girl! Your girl went *ham*!"

Lanai shook her head in pity. She knew she was going to miss the sentencing phase of the trial. She really didn't want to keep watching the spectacle that Sade had turned into. She silently prayed for God to touch Sade's heart and mind, for her to find some peace. The last thing that Lanai wanted to portray was perfection because she was far from it, but she definitely was working on being a better person. She'd recently learned that praying for someone would help them more than gossiping about them. She got up and led the way out of the courtroom.

As they got near her car, Katara suggested, "Let's go out to lunch."

"Go where?" Lanai asked, unlocking the doors from the keypad.

Katara shrugged, "I don't care. I just need a breather. Let's go to TGI Fridays."

Lanai agreed, "Okay."

They drove the few minutes to TGI Friday's and the parking lot was packed with lunch-goers. Lanai waited for a car to back out of the parking space, and said, "This is gonna take forever, Tara."

"It's not like we gotta clock back in," Katara pointed out, checking her phone.

They got out and went into the restaurant, having to ease around people that were waiting in the entryway to be seated. The hostess greeted them with a smile, saying, "Welcome to TGI Friday's. How many in your party?"

"Just the two of us," Lanai answered.

"It'll be about a thirty-minute wait for a table."

Lanai's head snapped around to Katara. Lanai said, "I'm not waiting thirty minutes just to be seated, then I gotta wait all over again to get my food."

"You big baby," Katara teased.

The hostess offered a solution. "We have seating at the bar."

As Lanai was about to object, Katara agreed, "Okay, we'll take it. Thank you."

Lanai looked at her sister funny, but followed her to the bar. They sat in the last two seats at the bar, with Katara putting her purse on the bar in front of her and Lanai holding hers in her lap. The bartender came over immediately, asking what he could get them. Katara ordered a double shot of Patrón and a Long Island Iced Tea. Lanai didn't hide the look of surprise on her face when she asked, "Celebrating something?"

Katara took the double shot from the bartender, almost before he could set it down, and downed it faster than he made it. She made a face as the harsh liquor burned its way down her throat. She shook her head no, as she sipped from the straw in the Long Island Iced Tea. The bartender asked Lanai what she needed and she said, "Uh, just water."

"You're not drinking with me?" Katara asked, taking a gulp from her straw.

"I gotta pick up the baby and go up to Thomas Jefferson this evening with Makai," Lanai explained. "He hasn't had a chance to get another vehicle yet, with everything that's been going on."

Katara nodded, waving her hand at the bartender to get his attention. When he came back over, she asked, "Can I get another double?"

"Whoa," Lanai said. "What's going on? You ain't drank like this in years."

"I'm thirsty," Katara commented just before knocking back the double shot.

Lanai took away the half empty glass of alcohol from in front of Katara and held it away from her. She said, "You're not getting it back until you tell me what's going on."

"Alright," Katara caved. When Lanai gave her back the glass, she said, "I'll tell you later."

"Oh, no," Lanai replied, reaching for the glass again.

Katara put up her arm to block her sister and laughed, "Alright, okay. I'll tell you. Damn."

When her sister didn't start talking immediately, Lanai gave her an expectant stare. Katara finally said, "Grammy is sick."

"Sick," Lanai echoed. "How sick? And why didn't you tell me?"

"Oww," Katara yelled when Lanai slapped her arm. "I didn't know how serious it was. I thought it was just a cough."

"What is it?"

"Lung cancer."

"Lung cancer!"

Katara nodded her head, taking another gulp through the straw. "And them niggas are still stressing her, acting a damn fool. Tyshawn, his baby momma and their three kids are living there, in that small one-bedroom apartment with her. BJ is supposed to be going to live there in a couple weeks, when he gets out for the seventeenth time. You know Craig has his own place, but Grammy is paying all his bills. I have no clue what that dummy is doing with all his money."

"I thought Grammy was moving," Lanai said.

Katara nodded. "She did. When she moved, they followed her."

Shocked, Lanai asked, "All those people are living in that housing for the elderly?"

Katara nodded again, draining the contents of her drink through the straw. She motioned for the bartender to refill her drink. When the bartender came back over, Lanai ordered two endless apps of boneless wings and Tuscan spinach dip. She knew Katara wasn't going to eat a meal while she drank, but she needed some kind of food to soak up the liquor she was drinking like water.

Lanai asked, "Why don't we just get her a place closer to us? Or she can just live with one of us."

Katara gave her sister an incredulous look. "Absolutely not! I will not be paying the bills for these niggas to live it up. She won't leave Baltimore, anyway. BJ's probation is contingent upon him staying in Baltimore County. She already told me he doesn't have anybody and she won't leave him stranded, as she put it."

Lanai shook her head. It was a sad, sickening situation. Katara's grandmother, the only grandmother that Lanai had ever known, had raised Katara and her brothers from birth, because their biological mother was a prostitute that refused to get her life together. She'd had no idea who their fathers were, and all four of them had different fathers. Katara had lucked out when Vi had taken her into her home and raised her as her own. All of Katara's brothers seemed to be content with sucking the life out of their grandmother, which drained Katara. She'd begged her grandmother for years to cut all of them off, but Grammy wouldn't hear of it.

Lanai asked, "So, what are you gonna do? I know you're gonna do something."

"Actually," Katara began, in between sips, "I have no idea what to do. I want to help her, but they're killing her and she won't let them go. I got nothing."

"I'll talk to her," Lanai conceded. "I'll talk her into moving down here and I'll get a bigger place. I gotta get a bigger place, anyway. They won't follow her to my house."

Katara chuckled, "Oh, but they will."

Exasperated, Lanai asked, "Well, what are we gonna do, Tara?"

"What can we do, Nai?" Katara returned, looking at her with drunken eyes. "I wanna help her, I do. But you can't help somebody fix something that they don't view as being wrong."

"You make a good point," Lanai agreed. "So what about this cancer? What are they doing to treat it?"

"Chemotherapy. She started treatments a couple months ago," Katara said, pushing her straw around in the glass.

"How is she doing with it?"

"Not good," Katara sighed. "Every time she has a treatment, she looks so drained. I just wanna take it from her. I'd rather it be me than her."

Lanai pointed out, "But if it were you, your daughter would have to go through what you're going through."

Katara nodded her head. Out of nowhere, she burst into tears. Lanai took her sister's face into her hands and pulled Katara to her, laying Katara's head on Lanai's shoulder. Katara sobbed, "I just want her to be better. I don't want her to have to suffer."

Lanai rubbed Katara's face soothingly. "Sssshhhhh, Tara. She's gonna be okay."

Katara cried, "She's not. She's dying. I know she's dying."

Lanai swallowed the lump that formed in her throat. She didn't want to admit it, but Katara was right. They both knew that Grammy wasn't going to live forever, but for her to have to die slowly and painfully was harder to accept. Lanai said, "You know she can't live forever."

"I know. I just want some more time with her," Katara said. "I just want her to live her last days without the burden and stress."

"We'll work together to lighten her load," Lanai promised.

Katara sat up and pushed her hair away from her face. She took a napkin and wiped her eyes. She said, "And me and Larry are arguing like every day."

"Since when?" Lanai asked, not hiding her surprise. She'd never seen Larry and Katara exchange an evil look, let alone argue.

Katara wiped her eyes with a fresh napkin. She revealed, "Since he feels like I'm spending all my time either working or being there for everyone else. He feels like I'm not there for him."

"There for him for what?"

"We don't do anything together anymore. We don't go anywhere. I'm always gone."

Lanai felt a pang of guilt. She knew that Katara constantly being there for her was more than likely the beginning of the strain on their relationship. She said, "Then you gotta make time for him."

"Grammy needs me," Katara answered.

"Well, I'll take turns with you taking her to chemo," Lanai offered.

Katara asked, "How? You got Makayla, Makai, his dad, work, and your own life."

"First of all, we need to bring Grammy closer. Period," Lanai demanded. "I'll make time. Let Tyshawn, BJ, and Craig fend for themselves. If they think they're bringing that madness here, I have another thought for them. We'll do our best to make sure that her last days are as enjoyable as they can be."

"I'll see," Katara said, not sounding convinced. "Let me talk to her."

Lanai responded, "No. Don't tell her anything. If you tell her, she'll tell them, then everybody's preparing to move to Delaware. Let's set it up and just go get her."

"You know Grammy doesn't like surprises," Katara reminded her.

Lanai shrugged her shoulders. "So what? Something's gotta give and you can't keep pretending like you don't have the weight of the world on your shoulders. You can't carry it alone. Let me help you, instead of you getting shit-faced at the bar."

Katara laughed and nodded her head. She crumpled up the napkin that she had wiped her eyes with and tossed it on the bar. She took down her purse, searching through it for her wallet. Lanai had gone into her wallet and pulled out her debit card. She handed it to the bartender and told her sister, "I got it. You just eat this food they're about to bring out."

When the food was placed in front of them, they finished their time at the bar laughing and reminiscing. They laughed so hard that they were in tears and their stomachs hurt. Lanai loved every minute of it. It had been a long time since she'd been able to just spend time with her sister, without work or other obligations interrupting them. She loved seeing Katara look relaxed for the first time in months.

They prepared to leave and Lanai asked, "Why don't you just take the rest of the day off, go home, and do something with Larry. Or do something *to* Larry. That's probably his problem."

Katara laughed, "You're probably right. It has been a while."

"Girl, you better go handle your business," Lanai exclaimed, getting into the driver's seat.

When they got back to the office, Katara got into her car after hugging Lanai extra tight and headed home. Lanai went back into the office to resume her business day. She went to her desk and checked her voicemails, her attention being drawn to one voicemail in particular. Jamal's voice came on the line:

"Hey, Lanai. This is Jamal. I know we talked earlier last week and you were waiting for the marble to come in. But I wanted to reach out to you to see what your schedule looked like. I was thinking maybe we could get some drinks or something. Just give me a call when you get this message. Have a good day."

Lanai pressed the number 7 to delete the message, feeling a little weird. If it had been a year ago, she would've hopped on the opportunity to go out for drinks with Jamal. Over the years, in the back of her mind, she'd toyed with the idea of what things would've been like with him, if they'd been able to explore. She had always considered him a friend, but she had begun to develop feelings for him. They'd spent so much time together, talking and getting to know one another, before Makai made her move to Dover. When she went through physical therapy, her thoughts went to the what-ifs a lot more often; she just never tried to look him up or get in touch with him.

She felt like it was unfortunate that they linked back up when she was no longer available. Part of her wanted to see where things would lead. That same part of her felt like he would've been good for her. She'd even wondered if her life would've taken such a drastic change, if she'd still had Jamal in her life. When she was in contact with Jamal all those years ago, she'd felt like she had an objective listening ear. She could count on Katara being there for her, but Jamal provided a male point of view that she valued. He helped her see things from a different perspective.

She blew a breath. It was a no-brainer. She'd have to call him back and let him down easy. If something could've been between them, that idea was dead. She was in a relationship with Makai. She wanted to give to him what she expected to receive. Regardless of the curves that life threw them, she intended to work hard on being the kind of woman that could look him in the eye, that could hold her head up, and the kind of woman that he wanted to marry. She wanted to give him her all, and building a relationship with Makayla was even more incentive to do the right thing. The phone call would just have to wait until tomorrow.

CHAPTER TWENTY-SEVEN

Makai flopped on the bed and took off his sneakers. He put them neatly up against the wall by the door and pulled his shirt over his head. He'd been stressed and tension seemed to take up permanent residence in his neck and shoulders. He rubbed the back of his neck with his right hand, heading for the bathroom. He figured that a hot shower should loosen up his neck and shoulders, if only temporarily.

He'd made dinner and put Lanai's plate in the microwave since she was working late. She'd told him that she had a client to see that could only meet after 5 pm. He'd gone and picked up Makayla from her new daycare that he wasn't completely sold on. Between going to the hospitals to watch the machines breathe for Ms. Hazel, and the machines breathe for his dad, Makai was ready to pull what little hair that he had out.

He'd put Makayla to bed after giving her dinner and a bath. She and Lanai were the only bright spots of his life lately. He went in the bathroom and turned on the shower to the hottest temperature. As he took off his undershirt, he heard the door, heels clicking on the floor, then nothing. In his mind, he knew that Lanai had stopped into Makayla's room to kiss her, before she came into their room. He figured that she probably had her bag in one hand and her heels in the other.

He took off his jeans, taking the belt out of the loops and tossing the jeans in the dirty clothes hamper, when Lanai appeared in the doorway. She smiled, "Hey, baby."

He returned a weary, "Hey."

"Awww," she said, dropping her shoes by the door and her purse on the bed. With arms outstretched, she walked over to him, smiling. She cooed, "Come here, baby. What's the matter?"

Annoyed, Makai said, "Not now, Lanai. I'm not in the mood."

She frowned and stopped in her tracks. She dropped her arms to her sides and asked, "What's wrong with you?"

"Nothing. I just wanna get a shower and go to bed," he answered.

He moved over to the dresser to get a pair of boxers and a pair of pajama pants. He felt like he had absolutely no energy. He flopped down on the side of the bed and dropped his head into his hands, blowing an exasperated breath. He just wanted to get a little relief, just a second for all the stress and bad news to go away. He'd always been strong, even when no one else was, but every part of him was drained. He felt like he had nothing left to give anyone; it felt like a huge task to breathe. Giving up had never been an option for him, but lately, he'd been having those thoughts.

He felt Lanai's hands on his shoulders as she stood in front of him, in between him and the dresser. She rubbed the back of his head, telling him, "Baby, it'll be okay."

Pushing his thoughts and feelings aside, he took a deep breath and sat up straight. He really didn't have time to dwell on his feelings. He looked up at her and with tired eyes, asked, "How was your day?"

"My day was awesome," she answered immediately. "But I don't wanna talk about that. I wanna talk about what's bothering you."

"I don't wanna talk about it right now," he replied. "I just wanna take a shower and go to sleep."

She lovingly rubbed his face. Respecting his wishes, she gave in. "Okay. We can talk later."

He heard his cell phone ring and asked, "Can you get that? It's over there."

She went around to the other side of the bed and picked his cell phone up off his nightstand. "Hello? Yes, hold on one second."

She brought the phone to him and he asked, "Who is it?"

She shrugged her shoulders and extended the phone to him.

He took the phone, asking, "Hello?"

"Hi, Makai?" the female asked.

"Yeah?"

"Makai, this is Hazel's daughter, Natalie."

"Hi, Natalie. How are you? How is Ms. Hazel? When I came up this morning, she still was unresponsive."

"Yeah..." Natalie sounded like she was having a hard time speaking for a moment. She said, "I wanted to call and give you an update."

"Okay," he said, not liking the tone of the conversation.

She continued, "It was a hard decision to make, but after talking with a few family members, we decided to take her off life support. We don't believe that she would've wanted to live like that, not able to live, breathe, or function on her own. I know you were close to her, so I wanted to call and let you know. I'll keep you updated with the funeral arrangements."

"Okay," was all he said. He wasn't sure if she was done with the conversation or not, but he put the phone down on the bed next to him. He felt like he was in a daze. He knew with her age that she wasn't going to live forever, but he thought he'd at least have the opportunity to talk with her one more time. He wanted to tell her thank you for everything; he wanted the chance to say goodbye. He didn't feel the tears well up in his eyes or the first one slip down his face.

Crying felt foreign to him, he hadn't cried since he was a little boy. He'd wanted to cry when he'd had his heart broken at 15, but he'd made himself redirect the feelings and energy. He remembered the tears welling up in his eyes when Lanai left him, but he'd refused to let them fall.

He would never have known the tear even fell, if it weren't for Lanai wiping it away. He looked up at her with lost eyes and she pulled his head to her, wrapping her hands around his head. He didn't want to give into the emotions that washed over him. He didn't want to feel what he was feeling; it was simpler just to push them away, go take a shower, and go to sleep.

He intended to push her away and go take his shower. His hands went to her waist, but instead of pushing her away, he wrapped his arms around her waist. The lump that formed in his throat made it difficult to breathe. With her rubbing his head like a mother would rub her son's head, it made it impossible to hold back what he'd been holding in for decades. Silent tears turned into body-racking sobs that made Lanai hold him tighter, her arms going around his shoulders.

She rubbed his back and whispered to him that it was okay to let it out. He held on to her like she was his life raft, and he was in the middle of the Atlantic Ocean. After so many years, he finally shed tears for the childhood experiences that he was cheated out of. His tears allowed him to let go of the hurt that Mya had caused by not caring enough, and putting her own selfish needs before the needs of the children that needed her.

He cried for the one woman that had loved him like a son. He'd only known her for a short time, but it felt like he'd known her all his life. Ms. Hazel welcomed him into her home, life, and heart. She'd treated him and Makayla better than family. He hated that Makayla wouldn't be able to see her anymore. He also carried around the guilt surrounding Ms. Hazel even being in the hospital. He felt like he was the cause of her being in the condition that she was in and he was sorry. It made him angry that he couldn't even tell her face to face that he was sorry.

Tears flowed freely for his father's car accident and a coma that he might possibly never wake up from. He had to accept the fact that someone else's poor decision not to drive safely might cause him to never speak to his father again, and could possibly take his dad away from him forever. There was so much more that he wanted to say and do. Since finding out that he had a little sister, there were so many questions that he wanted answers to. He knew that if Roger died, he more than likely wouldn't get those answers.

Lanai stood there between his knees and held him while he cried. She didn't say much; she didn't rush him. She patiently waited for him to let go of everything that he'd kept pent up forever. He wanted to be conscious of the fact that he was a man and he was supposed to keep it together all the time. Other than Ms. Hazel, Lanai was the only woman that he felt comfortable being vulnerable around. He knew that most women would be okay with a man crying around them initially, but would use that against them later. He wasn't a punk and crying made him feel like a punk.

He finally pulled himself together, releasing the hold that he'd had on Lanai and wiping his face. She helped to wipe his tears, telling him, "Babe, stop holding it in. It's alright to let it out."

Composing himself by taking a deep breath and rubbing a hand over his face, Makai assured her, "I'm fine."

"Honey, you're not fine," she argued in a soft voice. "You're walking around with the weight of the world on your shoulders. That's not good and it's not healthy. You gotta let go of it. Talk to me. Tell me what's wrong."

"I'm fine," he insisted, a little more sternly than he'd intended.

She leaned back so that they were eye-to-eye. Looking him in the eye, she said, "Listen, I know you don't wanna talk, and we work hard to compromise and not argue. But if you don't open up—right now—and tell me what's bothering you, I can promise you a huge argument that will last all night."

"I don't wanna talk about it," he said.

She rebutted, "And I don't like continuing to see you hurt or upset."

When he sat silently, she tried a different angle. She asked, "Didn't you say that you wanted to spend the rest of your life with me?"

He nodded. "I do. I am."

"Do you think we can be happy for the rest of our lives, not addressing what is really wrong," she questioned.

He said, "What's bothering me has nothing to do with you. What's bothering me is old and it ain't really bothering me. Ms. Hazel was taken off of life support."

Lanai nodded her head. "I figured as much. I'm sorry to hear that. But truth be told, that's not all this is about. I need you to trust me."

He rolled his eyes. "I do trust you."

She shook her head. She said, "You don't trust me enough to let me in past a certain point. You let me in as far as you want to; as far as you think is safe, then you shut down on me. You throw up those roadblocks and refuse to let your guard down."

"C'mon, babe," he pleaded. "I'm really not in the mood. I'm sure the shower water is cold by now."

She walked away and went into the bathroom. She turned off the water and the light, returning to the side of the bed where he was. Instead of standing in front of him, she sat down next to him. She said, "By the time you get done telling me everything, the water will have heated back up."

He blew an exasperated breath. They were both equally stubborn. Her stubbornness was attractive to him most of the time, but when he wanted her to let something go and she didn't, her stubbornness was a pain in the ass. He needed her to leave things how they were. He needed her to let him be, while he got himself together, but knowing whom he was dealing with, he knew that wasn't going to happen. Deep down, he was tired of carrying the burden of hurt feelings. As a man, and a black man in general, it wasn't feasible to talk about his innermost hurts and feelings. He'd conditioned himself to "get over it".

He said, "Ms. Hazel was like a mother to me; a mother I never had."

"Wasn't that your mom at the hospital?"

He nodded. "She left twenty-two years ago."

"I remember you telling me your dad raised you," she said. "I never knew it was because she left. Do you know why she left?"

He shook his head, "Nope. My dad didn't do drugs, he didn't beat on her, and he said he never cheated. She just up and left one day and never looked back."

Lanai was quiet for a moment. Then she asked, "How did that make you feel? How does it make you feel now?"

He shrugged his shoulders and made a face. He said, "Back then, I was confused, hurt, and angry. Angry was the emotion that stayed the longest. The other two didn't matter as much. I used my anger towards her to motivate me to make something out of myself. Now, I don't care."

"You care," she argued.

"Nah, I don't."

"You do," Lanai said, nodding her head. "If you didn't, it wouldn't hurt. Clearly, it hurts. I'm saying that from personal experience. You know I know hurt. Admitting what is wrong, releases the powerful hold that whatever it is has on you. Don't be afraid to admit it to me. You know your secrets are safe with me."

"I ain't scared of nothing," he replied, sounding like his pride had been hurt.

She put up her hands defensively, saying, "I'm not attacking your manhood. I'm sharing with you what I learned. I'm gonna love you regardless. In my eyes, you're always gonna be my Superman."

He halfway grinned and dryly said, "Thanks."

"I'm serious," she said.

He was quiet for a moment, thinking about what he actually felt. He said, "I hate her. I thought I was over her leaving, because it had been so long. A part of me wants to not care, 'cause I done came so far in my life. I've done pretty damn good without her help. But there's another part of me that is just pissed the fuck off and hating her. I hate her for being selfish. I could never leave Makayla for any reason, and I'm a man. She carried me and my brother in her body and still found it in herself to leave."

Lanai thought for a moment. She finally said, "You're gonna have to have a conversation with her."

Makai adamantly shook his head. "Fuck that. I ain't talking to that bitch. Fuck her."

"It's not for her, it's for you," Lanai pointed out. "You need to make peace with this, and the only way that's gonna happen, is for you to ask the questions you never got the chance to ask, and say what you never got to say."

He shook his head again and repeated, "I ain't talking to her."

"Then carry around this anger and aggression for the rest of your life," Lanai retorted. "Ruin your daughter's life with your bitterness. Grow into an old miserable man that can't find the strength to confront his past, and take control of the situation."

"I won't grow into an old angry man, 'cause I don't care," he said.

"I said an old *miserable* man," she corrected.

He waved his hand dismissively. "Same shit."

"It's gotta be done," she said quietly.

"I'm done talking," he announced, standing up from the bed and going into the bathroom. He turned the water on again, took off and he tossed his boxers into the dirty clothes hamper, and got in the shower. He wasn't sure what the future held, but he was definitely sure he wasn't going to keep dealing with the emotional bullshit. It was okay for Lanai to fall apart; he'd help her put herself back together. But he'd be damned if he continued to cry and deal with his emotions like a punk. He wasn't a bitch, and he wasn't going to start acting like one.

CHAPTER TWENTY-EIGHT

Lanai followed Makai's lead into Roger's hospital room, barely able to keep up with him. They still had on their clothes from attending Ms. Hazel's funeral, when he'd gotten the phone call that there was a change with his father. The nurse that had called him hadn't given him any other information, other than there was a change. They had raced from Dover, DE to Philadelphia, PA as fast as Lanai's car and the traffic would allow.

They were both surprised to see the head of Roger's bed up in an almost sitting position and Roger's eyes were open. Mya and Raegan were sitting on the couch next to the bed, smiling, until Makai and Lanai had walked into the room. Roger's eyes went to the cause of their change in expression and his eyes lit up. He smiled as much as the oxygen mask would allow him to at his oldest son. It looked like he tried to extend his hand to Makai, but all he managed was extending his fingers.

Makai seemed to know exactly what he meant. He went to the side of the bed and took his dad's hand. He said, "Hey, Dad. How you feeling?"

From behind the mask, he said, "Sore."

Makai chuckled. "You should be sore. Thank God you can feel."

Roger nodded his head in agreement, and it looked like it took effort for him to swallow.

Makai asked, "How long you been awake?"

Roger's eyes went to Mya as if to ask her how long it had been. He looked back at Makai and said, "A couple hours."

"You ate yet?"

Roger shook his head. "They got me on a liquid diet right now. I want a cheesesteak."

Everyone in the room laughed. Makai said, "Dad, you gotta follow the doctor's orders."

The noise of someone coming into the room drew everyone's attention to the door. They saw Malik and a woman walking into the room. Malik's worried expression was quickly replaced with relief when he saw that their dad was sitting up and talking. Makai stepped back and allowed Malik to stand next to their father and hold his hand.

Roger looked past Malik and partially smiled at Lanai. He said, "Hey, beautiful lady. How are you?"

Lanai smiled in return from where she stood and answered, "I'm good, Mr. Roger. How are you?"

"How many times do I have to tell you to call me Dad?" he chastised jokingly. "When did you cut that beautiful hair?"

As a reflex, she rubbed the back of her neck with a sheepish grin. She said, "It's been a while."

He made a sound, then looked to the petite, brown-skinned woman that had come in with Malik. She had big brown eyes and a reddish-brown wig on her head. He said, "Nina, how are you? How are my grandbabies?"

Nina nodded, smiling. "They're all good...missing their Pop-Pop."

"Give them my love," he asked her.

She nodded and promised, "I will, Dad."

Roger told Malik, "Son, take this damn thing off my face."

Both Makai and Malik protested. Makai said, "Dad, you need it so you can breathe."

Roger grunted and moved his head as much as he could, trying to move it on his own. He insisted, "Take this damn thing off, so I can say what I need to say. I'm breathing just fine."

Makai asked, with concern in his tone, "You can't lift your arms?"

"They want him to keep them straight because of the IVs," Mya answered, inserting herself into the conversation.

Lanai looked at Makai to see how he'd react to his mother's input. She saw that his jaw tensed when Mya spoke. Lanai really wanted him to address what was wrong so that he could get over it. She wanted him to forgive his mother, but she knew that concept might be a little too far-fetched for the moment.

Roger ordered, "Malik, take this mask off."

Doing as he was told, Malik took the oxygen mask off and slipped it over Roger's graying head, laying it on the top of the bed. Roger looked from Malik to Makai and said, "Listen. I got something to tell you boys—"

"We know we have a sister," Makai interrupted.

Roger shot him a glance that let him know not to interrupt him again and Makai stood there, silently waiting for Roger to say what he wanted to say. Roger said, "Yes, you do have a sister. I feel like I owe you boys an apology, 'cause I found out about her four years ago and I just didn't know how to tell you."

"Why was it kept from you for twelve years?" Makai questioned, apparently intending for the question to be a shot at Mya.

Roger said, "That ain't important. What's important is she's your sister and you need to get to know one another. I...I want..." The wheezing and coughs prevented him from finishing his sentence.

Malik rushed to put the mask back over Roger's nose and mouth. Raegan and Mya jumped up from the couch to stand closer to him, on the other side of the bed Mya rubbed his arm, telling him to take it easy and to breathe.

Makai remarked, "Dad, you're gonna have to keep that on. Talk around it or don't talk at all."

Roger concentrated on taking in the oxygen that came through the mask, but he also shot Makai a warning look. After a few minutes of taking the deepest breaths that his lungs could handle, Roger ordered, "Talk to your mother."

Makai's face looked like he'd just been slapped. Protest was written all over his face as he shook his head and asked, "For what?"

"Don't question me, boy," Roger said. "Do...do what I tell you to do."

"Dad—" Makai began.

"They'll talk," Malik interrupted. He saw that Roger was beginning to get more upset, and going back and forth with Makai was only going to make things worse. Lanai was grateful for Malik's interruption.

Roger gave Makai another look and nodded his head at Malik. Roger said, "You make sure they do."

Malik promised, "I will. Dad, you relax. Everything's gonna be fine."

Lanai carefully looked Makai over. She knew him and she knew that he wouldn't willingly talk to Mya. She knew that he respected his father, but talking to Mya was something he was going to avoid. Lanai watched as Mya, Raegan, and Malik encouraged Roger to take it easy and breathe.

Makai turned to her and asked, "You ready to go? We gotta go pick Makayla up."

Caught off guard, Lanai recovered quickly. She nodded and prepared to lead the way out the door.

Roger spoke up, "Kai, where you going?"

"I gotta go pick the baby up," he said. He wasn't entirely lying. She was with the babysitter they kept on standby for just in case, and Makayla was in very good hands. They didn't have to pick Makayla up until they were ready.

"Hold on," Roger wheezed. He pleaded, "Please talk to your mother. Malik talked to her."

Makai said dryly, "There's nothing to talk about."

"Forgive her," Roger croaked out.

"Dad, now ain't the time," Makai warned. "I'm glad you're awake. I'll be back tomorrow some time."

"Why can't you forgive her?" Roger pressed.

Makai blew a breath. Lanai could tell that he was being pushed to his limit. He said, "Because I don't want to. Can I go now?"

Roger shook his head no. "Fix this."

"Son—" Mya began.

"Don't call me that," Makai snapped.

Her head jerked back and her nose wrinkled up as if she'd smelled something putrid. She turned to Roger, "See? This is what I was talking about."

Makai's brows furrowed together. He asked in an accusatory tone, "So you up here getting my dad upset over some bullshit? You bothering him with this dumb shit?"

"It's important," she said.

"To whom?" he asked incredulously.

"To me," she replied. "And to your father."

"If it was important, you wouldn't've left your two sons. Nor would you have kept a child away from her father for twelve years," Makai pointed out.

Mya blew an exasperated breath. Her tone sounded annoyed when she said, "It's been over two decades. I can't change the past. When are you going to get over it?"

"What?" Makai asked.

Everyone in the room looked shocked that she'd been bold enough to say something like that.

Makai asked, "Are you serious? Were you raised by your mother?"

Mya nodded her head.

Makai asked, "So how would you know how we felt?"

"My mom raised me by herself," Mya said.

Makai pointed out, "At least she raised you. You left. And you kept his daughter away from him for twelve years. Ain't nothing you gonna be able to say to excuse that shit. You were wrong and you need to take responsibility for it."

"You have no idea of the circumstances that surrounded me leaving," she said, trying to squirm her way out of the confrontation.

"It doesn't matter. You left," he repeated.

The power of his words seemed like they were slowly sinking into Mya's head. She couldn't escape his anger, or the impact of his words. She looked at Malik, who was looking out the window to keep from having to give anyone eye contact. Barely above a whisper, she said, "I wasn't any good to you two."

"But you were good for her," he spat.

Raegan looked up with hurt in her eyes. Makai knew that she was innocent, but it didn't make any sense to be good for one child, and not be good for the two that came before her. He looked at his sister and clarified his statement, "No offense to you; I don't even know you."

Raegan looked at their mother but Mya kept her gaze on Makai. If looks could kill, Makai would've dropped dead, because she was definitely giving him a deadly stare. She asked, "What do you want from me?"

"Nothing," he answered simply.

"So you're just gonna carry around this hatred for the rest of your life?" she asked.

"How would you feel if it were you?"

She thought for a moment, then said, "I don't know. But because I'm your mother, I expect forgiveness and respect."

"You gotta earn respect to get it," he pointed out. "And any animal can give birth; that doesn't make it a mother."

His words hung in the air and everyone else was clearly uncomfortable. Makai looked to his father and said, "Dad, I'm gonna go get the baby. Call or text me if you need me." He looked to his brother and instructed, "Call me or text me if there are any changes before I make it back up."

Malik nodded and Roger didn't look too happy, but he didn't say another word. Makai didn't really care how anybody felt about what he'd said or how he felt. He wasn't apologizing to anyone, especially not Mya. He knew Lanai and Roger wanted him to make amends with her, but he didn't see that happening. He'd heard people talk about forgiveness wasn't for the other person. He didn't feel like she was worthy of his forgiveness, so he wasn't giving it to her. He was going to move on with his life, and he didn't need her to be a part of it. He left the hospital, walking away with a clear conscience.

CHAPTER TWENTY-NINE

Katara sat next to her sister as they sat in the waiting room of Christina Hospital in Christiana, DE, where Grammy got her chemotherapy treatments.. It seemed like every time they brought her to the hospital, she got weaker. They hated seeing her like that, but Katara had to admit that she wasn't ready to let go. She found herself asking God when she went to the altar or when she prayed, to allow her Grammy more time. Grammy stayed optimistic, though, regardless of the severe pain that she was in.

The chemotherapy process was horrific. Katara and Lanai watched as the effects of trying to cure cancer ripped families apart and traumatized them. It seemed to them that curing cancer was more painful than the actual disease. They'd seen kids moving in and out of the treatment center, which was one of the hardest parts. Katara noticed Lanai with tears in her eyes, watching the children and older people weak and listless, tears that mirrored her own. Cancer was hard on everyone involved, whether they had it or not.

Lanai worked on her laptop as Katara people-watched. Katara watched as a middle-aged white couple came in with a bald little girl. The pink and white sweatpants, white T-shirt, jean jacket with pink and white decorations, and the pink and white bow she wore on her head, were the only indication that the child was a girl.

Katara could see the stress on the father's face and the mother tried to be as bubbly as she could be. They let the woman at the front desk know what they were there for. When a nurse came out to take the little girl, the parents went over to the waiting area and sat down, not too far from Katara and Lanai.

Katara had a magazine in her lap that she'd been glancing at every now and again. She tried to give people as much privacy as possible, because she valued her privacy. She couldn't help what her eyes saw when she was bored with the magazine, or what her ears picked up on when she could hear people's conversations. The couple started out whispering after the dad blew an exasperated breath.

The couple's hushed whispers turned louder, and others overheard them. The wife asked, "What do you want me to do, John?"

"I want you to stop pretending like everything is perfect, Amy," John answered.

Amy said, "I have to be as positive as possible. You know this is taking a toll on Amanda."

"It's taking a toll on everybody," he pointed out. "Our son is failing in school because we spend all our time, trying to figure out solutions to balance Amanda's diet with this chemo."

Amy looked around quickly to see if anyone was watching them, then said, "Sssshhhh, John! The whole world doesn't have to know our business."

"It's true," he replied.

"Well, maybe if you spent more time with our son, he wouldn't be failing," she shot back. "Your whore can go a day or two without seeing you."

"Maybe if you'd stop shopping *every single day* like you didn't get fired seven months ago and spent more time with our son, he wouldn't be failing," John shot back. "I'm paying all the bills, including the bill for our daughter's treatments, your spending, and Jack's extra-curricular activities. I could use a little help. And FYI, I stopped seeing Megan more than a year ago. Remember, you made me pick up the bill for a psychiatrist that we don't need?"

"We needed someone to talk to. Instead of you coming to me and talking to me because I'm your wife, you went and cheated with a woman you work with," she argued.

"Did I go out and get a therapist when you cheated on me with my business partner, who I have to look in the face every goddamn day?" he asked.

Katara's eyes darted up to see Amy's face turn red and her jaw dropped. Amy said, "I told you it was one time."

"Does it really matter how many times it was," he questioned. "Point is; I did to you what you did to me. Now, I would be justified in picking up a spending habit, right? Or maybe I should just stop paying for everything?"

"Maybe you should stop being a jackass," she hissed. "You make it sound like we're such a burden on you!"

"Your excessive spending *is* a burden on me," he returned. "Get a job instead of trying to figure out new ways to drive me to the poor house."

"Get a penile implant and then I wouldn't have to spend excessively," she rebutted.

Katara choked on her spit in disbelief. She quickly brought the magazine up to shield her face, so the couple couldn't see her trying hard not to laugh. She had to work hard to make her snickering sound like coughing. Lanai pressed her lips together to keep from laughing, and tried to look as focused on her laptop as she possibly could. Under her breath, Katara warned, "Don't you do it. If you laugh, you know I'ma laugh."

Out of the side of her mouth, Lanai whispered, "I can't believe she said that to him."

Katara peeked from over the top of the magazine and saw that John's face was beet red. Looking like she felt like she'd won the argument, Amy had a smug grin on her face. She said, "I'm going to the gift shop to find something for Amanda. I'll be back in an hour."

John didn't say anything in response to her comment. He sat there fuming and when she was completely out of sight, he pulled out his cell phone. He dialed a number, put the phone to his ear and waited for someone to pick up. He pushed a few buttons and put the phone back to his ear. When someone came on the line, he said, "Yes, I need to report my wife's card stolen."

Katara's jaw dropped and she looked at Lanai, who was looking at her in pure amazement. "The shit that you see in the hospital," Katara mumbled, shaking her head.

Lanai shook her head. They both knew that people had problems, but the hospital waiting room was not the place to air it or hash it out. Katara and Larry had their problems, they even argued. But she would slap the shit out of him if he even thought about embarrassing her that way. Katara had to admit to herself that she was relieved it was not a black couple acting a fool in public. She continued to thumb through the Home Décor Magazine.

She felt her phone vibrate in her purse on her lap and she looked around in her purse for the phone, holding the magazine in one hand. She found it, pulled it out, and looked at the screen. She didn't recognize the number, but figuring it might be about business, she decided to answer. She slid the green icon across the screen, asking, "Hello?"

"Is this Katara?" a female asked with attitude.

Katara's heart dropped to her stomach. She and Larry had been arguing off and on about her being so busy. She'd been so busy lately, they hadn't had sex in a few months. She knew he was reaching his breaking point, because he didn't like to go without sex for more than two days. She didn't like depriving him; she just was so busy. Business had increased lately, they had to get Grammy settled in her new apartment, and she still had mommy duties. There were times when she felt bad that Larry was there more for Sariyah than she was able to be, but she did the best that she could.

Katara was always there to kiss her goodnight, and there when Sariyah woke up. She dedicated every spare second to helping Sariyah prepare for church. She hated that there wasn't much time left for Larry. But with him being a *grown man* she expected him to be understanding, even though he was more understanding than any man she'd ever met. He'd been understanding from the beginning, accepting her and her baggage. He'd helped her work through things, helping her to grow into the woman that she was.

She wondered if he'd gotten tired of waiting on her to make time for him. She wondered if he was sick of things between them being so hard. *What if he'd decided to seek comfort with another woman? What if he'd gotten fed up and decided that he didn't want to be with me anymore? What if his chick on the side was tired of being on the side and wanted to let me know who she was?* What if... Katara silenced the questions in her head. If he was cheating, she'd kill him. Period. She'd given that man a kid, a family, stability, and helped cultivate himself into the established businessman that he was. If he'd gotten weak and allowed temptation to take over, she was going to kill him.

She squared her shoulders, preparing herself for the nonsense that awaited her on the other line. She was going to handle the conversation like a lady, but Larry would have *hell* to pay when she saw him. She answered, "Yes, this is Katara. May I ask who this is?"

"This is Tonicka," the girl answered. "I'm BJ's girlfriend. Who the fuck are you, and why is my man calling and texting you?"

Katara exhaled in relief and chuckled. "You don't understand. It's not even like that."

Tonicka screamed into the phone, "What you mean 'it's not even like that'? You texting him you love him, and he telling you he love you! It's like something! Don't play with me, bitch! I'll find out where you are and fuck you up! I see you have a Delaware number. That ain't far from Baltimore."

"Look, little girl," Katara said through clenched teeth, "BJ is my brother."

"Uh-uh, fuck that! I don't play that brother-sister bullshit," Tonicka ranted. "My man don't have female friends or fake sisters. Fuck you think this is?"

Katara tried to hold on to her composure and not make a scene. She didn't want to make a spectacle of herself, but if the girl kept talking stupid, she wouldn't have to come to Delaware because Katara would go to Baltimore. She tried one more time to be rational with the girl on the phone. She said, "Honey, he really is my blood brother. I have a man."

"Having a man don't mean shit," Tonicka replied. "And if you're his blood sister, why haven't I met you? Why don't you have any pictures with him? Where was you when he was in County?"

Katara asked, "How long have you and BJ been together?"

"Four weeks," Tonicka said, sounding as if she'd said four years. "But I've been holding him down ever since my cousin's baby dad's nephew's neighbor's third cousin's best friend hooked me up with him."

Katara burst into laughter. She laughed so hard that she doubled over in her chair and the phone came down from her ear. She laughed so hard that everyone was looking at her. Lanai looked at her with an amused expression. She asked, "What is so funny?"

Katara shook her head and waved her hand, laughing. After a few moments, she was able to compose herself and put the phone back to her ear. She had tears in her eyes from laughing so hard. With her stomach muscles hurting, she asked, "Girl, are you serious? Is this a joke? Ask BJ who I am. I'm his little sister. You should do your research, before you call yourself calling and checking somebody."

More to herself than to Tonicka, Katara asked, "Four weeks? Are you serious? This is the most ghetto—"

"Well, I go through his phone on the regular and the shit didn't look right," Tonicka answered, her voice sounding unsure.

"Honey, you coulda just asked," Katara said. "Phone etiquette 101, don't call accusing someone unless you have all the facts. If you did your research, you would've found out that I am, in fact his sister. Four weeks together after making a jailhouse love connection, doesn't qualify as much in my opinion."

"Well, whatever," Tonicka mumbled. "You just don't text or call my man no more."

Katara laughed. "I will continue to text and call my brother as much as I like. You have a wonderful day."

Katara ended the call, still laughing. Lanai asked, "What is going on?"

"BJ found somebody gullible and dumb enough to host him out," Katara revealed. "He had to make her his girlfriend, I guess. He ain't even all the way home yet and she's acting like his parole officer. That girl is in for a ride."

"She thought you were somebody he was cheating with?" Lanai asked.

Katara nodded her head. She said, "It's sad. He probably ain't being faithful to her, but if he was, he won't be now. Not with her acting like that."

Lanai shook her head, returning to her work. Katara looked over at her sister, busy at work. She was proud of Lanai's progress. Lanai had gone from a confused, naïve little girl, chasing behind Makai like a lost puppy, to a beautiful and focused woman of God. Lanai had gone from addictions to both drugs and being in love, to being a role model for another woman's daughter. She'd taken her bad situations and feelings of helplessness and let God use her to turn it around. Katara felt like a proud mother. She knew that God was going to work on Lanai, but only if Lanai allowed Him to. Katara was so glad that Lanai had taken that step, because she seemed like she was so at peace.

Katara still didn't completely trust Makai, but she had to give credit where it was due. He treated her sister like she was a princess. He hadn't been caught in a lie since Lanai had taken him back. He was there for Lanai, every step of the way, it seemed. He was super supportive and he rarely told her no. He seemed to be giving Lanai everything that he'd taken away from her over the course of ten years. Deep down, Katara smiled. She wasn't going to let either of them know that she was happy about their relationship, because she didn't want Makai to get comfortable.

Katara thought about how happy Makai and Lanai were, and it reminded her of how happy she and Larry used to be. She missed the way they used to play and talk. She missed the late night conversations, surprise lunches and dinners, and surprise gifts. Larry didn't do it big like Makai did, but she didn't mind. The smaller things were more important to her. She would probably look at him sideways and cuss him out if he bought her something from Louis Vuitton or Gucci. That money could be better spent somewhere else or could go in their daughter's college fund. She'd told him if he wanted to make her happy, pay the mortgage up for a year.

She also missed his touch. They argued so much over the dumbest things that she dreaded seeing his number pop up on her phone. She wanted to be able to go home and have him just hold her. They didn't even kiss anymore. If he went to bed after her, she wouldn't even know he was in the bed until she woke up in the morning. They didn't tell each other that they loved one another anymore. She used to get nervous at the thought of Larry proposing, because she wanted it so bad, but refused to say it. The current state of their relationship had her wondering, if they'd make it to the beginning of the next week.

Thinking about the phone call that she'd received brought some things into perspective for her. She worried about finding out that he was cheating or another woman calling her phone, because she knew that he wasn't getting what he needed from her. Her conscience was working on her overtime. She constantly prayed for other people and their situations, she prayed for her family and friends, but she didn't once pray for her relationship. She prayed for Larry, but not for their relationship. She took for granted that things would fall into place effortlessly, because she wanted them to.

She put the pin number in to unlock her phone. As she dialed Larry's number, she thought about how one of their last arguments was about how Larry felt that she was trying to hide something from him with a pin number lock on her phone. She tried explaining to him that the lock on the phone kept people from seeing the ignorant text messages that popped up from him in response to her more ignorant texts that she sent him. She hated that they continued to disrespect each other and they had grown so far apart.

She was about to end the call, because he let it ring until it almost got to voicemail. He asked, "Yeah?"

His tone was so harsh that it made her cringe. She said, "Hey."

Annoyed, he asked, "What's up? What's wrong?"

"Nothing is wrong," she answered. "I just wanted to call you. Just wanted to hear your voice."

"Why?" he questioned, sounding suspicious.

"No reason," she said. After listening to dead air over the line for a few seconds, she decided to go against what she would normally do. Normally, she wouldn't have a personal conversation in public, but she definitely didn't want to be in Amy or Tonicka's position either. "Look, Larry. We need to talk."

"Talk about what?"

"First of all," she began, "talk about the way we talk to each other. I'm tired of fighting."

"I don't know what you're talking about, Katara," he said. "I got work to get done before it's time for me to pick Riyah up from daycare."

She offered, "I'll pick her up from daycare."

"I thought you were with your sister and grandmom."

"I am, but we'll be done in enough time for me to pick her up."

"You can't be late picking her up," he warned.

She rolled her eyes and stopped herself from saying something smart. She wanted to tell him that she wasn't an idiot; she knew that their daughter couldn't be picked up late. She was the one that had picked the daycare, enrolled her, and signed the contract. As calmly as she could muster, she said, "I know. I'll pick her up on time. Do you have plans after you leave the shop?"

"My only plans were to pick up Riyah and make her dinner," he answered.

"Well, can you come straight home?"

"I'm not in the mood to talk, Katara," he said.

Every time he called her by her name, it irritated her. She missed the nicknames and the love she used to hear in his tone. She asked, "Can you please come straight home?"

He let out a loud sigh. "Fine. Anything else?"

Shocked at his callousness, she took the phone away from her ear and stared at it as if it was a foreign object. She put the phone back to her ear and answered, "No."

Even if she wanted to say something more, she couldn't, because he ended the call abruptly. Feeling down, she dropped the phone into her purse. Lanai asked, "Tara, what's wrong?"

"Nothing," Katara mumbled.

"Lies," Lanai retorted.

Katara sighed. "This shit with Larry."

"What's the problem now?" Lanai asked, closing her laptop.

"I'm tryna have a conversation with him to hash out what's wrong," Katara explained. "I want to fix what's wrong. I don't like what's going on between us, but he doesn't wanna talk. He's just so nasty towards me."

"Well, you know what you need to do, right?" Lanai asked.

Katara shook her head no. She was truly at a loss because she felt like she'd tried everything.

Lanai said, "You need to get rid of Riyah for a night and put it on him. He's clearly deprived. Talking won't get through to him."

"Sex doesn't change anything," Katara said. "Our problems will still be there."

"You wanna bet?" Lanai challenged. "Sex fixes a lot. You told me that the arguments are dumb and petty. You said most of the time; you don't know what started it or what y'all are even arguing about."

"That's true."

"It's because both of y'all need to release that pent up aggression," Lanai remarked.

Katara thought for a moment. She knew that she needed some type of release, because she would sometimes start arguments or purposely be mean or nasty. She would be irritated over nothing. It was definitely time for a change, or somebody was going to end up in a body bag. She felt like she'd invested too much time, energy, and effort into him for to be with somebody else. Even though they weren't married, she felt like they were in it until death did them part; whether it was voluntarily or not.

Lanai offered, "I can take Riyah for the night. We can have a girls' night with Kayla. Cook that man's favorite foods, wear that man's favorite lingerie, and wear that man out. I guarantee you he'll be whistling tomorrow, cooking you breakfast."

Katara joined Lanai in laughter, but she knew her sister was right. She normally had the advice for Lanai to follow. Lanai had made so many bonehead decisions over the years that Katara had felt like the older sibling. Katara was grateful for somebody that would listen and give her sound advice that wouldn't have her regretting a decision or sitting in jail. Katara wanted to do whatever was necessary—as long as it was within reason—to get her relationship back on the right track.

Katara said, "Well, when we pick Sariyah up from daycare, you can just drop me to my car. I should have enough time to go home and cook something before he gets home."

"You should let me flat-iron your hair, too," Lanai said, fingering the hair that hung from Katara's ponytail.

Katara made the observation that she didn't even do her hair or put on makeup anymore. She touched her long, thick, curly ponytail. She said, "You know that'll take forever."

"We can go straight to your house," Lanai suggested. "You can put whatever you're gonna cook on, I can do your hair, and I can get Riyah's clothes."

"What about Grammy?"

"I can put her to bed."

"What about her dinner?"

"I know what to do."

"I know that."

"Stop being so overprotective. I got this," Lanai assured Katara.

Katara smiled, "Thank you."

"For what?"

"For being the brains."

"For once," Lanai laughed. "You know you don't have to thank me. It's easy to see another person's situation and help fix it. It's hard to see your own for what it is and what it needs. We all need help."

Changing the subject, Katara asked, "So how are things with you and Makai?"

Lanai answered, "Good. He pretends like the issues he has with his mother don't exist, and I'm sick of beating a dead horse with a stick. But other than that, he's adjusting to Ms. Hazel being gone, his dad is beginning to do better, and he keeps in contact with his brother constantly. He found out he has a sister and I told him it would be important to establish a relationship with her, but you know he has a head like concrete. He and I are good, though. We go out, we talk, we have no secrets, and we're building."

"Are you happy?"

"Happier than I have ever been," Lanai beamed.

Katara said, "You look happy. I see you're letting your hair grow out."

Lanai reached up and touched her shoulder-length hair. "Yeah, I was skeptical at first about letting it grow. I think the short is cute, but I also miss the long. I don't know. I might decide to cut it again. We'll see."

"I am so proud of you," Katara blurted.

Lanai smiled. "Why?"

"Because you've come so far," Katara admitted. "You allowed God to turn your mess into a message, and that takes courage. You're a grown woman now."

Lanai nodded her head. "I am. I thank God for it. I thank God for you. If it hadn't been for you, I would still be a mess."

"Stop it before you make me cry," Katara warned.

"I'm serious," Lanai said. "A good support system makes a big difference. Things that I used to be afraid of, I confront. I'm nowhere near perfect and won't pretend to be. But I am exceptionally blessed."

They continued to chat until Grammy was wheeled out into the waiting room in a wheelchair. Seeing her look so feeble, tired, and old pulled at Katara's heartstrings. She gave the girls a weak smile as they stood. Katara went over to the wheelchair and touched Grammy's wrinkled skin, which was softer than any skin she'd ever felt. She asked, "You okay, Grammy?"

Grammy nodded, touching her granddaughter's hand. "I'm ready to go home," she said.

"Let me go get the car," Lanai announced, kissing Grammy's cheek after Katara removed her hand.

Katara stood next to the wheelchair, holding Grammy's hand. Grammy said, "Baby girl, I need you to do me a favor."

"Anything, Grammy."

"I need you to stop living for everybody else and live for yourself," Grammy stated. "I ain't gonna be here forever. You don't owe me anything; you don't owe your brothers anything. Love that man that loves you and spend time with him."

How does she know about me having problems with Larry? Katara thought. But then again, how could she not know? Grammy knew everything. Katara loved the fact that Vi had taken her in, but she hated that it had taken her away from Grammy. Things that she'd wanted to learn and experience with Grammy, she missed out on.

Katara answered dutifully, "Yes, ma'am."

Grammy kissed the back of Katara's hand. She said, "You know I love you, right?"

"Yes, ma'am," Katara answered, kissing the back of her wrinkled hand in return.

"I don't have much longer," Grammy informed her.

Katara tried to stop her, "Grammy, don't talk like that."

"Listen, honey," Grammy said. "Our days on this earth are short. You know that. When I leave this place, I get to be with my Lord and Savior. Take comfort in that, baby."

Katara admitted, "I don't want to take comfort in you being gone. My time with you has always been so limited. I asked God to allow me time to make up for the time that I missed with you."

"Baby, you didn't miss any time with me. God answered my prayers when he sent Vi and Lanai your way," Grammy revealed. "I didn't want the streets to swallow you up like they did your momma. I hate that I failed her and I felt like God allowed me to right that wrong when he brought Vi along. He answered my prayers when He allowed you to be with a family that could give you what you needed. I don't know where I went wrong with your momma—"

"You didn't," Katara said, squatting down to eye level with Grammy. "You did the best that you could. You gave her life and it was up to her to do something with it. You went above and beyond, because you raised her kids. You introduced me to a relationship with God. That's the best thing you could ever do for anyone."

Grammy lovingly touched Katara's cocoa-colored face and smiled. The light in Grammy's eyes that Katara had always remembered was dimming. Grammy said, "Baby, I gave you what God gave me. But I want you to stop living your life like you owe everybody. You don't owe me anything."

"I owe you everything," Katara argued. "You were always there, doing what you didn't have to do."

Grammy waved her off, saying, "Hush now, child. I'm ready to go home."

Katara pressed her lips together, suppressing the rest of what she wanted to say. She had a reputation of saying whatever that was on her mind, except when it came to Grammy. She did whatever Grammy said, whenever Grammy said it. Grammy was one woman that Katara didn't argue with. Even if she didn't like it, Katara did what she was told without hesitation at all times. It had taken Lanai talking to and convincing Grammy to move to Delaware, because Katara had felt like she was being disobedient, having the conversation with her.

Hearing that Grammy was ready to go home made Katara nervous. She had a sinking feeling in her stomach that Grammy wasn't talking about the apartment that Katara and Lanai had just moved her into. Tears came to her eyes as she thought about Grammy dying. Her heart, nor her head, was ready to accept the possibility that Grammy wouldn't be around. She'd missed many years of physical contact with Grammy and she wanted to make up for it. She prayed that God allowed her that time.

Katara saw Lanai's car pull up in front of the doors and she walked beside the wheelchair that the nurse pushed out. As the nurse helped Grammy out the chair and into the backseat, Katara asked, "Grammy, can you promise me something?"

Grammy looked up from the backseat and asked, "What, sweetheart?"

"Can you promise me that you'll hold on a while longer? For me, please," Katara pleaded.

Grammy smiled, "Baby, that ain't my decision. That's up to my God."

Katara knew what the response would be, but she wanted Grammy to lie to her, just once. She needed Grammy to lie to her that one time to make her feel better. Katara felt like her heart was being torn in pieces. Grammy was the only parent that Katara had known. Even though Vi had taken her in physically, Katara and Lanai always had to fend for themselves. Vi had provided the essentials and Katara had felt like Vi had done to the best of her abilities.

Grammy wasn't physically there, but she always answered every phone call and had the best advice. One time, she'd walked Katara through a recipe that Katara had messed up. Grammy had been patient enough to talk her through fixing it, and Larry hadn't even known the difference. Katara wanted Sariyah to experience the love that only Grammy had to give. She wanted Grammy to outlive her. Realistically though, Katara knew that Grammy's days were numbered.

Katara got into the passenger seat and buckled her seatbelt. She pushed her tears away, along with the thoughts of Grammy dying. She thought about what she was going to cook for dinner, not really having an idea. She went over what she remembered being in the refrigerator and freezer, trying to remember what was easiest to thaw out. Larry didn't have a particular dish that he liked; he just liked when she cooked. She hadn't been doing too much cooking lately, either. She shook her head at herself. She wasn't doing anything lately and it was sad.

It took Lanai about 30 minutes to get from Christiana to Dover, where Sariyah's daycare was. It took Katara a few minutes to sign Sariyah out, then they were headed to Camden. When they arrived at her house, Katara helped Grammy to get out the car and walk up to the door of her house. After unlocking the door, Katara made Grammy comfortable in the sitting room before going to the kitchen. She looked through the freezer and deep freezer and found nothing that wouldn't take long to thaw out and cook. She checked the refrigerator and found some chicken breasts that Larry must've take out for his and Sariyah's dinner.

She took the chicken from the refrigerator, along with shredded cheese, and spinach. After preheating the oven to 400, and washing her hands a second time, she took the chicken breasts from the pack they were sold in, cleaned them, then cut them almost completely in half. Quickly, she took the spinach and shredded cheese, stuffing the chicken breasts and seasoning them. When she was done, seasoning the chicken in the pan and pouring chicken broth in to substitute for water, she slid the pan in the oven.

She liked to make her pasta sauces from scratch, but she was pressed for time. Katara decided to cook one of the Lipton Sides that she'd bought for Larry to cook if she wasn't home. She dropped some broccoli into a steamer over a pot of boiling water, putting seasoning on the broccoli. Lanai brought down the flat iron and plugged it up in the bathroom on the first floor. On her way to the bathroom, Katara pulled the scrunchy that she used to hold her hair in a ponytail out.

When she got in the bathroom, she sat on the closed toilet and prepared for it to take forever. Lanai worked as fast as she could, but it still took about an hour and a half. Katara kept looking at her watch, wondering if Larry was going to get caught in traffic, which would give her time to light the candles that she had placed strategically through the house years ago, but never used. She wanted to use everything available to show him that she was putting forth the effort, to make things better between them.

When Lanai was finished straightening her hair, Katara made a move to sweep her hair into a ponytail. Lanai smacked Katara's hand. "Girl, what are you doing? I ain't do all this for nothing!"

Katara grinned sheepishly. "I'm sorry. It's a habit."

"Alright, well, we're getting out of here before he gets here," Lanai announced. "Do you need me to do anything?"

Katara shook her head. "Just call me if there's a problem with getting Grammy straight. Are you sure you don't need me to help you?"

Lanai turned off and unplugged the flat iron, waving her sister off. "I need you to concentrate on knocking this man's socks off," she retorted.

Katara said, "I'm not sure we'll even get that far. Shit is bad between us."

"It ain't as bad as you think it is," Lanai replied, trying to encourage Katara.

"Honey, I live with that man," Katara said dryly, going into the kitchen to check on dinner.

Lanai disappeared upstairs and gathered clothes and pajamas for Sariyah to stay the night. Sariyah sat in the sitting room, talking Grammy's head off. Grammy looked like she was enjoying every single second, even though she had no idea what Sariyah was talking about. Lanai came into the kitchen, announcing, "Alright, Ms. Missy. We're leaving."

"Are you sure you don't need help with Grammy? I can do this another night," Katara said, stepping away from the stove after closing the oven door. She'd peeked in on the chicken and it wasn't far from being done. She turned the burner off for the steamed broccoli. She'd cooked the pasta before she'd gotten her hair done.

Lanai retorted, "What you can do is take your butt upstairs, wrap that hair, and get a shower. Put on some Vicky's Secret."

Katara turned her wrist over to check the time. She probably had about 15 minutes before Larry would be home. She nervously rubbed her damp hands on her pants. She felt like a teenage girl preparing for her first date with a boy. She knew that when Lanai, Grammy, and Sariyah left, she wouldn't have other people to focus on.

Lanai asked, "Are you nervous?"

Katara nodded slowly. "I don't wanna be putting myself out there for him to reject me. I hate rejection."

"Who doesn't?" Lanai mused. "You'll be fine, though. He still loves you; he never stopped. He'll feel appreciated tonight. As much as they like to pretend that it doesn't matter, men want to feel appreciated, too. Makai starts acting like a big baby when he feels like I'm neglecting him."

Katara nodded, soaking up the information that her sister gave her. She followed Lanai into the sitting room. She hugged and kissed Sariyah, reminding her to be a good girl. Katara helped Grammy out of the chair and kissed her cheek. She said, "I love you, Grammy. I'll see you in the morning."

"I love you, too, baby. Sleep in," Grammy advised with a wink.

Katara and Lanai laughed and Katara followed them to the door. Lanai said, "Go get ready. I got them. Riyah's gonna help me with Grammy, right, Love Bug?"

Sariyah nodded her head, sending her thick, long, jet-black ponytails bobbing back and forth.

Katara stood at the door, anxiously watching the three of them go down the walkway. She didn't close the door until she saw that Grammy and Sariyah made it safely into the car with seatbelts on. She waved at Lanai, who waved back as she got into the driver's seat. Katara closed and locked the door, letting out a breath. She went into the kitchen, found the long lighter, and set about lighting candles all over the house, turning off the lights as she did. When she was done, she wrapped her long, silky black hair up in a satin scarf. She loved the way that her hair felt as it swept over her shoulders. She almost smiled at the feeling.

She jumped in the shower, making it quick. She quickly put lotion on her already soft, cocoa-colored skin from head to toe. She didn't have much time to admire anything about herself, but rarely she got to admire how smooth and even-toned her skin was. She knew dark-skinned women that didn't like their complexion, but she loved hers. As she rubbed the lotion in on her leg, she turned it side to side, loving the look and feel of her toned limbs. Even though she'd had a child, her stomach was still flat, her butt was still high, and her breasts were still perky. After applying her lotion, she twisted and turned in front of her full-length mirror, continuing to admire how good her naked body looked.

For a second, she contemplated meeting Larry at the front door in her birthday suit. She knew that would get his attention. Feeling like that wasn't something "proper" to do, though, she moved over to the dresser drawer with her underclothes in it. She opened the drawer, digging all the way to the bottom to find her lacy underwear and bras. She moved the "everyday" underwear and bras out the way and searched through the "pretty panties and bras" that she hadn't worn in a long time.

She found a peach-colored lace bra and thong panty set. Slipping into the garments, she took a second to look at her reflection, twisting and turning again. It was amazing how good the peach looked against her chocolate skin. She pulled her scarf off and her hair fell down, falling all over the place. She used her fingers to move her hair out of her face and tousle the hair. She smiled at her reflection, looking better than any Victoria's Secret model she'd ever seen. After grabbing a white satin robe from the closet and applying a little lip-gloss to her lips, she bounded down the steps barefoot to take the chicken out of the oven.

Using the oven mitts, she took the chicken out and put it on the counter. She looked at the time on the oven, frowning. It normally didn't take almost two hours for him to get home. She took down two glass plates and put the food on them, trying to remind herself that traffic may have been bad. As she took a bottle of wine out the refrigerator and two glasses, placing them on the table, she tried to keep her mind from going to thoughts of him making a pit stop with another woman. She lit the long candles on the dining room table, placed their food and glasses on the table, and poured two glasses of wine. Subconsciously, she chewed on her bottom lip with the bottle of wine in her hand. As much as she didn't want to admit it, lately, Larry's behavior suggested he was cheating.

Tears came to her eyes, even though she had zero proof, other than constant arguments and bitterness between the two of them. She looked at the way she'd set up the dining room and thought about the lengths she'd gone through. She knew that he meant the world to her and she was more than willing to prove it to him. The thought of it being too late to show him that he meant the world to her and she wanted to fix what was wrong crossed her mind, causing a tear to slide down her cheek. *What am I going to do?*

As quickly as the tear had fallen, she wiped it away with a determined hand. She was going to pull herself together, that's what she was going to do. If he was cheating, she hoped it was worth it. She was a good woman—albeit a busy woman—and a good mother. If he didn't appreciate it, then that was his stupidity and his loss. She took a long swallow from the bottle she held in her hand, determined not to let her emotions get the best of her. She'd put a lot into her relationship, but one monkey didn't stop the show. She wasn't afraid to start over.

She squared her shoulders and put the bottle on the table. She made up her mind that she would go put some clothes on, put her hair back in a ponytail, then go about blowing out all the candles.

She decided to clean up the kitchen and put the food in the refrigerator after she put some clothes on. She headed towards the stairs, pulling her robe together as she heard a key in the lock. She froze in her tracks with her hand on the banister rail as the door came open.

Larry stepped into the house, closing the storm door behind him. He looked up with his hand on the front door to close it and was caught completely off guard. His eyes traveled from her pedicured feet, up her legs, taking in the lingerie showing through the open robe, and up to her straight hair. His eyes dropped back down to her cleavage and her flat stomach. His mouth dropped open slightly and he stood in the doorway with the door open in disbelief.

She smiled at him and barely above a whisper, she said, "Hey, baby."

"Hey," he responded, with his eyes traveling over her body again.

"Are you gonna close the door?" she asked, grinning.

As if it was registering for the first time in his mind that the door was still open, he said, "Oh, shit. Yeah."

He pushed the door closed and locked it, but never took his eyes off her. Putting her hands on her hips and twisting and turning to model what she had on, she asked with a smile, "You like?"

"Yeah," he answered quickly.

With one hand on her hip and the other beckoning him to her, she said, "Come here."

He wasted no time closing the space between them, sliding his hands around her waist to the small of her back and pulling her to him. She could feel his heart thumping against her hands on his chest. She looked up at him and asked, "How was your day?"

He kissed her fervently, instead of answering her question. He slid his hand into her hair, grabbing a fistful in the back of her head. He tilted her head back, deepening the kiss. It had been a long time since he'd kissed her like he missed her, but the kiss had her knees feeling weak. When the kiss was over, she was breathless. He lifted her off the floor and she wrapped her limbs around him. Caressing the smooth skin of her back, he murmured against the side of her face, "You always so damn soft."

She rubbed her face against the side of his face, loving the roughness of his beard and hair on the side of his face. She said, "I cooked dinner."

Taking her upstairs, he said, "Fuck that food."

She laughed, "It's gonna get cold."

Kissing the base of her neck on the way up the stairs, he said, "We have a microwave."

CHAPTER THIRTY

Makai blew hot air and hit the glass counter with his hand. He stood in Lanai's favorite jewelry store, TIFFANY & Co, trying to decide on the perfect ring for Lanai. He'd brought Makayla with him, but the toddler couldn't possibly be any help. He'd told Lanai to enjoy a day to herself, getting a massage and her nails, feet, and hair done. He liked that she was letting her hair grow back.

Over the years, he'd bought her countless gifts. He'd bought her "guilt" gifts to make himself feel better about the way that he'd treated her and lied to her. He remembered spending $250,000 on a rose gold watch from this same store. The rings, watches, bracelets, necklaces, and other gifts that he'd bought her weren't as special as the ring he was looking for. He knew what she liked, and what he liked seeing her in, but he wanted the ring he was looking for to express everything she meant to him. It was just a dumb-long process to find it.

He'd been looking for the perfect ring for a whole week. He hadn't liked anything that he'd seen; nothing caught his eye. It wasn't that the diamonds were big enough, because they were huge. The rings he'd seen didn't seem to be what he wanted her to wear for the rest of her life. He'd thought about it over the years and toyed with the idea of proposing. He'd told her that she was going to be his wife. But up until a week ago, he'd never been serious about finding a ring and making it official.

He stood there wondering if he should even go through with it. It wasn't like either of them were going anywhere. As far as he was concerned, the actual certificate didn't matter. In his mind, she was all he wanted; she was his wife. But he knew what it meant to her, so he knew he had to keep looking. The ring search was more about him than it was for her. He knew that she'd be okay with going to the Justice of the Peace with no engagement ring as long as they were married.

The young lady that stood behind the counter took out yet another velvet case with diamond engagement rings in it. She set it down, eyeing him suspiciously, because he'd hit the glass. She looked like she was contemplating calling security. She asked, "Sir, do you have any idea of what you want?"

Barely looking at the rings she'd placed in front of him, he answered absently, "Nah, I'll know it when I see it."

"Do you have a price range?"

He shook his head.

"Well, you know the pawn shops have a good selection," she said.

He shot her a look that could've frozen fire and she ducked her head down, pretending to be busy organizing the rings she'd just put back.

When he was about to give up, his eyes caught a big diamond in a platinum setting. He picked the ring up and asked, "What is this?"

"This is our Tiffany Grace. It's a two and a half carat, princess-cut diamond in a platinum setting. It's really a beautiful ring," the lady commented.

He looked down at Makayla and showed her the ring. He asked, "What you think, Munchkin?"

Clutching her sippy cup to her chest, she nodded her head back in forth hard, showing her approval. He could've shown her a ring pop and gotten the same response. He noticed that not only was it a big ass diamond in the middle, but smaller diamonds were around the platinum band. He looked at it, turning it over on the tip of his finger, contemplating. He looked up at the girl that was eyeing him closely. He said, "I'll take it."

Baffled, the girl blurted, "Sir, that's a $47,229 ring."

"Okay," he answered, not blinking. "You want cash or card?"

Quickly, she recovered, tucking her bottom lip in between her teeth. She got a ring box for it in their signature robin's egg blue, with the company's name on it. He gave her the ring and let her secure the ring inside the box. She moved over to the cash register, asking, "Will that be cash or charge, sir?"

"Do you have the earrings I asked about when I came in earlier?" he asked.

"Oh, I'm so sorry," she apologized. "I'll get them right now."

She scrambled to get the diamond studs that he'd picked out earlier for Makayla. She returned to the register with the earrings and ring box, looking at Makai like a dog expecting a bone from her master. Makai pulled out his wallet and gave her his black American Express card. He didn't want to draw too much attention to himself, by paying for the purchase in cash, even though he had it in his pocket.

She asked, "Can I see your ID, sir?"

He pulled out his driver's license and waited while she looked at his picture, then at him. She looked carefully at the name and signature, and compared it to the name on the front of the card and the signature on the back. When she was satisfied that he hadn't stolen the card, she gave his license back to him. She rang up the jewelry and looked up at him, telling him, "It comes to $47,728."

He gave her a quick nod, confirming that it was okay to charge the card. He knew she was waiting for it to be declined. He smiled inside as he waited calmly, because he knew he had excellent credit. In addition to taking his businesses serious, he was very conscious of his credit. He knew that most of the world thought that all black men, especially younger ones, were careless with credit. Even if others were, Makai wasn't. He wanted to give his daughter more than just promises and bills when he died.

The young lady swiped the card and subtly held her breath, waiting for the machine to connect with the host. After making some noise and taking a few seconds, a receipt printed out. She looked relieved as she tore the receipt paper off and gave it to him with a pen. He signed the receipt and gave it back to her, taking his small bag, his card, and his copy of the receipt. Picking his daughter up, he walked out the store, not even acknowledging her telling him to have a nice day. He put Makayla into the backseat of the 2015 smoke gray Chrysler 300 with tinted windows. After strapping her into the car seat, he closed the door and went around, getting into the driver's seat.

He put his foot on the brake, pressing the button to start the engine. Instead of pulling off, he took the ring box out of the bag, opened it, and looked at it for a moment. Part of him wasn't completely sure that marriage was for him. He felt like maybe he was rushing it. But then he was reminded of life was like without Lanai and his stomach sank. He looked in the rearview mirror at his daughter. Lanai wasn't just a major part of his life; Makayla was attached to her. He wouldn't want any other woman around his daughter. He snapped the box shut, deciding that he was definitely doing the right thing. He pulled away from the curb and headed back to Dover.

It took him about an hour to get back to Dover, feeling like he was floating every time he drove his new car. He'd wanted to get another truck, until he test-drove the car just for the hell of it. He fell in love with it almost immediately. The leather seats made him feel more like a boss than his executive chair. He loved the navigation system and the Bluetooth. He appreciated the fact that his phone automatically connected to the Bluetooth of the car as soon as he got in, because he still hadn't gotten around to buying a Bluetooth headset.

He pulled in front of Lanai and Katara's office, seeing that her car was parked in the parking lot. He knew she couldn't take a day off, regardless of what he'd said. He looked at Makayla in the rearview mirror and asked, "You ready, Munchkin?"

"Yes," she said.

Makai went around to let her out and closed the door as she ran up to and tried to open the office door. He threw the bag on the front seat and tucked the ring box in his right front pocket. He closed the back door and went to assist Makayla in opening the door, arming the alarm on his car. He let Makayla go in first, following her inside. Makayla ran straight to Lanai and jumped in her lap, giving her the biggest hug and kiss.

Lanai smiled, "Hey, my Sweetie Pie. I missed you." She smiled up at Makai, "Hey, baby."

He shook his head in mock pity, "Just couldn't stay away, could you?"

She shook her head. "I tried."

He was quiet for a moment, his palms beginning to sweat. He was nervous about what he was about to do, even though he was sure. He felt like he was on a roller coaster ride. He cleared his throat and said, "Come here."

A confused look crept over her face as she stood up, hoisting Makayla on her hip and coming around the desk. He told her, "Put her down."

Slowly, she did as she was told. She asked, "Why? What's going on?"

He put his hand in his pocket, closing his fingers around the box. He had to admit that he was scared as hell, feeling like he was awaiting lethal injection or the electric chair. More important to him than the feeling of freedom was stability for his daughter. Lanai's happiness meant more to him than feeling like a bachelor. He knew he'd never find a love like the one he looked at or woke up to every morning again in life. He knew it was now or never, because Lanai wasn't going to wait forever. He took a deep breath, took the ring box out of his pocket, and went down on one knee.

He took her shaky hand into his, looking up into her gray eyes that had gotten as big as saucers. He exhaled and took in another breath, trying to calm his nerves and say what he wanted to say before he passed out. He felt a little light-headed from the anticipation. He was sure she'd say yes, but there was always the possibility that she wouldn't.

He exhaled the breath he'd been holding on to and said, "Twelve years ago, nobody would've been able to tell me that I'd fall in love, let alone fall in love with my best friend. I don't even realize I'm doing it, but I thank God every day for you. I thank Him for allowing me another chance with you. You love my daughter like she was your own and I thank you for that. You give me a reason to live, and if you will be my wife, I promise I'll spend the rest of my life making you happy. I'll give you the world and then some. Will you marry me?"

CHAPTER THIRTY-ONE

anai slowly put Makayla down on the floor, a little worried about Makai telling her to put the baby down. He was always up to something, always being dramatic and keeping her in suspense. She'd given up on praying that one of his surprises would be a proposal a while ago. She wanted to marry him, but she'd decided that it would be best for her sanity to refocus her energy on something feasible.

It was rare for her to see anything in Makai's eyes except confidence. It made her nervous to see that he looked nervous. When he went down on one knee, her breath caught in her throat and her heart skipped a beat. Her hands began to shake and her eyes got huge. Her eyes saw what was going on, but her brain was having trouble processing it. *This can't be happening!* All she'd heard him say was "twelve years ago", before her brain shut off. She couldn't believe that he was down in front of her on one knee. *I don't believe it...that's ring's from TIFFANY'S!*

Her heart started beating so fast, she felt like it was about to come out of her chest. The blood pounded in her ears and she couldn't hear what he was saying. She saw his lips moving, but her brain was swirling, making it impossible for her even to read his lips. She saw him open the lid of the box and she damn near fainted. A 2.5-carat, princess cut diamond winked at her from the velvet inside the box. Her free hand went to her chest and her mouth dropped open. She felt like she was about to drop dead right there in the office. *Oh, my God! Oh, my God! Oh, my God! God, I'm gonna die! I am going to fall out!* Her breathing increased rapidly and her hands began sweating instantly.

She felt like she needed to take a step back, snatch her hand back, and do some breathing exercises to process everything. She would've snatched her hand back if she was able to move. Part of her brain told her this is one of his jokes; he would think was funny. But that diamond that kept winking at her, letting her know that it was definitely not a joke. Looking into his eyes and seeing the sincerity and nervousness that matched her own, let her know that the moment was real. Tears welled up in her eyes. After twelve years of the back and forth abuse from him, and from herself in multiple ways, lost babies, drug abuse, lies, disrespect, and other women, they were in the place she'd been trying to get to their entire time.

A tear ran down her cheek when his lips stopped moving. He looked at her expectantly and she stared back at him blankly. She would've loved to hear the words that he'd said to her, but her brain was still trying to process him being on one knee. He reached up and wiped her tear with his thumb and she blinked, snapping out of her trance somewhat.

He asked again, "Will you marry me?"

More tears fell from her eyes when she whispered, "Yes."

He took the ring from its holding place in the box, slid it onto her left ring finger, surprising both of them when it fit perfectly. He stood to his feet and enveloped her in his arms. He kissed her temple as she buried his face in his shirt. *It's a good thing that I wear good quality makeup, or his shirt would be ruined.*

Still in a state of shock, she leaned back and looked up at him, asking, "Is this real?"

He smiled down at her, assuring her, "It's real."

"Are you sure?" she sounded uncertain.

"Never been more sure about anything in my life," he replied, kissing her nose.

The knots that had formed in the pit of her stomach seemed to unravel and she released the breath that she'd been holding, dropping her head on his chest. In her head, she thanked God for giving her the desires of her heart. She didn't have a child of her own, but Makayla was the child that she'd always wanted. She loved that little girl as if she'd given birth to her. Makai had made the decision to grow up and be the man that she needed and deserved. They were happy together, grew together, and motivated one another. Even though things were never going to go back to where they were in the beginning, he'd worked hard to establish trust between them again.

He finally proved to her—before the ring and proposal—that she was a priority of his. He showed her every day that he loved and respected her. He had worked hard to redeem himself and she appreciated it. She also thanked God for a closer relationship with Him and the foundation that she didn't have for so many years. She thanked Him for every bad thing that had happened because it had made her into the woman that she was; the woman that Makai wanted to marry. She was finally able to look at herself in the mirror and appreciate the woman that she'd grown into. More than she loved the man that wanted to spend the rest of his life with her; she now truly loved herself. She could truly say that she loved herself, and she had God to thank for that.

CHAPTER THIRTY-TWO

"**B**abe," Lanai called from the bathroom of the master bedroom, her voice shaky.

After their engagement, Makai had put the house that he bought in Wild Quail up for sale. The two of them purchased a five-bedroom house with a two-car garage in the Camden, DE area. Lanai wanted to be closer to Katara and Sariyah, and Katara had told her that the Caesar Rodney School District was one of the best districts to have Makayla in when she started school in a few years. Lanai loved the house, but what she loved the most was that it felt like home. It was something that they'd bought together, with both of their names on the deed, and it wasn't something that he'd forced on her. The house had a warm feel to it, as opposed to the constant cold edge that the house in Wild Quail had.

Lanai had found out that she was eight-weeks pregnant right after they'd moved into the house. She had kept it a secret from everyone for as long as she could. She'd had so many instances where she'd gotten the hopes of everyone up, just to have to let them down, because the baby didn't make it for whatever reason. She couldn't hide it from Katara any longer, after her fifth month. Katara and Makai had asked her whom was she trying to fool, because they'd known all along. Neither of them would let her do much of anything; Katara even made Lanai retire her heels until after the baby was born. The doctor had said that the pregnancy was high-risk, and Makai and Katara made Lanai stick to every letter of his order.

Lanai acted like she hated it, but secretly, she loved the attention. She walked with a waddle and her belly looked like it led her around everywhere she went. Makai waited on her hand and foot when he was home; he'd even reduced his hours at work. He'd bought a car dealership, but he put his employees to work, because he wanted to make sure that Lanai did as she was told. He rubbed her back, belly, and feet. He would talk and read to her stomach often. They made sure that Makayla felt included and she was ecstatic about becoming a big sister.

Whenever he wasn't around Lanai, he would call and text so much that it would cause them to argue. She constantly told him to give her room to breathe. She tried telling him that if something was wrong, she would call. But it all seemed to fall on deaf ears because he continued to call and text every few minutes, checking to make sure she and the baby were okay. He bought her expensive sneakers that were supposed to have soles with a good grip, until her feet swelled to the point of her only being able to wear slippers. He made her wear a special kind of slip-resistant slippers so that she wouldn't fall. She'd told him over and over that he was going overboard.

Lanai was now nine days overdue, and she had to admit that she was ready to give birth. She was pregnant with a boy and felt like she'd put on a hundred pounds, though she'd actually gained thirty pounds. There were times when she worried about the weight gain, and how difficult it would be to lose the weight. She had her moments of insecurity when she would ask herself if he would still want her to marry him after putting on so much weight. She was happy that so far, the baby was healthy, but she honestly couldn't wait for him to be born. She was dying to breastfeed and exercise to get rid of the weight.

She sat on the toilet, feeling the constant flow of liquid. "Makai, come here now," she called out. She knew the distinct smell of amniotic fluid, and the fact that the quantity of liquid was too long for it to be urine, indicated that her water had broken. Dr. Yuri had scheduled her for a C-section for the next morning, because she was overdue, but now that wouldn't be necessary. Lanai was kind of happy that her water had broken on its own. When she didn't hear Makai coming, she called again, louder, "Babe?"

A few seconds later, Makai appeared in the doorway of the bathroom. He asked, "What's wrong?"

She looked up at him with wide eyes, "My water broke."

"It what?" he asked, shocked.

"It broke."

"Well, get up," he said. "Let's go."

"I'd love to," she replied sarcastically. "Only problem is the fluid is still coming out."

"Well, what do you want me to do? I can't stop the fluid."

"I didn't ask you to," she retorted. "Call the doctor and tell him my water broke. Tell him you're taking me to the hospital. Get my bag and the baby's bag."

Makai stood there, still listening for instructions.

Lanai said, "Babe, go now or I'm gonna have him on the toilet."

Makai nodded, snapping out of his daze, and went to do as he was told. She could hear him calling the doctor's office to let the doctor know they were on the way to the hospital, but then she couldn't hear him anymore. The flow of liquid had reduced to trickling. She was waiting for it to stop so that she could get up, pull up her panties, and go in the room. Makai returned to the doorway with bags in hand, looking at her expectantly.

She said, "It hasn't stopped yet."

He asked, "So now what?"

"Call Katara and tell her it's time," Lanai instructed. "Look under the sink and give me a pad, please. The nurse had said to put a pad on if my water broke."

He did as she asked, handing her an Always pad from under the sink. She unwrapped it, applied it to the seat of her panties, and attempted to get up. When she wasn't able to push herself up by pushing down on the back of the toilet with her hands, she tried to shimmy and shift herself to the edge of the toilet seat. When that didn't work, she held out her hands to Makai. He quickly went over to her and took her hands, pulling her up from the toilet.

She noticed that his hands were sweaty. She asked, "Are you alright?"

"Yeah," he said, trying not to sound as nervous as his hands had indicated.

She attempted to bend down and pull up her panties. When he saw that she was struggling, he pulled them up for her and held her hand as he guided her out of the bathroom. He asked, "Are you okay?"

She nodded her head, not feeling any pain. She said, "I'm fine. Just gotta get to the hospital."

Makai carefully walked beside her, careful not to force her to move too fast. It seemed like it took forever to get down the steps, and out the kitchen door that led to the garage. Once he got her settled into the passenger seat of his car, he pushed the button on the wall to open the garage door and got into the car. He rubbed her hand after pushing the button to start the car, asking again, "Are you okay?"

Trying to assure him, she said, "I'm fine. I don't feel any pain."

He backed out of the garage, asking, "Are you sure it's time?"

"I know what it feels and smells like for water to break," she told him.

"I was just asking," he said.

The drive to the hospital took about 7 minutes, and they went straight up to Bayhealth Kent General's Labor and Delivery section on the 5th floor. As they got off the elevator and approached the desk, Makai told them her name and the staff told them that Dr. Yuri was already there. The staff led Lanai through the double doors, asking when her water broke her name, address, and insurance information. She told numerous staff members that she wasn't feeling any pain. They took her to her assigned room, and sent her into the bathroom to undress. She took off her sundress and panties, struggling because her stomach had grown so big, put them in the bag they gave her, and waddled back out into the room.

She was about to climb onto the bed when a sharp pain shot across her stomach, causing her to bend over, suppressing a groan. Makai rushed to her side, putting his hand on her back and asking, "Are you okay? What's wrong?"

Through clenched teeth, she said, "Contraction."

The nurse in the room had joined him at her side, helping her to a standing position. She said, "Let's get you in this bed and hooked up to the monitor."

Lanai scooted onto the bed and Makai lifted her legs and swung them onto the bed. She scooted around, trying to get comfortable. The pain in her back had just started, but it had gone from a zero to an eight in a matter of seconds. She frowned at the feeling, not able to get comfortable or get a handle on the pain. A few nurses came in, buzzing around the room to hook her up to the fetal monitor, put an IV in her arm, and attach the blood pressure cuff. She tried to be as still as possible with the IV being inserted, but the next contraction hit so hard, it made her draw her knees up and she clenched her fist. She hadn't intended to, but she ended up jerking her arm. The needle scraped across her arm, causing a bright red mark to appear.

She yelled, "What the hell? Lady, what are you doing?"

Completely shaken, the tall, skinny nurse stammered, "Uh...ma'am...um...when you moved..."

"Look, dammit," Lanai replied. "You better hurry up and get this shit in. You scrape me one more time and I'ma...ugggggghhhh, shit!"

Another contraction hit and the tall, skinny nurse with the IV told her coworker, "I can't get this in while she's having contractions."

The next contraction seemed to come right after the one before and it caused her to roll over on her left side and draw up into the fetal position. She grabbed ahold of the bed railing, squeezing until her knuckles turned white, trying not to scream. She yelled, "Son of a bitch! Somebody do something! Give me some drugs or something!"

The tall, skinny nurse that was supposed to insert the IV backed away slowly from the bed, looking terrified. Lanai squeezed her knees together and held on tight to the bed railing, clenching her teeth. Makai stood there looking helpless, as she growled and grunted through the next contraction. Pains were hitting her nonstop in the back and across the stomach, bringing tears to her eyes. She cried, "Oh, my God! Please, somebody do something!"

"Ma'am, there's nothing we can do. You have to be still in order for us to get the IV safely in," the tall, skinny nurse told her.

Lanai flipped onto her back, demanding, "Y'all better do something quick! I can't take this shit!"

The tall, skinny nurse with the IV started to move towards the bed until Lanai gripped the hospital gown, screaming out in so much pain that she almost sat up completely. When the contraction was over, she flopped back on the bed, panting and sweating. Her eyes rolled up to the ceiling and she asked God to help her. She didn't know how close the baby was to coming, but she knew that the pain was excruciating. She didn't remember being in as much pain when she'd had to push out her first son. She felt someone's hand on her temple and looked over to see Makai looking down at her with concern etched all over his face.

He took her hand in his and said, "Just squeeze my hand when you feel another one coming."

Another contraction hit before she could respond. She snatched his hand and squeezed it for dear life, raising her top half up off the bed. She knew the nurses in the room standing around watching her, were supposed to be doing something other than watch. Between panting breaths, she asked, "Isn't somebody supposed to be checking me or something? I mean, these damn contractions are coming a little quick, don't you think?"

Her chastisement seemed to bring the nurses to life and they began moving again. She couldn't understand how she got stuck with three dumb asses all at the same time. One of the nurses left and came back with another nurse. Lanai squeezed Makai's hand and bit down on her lip, trying her best to ride out the contraction. It was taking all of her energy and her body was covered in sweat. She felt like she was becoming delirious, shaking her head from side to side because it hurt so bad. All she wanted was for the pain to be over.

She began to call out, "God, please help me. I need You to take this pain away, in the name of Jesus. I feel like I'm about to *die*!

God, I need You to get this child out of me. I promise if You do, I will *never* have sex again in my life. God, get this little nigga outta me!"

The nurse had gone to the end of the bed and touched Lanai's knee, telling her, "Ms. Wilson, I'm going to check your cervix to see how much you've dilated."

Shaking her head from side to side, she panted, "I don't care what you do. Just get it outta me, *now*!"

The nurse moved her legs apart, and with her gloved hand, she inserted two of her fingers. She looked at the nurse standing next to her and ordered, "Get Dr. Yuri in here right now. This baby is crowning."

Just as the nurse had finished her statement, Dr. Yuri came into the room, suited up and ready to deliver a baby. Another contraction caused Lanai's legs to snap shut with Dr. Yuri's hand between them. Lanai let out a piercing scream and when Makai tried to soothe her, she slapped his hand away. With tears flowing, she accused, "This is all your fucking fault! I hate you! *Get away from me!*"

Makai began to back up, but another pain hit her and she reached out, grabbing his shirt and yanking him to the bed, as she screamed through clenched teeth. Dr. Yuri pried Lanai's knees apart and the nurse next to him tried to console her, telling her, "Honey, you're gonna have to push. He's right here. You gotta push him out. When you feel the next contraction, push."

Before the nurse could finish what she was saying, Lanai grabbed the bed railing with her free hand, held on tight, and pushed down with all her might.

The nurse asked, "Did you just have a contraction?"

With her face flushed, Lanai answered, "No."

The nurse grinned, "Wait for it."

A second later, Lanai felt a contraction and with a handful of Makai's shirt, she yanked him down to her level. She squeezed the bed railing, pressing her lips together, and bearing down, she pushed as hard as she could. The nurse watched the monitor and told Lanai when to stop. She told her, "Ms. Wilson, just breathe and relax."

Lanai looked at the woman like she'd lost her mind. With her hair all over her head and stuck to her face and neck, her eyes were wild and she looked like a mad woman. She said, "I'm not doing that. I want this shit over."

One of the nurses interjected, "But, you gotta..."

It was too late because Lanai had already started pushing again. She was determined to have the horrific experience over as soon as possible. Lanai pushed down, counting out ten seconds in her head, stopped for a few seconds to take a few quick breaths, then went right back to pushing. This nurse had to be out her ever-loving mind if she thought Lanai was going to keep waiting. If the baby was right there, she was going to help his little butt to come out; besides, she couldn't wait to meet him.

After about four more pushes, she felt a gush of warm liquid and Dr. Yuri said, "He's out!"

Dr. Yuri caught the baby as he came out and held him up, looking at Makai. He asked, "Do you want to cut the cord?"

One of the waiting nurses had a pair of surgical scissors ready, handing them to him. Lanai had collapsed onto the bed, out of breath, but she hadn't let go of his shirt. Taking the scissors, he leaned over and clipped the umbilical cord. The nurse closest to Lanai took the nose syringe offered by one of her fellow nurses, suctioned the baby's mouth and nose, and turned him over.

Lanai's head came up off the bed. She asked, "Why isn't he crying? What's wrong with him?"

Dr. Yuri gave him a smack on the butt and he screamed. The nurse standing next to Dr. Yuri laughed, "I think he was asleep."

"Asleep?" Lanai asked, baffled. "How can he sleep coming out?"

"Honey, I've seen stranger things happen," the nurse said, passing the crying baby to the short, fat nurse waiting near the baby bed with the warming lamp.

Dr. Yuri pushed down on Lanai's lower stomach, telling her, "Give me one good push."

Lanai rolled her eyes. She remembered that the placenta felt like another child coming out. A few more pushes and the placenta plopped out onto the bed, with the other blood and fluids that were all over the sheet. Lanai noticed that she didn't hear the baby crying anymore. She looked around, anxious to see where he was. She saw the short, fat nurse putting a T-shirt on him and he had a diaper on. Lanai could see that his eyes were open; he just wasn't crying.

She looked up at Makai in a panic, and asked, "What's wrong with him? Why isn't he crying?"

"He's fine," the nurse next to her assured her. "He's just not a crier. You better thank God he's not a crier."

"I wanna hold him," Lanai said, not believing that he was okay.

The short, fat nurse brought the baby over to Lanai and gave him to her. The nurse suggested, "You should try and breastfeed within an hour or two, if that's what you want to do."

Lanai took him into her arms and put her face to his. His skin was so soft and warm. His jet-black hair was soft. She did a quick check of his fingers and toes to make sure they were all there. He looked at her with unblinking eyes and she smiled at him. She felt his little body rise and fall with his breathing; breathing that he didn't need a machine to do for him. She put her hand on his chest and felt his little heart beating, which was something she didn't get to experience with Makai, Jr.

She looked over his features, noticing how much he had in common with his brother and sister. Makai's genes were definitely prominent. Her son had only been in the world for ten minutes and she was in love. She kissed his forehead. Looking at him move his fingers and stretch his mouth, she knew that he was the blessing that God had promised her. She knew that God had—at that moment—given her the last of the desires of her heart that she'd given up on. She'd made peace with the fact that she may never experience motherhood. And God was yet again, shocking her to her core, yet again.

She felt so overcome with emotion and joy that she wanted to jump out of the bed and shout. She wanted to thank Him and praise Him over and over. She wanted to express her gratitude for God having mercy on her and blessing her with the one thing that she'd always wanted. More than anything in the world, she wanted a healthy child. God gave to her what He wanted her to have, when

He wanted her to have it. But He'd also given it to her when she was mature enough to receive it and accept it.

She knew that if God had allowed her to be a mother over the years, she would've put that child through unnecessary nonsense. She never would've been able to appreciate it. But with her being a grown woman—in every sense of the word—she now could appreciate the blessings that God had for her. She prayed that He continued to protect and guide her family. She'd learned that the price of being redeemed was a price worth paying.

ABOUT THE AUTHOR

Regina Bumbrey has been writing since she was 12 years old. Writing has always been a passion of hers and it has allowed her to escape.

She comes from a family of 13 children, six living in one house. Writing was her way of staying out of trouble and to keep from remembering how hard it was to fit in at home and school.

Her dream since she was about 15 years old was to become a published writer. She never took it seriously until she became a parent herself. She aspires to be able to show her children that if they follow their dreams, put in the hard work necessary, and stay focused, anything is possible.

She has an Associate's Degree in Business Administration and plan to obtain a Bachelor's Degree in Human Resource Management.

Follow Regina Bumbrey on her social media sites:
Facebook, Twitter, Instagram, Google+: Regina Bumbrey

Visit her website
www.authorrbumbrey.com